Three Exciting NEW Talented Writers

Three delightful NEW novels
introduced by
international bestselling author
PENNY JORDAN

Mills & Boon
Presents...

ROBYN GRADY

JOANNA FULFORD

JANICE LYNN

Mills & Boon
Presents...

ROBYN GRADY

JOANNA FULFORD

JANICE LYNN

M&B™ and M&B™ with the Rose Device
are trademarks of the publisher.
Harlequin Mills & Boon Limited, Eton House,
18-24 Paradise Road, Richmond, Surrey TW9 1SR

MILLS & BOON PRESENTS...
© by Harlequin Enterprises II B.V./S.à.r.l. 2009

Baby Bequest © Robyn Grady 2008
The Viking's Defiant Bride © Joanna Fulford 2009
The Nurse's Baby Miracle © Janice Lynn 2009

ISBN: 978 0 263 87544 7

009-1009

Harlequin Mills & Boon policy is to use papers that are
natural, renewable and recyclable products and made from
wood grown in sustainable forests. The logging and
manufacturing processes conform to the legal environmental
regulations of the country of origin.

Printed and bound in Spain
by Litografia Rosés S.A., Barcelona

Introduction
by
New York Times **and** *Sunday Times*
bestselling author
Penny Jordan

Welcome to *Mills & Boon Presents…*
Robyn Grady, Joanna Fulford and Janice Lynn.

Introducing new writers to the readers makes me feel excited and proud. It takes me back to my own early days as a writer.

The actual process, as I experienced it, of having my first book bought by Mills & Boon was very different in my day. I'd read in a magazine that M & B were looking for new authors; I loved the books and had been trying to write one for ages, so knowing that Mills & Boon wanted to expand their author base gave me the impetus to really focus on writing my book.

When I hadn't heard anything several months after submission, I assumed that the book wasn't good enough. However – uncharacteristically for me – I actually telephoned London and, to my disbelief and my joy, I was told that the editors liked my book; that there would be some editorial revisions and would I like to visit to discuss them?

Would I !!!! I could hardly take it all in.

I duly went to London, where I met Jacqui Bianchi, the Editorial Director at that time, who went through with me the revisions that needed to be done.

Obviously, as a keen reader, I already knew how my book would be presented visually and I was thrilled when mine came out. And when I see the first copy of one of my books, I still feel the same sense of disbelief and joy I felt that first time.

I had lunch with Alan Boon after I had been writing for some time. It was a huge honour and I still cherish the memory.

The internet has changed the process since my first book was accepted. When I first submitted, authors did not have much contact with one another – there were no loops celebrating 'the call', etc., for instance. For me, after the thrill of my first acceptance, I was terrified that it was a fluke and that I'd never be able to write another book that would also be accepted. Even now, one is only as good as the last book and the readers' response to it. I am truly grateful to our readers for the support they have given me and continue to give me.

What *hasn't* changed is the dedicated help that authors receive from the Editorial Department and which is much appreciated by us all, but especially by this author. The editor's overseeing eye can spot things that the writer is often too close up to a book to see.

Similarly, the authors I have been privileged to mentor were already good writers. I simply helped them to highlight their strengths in the context of a Mills & Boon® book and I am very proud of my small contribution to their success.

When I am asked, "What one or two pieces of advice would you give someone wanting to write?", I respond: know your genre and really feel that you are writing in the right genre for you.

Romantic fiction as a genre is eternally popular. The need to give and receive love and to have a mutually loving relationship with a partner is in itself eternal – as I write I merely reflect people's feelings, I don't create them. In every story I ask myself to remember how it felt to fall in love and to long passionately for that love to be returned.

Robyn Grady, Joanna Fulford and Janice Lynn, the new authors featured here, all write for different 'home' series – Desire™/Modern Heat™, Historical & Medical™ – but I think every great romance contains the writers' conviction that their hero and their heroine have to be together no matter what conflicts may separate them.

I wish I hadn't been asked to let Robyn, Joanna and Janice know what their typical day might be like – I don't want to put them off – many hours of sitting in front of a computer worrying about one's book. But once it's finished and you swear you will never be able to write another, somehow up pops another 'idea', another story demanding to be told, another hero who needs the love of a

Mills & Boon® heroine in his life.

As a writer who has been around for some years, I feel I am more in need of advice from writers starting out rather than the other way around. New authors have a fresh eye and a take on our genre that inspires and excites me, both as a reader and a writer.

Mills & Boon receive many submissions from all over the world and a few special new writers are published every year. This year *Mills & Boon Presents...* showcases *Baby Bequest* by Robyn Grady, *The Viking's Defiant Bride* by Joanna Fulford and *The Nurse's Baby Miracle* by Janice Lynn. Here you can read the books, the authors' biographies and even see some of the editors' comments. Enjoy!

Thank you so much,

Penny Jordan

ABOUT THE AUTHORS

ROBYN GRADY

Robyn's Editors Say:

"It's easy to see that Robyn's fresh voice and surprising, sexy set-ups are a wonderful draw for Desire™ readers."

"Robyn writes very sexy, dramatic and layered stories. She has a style that is so captivating you can't help but finish the book right then and there."

What stood out for her editor when *Baby Bequest* was bought was "that she had managed to balance drama and conflict perfectly. She had a very fresh voice, and her writing oozed a fluidity that engaged the reader from page one."

Robyn Says:

When I set my mind to something I'm not easily swayed. From the outset, I was determined to be a Harlequin/Mills & Boon author. They publish my favourite authors, offer a line to suit every mood and are the biggest publisher of romance in the world. Once I began to learn more about the craft and joined groups like Romance Writers of Australia, I couldn't stop. I often wrote clear through the night!

After seven years of submitting, I received two phone calls from London regarding revisions on separate manuscripts, neither of which sold. In 2006, I was a finalist in thirteen US contests, but I couldn't seem to make it over that final line. During a what-have-I-got-to-lose moment, I e-mailed a New York agent who, to my disbelief and delight, took me on. Three weeks later, on the morning of 5th December, I received three e-mails from my agent. The last read, "Offer from Desire"!

I could've fallen off my chair! I think I cried. Of course I accepted. I spoke to my husband and a couple of friends on the phone, sent a few e-mails to more friends, but because it was the big last-day-of-school, including a junior school graduation, I couldn't get back to my computer until 11pm. Hundreds of congratulatory messages were piled up in my inbox. I've kept, and prize, every one. I sold to London in a two-book deal the following month. *Baby Bequest* is my fifth book. I'm currently writing my ninth. Two years on from my first sale, it's still wild and wonderful to know my dream came true in such a stellar way.

I realise now (as, no doubt, many writers do) this is who I was meant to be, what I was meant to do. I love when a book hits the bestsellers list. I love when I see the different covers from countries all over the world. Best of all, I love when I receive feedback from readers who've enjoyed a particular story and are looking forward to the next.

Baby Bequest

Twelve years ago, the 'bad boy' Jenna Darley adored disappeared without so much as a goodbye note. When Gage Cameron returns, now incredibly successful and offering to help Jenna fight for custody of her niece after a family tragedy, she's ready to tell him where to get off. But Jenna comes to discover that true love can survive the toughest of tests. Gage has an even more remarkable lesson to learn – and it begins with trusting himself enough to let go of secrets that could hurt Jenna even more.

The story takes place in cosmopolitan Sydney, Australia. The premise and overall tone are deeply emotional, but there are also light moments where the story's more serious themes are balanced alongside the irresistible thrill of 'rediscovering the love of your life'. Ultimately *Baby Bequest* is about time healing all wounds. About love winning out and growing stronger.

JOANNA FULFORD

Joanna's Editors Say:

"Joanna Fulford is a UK author. *The Viking's Defiant Bride* is her first book!

Keen historian Joanna is an exciting new voice for the Historical romance series – she just sweeps the reader along with her fast-paced, compelling writing. She paints an evocative picture of the period, bringing it to life beautifully through the eyes of her strong and hugely appealing characters."

This book is a page-turner to the very end! The vibrant characters and rich historical setting instantly stood out to the editor. The heroine Elgiva is strong and determined, while Wulfrum – wow! He's just gorgeous – is a powerful Viking earl, self-assured with a steely core – and a vulnerability hidden away that only

Elgiva can touch. Joanna creates a fabulous relationship between sworn enemies who the reader just knows are meant to be together.

Joanna worked diligently on the revisions needed for *The Viking's Defiant Bride* and impressed the editor with her determination and professionalism. "It was a wonderful moment to finally give her a call and tell her that we wanted to buy her first book! She was absolutely thrilled and is already buzzing with ideas for future stories!"

Joanna Says:

I have been a scribbler all my life but a full-time author only for the past four years. It is a solitary business, but I wouldn't swap it for any other. Although writing is hard work, it is also enormous fun. To quote Terry Pratchett: "Writing is probably the most fun you can have with your clothes on." When the creative muse is on form and the words are flowing, there's an incredible buzz to be had. Of course, the downside is when the flow becomes a trickle or dries up altogether. Fortunately that happens rarely now. The more you write, the stronger your writing muscles get. I've also been fortunate in joining a writing group whose members provide moral support and encouragement as well as useful feedback on work in progress.

As I have always enjoyed reading historical novels it seemed logical to write one. The idea for *The Viking's Defiant Bride* came to me on a trip to Northumberland. I'd ducked into a gift shop to avoid a heavy shower and, while browsing, found a copy of Roy Anderson's wonderful little book, *The Violent Kingdom*. One paragraph and I was hooked. The history of Northumbria is utterly compelling, particularly the great Viking invasion of 865 AD. As soon as I read it I knew what my own story was going to be about. I could already see its hero, Wulfrum, leaping ashore from one of the sea dragons, sword in hand, ready to stride into a new adventure.

Having written the book, I sent the opening chapters to Harlequin Mills & Boon. Not only did my story seem to fit their spec, but I knew that, unlike many publishers, they would at least read the manuscript. In fact, they asked to see the rest. What followed was a long apprenticeship. It took eighteen months and four rewrites before the novel was finally accepted for publication. Getting that phone call was the greatest buzz of all and what made it special was that the editor sounded just as excited as I was. The high lasted at least a week.

Since then I've written my second book, a Regency romance this time, set against the background of the Luddite riots. It was a turbulent period and provides another ready-made source of conflict against which to set the central love story. *The Wayward Governess* will be published in December 2009.

I have numerous ideas for other stories, other heroes and heroines in other times. The richness of English history offers an endless source of possibility. While you need a good handle on period, it is important not to get bogged down in research. As Bernard Cornwell said, "It is not the business of the novelist to give a history lesson. The important thing is to tell the story." And that's exactly what I do. If there's a point I don't know about, I make a note and look it up later.

Having got the story down, then you can go back and edit those areas that need more work. It's easier to do that when you have an overview of the whole novel. For the purposes of editing you need to develop a critical eye and be prepared to murder your darlings. It is tough to have to cut a chapter or a scene that you've sweated over, but if it tightens up the story it's well worth the pain.

Finally, and most important of all, are determination and perseverance. As a writer you have to be prepared for the long haul. I suspect that all over England are partially completed novels gathering dust in cupboards. Some of them could be potentially great books, perhaps works of genius. We'll never know. Don't let yours be one of them. Lay in a supply of chocolate to help you through the tough times and get on with the writing. Good luck.

For more information go to www.joannafulford. info

The Viking's Defiant Bride

When the Vikings invade England in 856 AD, a Saxon estate becomes the spoils of war for a powerful Viking warrior – as does its feisty, courageous mistress, Elgiva of Ravenswood, whom he intends to take as his bride! Wulfrum may be the conqueror, but he wants Elgiva to come willingly to him – especially as he knows she feels the heat between them as well as he. An electric battle of wills ensues, complicated by all-consuming desire, tumultuous emotions and divided loyalties!

JANICE LYNN

Janice's Editors Say:

Janice Lynn lives in the southern United States, in Tennessee, and *The Nurse's Baby Miracle* is her fifth book for Mills & Boon® Medicals!

"Janice is such an exciting new voice for the Medical™ romance series – she writes compelling, intense medical drama and draws you into her stories with her sparkling, likeable heroines and strong commanding heroes that you'll fall in love with instantly. Her stories are powerfully emotional and sweep you along on an emotional roller-coaster ride towards a fabulously sparkling ending.

This story was compelling from the very first page; Natalie and Caleb meet whilst working as medical staff on a three-day fundraising walk for breast cancer, a subject very close to the author's heart, and the buzz of the participants and the adrenalin of the volunteer staff made you feel as if you were right there with them! You had so much sympathy for Natalie: a tragic accident left her convinced that she had only this one chance to conceive the baby she's always longed for. And as soon as the oh-so-sexy Dr Caleb Burton strode on to the page you knew they were destined for their very own happy-ever-after!

Janice bubbles over with enthusiasm and energy and she truly loves writing – and reading! – romance. It's always a wonderful moment to finally call an author and tell them we want to buy their first book – and Janice was no exception! She has been an absolute pleasure to work with ever since."

Janice Says:

In October 2006 I volunteered for my first breast cancer fundraiser – a three-day sixty-mile walk in Atlanta where we walked all day and slept in tents at night. From the moment I arrived, I knew I'd someday use my experience as the backdrop for a story. Later that year my dream of writing for Mills & Boon came true when I sold my first Medical™ romance.

Although I walked (and walked and walked) during the event I participated in, Nurse Natalie Carmichael and Dr Caleb Burton volunteer as part of the medical crew and tend to the walkers, many of whom are breast cancer survivors. During their three-day stint, they change each other's life.

The father of a small daughter, Caleb is a widower of a breast cancer victim and isn't sure he can give his heart only to possibly lose his love a second time. Natalie has secrets of her own, secrets that throw Caleb into an emotional tailspin.

Because my grandmother is a breast cancer survivor, this story holds a special place in my heart. If you've never participated in a cancer fundraiser, please consider doing so by walking or donating funds for much needed research.

I love to hear from readers. Please e-mail me at Janice@janicelynn.net to let me know what you think of Caleb and Natalie's story or to just chat about romance. Or visit me at www. janicelynn.net to find out my latest news.

Happy reading!

Janice

The Nurse's Baby Miracle

In *The Nurse's Baby Miracle* it seems that nurse Natalie Carmichael's dream of motherhood may have been cruelly snatched away by a car accident. Then she meets drop-dead-gorgeous obstetrician Caleb Burton… The attraction between them is utterly irresistible and they spend one wonderful night together – a night that leaves Natalie pregnant with Caleb's baby! How will Natalie tell this gorgeous baby doctor he's about to become a daddy? But there's another shock in store. The miracle hasn't ended there – Natalie is expecting twins!

With thanks to Tony Mansueto for his expert
advice on helicopters.

Melissa Jeglinski, Jennifer Schober and
Shana Smith – thank you all for helping make
Baby Bequest my favourite.

Baby Bequest

ROBYN GRADY

Robyn Grady was born in Brisbane, Australia, the third child of four. While she didn't come from a family of bookworms, Robyn fell in love with the magic of storytelling from the moment she discovered *Cinderella*.

She was educated at Corinda Primary and High Schools and, having done well in business subjects, decided to follow her sisters' paths and become a secretary. By age nineteen, she was personal assistant to the publicity and public relations manager of a metropolitan television station. Then came a move to production, where she helped produce and direct children's programmes, game shows, sports broadcasts, the nightly news and current affairs. When the network was sold, the majority of staff was retrenched the week before Christmas...a blessing in disguise.

She moved to Queensland's Sunshine Coast to be closer to family. Remembering her love of romance books, she decided it was high time she wrote one...then she wrote another. Now she plans never to stop.

Robyn has majors in English Literature and Psychology and lives with her own real-life Prince Charming. Her life is kept busy with writing for Modern Heat™ and Desire™, as well as caring for three beautiful (and extraordinarily different) daughters, Ashleigh, Holly and Tabitha. She enjoys the ocean, the theatre and catching up with friends over lunch.

You can contact Robyn via her website www.robyngrady.com

CHAPTER ONE

"IF YOU'RE here about my father, you're too late." Jenna Darley took time enough to bite back tears and lift her chin. "I buried him two days ago."

Gage Cameron glanced over from where he was crouching on the lawn, introducing himself to the Darleys' curious Alsatian. A moment after his ice-gray gaze found hers, his square jaw relaxed with a smile that was supportive and, in spite of it all, faintly seductive.

Unbidden heat curled low in Jenna's stomach.

Suits worth thousands had replaced the bad-boy jeans he'd worn twelve years ago, but clearly the lone wolf she'd once loved hadn't vanished completely. Good thing she'd made the choice to grow up. Move on.

Too bad he'd done it first.

With a final ruffle of Shadow's ears, Gage pushed to his feet. Taller than she remembered, he brushed his large tanned hands and surveyed the extensive manicured grounds of her family's Sydney home. Not that it belonged to "family" anymore.

Her father, twin sister and brother-in-law were all dead, victims of a freak helicopter crash. Although she'd received the news ten days ago, Jenna still had trouble believing it. Half the time she was crying, or close to it; the other half she felt...*numb*. The horror was real, yet it wasn't.

Earlier this week, while she'd sat, dazed, in a lawyer's office, she'd discovered that her father's entire estate had been left to her stepmother, a polished middle-aged woman whom everyone adored...everyone but black sheep Jenna.

The nightmare didn't end there.

Gage sauntered over, the broad ledge of his shoulders moving in a languid, almost predatory roll. When he stopped an arm's length away, his head tilted and chin tipped lower as if she were somehow broken and he could spare the time to fix her.

"I was tied up in Dubai when I heard," he said in a rumbling voice that had deepened over the years. "I flew back as soon as I could."

Jenna twined her arms over her ribs and pressed the sick, empty ache in her stomach. "A waste of your time, I'm afraid."

Jump on your private jet and fly back to your high-powered lair, she thought. *There's nothing for you here.*

His gaze sharpened as if he'd read her mind. Still he persisted. "If there's anything I can do..."

Her bland expression held. "Thank you. No."

Nowadays Gage raked in millions the way other men raked up leaves. Although his base was Melbourne, Australia, his soaring success was praised in every medium all over the world. From Paris to Penang, wherever Jenna traveled for her freelance writing, Gage's rugged good looks, those piercing gray eyes, seemed to find her—today in the unforgettable flesh.

Unfortunately nothing, including status and wealth, could bring back three members of her family she missed so deeply that she couldn't see this darkness ever lifting. But there was a fourth and final member—her three-month-old niece. It was little Meg that she must concentrate on now.

Anchoring his weight, Gage slid both hands into his trouser pockets. "I'm staying in Sydney for a few weeks."

Through bleary eyes, Jenna tried to focus. "You have business to conduct?" *A few more million to make?*

Raw magnetism radiated from his tall and impressive frame while little other than cool detachment shone from the depths of those crystal-cut eyes. So commanding and assured. She could only imagine how ruthless he'd become.

"Your father would want me to make sure you're all right," he replied.

Her mask broke.

"You were the housekeeper's son, Gage. My father gave you a bed, an education, and you left without so much as a goodbye. I'm sorry, but why do you think he would care *what* you said or did now?"

His eyes narrowed so slightly, so briefly, she wondered if she'd imagined it.

"If I thought it would make a difference," he said, "I'd tell you."

She pinned him with a jaded look then turned and sank onto the wooden slats of a nearby garden bench. "Whatever."

If that sounded dismissive or rude, she simply couldn't help it. What little energy she had left needed to be spent on one thing and one thing only.

Meg.

Guardianship.

What do I do now?

She was that little girl's blood, not Leeann Darley. It was wrong that her stepmother should raise Meg, no matter what that stony-faced lawyer or those wills had said. True, these last ten years she'd had no fixed address, and at present she had no legal right to Meg.

She also had no intention of giving up.

Elbows on knees, Jenna gnawed around a thumbnail. When her restless gaze landed on a stick, she picked it up and tossed it for Shadow to fetch while Gage slowly circled her.

"You and your father always locked horns," he said after a long, considering moment. "Everything was left to his wife, wasn't it?"

A withering, dizzy sensation ran through her. *Everything* was right.

But then she studied him more closely. "What was that? A good guess?"

His mouth tilted. "Surely you've heard of my sixth sense where finances are concerned."

She thought it through and had to concede. Of course Gage's intuition with regard to money matters was well known. Aside from that, it wasn't unusual for a husband to leave the majority of his worldly goods to his wife, including the family property and everything in it.

A dry eucalyptus leaf dropped into her lap. Jenna covered the leaf in her hand and broke it in her fist. The trees had been saplings when they'd first moved here. It seemed that as they'd grown taller, she'd grown more unhappy until one day she'd simply up and left. The frustration of trying to fit in with a blended family…the deep sense of loss whenever she thought of her mother... What she wouldn't give to turn back time to when they really *had* been a family.

But fairy tales were for children. And sometimes even children missed out.

"I don't care about my father's possessions," she said. There were things far more important than money.

"Tell me, Jenna, twelve years on, what *do* you care about?"

She gazed up into that strongly hewn face, at the faint scar nicking his upper lip. "If I thought it would make a difference," she quipped, "I'd tell you."

A lazy grin reflected in his eyes. "Try me."

God help her, she was tempted.

She was light on friends—hopping from country to country didn't nurture long-term anything—and she did have an overwhelming urge to confess to someone who knew her background that she'd forgiven her father for re-marrying so soon after her mother's death. It hurt like hell that she'd lost the chance to tell him that she loved him, despite their ongoing feud.

Worse, she would never talk to her sister again, the one person she'd truly trusted. Amy had been more than a sibling, more than a friend. She'd been a *part* of her. And an important part of her sister lived still.

The inescapable truth spilled out. "I have to fight for her child."

His eyebrows nudged together and his hands emerged from his pockets. "What did you say?"

Jenna bit the inside of her cheek, but she couldn't take it back, just as she couldn't will away the salty trail curling around her chin.

She knocked the tear aside. "These last few days have been…difficult."

His frown deepened. "What are you talking about? Whose child?"

"Amy has—" She swallowed against the wad of cotton clogging her throat and rephrased. "Amy *had* a three-month-old."

He sank down beside her, too close and yet, in other unwelcome ways, not close enough. "He didn't mention a baby."

Jenna's attention caught and she looked at him. "Who didn't mention a baby?"

His preoccupied gaze blinked back from some distant point. "I mean the newspaper report my second-in-charge passed on. It only cited your father's widow, yourself and the three passengers who'd flown out to survey a development site."

She nodded as the details looped their well-worn groove in her brain. "Brad, Amy's husband, wanted Dad's opinion on some acreage he was interested in buying. They left at ten in the morning. Meg stayed with my stepmother."

Jenna had originally booked a flight for her niece's christening next month and had planned on staying a while. Amy had been so excited. The sisters saw each other regularly, but as Jenna had grown older—particularly now that she was an aunt—it hadn't seemed nearly enough. But when she'd received news of the accident, she'd boarded the first flight to Sydney.

Before arriving last week, she'd seen photos of her niece. Since the accident, she gazed at them constantly. Her favorite was Meg's first bright-eyed smile, hugging the panda bear her auntie had sent by Express Mail the day Margaret Jane had been born.

Now that little girl had lost both her parents and was living with a woman who cared more about facials and status symbols than lullabies and kisses good-night. At the funeral, Leeann had mentioned that she and Meg would be flying to San Francisco to visit her aging parents for Christmas; she wasn't certain when they'd return.

Christmas was only three months away.

Jenna clutched the bench slats at her sides and prayed. *I'll do anything, give anything. Just help me find a way.*

Shadow trotted back and carefully placed the stick at Gage's polished shoes. He stooped, cast the stick spinning with absentminded skill, then laid an arm along the back of the bench. The heat of his hand radiated near her nape and some crazy, needy part of her almost leant back to absorb it.

"Who has the baby now? Leeann?"

She nodded then forced her mouth to work. "She's always wanted a child of her own."

Leeann's parents had shuffled her off to boarding school at a young age. Jenna and Amy had decided that because Leeann hadn't felt loved growing up, there was a great gaping hole where her heart ought to be, and Leeann thought a child would fill it. A couple of years back, in her early forties, Leeann had faced the fact she might never conceive—which couldn't be a bad thing. From what Jenna had sampled of Leeann's parenting skills, a starving rat would treat its young better.

"Amy told me that Leeann was getting desperate," Jenna continued. "She'd looked into in vitro fertilization and even adoption."

After doing a story on an orphanage in the Jiangxi Province last year, Jenna had wanted to adopt every dewy-eyed child there…so vulnerable and innocent. Now there was another orphan in the world.

"She's the testamentary guardian?"

Jenna's burning gaze drifted up from her sandals. "My father and Leeann were both named as Meg's guardians in her parents' wills."

"Not you?"

"I guess Amy and Brad thought if they'd ever needed someone to step in, my father was settled here, while I wasn't in one place long enough to take care of the day-to-day needs of a child."

"They were right." When she slid him a look, Gage shrugged. "I've seen your byline on travel articles from all over the world. The ones I've read were very good."

The compliment sank in. Perhaps she should thank him, but she didn't want flattery. What she needed now was a solution.

"Brad had no living relatives," she continued, peering past the pines to the orchid hothouse her father had loved. "I know they both trusted Dad, and Amy wasn't the type to hold grudges, not even against Leeann." Family fractures had been Jenna's specialty. "But Amy would never have meant for Leeann to take sole responsibility for Meg. No one could've foreseen this kind of tragedy—all three gone. If she had, Amy would have known I'd give up *everything*—" Her rush of words ran dry. "You wouldn't understand."

"Because I didn't have a family I was close to?"

Although he'd crushed her heart when he'd left, she scanned his questioning gaze now and found she didn't want to hurt him. But the truth was too obvious. She pressed her lips together and nodded.

He broke their gaze, threw the stick, and Shadow sped off again. "Have you spoken to a lawyer?"

"My father's. He said babies are a full-time job, and Leeann has the resources and sense of commitment Meg needs. But he's being narrow-minded. There's no reason I couldn't find work here and settle down."

"Would you want to?"

Images of Hawaii at sunset and the iridescent greens of Germany in spring clicked like snapshots through her mind, but she pushed them aside. There was no question. She would give it all up tomorrow.

But if Gage had implied that people who moved around somehow lacked a sense of responsibility… "I doubt you're in a position to cast any stones," she replied.

He flicked open his jacket button and his deep chest expanded beneath his crisp white shirt as he leant back more. "Oh, I understand a wandering spirit, Jenna. Owning stock in companies across the globe gives me a reason to migrate regularly and often. I don't like to grow roots." His approving gaze brushed her cheek. "Neither do you."

A tingling rush swept over her skin, but she wouldn't respond based on physical awareness. Instead she fell back on cynical amusement. "Well, who'd have guessed? We're practically a match made in heaven."

"Heaven's a little too tame for us."

When his eyes crinkled at the corners, a delicious warmth seeped through her veins.

So, after all this time, at their deepest level, they knew each other still. She felt so fragile—so much in need of his strength—she could almost forget the heartache of that summer, fall into those powerful arms and actually forgive him.

A phone rang. Gage slipped the cell from his belt and checked the display. "Excuse me. I'll be five minutes. Ten tops."

Letting go of the tension, she inhaled a lungful of pine air and Gage's frighteningly familiar scent. Then she stood and moved away, leaving Gage to his call.

Her laptop and Internet connection were still open in her father's study. She'd been about to hit SEND and decline an offer on a story about a chain of bed-and-breakfasts from Tuscany down through to Campania when Shadow had barked and she'd crossed to the French doors. A tall dark stranger had been walking up the path from the arched iron gates. Two disbelieving seconds later she'd realized her visitor was none other than the man she'd fallen in puppy love with after her first year of college.

Jenna passed through those French doors now, crossed the spacious room decorated in forest-green leather and handcrafted oak, then folded herself into the chair set before her laptop. Her gaze settled on the photo her father had kept on his desk—herself and Amy, aged eight, in Cinderella dress-up. Amy, the nurturing one, was fixing Jenna's lopsided tiara.

Jenna picked up the photo, as she'd done so often these past days. But this time her thoughts drifted back to her visitor.

Gage and his mother had lived in a house next door, which had been supplied by her father. For five years she'd glimpsed her young male neighbor only at a distance. Then she'd come home from college that

summer and the brooding ruffian had grown into a man—
deep-chested, muscled and sexy in a dangerous way that
had left her breathless whenever he'd looked at her with
a slanted smile that said he'd noticed her too.

Puppy love. The term was too naive for the wonderfully
wicked feelings he'd planted and nurtured within her. Far
more explicit phrases came to mind.

The simmer of remembered longing trickled through
her bloodstream then swirled and sparked like a lit match
down below. But she shrugged off the smoldering sensation. Her father had said Gage wasn't the type of man a
young woman should get involved with.

Jenna rested her forearms on the desk.

Twenty-nine wasn't so young.

"I managed to end that call sooner than I'd thought."

Jenna jumped at the deep voice at her back. She swung
around and felt her heart beat faster. Gage's striking sil-
houette consumed the doorway, eclipsing a good portion
of the golden afternoon light.

How many lovers had he had in twelve years? How
many times had she secretly wished she'd sampled him
herself?

As he moved forward, she tamped down that thought
and, after replacing the photo, eased out of her chair.

She searched for something to say. "So, another
business deal in the bag?"

"Afraid not. And I won't lay more chips on that table
just yet." He flicked back his jacket, set his hands low on
his hips and took in the room—the wood-paneled walls,
the limestone fireplace, the wingchair where she'd once
curled up on her father's lap while he read his botany
books and explained the pictures.

"So was Leeann bequeathed the house as well?"

Jenna slid her attention from the chair back to Gage and gave him a wry smile. "Leeann's been generous enough to let me stay while I'm here. She and Meg are in the penthouse in town."

"Do you have savings? I presume you won't starve."

She might not be wealthy by his standards, but who was? "I haven't lived off my father since I left college and found my first freelance job overseas."

He came closer and her center warmed as that lit match flickered and leapt high. It wasn't the place—certainly not the time—and yet the burning physical response to his being near was automatic, a literal knee-jerk reaction. Did he have that effect on all women? The answer was obvious: *no question about it.*

"You really don't care about the business, the house?" he asked, a curious light in his eyes.

That inner warmth wavered and fell away.

"My family, bar one, are gone. No, Gage, I don't care about the money."

Landing back in reality, all the pain fresh again in her mind, she crossed to the door. For more reasons than one, it was time to end this reunion.

"Thank you for making the trip. If you don't mind, I think it's best you leave now."

Deep in thought—also ignoring her suggestion—he moved to the desk. "I'll speak with my lawyer."

Over a decade on and *still* he didn't listen. "I just told you—"

"Not about the money. About your niece."

She shut her eyes and groaned. "Please don't."

The last thing she needed was a Family Court judge

bristling over the heavy-handed tactics of a multimillion-aire who thought he could buy anyone and anything.

He eased a thigh over one corner of the desk and laced his hands between his long, clearly muscular legs. One dark eyebrow flexed. "What if it means getting custody of your niece?"

"Gage, please. This isn't a game."

But the steely look in his eyes said he was very serious.

He picked up a miniature globe and spun the sphere. Asia, Europe, America flew round in a blur of bright colors. "I must say, I'm not wholly convinced you'll be happy giving up your lifestyle. God knows, I wouldn't be."

Self-righteous heat scorched her cheeks. "No problem for you." Her smile was thin. "Stay single."

His lips twitched as if she'd said something amusing. "I don't see marriage as an issue, necessarily." He set the globe down. "But children need a stable home life."

"Then I suggest you be extra careful about contraception."

The air between them condensed and crackled before he grinned and assured her, "Always."

His hip slid off the desk and he drew up to his full intimidating height while Jenna remembered his mother—wiry hair, vacant expression, a vague smell of whiskey whenever she spoke. If Gage didn't want the responsibility of having a family, she shouldn't be surprised. He'd been sorely deprived of role models. Jenna's own reasons for remaining single were something else entirely.

"We were talking about your niece," he said in a meaningful tone. "I have a way to get you what you want."

His cool eyes sparkled and she was reminded again of the lawless rebel she'd once known. Then, as now, he'd rippled with the promise of a thousand possibilities. At seventeen, almost eighteen, she'd been entranced by it.

Feeling that same tug, she leant further back against the doorjamb. "Just so we're on the same page, kidnapping's not an option."

He didn't crack a smile. "What I propose isn't completely honest, but it's far from a federal offence."

Now she was intrigued.

Weighing the pros and cons, she searched his eyes and finally murmured, "I'm listening."

"Wherever possible, judges like to comply with last wishes. But you *are* this baby's blood relative."

Her shoulders sagged. She'd been through all that. "Dad's lawyer said that's not enough. And the longer Meg stays with Leeann, the less likely the courts will be to uproot her."

"But if you had a suitable place of your own, as well as the legal brains and money to push forward and make an immediate request…"

She frowned. Waited.

"And…"

"You need a secret weapon," Gage said, "that will shoot you ahead in the guardianship stakes."

"A miracle?"

The scar on his top lip curved up. "A husband."

CHAPTER TWO

"You're suggesting I get married?" Jenna's hand went to her forehead and she coughed out a laugh, a baffled sound. "I'm sorry. This is taking a moment to absorb but…what would my marrying accomplish?"

Gage's gaze skimmed her shoulder-length dark-blond hair. The soft curl was pretty, but he preferred her hair long, framing a face he'd remembered as saucy, not tearstained.

"For a start," he explained, "a marriage license would tell the court that you're serious about settling down. It would also imply that the child would enjoy the benefits of having a father."

He'd often wondered how different his life might have been had he known positive paternal guidance. Chances were he wouldn't be absurdly rich. Then again, he wouldn't have needed money as a substitute for other, less definable things. Things he'd once wanted to give Jenna but knew now he could never provide.

"Isn't that rather drastic?" she asked.

Gage inhaled her perfume, a scent that reminded him of crushed berries—wild and sweet—then he cocked his head. "I thought these were drastic times."

He looked at her expectantly, but her troubled gaze held far more suspicion than hope.

Hell's fire, the last thing he wanted was Jenna's distrust, even if he well understood it. Twelve years ago he'd vanished like a thief in the night. The time for excuses was long past. But he'd come here today with a plan to help make it up to her. Oh, not entirely—not even close. But maybe, hopefully, enough.

He had it on good authority that Darley Realty, the residential development company her father had founded twenty-five years ago, was in dire financial straits. Gage also knew that Jenna's father had intended to change his will; in the event of his death, the vast majority of Raphael's assets were to pass on to his daughters, not his wife. With Amy gone now, too, Gage had assumed Jenna would be the major beneficiary.

He'd come today to offer to buy Darley Realty for a generous price. He'd wanted a speedy transaction, the idea being Jenna could continue her hassle-free life without learning about the company's problems and consequently suffering any unnecessary sense of embarrassment or gratitude over his offer. He'd had little doubt that Jenna would accept; her profession was writing, and her life was overseas. But apparently Raphael hadn't had time to change his will before the accident. And it seemed that Jenna couldn't care less about the money. After her loss, she had her heart set on one thing and one thing only.

A baby.

Not easy given the circumstances, but he'd learned that almost anything was possible. He'd make it his mission: before he walked away a second time, he would see Jenna happy. He would give her what she wanted most. Then maybe he could close that book—bury that ghost—and at last get on with his life, conscience clear.

She edged toward the middle of the room, hands clasped at her waist. "Say you're right. Where am I supposed to find this husband?"

He tipped an imaginary hat. "At your service."

She smiled. "Now you *are* playing games."

His earlier years had been about survival, pretending off-handed acceptance when mostly he'd been drowning with weights tied around both feet. These days he called the shots. With every breath, he intended to keep it that way. If Gage Cameron played games, it was only ever by his own rules.

"Will you at least listen to my plan?"

"Fine." She nodded. "Go ahead."

"First we'll make it known to Leeann that we're reunited lovers."

Her slim nostrils flared. "First lie."

Not through any lack of desire on his part. But success was bred through a combination of flexibility, critical timing and restraint of emotion. Now he was a master. Now he always won.

"We'll announce our engagement," he went on. "As soon as possible, we'll marry and file a petition for guardianship of Meg. The judge will see that the baby won't need to worry financially—"

"Meg wouldn't need to worry about money with Leeann as a guardian either."

"You said you'd listen," he chided.

Given the way her fingers wound around and strangled each other, she might want to slap him for suggesting any part of this. Instead she nodded again and he strolled toward her.

"Our petition," he continued, "will state that you're not only a blood relative but are also the mother's twin sister. We'll dig up an expert or two who will testify that you're the natural choice to replace the child's biological mother. They can list the benefits the baby would enjoy with regard to face as well as scent recognition. As identical twins, yours and Amy's would be similar."

Her mouth dropped open. "How on earth do you know about such things?"

"I read it somewhere." Since he'd known Jenna, the subject of twins had fascinated him. He'd be happy to recite some eye-opening facts he'd mentally filed away regarding studies on twin science; he bet she'd be interested. "Another advantage is age. You're fifteen years younger than Leeann."

Her eyebrows knitted. "That sounds like discrimination."

"Statistics will bear out the probability that you'll be around longer, which equates to more stability for Meg."

"More stability," she murmured, understanding. "I see."

"Plus you'll have the unswerving support of a marital partner…a past associate of the family."

Her eyes glistened, probing his as she soaked it all in. She'd become far more beautiful than he'd ever imagined. In her female prime, she was lush and challenging, unlike the first time when she'd been young, eager and way off-limits. Her father had been right about one thing: his young blood had run hotter, faster, back then. If he hadn't left that night…

"Why are you doing this?" she asked.

He willed his gaze to track up from the beating hollow of her throat. "You want your niece."

"I could tell the greengrocer that. He's not going to propose."

How to explain?

He tugged an earlobe. "Your father…"

"My father would roll over in his grave at the thought of us marrying. You know that as well as I do."

The knife twisted in his gut but he didn't flinch. A poker face was a strategist's best friend. "When we first knew each other, no doubt. But money changes a lot of things, including people's opinions."

"It doesn't change the past."

He knew the questions that shone from the depths of her eyes: *Why did you leave? Why didn't you have the decency to tell me?*

Would she believe that he'd had no choice? Twelve years ago, for the first time in his life, he'd made the smart choice instead of the rogue one. As a consequence, he'd discovered who he was—who and where he needed to be. Free, alone and reasonably happy. He was wise enough now not to wish for more.

He edged around her unspoken question. "If I'd said goodbye, I wouldn't have wanted to go."

God knows, that was true.

Her lips hardened to a flat line. "Here's a cliché that works. I was young and foolish. I thought you cared. It might be even more foolish to believe that you care to this extent now."

"You think I'd offer something like this then walk away?"

Her eyes held his. "Yes, I do."

"I give you my word."

"Honor was never your strong suit."

But she was forgetting...once when he could have taken her, a virgin, he'd left her alone. Hell, his mother had come from a nice family too until his father had ripped it out from under her and left her with an addiction as well as an infant she couldn't care for.

He inhaled deeply.

All that was done with, buried. Dead. Obviously so was this discussion.

"Then I take it your mind is made up," he stated with a smile that held no offence. When all was said and done, there wasn't a reason in the world she *should* trust him. Regrettably it seemed too much had happened and too much time had passed to change that now.

"My deepest condolences on your loss," he said, "and best of luck with your niece."

But when he turned away, she caught his arm. Even through his jacket sleeve, the evocative warmth burrowed into his flesh, causing his skin to tighten and heat. Angling back, he studied her red-rimmed eyes and saw the same charged awareness that he felt, as well as thinly veiled fear.

Her throat bobbed on a swallow. "I'm just not certain this is the way."

"What other way is there? You've already said that kidnapping's out."

It took a moment for her to return his crooked smile. But he didn't miss the fine sheen erupting on her hairline.

Finally she blew out a breath and her hold on his arm slid away. "What would this...*marriage* entail?"

He faced her full on. "Being seen together. Buying a ring. Setting a date."

"What about your work?" Her eyes dulled with skepticism. "Do you have time for this kind of charade?"

"I do have several important business transactions coming up, but, as I said, I'll be in Sydney for a few weeks. I'll try to limit my travel after that to keep the pretence up. And once you have guardianship of the child, and there's no chance of things unraveling, we can go our separate ways."

She rubbed her palms down the sides of her jeans. "Do you actually believe we can convince people that our engagement is real?"

"Absolutely."

Her eyebrows lifted. "Because in business you're used to bluffing?"

Because since I laid eyes on you again, all I can think about is taking you in my arms and kissing you senseless.

His thoughts might have shown on his face since she blinked several times and a blush crept from her cleavage all the way up the column of her throat.

He rapped his knuckles against his thigh and crossed back to the desk.

One step at a time.

"We'll need to show the world," he explained, "that we've fallen in love. That we're committed to each other."

He collected a silver framed photo next to the globe and clenched his jaw.

What a waste. Amy had been a nice girl; *too* nice for his tastes. It had always been Jenna who'd caught his interest, the teenager with a wiggle in her walk and a sense of right on her side. Once upon a time he'd honestly hoped they would marry. If only things had been different…

He pushed *if onlys* from his mind, set the frame down, and met Jenna's gaze again.

She seemed to be sizing him up. "And what precisely do you get out of all this?"

He merely smiled. "I get to help an old friend."

"That's not a very good answer."

"It's the only answer I have."

"You mean it's the only one you're prepared to give. Forgive me if I'm a little skeptical of your motives."

"What other motives could there be?"

She pressed her lips together as if they'd gone dry. "You wouldn't expect us to…I mean…you're not thinking that…"

An adrenaline surge threw his heartbeat into a cantor. "You're asking if we'll need to embrace…to kiss?"

Make love?

He crossed back and invaded her personal space until her neck arced slowly back. Gazing down into her eyes, he enjoyed a deep stir of desire—the same as long ago, yet somehow deliciously different.

"Jenna, we need to get something out in the open. Two people know when they're sexually compatible. We were compatible then. We still are now. It would be crazy to deny it. And, yes, we will need to show affection in public. But I won't take advantage of the situation."

Naturally he wanted her, but that could only happen if she wanted him, too. And not out of comfort from grieving, or impossible dreams of *happy families,* but from a mutual hunger that deserved to be satisfied, once…possibly twice. That was the limit. That would be safe.

Calm, mingled with curiosity, washed over her face. "You're a complicated man, Gage Cameron."

"That's where people come unstuck." He grinned. "I'm easy to work out."

He imagined his palm sliding down over her curves, his head lowering and insides smoldering as his mouth captured hers. She was frightened, filled with pain and a desperate need for reassurance. How easy it would be to meet her lips and give her some relief.

He bit down and moved away.

Time to go.

"I can get things underway tomorrow," he said, almost to the door. "I'll collect you at ten."

"Gage?"

He turned back.

"I'm not sure I won't regret this, but…" She hesitated then slowly smiled. "Thank you."

He nodded and left, the dog trotting at his heels.

When Jenna had what she needed—when there was no question—he would walk away, just as he was walking away now. Because her father had been right. Long term he was bad for her.

Hell, too close for too long, he was bad for anyone.

CHAPTER THREE

THE next day Jenna accepted Gage's hand and let him help her out from his black imported coupe onto the sidewalk that surrounded her stepmother's apartment building. Peering up at the top floor, she sucked in a nervous breath and straightened her conservative, pale blue dress.

She hated conservative. A T-shirt and jeans suited her far better. But denim would look decidedly out of place today alongside Gage's craftsman-cut suit. Not that his long, powerful legs wouldn't still look exceptional in faded hip-riding Levi's. Whenever she'd seen him during that summer long ago, hunched over the open bonnet of his eighties model Ford—his broad, bare back glistening and brown—she'd practically melted.

"We don't need to do this today." He placed a warm palm between her shoulder blades. "You can give yourself another day or two."

His words, and touch, almost melted her now. And after yesterday, when he'd stood so close and had spoken about *affection in public* and *sexual compatibility*, she was certain any significant physical contact between them would be as dangerous as ever. Yet, for the sake of authenticity leading up to their "marriage," he'd made it clear they needed to play, and play well, at being lovers.

So how soon before he brought her close to him? How soon before they kissed?

"After hearing your lawyer's advice half an hour ago," she said, forcing herself to focus, "seeing Leeann sooner is definitely better than later."

He walked in step beside her. "Lance sounded more than optimistic about our chances."

She clutched her handbag to her chest. Her stomach was a constantly churning ball of nerves. "I'm not sure he bought the reunited lovers story."

She wasn't any more certain Leeann would. Jenna loathed being deceived and hated deceiving anyone else. But as Gage had pointed out, these were desperate times. And the next few weeks weren't to benefit herself but her niece. Despite the guardianship directive, in her heart she knew Amy would have given more than her blessing— she'd have been cheering her on every step of the way.

Gage sent her a lopsided *trust me* smile that made Jenna's heart skip a beat. "My lawyer isn't the one who counts. We need to convince Leeann that we're serious and she's in for one hell of a fight if she doesn't consent to handing Meg over. She'll back down."

Jenna wasn't so sure. "Leeann had three miscarriages early on. I can't see her simply handing over what she wants more than anything." She glared straight ahead. "All the better if she thought it hurt me."

He swung open the building's pedestrian gate and ushered her through. "Leeann can be a possessive and spiteful woman."

Curious, she stepped under the bridge of his arm into

the neat sandstone courtyard. "I didn't realize you knew
her that well."

"I know enough."

Possessive…spiteful. Could he really help her get
custody of Meg from Leeann? Jenna knew where her niece
belonged, and not purely because she was kin. She'd never
liked or trusted Leeann. Her skin crawled to think of Amy's
daughter growing up with a woman who'd reminded her of
a prickly, well-dressed praying mantis. She wondered how
her father had ever fallen in love with such a woman when
her mother had been so sweet and giving—so much like
Amy.

They stopped before the building intercom. He gazed
down at her, one imperious eyebrow raised. "You ready?"

"No," she replied. "Are you?"

He grinned, slow and sexy. "I'm looking forward to it."

While he buzzed, Jenna wrung her purse and told
herself to breathe, just breathe. It didn't help. Would all
this subterfuge blow up in her face? Could this hurt her
chances with Meg rather than help?

Perhaps she needed more time to think it over.

"Maybe we should have called," she reasoned, "to let
her know we were coming."

"No. We should let her enjoy the surprise."

Like the way he'd surprised her yesterday, by showing
up unannounced then suggesting they get married? Gage
had let her know that he had no intention of finishing
what they'd started all those years ago: he didn't plan to
seduce her. A big part of her—the pride-filled part—
rejoiced. She'd been a fragile teenager when he'd left her
love for him high and dry; she hadn't thought she would
ever recover.

Yet a more reckless side remembered the feel of his hard, hot chest, the way his shadowed jaw had grazed a delicious path along her skin. What would it be like to enjoy the penetrating pleasure of his kiss again? Would it feel different now that they were older?

The intercom clicked and Leeann's voice purred out. "I'm busy. Come back later."

Gage leant closer. "Mrs. Darley, this is Gage Cameron. I'm with Jenna. May we come up? We won't take more than a few minutes of your time."

A torturous silence stretched out. Jenna imagined her stepmother's mind spinning at the name from the past, connecting it with "multimillionaire" then wondering why the heck he was troubling her almost two weeks after her husband's death.

The intercom snapped again. "I really am stretched for time."

Jenna set her teeth. She was so over Leeann's lady-of-the-house routine. She'd been over it years ago. Today, for her niece's sake, she wouldn't tolerate it.

She spoke directly at the grill. "We've come to see Meg."

Large hands on Jenna's shoulders tugged her back. Gage's slight frown said, *I'll handle this.* "Mrs. Darley, I'm on a tight schedule, too. We would appreciate a few moments."

Jenna had all but given up when the door buzzed, and her high-strung nerves loosened a knot. Gage shouldered the jamb and swept Jenna inside the building. At the lift, he punched the *up* arrow.

Threading his hands before him, he gazed at the light passing down the floors—so cool—while she felt ready to dissolve like a sandcastle smashed by a succession of waves. But this morning, whenever her mind had funneled down into grief-stricken thoughts over losing her father and sister, she'd ordered herself to think only of Meg. More resolute than ever, she did that now.

Beside her, Gage rocked back on his heels. "Why did you cut your hair?"

His question threw her. She looked over at his classically chiseled profile—the straight nose and firm jaw angled up as he watched the lift light blink down.

"I'm sorry," she stammered, "what did you just say?"

He looked at her, the same way he had yesterday—evaluating, wondering. Dangerous and sultry. "When I left, your hair was a thick wavy river down your back."

What on earth?

Gathering herself, she forced her eyes away from his and dead ahead. "Most places I stay don't have dryers. It was difficult to manage."

"It was beautiful."

The breath caught in her chest. Was he doing this deliberately—putting her off-guard, now of all times? Or was he setting the mood for their performance in front of Leeann? Either explanation made her less than comfortable. In fact, it made her highly *un*comfortable.

She blew a wave off her damp forehead and concentrated on the cold metallic doors. "My hair isn't important."

"I liked when you wore it out, wild and tangled."

"It's much easier tame and shorter."

Out of the corner of her eye, she saw him appraise her, from crown to toe, before he peered back at the lift light. "You should let it grow."

Heat consumed her cheeks. Feeling herself being towed away, Jenna briefly closed her eyes and tried to tamp down images of him curled over her, his hands in her hair—long, short…what did it matter? Making love with Gage would be ecstasy any way it came.

The lift doors whirred open. They stepped inside and traveled to the top floor in simmering silence. The space seemed way too small to accommodate her, him and the electric charge humming between them.

When the lift stopped, she strode out a step ahead then had to tell her heart to quit thumping all over again. Leeann was parked in the doorway of what had been, only a handful of days before, her father's apartment.

Jenna had always disliked the beauty mark that sat on the steeple of Leeann's left eyebrow. She detested it more now as that eyebrow lifted along with her stepmother's intrigued smile.

Leeann spoke to Gage. "Well, *you've* grown up."

"In every way that counts." Gage linked an arm around Jenna's waist and moved them both forward.

Jenna was normally a patient person, but she didn't want to waste time on pleasantries now. As they crossed the threshold onto white Italian marble surrounded by sumptuous furnishings, as politely as she could, she came right to the point.

"Where's Meg?"

After closing the door, Leeann led them into the living room that boasted a panoramic view of the glistening blue harbour and majestic giant shells of Sydney's Opera House. Her father's portrait hung on the far wall and the bonsai plant her mother had given him the year she'd passed away sat on the wet bar. The leaves were tinged brown.

"You should have called and let me know you were

coming," Leeann explained, her voice saccharine sweet. "The baby's out, I'm afraid, getting some fresh air with the nanny. She's a woman with impeccable qualifications and references. Expensive, but my granddaughter deserves the best."

"So, you're not caring for Meg yourself?"

Jenna's gaze snapped over to Gage and she smiled. *Good question.*

"Given that I don't have any firsthand experience with infants," Leeann replied a little stiffly, "I wasn't too proud to seek assistance." She brought her hands together, a terminating gesture. "I'd offer you refreshments, but I have an appointment with my lawyer in an hour."

Jenna's lip curled at the same kind of dismissal she'd heard from this woman too often in the past. Then she noticed something out of place—a jacket lying over a dining room chair. A heavy jacket…leather. Big.

She moved toward it, assessed the jacket, then Leeann. "Unless his tastes changed radically, this didn't belong to my father." It smelled of oil or grease.

Leeann stood very still, as if she were holding her breath. "That belongs to the nanny."

"Don't nannies wear pinafores and carry umbrellas?" Jenna asked skeptically.

Leeann manufactured a laugh and patted her blond chignon. "I meant the nanny's boyfriend."

Somebody's boyfriend, Jenna thought, but not the nanny's. Seemed it hadn't taken Leeann long to fill her poor father's shoes.

Her chest constricted.

Or perhaps Leeann had been seeing someone on the side all along.

Leeann swung her attention to Gage. "I presume you made the journey to pay your respects to my husband. A little late for the ceremony, I'm afraid."

Gage nodded. "Jenna's father was very generous to me."

Leeann's green eyes lowered even as they gleamed. "And to me."

A weak mewling leaked out from behind a partly closed bedroom door. Jenna stilled, heard it again, then held her stomach. *Meg.*

A fierce protective instinct surged up and she pushed past Leeann into the room. In the darkened far corner stood a cot, pretty with lace and a hanging mobile of colorful clowns. Tiny fists waved above the mattress and the crying grew louder.

Heart squeezing, Jenna rushed to the cot.

Leaning over the rail, she carefully scooped the baby out and cradled her close. Meg hiccupped out another cry, but her big blue eyes, wet with tears, opened to gaze into Jenna's. Did the baby recognize her? Did Meg think she was her mother?

For the most part, Leeann had made Meg unavailable for one reason or another, although she had been uncommonly generous the day of the funeral; Jenna had held her niece right through the service and afterward at the wake. But that day Jenna had been in a different zone, barely functioning. Now, however, she felt the connection between them as if she'd been zapped by lightning—strong, bright and formidable.

Tucking Meg close, Jenna breathed in the scent of powder and felt the deep-rooted knowledge of kinship. "It's okay, sweetie." As the crying petered out, she smiled softly down as her throat thickened. "You look so much like your mother."

Behind her, she sensed Gage's towering presence, then heard the comforting rumble of his voice near her ear. "And her aunt."

From the rear of the room, Leeann made her excuse. "I'd just put her down and didn't want her disturbed. I wasn't sure you'd understand."

You're right, Jenna thought. *I don't.*

But she kept those comments to herself. Leeann's explanation might be embarrassingly lame, but Jenna didn't want anything upsetting the baby again.

In the absence of a challenge, Leeann went on. "She's sleeping through the night now. Amy used to speak often about what songs Meg liked to hear, the nightlight she preferred left on. Amy might have told you, too, Jenna…over the phone or in a letter." Her voice crept closer. "When did you say you were heading back overseas?"

Jenna curled a finger around Meg's silken cheek. "I'm not."

She smiled at the baby gripping her finger as well as Leeann's stunned silence. In the past she'd never gotten the upper hand as far as this woman was concerned. That's why she'd left home so soon after finishing college. No matter the disagreement—bar two—her father had sided with his new wife. He'd valued their marriage, as he'd valued Jenna's mother until her death. He'd told his daughter he didn't want any upsets in the family home, then had asked why she couldn't simply be polite and get along.

Her father couldn't understand that Leeann had seen his strong-willed daughter as a threat. When they were alone,

Leeann had made it clear there was room for only one mistress in the Darley household. The frosty glares, the subtle yet painful barbs… Having been brought up by a quiet and gentle woman, Jenna hadn't known how to handle a female relationship based on rivalry. In the end, she'd handled it by throwing up her hands and walking away.

But she wouldn't walk away from this fight.

"Wasn't there an assignment," Leeann stammered, "in Italy? You mentioned it at the funeral…"

Gage blocked Leeann's progress toward Jenna. "She declined that assignment. Although we have talked about visiting Venice during a brief honeymoon."

Every inch of Jenna glowed warm. Those words were simply part of an act to get Meg and keep her where she belonged. Yet it seemed like only yesterday that she'd gone to sleep dreaming of sharing a honeymoon with Gage. A young and foolish girl's dream. She had never featured in his bigger plans.

Now Gage was an important man, and pedal-to-the-metal busy.

Why *was* he helping her?

Ashen-faced, Leeann navigated around Gage and planted herself before Jenna. "Did I hear right? A honeymoon?"

Gage cupped Jenna's shoulders and his heat radiated through to her very bones. "When Jenna and I met again, the old sparks fired back up." He looked down at her and smiled. "We've wasted so much time, haven't we, darling?"

His earlier comments about her hair rose in Jenna's mind. Finding the emotion she needed, she bit that bullet.

"When Gage asked me to marry him, I...I knew it was right." She turned, steadied herself upon facing the solid heat of Gage's frame, then placed the baby in his arms.

Strong chin tucking in, he held Meg a little away from his broad chest...until the baby gurgled, then he cocked his head, his mouth curved slightly at one corner, and he brought her close.

A tower of a man holding such a tiny life. The picture made Jenna's heart beat fast. Gage had no intention of fathering children. As he'd said, he valued his freedom too much and a child needed stability. Still, it was a shame that a man who possessed Gage's more admirable qualities— leadership, intelligence, vision—would never pass those genes on. This situation with herself and Meg would probably be the closest he would come to fatherhood.

A shiver chased up her spine.

Gage could walk away. But, as young as she was, would Meg grow attached?

Would her Aunt Jenna?

Although Leeann was inches shorter than her step-daughter, she managed to look down her long nose at her. "I don't see a ring on your finger, Jenna."

Gage directed his smile and attention toward Meg but spoke to Leeann. "That's where we're headed next."

Clearly agitated, Leeann patted her chignon again then moved to pry the baby from Gage's arms. "Then I suppose you'd best be on your way."

The baby squirmed, but Leeann propped Meg upright against her shoulder, facing her away from the couple she was obviously seeing more clearly as a threat. When Meg mewled, Leeann rubbed the back of her pink playsuit a little too vigorously. The truly tragic part was that Jenna knew how genuinely Leeann wanted to keep the baby, too. Leeann thought Meg could fill that empty place inside of her—the part that hadn't received or learned how to love. If Jenna hadn't experienced Leeann's narcissism firsthand growing up, she might even feel sorry for her.

"You'll both be living in Melbourne?" Leeann asked, her eyes assessing the two of them.

Jenna's mind went blank. Now that she was back, she had no intention of leaving Sydney again; this had been Amy's home. It would be Meg's home too. But Leeann would be aware that Gage's headquarters were down south.

As if reading her thoughts, Gage came up with the perfect response. "Jenna would like to stay in Sydney, and I already had plans to relocate my head office here."

His arms circled Jenna's waist and brought her closer. As he smiled down into her eyes, her heartbeat tripped over itself. He was so convincing. She had to remind herself that these simmering looks were merely for show.

Leeann cleared her throat; their display obviously irritated her. "I read in this morning's business section that you were wrapping up a secret negotiation." The baby whimpered and Leeann began to jiggle her. "I'd have thought your time would be needed in Melbourne twenty-four seven."

When the baby cried, Leeann shh'ed louder and jiggled faster, and Jenna's paper-thin patience tore down the middle.

She couldn't do it. Legal guardian or not, how could she leave Amy's baby here even one minute longer?

She was about to lever Meg from Leeann's arms when a young woman rushed into the room.

"I'll take her if you'd like, Mrs. Darley."

The woman's glasses sat crookedly above the bump of her nose, but her bearing, as she held out her hands for the baby, was firm and confident. Although she didn't want to, Jenna took a step back and let the woman—Meg's nanny, she presumed—take her niece.

Behind small oval lenses, the younger woman's large dark eyes appraised her, but Jenna couldn't quite decide whether it was with approval or mistrust.

"You must be Meg's aunt." The nanny smiled down at the quieting baby and tickled her chin. "I can see the resemblance." She turned to Leeann. "I had trouble finding the right formula. I'll make a bottle then put her back to sleep."

Leeann's chest expanded with a shuddering breath as she set a hand to the bodice of her raw silk jacket and visibly composed herself. "Thank you, Tina. We'll leave you both alone. My guests were about to leave."

Gage drew a card from his jacket's top pocket. "My lawyer's number." His grin was cold. "In case you need to contact us."

Traveling down in the lift a moment later, Jenna couldn't stop quaking. She crossed her arms, raised a fist, and tried to find a finger with any nail left to bite. She hadn't chewed her nails since ninth grade when Amy had bought a DIY French tip set to help her quit the habit. Amy had said there was no excuse for biting nails...she had to be strong...had to take it one day at a time...

Tears thickened in her throat.

Meg crying, the nanny's judgmental gaze, Leeann pushing them out... She should have taken her father's bonsai and *smashed* it against the window of that damn million-dollar view! Or better yet, she should have brought it back home where it belonged.

She closed her eyes.

Oh, Meg...

Gage wound an arm around her bent shoulders and brought her close. But the swelling bank of tears only rose higher. He felt so strong and sturdy, a pillar she could lean on. Lord in heaven, she needed that so much.

Releasing a breath, she relented and buried her face against a chest carved from warm granite.

"This is so wrong," she groaned against his lapels. "Meg doesn't belong there."

Gage's large hand stroked her hair.

The sheer strength of him...the smell. How easy it would be to forget the past and believe this incredible man truly wanted to marry her, and not merely for pragmatism's sake.

Her hands curled, fisting in his jacket.

Oh, I really am in a bad way, she thought.

As the doors parted, he gently drew her away and gazed deeply into her eyes, reassuring her. "The nanny seems nice."

Wishing away the hollow ache in her chest, Jenna accepted the handkerchief he offered and dabbed her wet eyes; she could imagine the puffy smudges partially covering her hideous dark circles. God, she needed sleep.

She sniffed. "I guess things could be worse."

But not much.

After she returned the handkerchief, Gage took her hand and, with a determined stride, marched one step ahead out of the lobby and into the street.

Behind his striding size twelves, her heels clacked on the sandstone. "Where are we going?"

"You weren't listening earlier?"

Her mind rewound and a wave of butterflies released in her stomach. "We're going to buy a ring?"

"A diamond so outrageously large that no one, including Leeann, can miss it. Then we have another stop to make."

He swung open the car door and indicated that she should take the passenger seat. She eased in and peered up at him. "Another stop? Are you going to tell me?"

Before shutting her door, he winked. "You know how I like surprises."

CHAPTER FOUR

JENNA gazed at the glamorous, princess-cut, white diamond ring Gage had slipped on her finger an hour ago and swallowed a great lump of nerves.

"Gage, maybe we're moving too fast."

Sitting across from her at a city mall café, her companion's gaze slid from the waiter delivering his coffee directly onto her.

"You heard my lawyer this morning," he said, a line cut between his brows. "Our best chance of claiming your niece means moving forward now. That translates into getting married immediately."

Jenna propped her pounding head in her hand.

One week, two tops, and I'll be Gage Cameron's bride, she thought. The scenario was surreal. So much had happened lately—the accident, the fallout from the wills, Gage showing up out of the blue. Her poor mind could barely keep up.

Jenna pushed three travel brochures around the tabletop while the diamond sparkled up, dazzling enough to hypnotize.

The Beauty of Bermuda.

New Zealand Honeymoon Retreats.
Marry in Las Vegas!

Time was of the essence, so Gage had suggested countries whose marriage laws required less lead time than Australia's one-month proviso, yet were still recognized here. It made perfect sense. Yet it all felt so…rushed.

Her fingertip trailed down a bright Bermuda beach. The pamphlet featured a couple kissing, their embrace framed by the halo of an orange setting sun. She pictured herself and Gage in that shot and the frazzled knot in her stomach pulled tighter.

"I know this marriage is all for show. I mean, I know this isn't for real." It certainly wasn't for forever.

Although his face was set, the assuring slant of his mouth was still killer sexy. *Darn the man.*

"You shouldn't look at this in terms of a conventional union," he told her.

Jenna sighed. "That's my problem. I'm scared to death no one will see it as conventional. Just phony."

"You're forgetting our chemistry." His gaze rested on her lips, making them tingle, before his attention drifted toward finding his coffee cup and spoon. "If we let that chemistry work for us—"

"Then I could be in even deeper trouble," she muttered under her breath.

He dropped in sugar and stirred. "I don't see how."

Well, she could start with how he'd described her hair when they'd stood outside that lift earlier today…the way his graveled confession of how he preferred it wild and tangled had made her heartbeat race and palms grow damp. He was trouble…trouble with a capital T.

The last thing she needed was to fall in love with Gage

Cameron again, particularly when she felt more vulnerable than ever before. She needed to be strong, shore up her defenses, and remember he was here only for the short term. She couldn't handle another dose of heartache—not on top of everything else.

"I don't want this…*relationship* to do more harm than good," she explained. "I don't want it to get out of hand."

"Out of my hands, Jenna, or yours?"

As he sipped his coffee, the power of his lidded gaze seemed to rope around her and tug her in. The awareness glittering in his eyes was so magnetic, so intense, he might as well have thrown a lasso.

She slowly sat back.

Twelve years ago he'd left without a word. Yesterday he'd made it clear he didn't want a family. So, why say in one breath that he wouldn't take advantage of this situation then openly flirt with her the next? He didn't make sense.

Unless…

Gage lowered his cup and scraped back his chair. "We won't waste time arguing the point. If you're unhappy, I'll tell the travel agent to nix the Las Vegas itinerary."

Words sat on the tip of her tongue, but before she could call him back and blurt out heaven knew what, he moved off. Two seconds later, his cell rang.

He'd left the phone on the table when his office had called earlier. He hadn't been pleased at the interruption. In fact, he'd seemed hard-pressed not to hurl the phone at the floor.

Jenna willed the hot-wired tension from her body. Gage was already passing through the travel agency doorway. Whoever it was could leave a message. With Gage gone, she had a little time to mull over her earlier assumption.

Setting her chin in her palm, she fingered the corner of the New Zealand pamphlet.

If it meant getting Meg back, of course she would marry Gage. She was grateful for his help. And if she had to choose, New Zealand's Mt. Ruapehu, with its fairy-tale top-of-the-world chateau, would've been her pick. But from the moment he'd suggested a wedding, a question had sprouted and grown until finally the answer pushed its way into the light.

He'd said he wouldn't take advantage of this situation. That didn't mean he would object if his bone-melting magnetism worked its inevitable charm and she ultimately threw herself at him, either to show her appreciation for his help, or for even more fundamental reasons than that.

Sexual attraction.

Carnal satisfaction.

Gage had found tremendous material success; there were few people to rival his seemingly effortless ascent in the business world. Yet somehow she got the impression that he was secretly looking for a different kind of challenge. Perhaps something over which he'd contemplated as often as she had.

Maybe he did want to help an old friend.

But maybe he also wanted to help himself.

His cell phone beeped, and Jenna's heart leapt to her throat. A message flashed on the miniature screen… and kept flashing. Her gaze snapped over to the travel agency. No Gage yet. When the cell phone beeped again, then beeped louder, an elderly man at the next table frowned at her over his bifocals.

Smiling an apology, Jenna rested her hand over the cell, hoping to muffle the sound. But the buzz vibrated up through her hand; it simply wouldn't be ignored.

More heads turned. Desperate, she swept the phone up. Which button of so many would stop the noise?

About to stab a red key, she froze. A word in the text message caught her attention.

Progress on the Darley bid?

Her world tilted and she almost slid off her chair. Head spinning, she read it again. She held her breath as another message flashed.

Need projection figures for next quarter if proceeding with purchase.

"Anything wrong?"

She tossed the phone as if it were a hot coal. It spun in a wild circle and landed in front of Gage as he joined her again at the table.

Drawing in his chair, he glowered at the phone then at her. "You look as if you'd seen ten ghosts."

"That message..." she managed. "It's about Darley Realty." Trying to make sense of it, her next words squeaked out. "Had you been speaking with my father about his company before the accident? About taking it over?"

The corners of that sensual mouth pulled down as he scanned the message. Then that faint scar twitched. She heard the rasp of his beard as he rubbed his jaw, then growled and thumbed a button.

Gage, answer me, damn it! "Was Darley Realty the secret takeover Leeann read about in the paper?"

Had she been mistaken about the kind of challenge Gage was chasing? Was taking over her father's company Gage's true secret agenda?

After a strained moment, he loosened his tie and nodded. "Your father was interested in selling."

Jenna expelled a lungful of pent-up air.

Her father had been tight-lipped about his business dealings at the best of times. Given their strained relationship, there was no reason Jenna should have known about a possible sellout. But Leeann might have known. More to the point…

"Why didn't you tell me?" As her pulse thudded in her temples, she narrowed her gaze and tried to decipher the truth behind the pale shadows in his eyes. "Is it because you still want Darley Realty in your portfolio?" Pain stabbed low in her throat. "Were you planning on seeing Leeann about that, too?"

Gage cursed and looked away. "Of course not."

"The thought didn't cross your mind?"

He collected his teaspoon and tapped it against the table. "That's not the point."

"You know, Gage, it really is the point."

A very sharp, potentially ugly point. She needed to know what this was about. These last few days, she'd had more than enough of being set aside.

"You realize that marriage to me and guardianship over Meg won't give you control of my father's firm. Leeann still gets to keep all the assets, no matter who wins custody of Meg."

He swept his spoon away and growled. "You're blowing this out of proportion. Your father's business doesn't even come close to other businesses I control."

"Then why did you want it?"

Heck, maybe his cronies had learned her father's Western Australia property was riddled with gold. Maybe Gage had some twisted megalomaniacal wish to absorb everything that had belonged to the man who'd once offered him charity—food, an education, a roof over his head.

He didn't meet her eyes. "It doesn't matter now."

"Just because you say so?"

His gaze snapped up. "We have more important things to discuss—like guardianship hearings."

She wasn't finished with this hearing yet. Gage had been after her father's business. He couldn't sweep that under the mat. She knew there had to be more to it…something to do with her and Meg.

"I want to know, Gage. I deserve to know."

His cup, almost at his lips, clattered back down, splashing coffee into its saucer. His expression hardened. "Your father…" He seemed to search for words. "He helped me."

Holding her breath, she waited for him to go on and pushed when he didn't. "Helped you? You mean after you left Sydney?"

His voice lowered. "This is complicated."

She crossed her legs and pretended to get comfortable. "I'm sure you've faced worse."

He exhaled and finally nodded. "You remember how we got…close that summer."

Heat scorched her cheeks. She wasn't that naive teenager anymore, the college girl heartsick for the hired help's son, yet the mere thought of how they'd held each other that last time, with the warm air drifting in through the open pool house, sent blood coursing through her veins like molten lava.

She lifted her chin. "I remember."

"Someone else had her heart set on a little clandestine fun, too."

As understanding slowly dawned, her legs uncrossed and her hands gripped the chair. "I don't believe you," she growled. "Amy wasn't even home that summer—"

"Not Amy. *Leeann.*"

Her head kicked back. The sting was so sharp, he might have physically slapped her.

"Leeann made a pass at you?" The idea was so off, so ridiculous, she almost gagged. But then she remembered the way Leeann had looked at Gage today, as if all her lewd Christmases had come at once, and her heart hit the ground.

Dear Lord, it was true. Her father's wife had propositioned the bad boy next door.

She found a thready voice. "What did she say?"

What did she *do?*

"My mother was out. I was in the backyard, working on my car. Leeann called in on the pretence of discussing requirements for a special dinner for some of your father's business associates. She said she wanted to leave a note. I led her to the kitchen, turned back to find a pen…"

When his words trailed off, Jenna finished for him.

"She kissed you."

He rubbed his temple. "I froze, then she snaked her arms around my neck…"

Uneasiness rolled through her, and Jenna waved her hands. "That's enough. I get the picture. But what does that have to do with my father helping you? With you being here now?"

"Leeann's first pass wasn't her last. But I was prepared when she came knocking again. I was inside and didn't let her through the front door. She got annoyed." His bristled jaw shifted. "You know what they say about a woman scorned."

Leeann had known about her crush on Gage, as had her father. Jenna remembered how particularly snide Leeann had been that summer before Gage had vanished and the pieces fell into place.

She'd been jealous.

Gage went on, "Leeann said if I didn't comply she would tell her husband that I'd cornered her in the grounds and forced myself on her."

Jenna's lip curled as she muttered, "And my father loved this woman."

"She kept her word and the next day your father confronted me. Said Leeann had told him everything. I could see in his eyes he didn't believe her. Nevertheless, as her husband, he had no alternative but to act. He told me to pack and be gone within the hour. Along with that, he gave me a good deal of cash and said not to come back unless I could prove my worth."

But Gage hadn't come back...not until yesterday.

"Your mother never knew?" she asked and he shook his head. "She died during my second year of college, didn't she? I was away in Canberra." She'd changed universities, not because of faculty choices, but because she'd wanted to get as far away from home—her unhappy family life and memories of Gage—as she could.

"Your father gave me his word he would look after her," Gage said. "I sent money every month and from my mother's return letters, Raphael kept his word. But it was no secret she was an alcoholic. The addiction took its toll. I came back briefly for the funeral, but Raphael Darley and I only exchanged nods."

She imagined her father's appraising onyx gaze. Had Gage experienced his first business success by then? Had he worn budget trousers to his mother's funeral, or a tailored suit?

She would have come home to pay her respects to Mrs. Cameron—she'd been a kind woman, just so very sad and broken. But her father hadn't told her of Mrs. Cameron's death until some weeks after the event. No doubt he'd wanted to keep the distance between his willful daughter and the young man his wife had accused of attempted rape.

Now Gage had returned home because of three more funerals.

She swallowed the block of wood stuck in her throat. "How long had you been talking with Dad about the possibility of a buyout?"

"We spoke before I flew out to Dubai. Raphael said…" Gage hesitated then continued with more conviction. "He said he was tired and wanted to retire. I said I'd see if I could help."

"And now?"

He leant forward. "Now we have more important things to focus on. Like a white dress and a baby."

His hand rested near hers. When his index finger grazed her pinkie, a jet of nerves and abject longing flooded her system. It was just a touch and yet the anticipation and heavenly heat it caused invaded every cell in her body, making her beat and glow from the inside out.

A white dress…

After a wedding day came the wedding night. He'd said that they would need to put on a show, but was even a portion of her earlier intuition correct? Did Gage have something more than conversation scheduled for behind closed doors?

An image of two bodies, naked and consumed by

heightened passion, swam to the forefront of her mind. Fire bloomed in her cheeks, smoldered up her limbs and blew a flame at that private place, low and deep inside.

She set her teeth.

For heaven's sake, think about the baby.

Averting her gaze, she drew her hand away and threaded her fingers in her lap. The diamond twinkled up at her, the embers smoldered again and she looked into Gage's eyes.

"I'm certain we should marry in Australia," she told him in a firm voice. "Leeann will have enough objections and suspicions. We don't need to give her an opportunity to stir trouble over whether a wedding conducted on foreign soil is recognized here, even if it is. It might even delay matters rather than push them forward."

A muscle jumped in Gage's jaw before he shucked back one broad shoulder. "It's your show." He collected his phone. "I'll have my personal assistant track down a good marriage celebrant and make an appointment. We'll get the paperwork filed today."

After thumbing a couple of buttons, he frowned at the screen. "Message from my lawyer." He pressed the phone to his ear. One eyebrow slowly lifted then his face turned dark.

By the time he disconnected, Jenna's heart was pounding in her ears. "What is it?"

Was it about Leeann?

"Your stepmother doesn't waste time," he told her, setting the phone down. "She wants you out of that house. You have a week to find alternate accommodations so Leeann can move back in. And that's not all. She wants to see me two weeks from today at the Darley Realty head office." He grinned. "Let the games begin."

CHAPTER FIVE

"WELCOME to your new home."

As Gage fanned open the door of his three-story penthouse, he fought the impulse to sweep Jenna up, carry her across the threshold and make a beeline for the master suite. Even if he could restrain the urge, the primal messages pulsing through his body didn't lie. He wanted her lines and curves against him. Wanted to hold her, fully, and for the longest time.

This past week had been a blissful kind of torture.

Jenna took a wary step inside and looked around. Curling a wave of hair behind her ear, she took in the extravagantly high ceilings, the king-size crimson-and-cream sunken lounge, then lifted her chin to scan beyond the sheer-curtained glass wall to one of the penthouse's four extensive balconies.

"I really could've found a place of my own. Something slightly less grand than the Taj Mahal," she said, pivoting around. "I'd hate to see your country estate."

He smiled. Maybe one day he'd show her his acreage in Colorado, though he didn't doubt she'd already seen Aspen's spectacular scenery during her travels.

He shut the door and strolled beneath the shadow of a Swarovski crystal chandelier. "We agreed. This is the best-fit solution. Living together is another way for Leeann and her lawyers to understand that we're serious about our relationship."

Her round eyes asked, *How serious?*

He almost stroked her silken cheek as he passed.

Serious enough.

After visiting her at the Darley address, dining out at casual venues and posing for the press like a regular couple in love, he sensed Jenna was beginning to trust him. No mean feat. He'd hurt her once, but he'd returned to make recompense.

If she decided that she wanted to take this rekindled friendship to the next level—to its delayed but natural conclusion—he wouldn't object. As long as she was fully aware of her actions and his limitations. Whatever they enjoyed, however many times they enjoyed it, it wouldn't be "till death us do part," no matter what papers they signed.

From his first memory he'd wanted to escape—his background, his dead-end life, his sometimes loving, sometimes neglectful mother. When they'd lived alongside the Darleys, Jenna had given him a reason for hope, a reason to stay. Then Leeann had accused him of attempted rape and Raphael had sent him on his way with more money than a regular guy could earn in a year.

The ugly truth was...

At twenty-one, he was relieved to leave "home," and thankful that Jenna had been spared from his less than stellar influence. She'd been way too good for him, a bright young woman from a respectable family. A virgin he had no right to deflower, yet no doubt would have if he'd stayed around for much longer.

As the years rolled on, another truth had bloomed.

No matter how many homes he owned or how powerful he became, the gap between himself and Jenna would never be bridged. He would always feel half-empty inside, missing the ingredient that made other people whole. Whoever's fault that was, it didn't matter. Long story short: his kind shouldn't reach for things they could never hope to have, and shouldn't damage other people when they tried but failed.

Loners shouldn't have families.

If Jenna didn't have her heart set on bringing up her niece…if she didn't want children of her own…well, maybe then. But if he hadn't been good for Jenna back then, he was definitely no good for her now…except where fighting for Meg—her family—was concerned.

An ironic twist, to be sure. But life, he'd learnt, was full of distortions.

"In three weeks," he said, checking the nearby high-tech facsimile for mail, "we'll be Mr. and Mrs. Cameron. Soon after that, you'll gain guardianship of Meg." He turned and offered a teasing grin. "If we're lucky, it might happen even sooner."

While her eyes sparkled with fragile hope, her hands joined, as if in prayer, and pressed against her mouth. "This is about your meeting with Leeann next week, isn't it? You've found something out."

A thread of doubt wove down his spine. But he'd held back these last bits of information long enough. Some she would like, but others…

Regardless, it was time.

"My sources say Leeann wants to sell Darley Realty."

She nodded slowly as if expecting more. "I wasn't sure whether she'd like the idea of being the female figurehead of a successful company like Darley's, or whether it would interfere with her lifestyle. Guess it's the latter. But what's that got to do with our chances of getting Meg?"

He spun a finger in the air. "Rewind a little."

"To what part?"

"The part where Darley's is successful."

Her brow creased. "I don't follow."

"Remember I said your father was tired and wanted to retire? That was only half of it."

Jenna's complexion faded from peaches and cream to the alabaster of the walls in one second flat.

His gut wrenched, but he resisted the urge to comfort her, even while her trembling lips seemed to beg him to do just that.

"Was he sick?" she asked.

He stuffed his hands in his trouser pockets, out of harm's way, and moved forward. "Your father was under a lot of stress. His company had suffered a succession of financial blows, a combination of bad advice and worse luck."

Her face pinched with disbelief. "And he asked you to bail him out?"

He nodded.

Her delicate shoulders, in that simple white T-shirt, stiffened. "I'm still missing a piece, aren't I?"

He hesitated. Should he come clean? Out of necessity, Raphael had told him everything, then had sworn him to secrecy. But Raphael was dead, and Jenna had said it herself: she deserved to know.

He stopped before her and held her eyes with his. "Your father suspected that Leeann was having an affair."

Jenna withered onto the nearby settee as if her legs had dissolved beneath her. She gazed at the floor, her white-knuckled fists clenched at her sides.

"The leather jacket." One fist punched the cushion. "I knew it."

Yes, he'd known it too, particularly given his own experience with Leeann. "I'm not at all sure that your father was still in love with his wife. He was pretty convinced of her infidelity. He wanted to sort out his affairs. Amy's share was already taken care of in his will, although I believe her husband had been wealthy in his own right. But Raphael admitted that he'd written you out after you two had had an argument and you'd left home for good."

He broke off.

Her pallor was much worse.

"You could do with some water," he said. "Or maybe something stronger."

He started toward the black granite wet bar, but she caught his forearm, bare beneath his rolled-up sleeve. The contact was a charge…startling, electric. He inwardly groaned as it shot a white-hot arrow to a highly responsive part of his anatomy.

Tugging, she drew him down to sit beside her. Her voice was a hoarse whisper. "I don't need a drink, Gage. I need to know everything."

The details would hurt but, a week on from their meeting again, he sensed that her strength had returned enough to cope. It had been her personal strength that had initially attracted him to Jenna. Then he'd discovered the power of her smile, the magic of her sigh. How he'd managed to hold off from easing himself fully inside her that last night was nothing short of a miracle.

He took a deep breath.

Stay focused, Cameron.

"Your father was ashamed of writing you out and more ashamed that he'd been too pigheaded to change his will back. He wanted to make amends. He wanted you to come home so he could tell you he was sorry."

As her eyes filled, the muscles in his chest and back tensed. He found her left hand and covered it with his right. That charge again, more intense this time, quickened his pulse to a gallop.

Her glistening eyes questioned his. "But something doesn't fit. If you already knew about the will, why did you pretend to *guess* a week ago that my father had bequeathed everything to Leeann?"

He stroked the top of her wrist with his thumb as he'd done twice before this week—once in his lawyer's office, the second time when they'd visited their marriage celebrant. If the intimacy of that touch was overstepping the line, she'd have let him know. Instead she seemed to take comfort in it. She wasn't the only one.

"The last time we spoke, your father was set to change his will, but he also thought the sale of Darley's might be the sounder option for his purpose of ensuring that his daughters received their inheritance. He wanted to forgive the past and its mistakes and give you, as well as Amy, the proceeds from the sale straight away to save any arguments later. We were going to sign papers when I arrived back from Dubai."

Hanging on each word, she nodded. "But he died before he could change his will or close the deal with you."

"On a business that I still believe will be very profitable when the right measures are in place. Your father…" How to put it? "On top of his suspicions over Leeann, I think he'd simply had enough. I was in a position to help."

"And pay him back for the money he gave you to make your start twelve years ago?"

He shrugged. "It would've been a win-win situation. I get to repay an old debt, attain a company I could build on, and you would've been taken care of." Her hand moved slightly beneath his and that hurtling arrow hit its mark again, the burn hotter and longer-lasting this time.

"I told you before," she said with a reproving but also grateful note, "money isn't important to me."

"But money *is* important to Leeann. She must know now the state of affairs. That there's work ahead if Darley's is to survive. The negotiations were confidential between the two principals, our financial controllers and a couple of my head people. No doubt Darley's man has informed her of the option her husband was looking into."

He sat back against the cream, tasseled cushions. She did too, her lips slightly parted as she listened.

"I'd prefer to win back Meg without this kind of bargaining," he said, remembering the grilling he'd received from Jenna a week ago regarding any plans he may have had to speak with Leeann about a buyout. "But since Leeann has set the agenda, now I'll let her know that I'm willing to pay dearly for the privilege of owning Darley Realty. Then it'll be a question of how dearly Leeann prizes her privileged lifestyle."

"You think she'd exchange Meg for money?" Jenna slipped her hand from his and waved it as she shook her head. "She might not make a cat's mother but she wants a child. You saw how much. She'd have enough funds without your offer. There's the house, the penthouse, Dad's investments—"

"The house is mortgage-free," he said, trying to ignore how much he missed their recent skin-on-skin contact. "But the bank owns the penthouse. The other investments have been converted into funds to buoy a dangerously high overdraft."

He'd been through all the financial details with Raphael. The company was caught in a downward spiral of debt and interest. Only a massive injection of funds could pull it out of the vortex now.

Her jaw was hanging. "Everything gone? Even his holdings in Western Australia?"

"The company still owns that piece of land, but initial reports tell me it's hardly a prime piece of real estate."

"So now we wait and see if Leeann takes the trade?" She winced. "Oh, God, that sounds horrible." Then her back straightened. "But, damn it, I don't care."

He smiled. "That's the spirit." The take-no-prisoners attitude he'd loved so much about her…that was drawing him toward her now, like a line reeling him in.

His groin flexed.

Dear Lord, damming his impulses where she was concerned would never get any easier. In fact, it could only get harder.

Maybe it was time to get things out in the open before he did something he would very much enjoy but quite possibly regret. He'd said he wouldn't take advantage of the situation. It's time he was frank.

Jenna, too.

He threaded his hands and, leaning forward, angled his

forearms on his knees. "There's something else we need to discuss about this arrangement. Jenna, we need to discuss us."

A blush crept up her throat and her pupils dilated. She wasn't immune to the heavy-hot strum resonating between them. Clearly she knew what was coming; he merely wanted to know whether to act on it. Was she as curious and flat-out frustrated as he was?

"I need to explain some things about myself," he told her, "and how I feel about you."

Her gaze flared then dropped away to land on the coffee table. She absently collected a pack of cards, which he'd left out this morning, and started to shuffle. "Explain?"

Distracted by the cards, he frowned. "Yes."

"Remember when you explained how to play poker?" She forced a smile as the cards slotted back and forth into her bejeweled left hand. "We stayed up till four one morning. I won."

Frown deepening, he scratched his temple.

From her avoidance tactics, it would appear he'd spoken too soon, if, in fact, there would ever be a right time to speak about the lightning-infused fever that brewed inside him whenever Jenna was near.

Still, he couldn't forget how he'd managed to make her laugh this past week, and how she fit so snugly alongside him whenever they walked. Last night at the movies, when the heroine had walked away from the hero just before the credit roll, Jenna had looked at him. He'd looked at her. Time had sped up and simultaneously slowed to a thick sweetly pitched crawl. He'd come so close to kissing her. He still believed she'd wanted him to.

He sucked down a breath.

He'd been right the first time. They needed this building awareness out in the open. Now.

He reached to take the cards from her hands, but she dodged and shuffled more quickly.

This time, he wasn't put off. "I don't want to discuss poker, Jenna."

Her attention remained on the blur of cards. "You've been playing solitaire, haven't you? That was your favorite. They have that game on software, you know. You can install it on your laptop. You don't need to play the old-fashioned way."

He swept aside a wave curling around her cheek. "I prefer the old-fashioned way."

Her hands stopped moving. Through her white T and fine lacy bra, her nipples visibly tightened. All those years ago, he'd lovingly caressed them. Once, only once, he'd run his tongue around their peaks, grazed his teeth over their ripened swell. Lord have mercy, he could feel their warmth pressed against him now.

"Times have changed." Her voice was uneven, a little breathless. "Don't you think it's only right that we try to change, too?"

This time she let him take the cards and set them on the tabletop. "I don't work that way. How about you?"

Would you like to play, Jenna? The way we used to... Even if it's just once...

He leant forward, inviting her to read the intention in his eyes...to sense how strong that intention was.

Her expression softened, even as her blue eyes grew darker, hotter. Her lips parted and she silently drew down some air. His gaze lingered on her mouth while his surroundings receded and the magnetic field urging them nearer wound up another sizzling degree. He tipped closer, ready to speak.

Ready to kiss...

Two palms met his chest, blocking his advance. "You said you wouldn't take advantage of the situation."

The high-voltage buzz zipping through his veins screeched then fell suddenly quiet. He pulled away, focusing on her words. "If that's what I'm doing—taking advantage of you—I apologize. But, Jenna, we really ought to talk about—"

"You want to *talk?*"

When her lips twitched with skepticism, Gage blinked twice then set his jaw. "After the week we've spent together, the way we've reconnected, I thought you might want to hear what I have to say."

Her gaze flicked over his face. Her expression eased, and for an instant her heart seemed to show in her eyes.

She slowly nodded. "Go on."

He bunched his hands to keep from bringing her near and instead laid an arm behind her over the settee. She didn't move away.

"Like anyone else, I have regrets. I've thought about you, Jenna—about us—a lot over the years."

"It's surprising that you found time to make your fortune."

He saw the flash of regret on her face over the barb, but she didn't take it back.

He conceded. "Guess I deserve that."

"Maybe. I really don't know anymore. I suppose it depends on what you say next."

The strength Gage so admired radiated out, and he caught himself. But he could only be truthful about how he felt. About what he could offer and what he could not.

He wanted to be with her, for her to share his bed, to know each other at last. "I want us to go back and claim what was denied us years ago." By age and class structure, by Leeann and his own shortcomings. "I'm asking if you want to finally live out that experience too."

He paused to find the words that would bind their feelings of the last few days rather than unravel them. He was committed in their efforts regarding Meg; he would be there for her in all things, the very best way he knew how. The thorn in the side of that commitment?

Making love with Jenna and helping her with Meg couldn't transform him into something he was not. He'd been born to be exactly what he was—nothing less, nothing more. For everyone's sake, he needed to remember that.

Against his better judgment, once he'd tried the traditional way. It had ended in the worst kind of disaster.

Rule number one: learn from your mistakes.

He was about to speak when Jenna tipped forward and set her forehead in her hands. Gage shunted closer and his hand lowered from the back of the settee to settle on the warm curve of her back. *Oh, hell.*

"Jenna…?"

She shook her head fiercely. "I can't do this. I want to, God help me, but I can't."

His heartbeat stopped before thudding harder against his ribs. Her words were muffled but he'd heard her well enough.

"I understand now why you left," she went on, "but it still hurt. Gage, it hurt almost as much as anything I've ever had to face."

Anything she'd had to face? Like the accident.

Christ.

Like losing her mother.

His hand came away.

"I can't risk that again," she ground out. "Not when Meg is relying on me. You said it yourself. If we acted on…" She groaned softly and her voice lowered. "On what we're feeling now, it would only complicate matters. The very last thing I want is more complications. I don't need to be hurt again, especially now."

Gage's fist dropped onto the settee with a soft thud.

He'd arrived on his white charger, decked out in shining armor, promising to rescue her. Determined not to hurt her. His goal had been to make her happy. Set things right. Release the ghosts then get on with their lives.

Yet here he was, putting tears back in her eyes. She might still be attracted to him, but she didn't want to take that next critical step. More to the point, she didn't want him to either.

Which meant *hands off.*

Get over it.

Move the hell on.

As she pushed to her feet, her knees in their fashionably tatty jeans bumped the coffee table. The cards, balanced on the timber's edge, fell, spilling over the marble floor.

She kept her eyes on her track shoes. "Which is my room?"

Finding his feet, and his center—the solitary place he always fell back upon—he gestured toward the gold-handled double doors to their right.

"Are my belongings in there?" she asked.

He'd had the bellhop bring her case straight up. He nodded. "Yes."

She hugged herself, a gesture conveying a need for distance. "Then, if you don't mind, it's been a long day. I'd like to take a shower."

He blew out a breath.

Make it a cold one and that's not a bad idea.

Forty minutes later Jenna emerged from her private suite, her hair damp, her creamy skin fresh and radiant. Dressed in a tank top and a pair of faded sweats, the years seemed to melt away. She didn't look a day over twenty.

Decked out in a crisp tuxedo, Gage came in from the balcony and unhooked her surprise, which he'd hung earlier on a curtain rod.

Her expression opened—more disbelief than wonder. She stopped fluffing her hair with the towel. Those pink-polished toes edged another step closer. "What's that?"

"An evening gown."

The dress rustled as he laid it over his arm and moved forward to present it.

"We have seats waiting at an exclusive special event," he told her. "We're going out."

CHAPTER SIX

"MATE, why didn't you tell me about her?"

Amidst a room full of tinkling crystal and clinking silverware, Gage slid Nick Farraday a look.

His friend, and second-in-charge in Sydney, pulled in his chin and put up both palms. "I take that back. Your personal life has always been just that—personal. Let me say, though, I feel privileged to be one of the first to meet your bride-to-be." His boyish smile curved upwards. "Jenna and my fiancée seem to have hit it off."

Nick tipped his head toward the ladies who sat, deep in conversation, at the romantically lit table. Tonight's event had been organized to raise funds for cancer research. Seating was intimate. Numbers restricted. Only the wealthiest or most influential in New South Wales had been invited.

The band's swing tune was subdued and pleasant. On a generous square of timber flooring, set beneath silver moonbeam lights, several couples swayed cheek-to-cheek. Which seemed like a rather good idea.

Earlier Jenna had made herself clear. No sex. No way. However, she hadn't ruled out dancing, which, aside from soothing his wound, would also add another convincing touch to their happy-couple front.

Forcing his gaze away from the delicate curve of Jenna's jaw, Gage focused on the advice he'd given as they'd entered the building's foyer this evening.

If we're to succeed, we must pretend to everyone. No exceptions.

"Jenna and I were meant to be," he told Nick with a sincere smile. "We realized it when we met again after I flew in to pay my respects."

The younger man leant closer and lowered his voice more. "What a tragedy. Her sister, the brother-in-law and her father." Elbow on the chair's arm, he positioned a hand near his mouth and murmured, "Guess there's no need for us to pursue Darley Realty. Your marriage will square that one away. Not that I'm suggesting this engagement has anything to do with that."

About to reply, Gage was interrupted by Nick's fiancée, Summer Reynold. "I'm so excited for you both. Jenna will look like a princess on your wedding day."

She looked like a princess *tonight.*

The woman he'd spoken with earlier today had said the gown was an original from a Brazilian designer's collection. The sleeveless silk bodice was jewel-encrusted, the pleated chiffon skirt falling from high on the waist. In the exclusive boutique's window, the gown appeared to be an ideal fit—long and busty. Guessing Jenna's shoe size, he'd told the assistant to include matching heels. Both had arrived unexpectedly after Jenna had gone to shower.

The gown hadn't been meant for any specific occasion, however, given this afternoon's awkward interaction, it had seemed wise to avoid confined spaces. Hence the last-minute decision to make use of the tickets he'd arranged for months back and join Nick and Summer this evening.

"I mentioned to Summer that our wedding will be a private ceremony," Jenna explained, her eyes reflecting the lilac folds of the gown. "Not too many guests."

Gage picked up the thread and carried it through. "There'll be just the celebrant, Jenna, myself and two witnesses."

Summer's hand found Nick's on the white tablecloth. "Well, if you're stuck for those two witnesses and we can help…"

Gage smiled. He couldn't be happier for Nick— Summer was a gem. An attractive woman, intelligent and apparently thoughtful. He understood why his friend was so clearly hooked.

He and Nick had met at a convention on the Gold Coast six years ago. Gage had hired him a week later, and Nick had proven many times since then that loyalty was his middle name. On top of that, he and Nick were on the same wavelength, always saw the same picture, big or small, perhaps because they'd both started out with nothing. If Gage had envisaged a brother, Nick would have been him.

Gage poured ice water into Jenna's glass then his own. "As a matter of fact, I would be honored for Nick to be my best man."

Nick's face broke into a wide smile. He stuck out his hand and Gage happily accepted. "With bells on, mate." His grin turned curious. "Want me to arrange for a bachelor's evening?"

"Girls jumping out of cakes and a bawdy night on the town?" Gage grinned back. "You know that's not my style."

Nick raised his glass in salute. "Just checking."

Jenna seemed to freeze for a moment before turning toward Summer. "And I'd love for you to be my maid of honor."

Gage's chest squeezed. Jenna would be thinking of Amy—of how much she'd want her twin by her side on her wedding day, particularly given the reason for this marriage. But who could say that Amy wouldn't be there? Love, and belief, were said to be powerful things.

Summer beamed, took hold of Jenna's hands and drew her up as she pushed to her feet as well. "I'll make sure you look beyond beautiful." They moved off toward the powder room, Summer explaining to Jenna, "I've never been a bridesmaid before. None of my friends are married yet, and I don't have any sisters…"

While Gage kept his eyes glued on Jenna's profile, waiting for her reaction to Summer's last comment, Nick picked up on his train of thought.

"Don't worry, mate. Knowing Summer, she brought up family to give Jenna a chance to mention the accident…or not. She won't push." He exhaled audibly and sat back. "One thing… Jenna's fortunate to have you to look after her father's business now."

Gage sucked air between his teeth. "Jenna wasn't bequeathed Darley Realty."

Nick's forehead creased before a look of comprehension dawned. "Darley's widow?" Gage nodded and Nick's palm slapped the table. "With mixed families, it can go either way."

Gage flexed his brows. "It went all the way with Leeann Darley."

"Will Jenna contest the will?"

Gage gave a considered reply. "Not that aspect."

"Well, from the way you look at her, I doubt she'll want for a thing, now or any time in the future."

While Nick sipped his wine and focused on the band, tapping his free hand to the tune, Gage wondered. He'd told Jenna the connection they shared was palpable, but did the tug he felt toward Jenna show that much?

He would never enjoy that depth of feeling with anyone else. These past days that enjoyment had grown to such an extent that the sizzle of his early twenties glowed like a kid's birthday candle compared to the twenty-story blaze he'd recently endured.

Of course, now she'd held up the stop sign, and he had to douse the flames. Not easy, but doable.

He downed three parts of his water.

Definitely doable.

Nick turned to him. "Guess I can come clean now, but I never thought I'd see you married. I know you've dated," his eyebrows jumped, "some real beauties, if you don't mind me saying. But you never commented on any of them, and now I know why. Your heart was already taken. Just goes to show. I never pegged you for a romantic."

Gage felt the smile of satisfaction move across his face then shook himself.

Hell, he was believing his own publicity! Yes, Jenna had held a place in his heart no other woman could hope to fill, but that didn't mean he was meant for marriage and a family of his own, not long term, anyway. Whether or not he wished it were different, he was a loner, of necessity living life by his terms and no one else's. When a man married he had to compromise, give up a part of himself. Good luck if he could do that. But Gage knew himself too well. If he tried to pretend to either Jenna or himself that this coming marriage was anything other than pragmatic, someone would get hurt. Again. The whole idea of them being together was to make up for a wrong, not slip up and make matters worse.

Baby Meg could steal anyone's heart. And she deserved someone who could give his heart right back.

Nick swiveled more toward Gage. "I know this probably isn't the time, but did you get in contact with James today? He's been on my case all afternoon."

Gage smothered a twinge of guilt. He'd known James, his right-hand man in Melbourne, had been trying to track him down. He'd turned off his cell phone but there'd been messages left on his hotel extension, on the fax, his email. He hadn't listened to or returned any calls these past days unless they were related to Jenna's situation. Not usual practice. In fact, highly unusual. And unacceptable. He mightn't have had a vacation in too long to remember, but that was no excuse. People relied on him to give 110 percent.

"I'll check in with James tomorrow," he said.

"Just so you know…our Emirates business deal has hit the fan."

Gage's fingers bunched up the tablecloth.

Not possible. "Everything was set."

"Apparently not. I'll let James explain, but he mentioned if you want to keep the deal, you'll need to fly to Dubai ASAP and stay there until the negotiations with the government are settled and stamped."

Gage's mind zeroed in on possible problems and solutions to the billion-dollar hotel contract he'd spent two years putting together. He would jump on his jet first thing tomorrow and—

Laughter caught his ear and jerked that thought clear

from his head. The ladies swept back over to the table, chatting like old friends. Gage's fist, and the bunched cloth, relaxed.

Jenna needed friends, people to connect with. And if she and Summer got along, there was every reason to believe they would continue the relationship after...

Well, after he and Jenna had reached their goal and Meg was where, and with whom, she belonged. Where Jenna belonged too. Finally home.

Before Jenna could sit, Gage thought of Dubai, of the limited time they had, and pushed back his chair.

On his feet, he claimed her hand and began to move off. "We should dance."

She pulled back her weight. "Dessert's just arrived." A tilt of her chin indicated the uniformed waiter delivering passion-fruit cheesecake and chocolate torte drizzled with raspberry coulee.

He circled her waist and ushered her away. "Dessert can wait."

Jenna quivered from her head down to her new high heels as Gage took her in his arms and, beneath a shower of smoky light, drew her near.

His left hand rested against the dip in her back. Her mouth went dry when his thumb circled the silky fabric inches above her behind—then stopped. But there was still the smell of him...the raw and tangible heat. The entire package did sinfully sweet things to every dimension of her body. Though he kept his eyes straight ahead, she knew he felt it too.

Question was: after this afternoon's confrontation, could she trust him not to act on it?

His thumb rubbed—stopped again—and Jenna trembled.

Lord, oh, Lord, think of something else.

"Nick's lovely," she blurted out. "I'd imagined a Jerry Maguire type but he's more a Sir Galahad. And Summer's so friendly."

"I'm glad you two get along well."

His chin grazed her temple as he spoke. Clearly he'd used a razor before donning that tux—which happened to fit his body like a Hollywood dream—yet already the shadow and rasp of his beard was evident…and very sexy.

Jenna closed her eyes.

How she yearned for a blank slate to give her peace. Instead pictures of his perfect forearm, from when she'd caught him earlier that day, swam in her mind. Another image followed of the coarse hair below the hollow of his throat. Today, directly after Gage's admission, how dearly she'd wanted to reach out and rub those crisp strands against his hot, tanned skin. She almost had.

Above the music, his deep voice infiltrated her daydream. "That was nice."

She heard the smile in his voice. Then guilt convulsed in her throat and her eyes flew open. She inched away from the hard plateau under his dress shirt, the masculine lure of his hips.

"Sorry, what did you say?"

His brow buckled before amusement hooked up one side of his mouth. "Asking Summer to be your maid of honor," he explained. "That was nice."

She sighed and smiled. "Oh. That."

His brow wrinkled again while his own smile widened. "What did you think I meant?"

The press of his hand on her back increased so subtly, she might have imagined it. Of course, she might not have imagined it either.

Her gaze skated over to the band.

Subject change—*quick.*

"I love this song."

She felt the heat of his eyes on her, trying to penetrate her veneer. "So I was right in asking you to dance."

She inwardly groaned. The simmering effects of slow dancing did little to strengthen the answer she'd given to his tempting but unacceptable suggestion this afternoon.

She cocked her head and thought more deeply.

But he wasn't acting improperly now. Merely adding to the picture they were building on. Reunited lovers. The we-simply-couldn't-deny-our-feelings-any-longer façade.

At least it was supposed to be a façade.

He rocked her around in a tight circle. When they returned to more regular steps, she was closer, the bodice of her gown touching his shirt. Through the sheer fabric, the tips of her breasts rubbed rhythmically back and forth, and when he threw in a fancy one-two-three, they rubbed a little harder.

The points of contact began to burn. The burn became an ache.

She broke from his hold.

Enough!

"I think we should eat dessert," she told him firmly.

He cut such an impressive picture, silver beams of light casting shadows over the chiseled planes of his face and dynamite cut of his tux. Without a scrap of effort, his presence dominated the massive room. The energy of his masculinity was lawless.

And dangerously close to irresistible.

He smiled as his hand reached for hers. "Our dance isn't over."

She gave him a wide berth.

Oh, yes it is.

Heartbeat clamoring, she wove through a field of besotted couples to find their table.

This was much worse than she first thought. Now that she knew his mind—that he wanted her in his bed—it wasn't enough that she'd made a choice. No matter how he tempted her, she couldn't jeopardize her chance with Meg by getting mixed up with Gage on a sexual level. She needed to be sharp, not lovelorn. And yet...

After just one dance, her breasts were on fire and her mind was spinning like a top. All her poor brain could register was the agony-ecstasy of being embraced by the only man who could make her feel like a woman should feel. Desirable, unique. Wanted...cherished...every inch...every minute.

The waves of arousal that had swamped her in her teens were back with a devastating vengeance. Yet, if she gave in to the pleasure and allowed herself to be carried away, no doubt about it—she would drown. Twelve years ago she'd come close to sinking, and the stakes were far higher this time.

She smiled as warmly as she could at Summer and Nick and folded back into her seat.

Summer's spoon fell against her dish with a *click.* "Well, that was the world's quickest dance."

Gage appeared and pulled his chair in, too. "Seems my skills on the dance floor can't compete with my fiancée's sweet tooth." He gave his napkin a sharp flick and set it on his lap.

Nick slid Summer a questioning look. Summer

conveyed a secret shrug. Gage downed the rest of his water and Jenna shifted in her seat.

Awkward moment.

"If I recall correctly, you have a sweet tooth, too, Gage," Jenna injected brightly to cover everyone's discomfort. He opened his mouth to speak but Jenna talked over him. "Now, don't deny it."

A muscle in his jaw clenched as Gage slid his plate closer. "I was about to say you were the one who changed my mind. I didn't think I liked dessert until I met you."

Jenna went limp.

She watched him sample the torte, suck some cream off his thumb, and got the strongest feeling his line wasn't the least manufactured. One week after they'd first kissed all those years ago, she'd bought a tub of ice cream to share while they watched TV in the pool house—their after-hours hideaway. He'd told her he didn't like sweet food, only savory—steak, potatoes, thick crusty bread. He simply was not interested in toffee brittle or cupcakes.

But she'd pounced and force-fed him a mouthful of premium French vanilla. Laughing, he'd rolled her off his chest, then swallowed and finally hummed out a big smile.

He'd been so sure about not liking sweets…but a week together and she'd changed his mind.

"Something wrong with your cheesecake?"

At Summer's murmured question, Jenna brought herself back. She focused on her plate and inhaled the tangy scent of passion-fruit pulp. "I'm sure it's delicious."

Gage dabbed his mouth and kicked off a conversation with Nick regarding the strength of the Australian dollar against the greenback. He drew Summer, a leading chartered accountant, into the conversation, too.

A chill crept up Jenna's spine.

Was he giving her the cold shoulder, annoyed that she'd left him on the dance floor? Or was he frustrated over her unwillingness this afternoon to let him clarify his feelings more fully? Had he changed his mind? Not about ice cream this time, but about spending the rest of his life alone?

Nick's voice came from far away. "Mate, she doesn't look too well."

"Perhaps we should call it a night," Summer suggested.

Jenna touched her forehead and found it damp. Her smile quivered. "Maybe I shouldn't have had that second glass of champagne with dinner."

But champagne bubbles hadn't lit the fires sparking through her system. A different, unanticipated new spin on things had.

Gage tipped close. "Would you like to leave?"

She nodded then spoke to Nick and Summer. "Sorry to be a bore."

Nick got to his feet. "Not at all. We can do this again soon."

Summer stood too and kissed Jenna's cheek as she rose. "In just under three weeks, in fact. But we won't be eating torte that day. It'll be a scrumptious wedding cake."

They all left the building together. Nick and Summer slipped into a cab while Gage turned in the direction of his penthouse.

But Jenna held back. "Do you mind if we go for a walk?" A blush singed her cheeks as he studied her, and she added, "I could do with the fresh air."

"You won't be cold?"

Little chance of that with her internal furnace working at maximum capacity whenever he was near.

She smiled. "I'll be fine."

They strolled in silence down a busy city street, headlights flashing in their faces and the Harbour Bridge twinkling like an arc of supernova stars in the distance. Within minutes, they reached Darling Harbour. Al fresco restaurants hummed with life while, farther down, the replica of Captain Cook's *Endeavour* sat quietly moored outside the Maritime Museum.

The wind picked up, flapping the massive sails and swirling around Jenna's hem.

Gage shrugged out of his jacket and draped it over her bare shoulders. "Don't argue," he chided when she went to object. "The breeze is chilly coming off the water."

Standing behind her, he positioned the jacket's big shoulders to fit her far smaller ones.

"Thank you." She hugged the jacket close, taking secret pleasure in the male scented warmth enveloping her. "And thanks for the lovely evening. I had a nice time."

"I'm glad you enjoyed Nick and Summer's company."

"I enjoyed your company, too."

A dark eyebrow lifted. "As long as I don't get too close," he observed as they resumed walking.

She tingled, remembering his arms around her, his granite chest and sizzling body heat so agonizingly tempting. What was the safe answer?

She decided there wasn't one.

The diamond on her finger flashed beneath the city lights and she found herself smiling.

"Jenna Cameron... It has a nice ring to it." She'd always thought so.

"Cameron was my mother's maiden name."

Jenna felt a stab of pain for him—over the loss of his

mother, growing up without a father, of being unable to share a father's name.

"I didn't know that," she murmured.

He nodded. "Whenever my mother had one too many and got out the old snaps, she'd insist that our line of Camerons had descended from kings." He chuckled and kicked a pebble with the toe of his polished lace-up shoe.

"Perhaps it's true," she said, but his wry smile said he doubted it. "Have you ever tried to look up your family tree?"

His smile changed. "You're kidding, right?"

She took him in, the uncompromising jut of his jaw, the lock of inky hair lifting in the salty breeze. "You might discover she's right and you do have royal blood in your veins."

That might help explain his exceptional abilities as a leader.

"More likely I'm descended from convicts. Only took a dozen generations to crawl our way out of the squalor."

He grinned but she didn't see humor in the single line bracketing his mouth.

"Guess it doesn't matter where we came from. Just who we turn out to be."

He stopped just as a cloud swallowed up the moonlight. "Jenna, where we come from *is* who we are."

"If that were true, you'd be wearing some type of crown or dragging chains."

"Yes," he said, "I would."

Dropping his gaze, he kicked another pebble. It skipped clear across the ground and plopped in the water. Needing a little time to think over his last remark, she followed it toward the water's edge, but he called her back.

"Hey, I thought we were walking."

She shrugged. "I walked over here."

"I prefer dry land. Blame the psychogenetic memory of great, great granddaddy locked in the hull of that convict ship. I don't think he could swim, either."

She laughed. "I promise not to push you in."

His arms raveled over his chest.

Jenna grinned.

Stubborn man.

She moved back and, equally determined, set her hands on her hips. When her elbows jutted, the jacket dislodged. Jenna grabbed to save it, but Gage moved first. He caught the sleeves, pinning them against her upper arms. The action also drew her in and toward him—wonderfully, dangerously close.

With his chest inches from hers, he searched her eyes. Her toes curled as sensual longing ignited a sizzling trail through her body. It was all she could do not to press a little closer, a little harder.

"Let's keep walking," she murmured, and then to ease the tension, "You can impress me with your knowledge of yachts."

"I know nothing about yachts." But he loosened his hold, rounded the jacket up over her shoulders, and they began to walk down the pier.

"You don't have a hundred-foot cruiser?" She'd seen pictures of the excessive luxury available on such vessels. Surely Gage would have one or two documented on his assets list.

"I don't like water, remember? Italian sports cars, corporate jets, no problem. Boats? Not even a little bit."

She hadn't given it much thought at the time, but

whenever he'd visited her at the pool house years ago, he had always stayed well clear of the pool itself. He really didn't like water? But why? There must be some good reason.

The pocket of his jacket buzzed—his cell phone. Jenna grinned. As if he would ever leave that behind.

After asking permission, he dug into a pocket and checked the cell's screen. "Excuse me." He thumbed a button. "This is important."

As he spoke—something about Dubai—she breathed in the briny air, examined the rows of vessels and stole sidelong glances at his profile, wondering. Maybe even hoping.

Phone pressed between his shoulder and ear, Gage asked permission again to rummage through his jacket. This time he retrieved a pen and scribbled a few words on his hand. Another few seconds and he disconnected.

"Guess the Cameron shop never shuts down," she said.

He reread the message on his hand. "I've neglected a few matters."

He was about to slot the pen away, but it flashed in a pier light and, on impulse, Jenna reached for it. He seemed reluctant to give it up.

She weighed the pen in her palm. "Hmm, heavy. It's not pure gold, is it?" His expression was noncommittal and she looked closer. "It *is* pure gold."

"That's not so unusual."

"Maybe not for you. What's this?" She rotated the pen and squinted in the hazy light. "An inscription? No. A symbol of some kind." She passed over it with her fingertip. "A vertical line with an arc at one end. It's a tree. Or an anchor."

"It's a plane. Why would I buy a pen with an anchor etched on it?"

She rolled her eyes theatrically. "Oh, that's right. You don't like water. But you do like jets." And your Maserati. Leading examples of speed and power.

He reached for the pen. Unprepared, she fumbled and it fell then bounced on the rough decking. Gage swooped and caught it a second before it might have rolled off into the harbour, lost forever.

Horrified, Jenna's hands flew to her mouth. "Gage, I'm so sorry."

He rose from his haunches. "No harm done. I would've hated to see you jump in there to get it though."

When he grinned, so did she.

But her smile faded. "It means a lot to you, doesn't it?"

He slipped the pen into his trouser pocket. "I bought it on a whim after a stock market gain, and signed my first big contract with it. I used it constantly until it started to wear. Now I generally keep it for important documents."

Yet he carried it around with him even when there were no contracts in sight? "Sounds like that pen is your good luck charm." And quite possibly more than that…a connection.

He shrugged. "Either way, I don't want to lose it."

"The pen with the plane, not the anchor or tree."

He winked. "Now you're catching on."

"Am I?"

As their gazes held, the atmosphere changed from relaxed to suddenly steamy. The heavy weight of lost years shrank and crystallized into a single, bright, hypercharged moment.

Was she reading too much into how adamantly he defended what that pen represented? Wealth, travel, independence, freedom. All the things he'd let her know were important to him a week ago.

Ice cream was one thing, life choices another. And, no matter how much she secretly wished it were otherwise, Gage seemed set on his choices. Beyond that? He was quite simply a magnificent enigma. No matter how many times she second-guessed herself, she would never know Gage Cameron. The reality was—to try might mean her downfall.

A cold, wet drop fell on Jenna's nose. At the same moment lightning flashed and a roll of distant thunder rumbled. Distracted, she looked up, and as if on cue, the rain came down.

When she shrieked, Gage swept the jacket over her head. A second later, he cursed and also ducked under cover.

While his arms made an awkward umbrella of the jacket, her palm landed against the hard wall of his chest. His heartbeat resonated through her fingers then spread like an electric current through her body. Crazy, and yet, for the first time in too long, she felt…safe.

His big shoulders were hunched. "We're soaked through."

She grinned. "I noticed."

"You said you wouldn't make me swim."

She grinned more, then couldn't help but think, *Would it really be so scary to swim, Gage? Couldn't you get used to it?*

This seemed the ideal as well as the most inappropriate moment to ask. "Why do you have such an aversion to water?"

"Ever wonder about the scar on my lip? I knocked three of my baby teeth out when I was washed down a storm pipe at age five. On top of swallowing a whole lot of mud, I almost drowned."

Jenna gasped. She couldn't imagine how terrified he must have been. "Did you ever think of seeing a professional to help you get over your fear?"

He smiled in grim amusement. "Avoidance has worked very well up till now."

Yet they continued to stand in the downpour, beneath the jacket. They should have run for shelter, but neither one moved while the rain pounded at their feet and his heart thudded near her palm.

"Jenna?"

In the dark, she imagined his mouth was incredibly close. "Yes, Gage?"

He seemed to move nearer.

She did the same....

CHAPTER SEVEN

STANDING in the pouring rain, both huddled beneath his tuxedo jacket, the reality was unavoidable. Gage was going to kiss her.

How would she react? Jenna couldn't think past the frantic beating of her heart, or the way her every fiber cried out for him to do it *now*.

She held her breath, waiting...

Then Gage groaned deeply and took her hand. "We've had enough fresh air."

The jacket came down and they ran off together, splashing through the puddles.

Ten minutes later, they entered the penthouse, shaking their wet hands and slipping off sodden shoes.

"Can I get you a towel? Something warm to drink?" Gage crossed to the bar, threw the drenched jacket over the back of a stool and reached for a crystal decanter. He poured himself two fingers in a heavy glass. No ice.

A convulsive shudder rippled up Jenna's spine. She was freezing, but a hot chocolate would suit her far better than scotch.

She inspected the puddle forming around her feet. "I think I'll change before anything else."

He thumbed a switch on a wall panel—the internal heating, she suspected—and downed half his single malt.

His shirt was plastered against the musculature of his deeply tanned chest and arms. Every knockout ridge and bulge was on display, presented in glorious prime-time relief. As he moved forward, more than the line between his brows told her he was uncomfortable. At being caught in the rain, ending up sopping wet? Or something, perhaps, not quite as obvious.

When they'd taken shelter beneath his jacket, he'd almost kissed her. Worse, she'd almost let him.

And he knew it.

Closer now, he lifted his chin to unravel his bow tie and flick open a button.

"It's getting late." He stopped before her. "Guess you're tired."

He took another quick sip and swallowed, waiting for her reply. Waiting for a sign. A look.

A touch.

She should go and change, yet she stood immobile, thinking of the heartache she'd lived through when she'd known Gage Cameron last. His life wasn't one she could ever share. And yet…had she changed her mind about becoming intimately involved? Down by the pier, she'd been tempted. Heck, she was tempted now.

Guess you're tired.

She gave a cryptic reply. "That sprint seems to have woken me up."

His eyes searched hers. "Me, too."

Behind him, the facsimile machine beeped. His gaze flicked over her face before he moved to retrieve a sheet from the tray. After scanning the message, he set down his drink and ran a hand through his glossy wet hair.

She inched closer. "Is it the Dubai problem again?"

Jaw clenched, he nodded at the page. "Sorry. You get changed. I need a moment here." He sank into a chair, found a pen on the desk and started making notes.

Jenna let out a sigh.

Perhaps she should take his reaction to this fax as a sign. He gave a good impression of a dedicated fiancé, but Gage would always be devoted to business.

He'd go for the plane, not the anchor, every time.

It should be enough that he'd offered to help her with Meg, and that he still found her desirable, although not at the moment. Head down, concentrating on the fax, he looked set for the duration.

Raising her dripping hem, Jenna padded a barefoot trail over the cold tiles into her carpeted room. She stripped off the dress and inspected it for damage; into the dry cleaners tomorrow, first thing.

After changing into the men's shirt she preferred to a negligee, the laptop caught her eye. She sat down and found her email inbox full. Proposals for overseas work, a free offer from a shoe store, a message from Leeann…

Her heart jackknifed into her throat and her shaky finger slipped over the mouse to click the message open straight away.

Letting you know, I've had to step up my plans to visit San Fran. My poor mother is ailing and begging to see our Meg. Back after Christmas—all going well.

That crippling, hopeless feeling gripped as if it had never been away.

All going well, be damned! Leeann had no intention of returning after Christmas.

It was happening, just as she'd feared. Leeann was leaving the country with Meg, for how long, she couldn't hope to guess. And what the hell could she do about it? Nothing. A big fat zero. As far as the law was concerned, Leeann was Meg's rightful guardian.

A light appeared in the darkness and she pushed to her feet.

Gage would know what to do.

She flew out the door. He hadn't moved.

"She's taking Meg away," she shot out. "I don't know when exactly, but she won't be in a hurry to bring her back. Maybe we should go see her. Petition for a special hearing or something."

Anything. Just as long as it was soon.

Gage pushed to his feet and braced her shoulders. "Slow down. What do you mean, taking Meg?"

Unshed tears stung her nose. Yes, she should stay calm—not exactly easy given the bloody great pit gaping before her.

Grabbing his hand, Jenna headed for her room. "Read for yourself."

In her room, Gage concentrated on the screen while Jenna paced back and forth.

"She has no intention of coming back," she said, pressing her throbbing temple. "Not until she's good and ready anyway. It's no use me flying over there to see Meg. Why would she let me through the door? I doubt the American police would be too eager to get involved in this kind of custody issue. She'd be in total control."

The way Leeann always liked it.

Jenna thought of Amy's gift to her on their fifteenth birthday. Leeann had fallen in love with the beautiful lovebird too—everyone had. One day Jenna returned home from school to find Tulip's birdcage not in her bedroom but the family room. A week later, the cage had migrated to Leeann's sitting room. Their father had intervened—the first of only two occasions. The following month, Leeann had taken it upon herself to clean the cage and Tulip had "accidentally" escaped. Over time, Jenna had replaced her hurt with a vengeful wish: soon she would fly away too. And never ever come back.

Gage straightened from where he leant on the back of her chair and rapped his knuckles several times against his outer thigh. Jenna's gaze scanned up from the movement. Her pulse rate tripled and mouth went dry. Some segment of her consciousness must have noticed, yet it hadn't registered until now. He'd discarded his wet dress shirt. From the hips up, he was naked—bronzed. Unbelievably built.

"Don't panic," he said. "It's more likely she's being manipulative and trying to call our bluff. *Give me what I want or you might not see your niece again.*"

Jenna wet her lips. "You mean she's threatening us?" Well, that made sense.

In the muted lamplight, she watched him grin. "But her threat carries no weight. She won't find another buyer for Darley Realty in the state it's in. She'd have more than enough to get her to the States, but if she wants real money, she needs to listen, not talk."

His drying hair was disheveled as if, while they'd been in separate rooms, his fingers had thrust through its thick crop several times. The unruly look suited him as much as it had in his youth, if not more.

Jenna shook herself and connected her runaway thoughts to Meg's situation.

"So, if Leeann takes the deal—Meg in exchange for an easy, generous sale—we don't need to get married."

Despite the silly pang of disappointment, that had to be a good thing.

Right?

Expression earnest, he took her hands and squeezed. "Jenna, we not only need to get married, we need to do it quickly and get that petition in and fast-tracked for the earliest possible hearing. If there's one thing I've learned it's wherever possible, don't put all your eggs in one basket."

In other words, despite his assurances, he wasn't certain what Leeann would do.

"So if she decides having Meg means more to her than the money…then if a judge decides to abide by the will's directives…"

She thought of Meg…of her little bird…

He brought her hands to his chest and pressed them close. "That won't happen."

His words, and steady strumming of his heart, brooked no argument.

But she couldn't be a Pollyanna now. If she kept thinking about it, rehashing all the options, making alternate plans…maybe if she prayed hard enough, long enough, God wouldn't let this happen.

Hot tears welled in her eyes. "But what if it *does* happen?"

What if this were punishment for her willfulness? If she'd put her family first and pride last, she would have stayed in Australia. She would be settled, Amy and Brad would've put her name in their wills and Meg wouldn't be stuck with a guardian who'd turned into the worst kind of witch.

Gage thumbed aside her tear as it trickled down her cheek. "It won't happen. We'll find a way."

Her mind jumped again.

"And how long do we try? A month, a year, two, ten?" How long before Meg began to see Leeann as her parent? At some point it would be unfair to take her from the person she'd come to see as her mother, no matter how unworthy.

When a small sob escaped, Gage wrapped his arms around her, and Jenna remembered a time when he had been all that she'd needed. She inhaled his clean musky scent, and her hands slid up to the broad flat rocks that defined his chest.

He felt so good. Made her feel so safe.

His hand smoothed over her hair then he murmured against her head. "One day at a time. I'll fix it. Trust me."

She scrunched her burning eyes shut.

Can I trust you, Gage? Can I trust myself?

His mouth grazed her temple, then again and again.

After a long moment, he held her even tighter and said, "I'm here. We'll sort this out tomorrow."

She lifted her face and, yes, his supportive smile *was* there. But along with that look came awareness—the same intense knowledge that had always pulsed and steamed between them. His expression changed and the heat of his body, pressed against hers, built until she could barely breathe.

His head lowered slightly, hers tipped up, then his mouth was closing over hers...taking her...kissing her...*thank God,* finally.

She was already melting when he broke from their embrace.

He stepped back, the cords in his neck strained. "You're upset. You need to rest."

She shook her head. "Right now what I need is you."

Ready to be kissed again and forget her problems, if only for a moment, she offered up her lips.

He held her back and groaned as he'd done beneath the jacket in the rain. "Damn it, Jenna, right now what you want is a friend, not a lover."

It was easy to read between the lines: He was telling her he wouldn't take advantage of her when she was emotionally vulnerable. Just as he wouldn't think of taking advantage of a woman who'd had too much to drink.

Or was under age, as she'd once been.

In the pool house that night, she'd begged him to go all the way. She'd felt his body lock and tremble above her, his physical need doing hellish battle with his scruples. She'd cursed him when he'd left Sydney without a word, and yet there was a noble deed to acknowledge too: Now she could admit that he'd respected her enough not to take what he wanted and screw the consequences.

But she was no longer a teen. She was an adult facing the biggest challenge of her life. She knew what she was doing here, tonight, and now nothing stopped them from finally enjoying it.

If she did lose Meg…

No! She couldn't bear to even *think* it, and she had the perfect diversion—making love to the only man she'd ever wanted…would ever want. Arms looping around his neck, she pulled herself up and set the tip of her nose to his.

"Forget what I said this afternoon. I want this. And I get it, Gage. I get *you*. You don't want to grow roots, and you don't want to take advantage of me. Thank you, but believe me when I say, no regrets, I promise. Like you said, let's finally just find out."

She angled her head and this time *she* kissed *him*.

The tension left his jaw. With a soft inner smile, she shimmied nearer and welcomed his full surrender. But he'd already taken the lead, deepening the kiss as his hands slid a sensuous path from where he cupped her face to the curve of her neck, then lower, sculpting the tingling slope of her shoulders.

When his hot palms skimmed down the full length of her arms, her shirt—and total submission—came, too.

CHAPTER EIGHT

ANY RESERVATIONS Gage had evaporated like a blast of high-powered steam.

Jenna had a change of heart and now everything seemed perfectly clear...the wonderful way she felt in his arms, the wild berry scent of her filling his lungs, filling him with life. He could go on kissing her till doomsday, but for one tiny problem.

Other delights should be shared aside from kissing, and tonight he intended for them to enjoy every one.

As he carefully turned her to face away from him, the oversized shirt, which he'd already slipped from her shoulders, fell completely from her body. He scooped his arms up under hers and crossed them over her ribs. Then he closed his eyes, created an image in his mind, and lovingly molded his palms over her breasts as a dedicated artist might test and shape his work. They were fuller than he remembered—heavier, but just as beautiful...and even more arousing.

With a sigh—a sound of pure pleasure—she reached up and back to coax his head down. As he kissed her neck, her fingers wound through his hair. "I've dreamt about you so often, but this is a hundred times better."

He smiled at her admission. "Only a hundred times?" He rolled her nipples.

She quivered and sighed again. "Make that a thousand. A *million*."

"Now we're getting close."

His palms grazed a wide circle across each peak before slowly riding down over her ribs, his fingers forming arrows tracking toward the juncture of her thighs. As his chest grazed down her back, his lips trailed the scented curve between ear and shoulder, and his hands discovered her inner thighs; his pulse rate spiraled as his thumbs delved between to gently edge them apart. He pressed her firmly against his pelvis then rode his touch higher, between her slick soft folds.

She was so ready. And he was way beyond ready for her.

Finding that hypersensitive spot, he began to work some heartfelt magic and her lower half tipped forward. When he increased the pressure, varied the motion, she started to move, a sensual, barely perceptible roll of her hips.

The heat between them rose and her movements grew bolder until she stilled then trembled, her energy and concentration obviously strung piano-wire tight. Time to pull back. He wanted this to last. Although she was close, ultimately she would appreciate that kind of delay, too.

They had all night.

As he eased her back around to face him, an appetizing thought struck. He cupped her bottom and nipped her lower lip. "So, you don't wear panties to bed."

Her eyes were dark and drowsy with desire. "I didn't know that was a crime."

"Not if I'd been around to enjoy the benefits."

Her grin was mischievous. "That sentiment works both ways."

He felt a tug and looked down.

She'd helped herself to his zipper.

The fly came down, her hand went in and the testosterone explosion almost took off his head.

This woman was bold, as she'd been all those years ago, but now there was no hint of fumbling or blushing. Jenna seemed to know precisely what she was doing and how she would do it.

A vision came to mind but he stomped on it quickly. He couldn't think of her with anyone else. He would only think of now—not the past, or the future—because this very minute that big empty space was finally filling with light.

Tonight he felt reborn.

He swept her off her feet at the same moment his unzipped trousers fell. He stepped from the pooled legs and carried his fiancée to bed.

As he walked, he kissed her, long and slow and deep, with every ounce of feeling he'd ever boxed in. Then he laid her on the sheets and watched her glow in the lamplight, dark-blond hair arced over white satin pillows, her lips slightly parted, wet and inviting.

When he was completely naked, he lay beside her and finally pulled her close. As one long shapely leg eased up to hook over his hip, he took her mouth again and her arched foot on his behind urged him on. Not that he needed persuading. His blood was on fire, every cell in his body ablaze with a desire that would devour every inch of her before coming even halfway close to containment.

Their kiss broke down into desperate snatches, his mouth tracking over her jaw, down her rain-scented neck and lower, until he dotted airy kisses over one perfect breast then the other.

She fisted her fingers in his hair as she writhed beneath him. "You need to know…you're driving me insane."

He didn't stop, or slow, or even think. He merely smiled as the tip of his tongue tickled her nipple. When the peak was hard and distended, his teeth grazed and gently tugged. Then, at long last, he drew the cherry into his mouth, burning the memory of sublime pleasure into his heart and mind forever.

Arching toward him, she whispered something half decipherable and incredibly sexy. His pounding erection hardened to stone. When her knee edged higher on his hip, he clutched her leg and ran his tongue all the way down her middle, lowering himself over her body and the bed until he landed smack-dab in heaven.

She tasted exactly as he'd imagined…fresh and provocatively feminine. He fanned her thighs wider, settled in and focused on making her happy.

He smiled at her reaction.

Yes, he was definitely making her happy.

All too soon, the pressure in his groin pulled mercilessly tight. Given the way her fingers dug into his shoulders, Jenna was teetering on a crumpling edge, too.

Summoning control, he pushed up and leaned over to rummage in the bedside drawer. She moved beneath him, her body inching lower as she trailed moist lips across his ribs, down around her navel, lower still until she hit solid rock.

Sweat broke out beneath his shoulder blades and at the

backs of his knees. Swallowing a curse, he bit his lip and with a single arm dragged her all the way back up. The tit-for-tat she had in mind would be a wonderful encore, but right now he was too close to the finale.

In the drawer, he found a small square wrapper. Hovering on top, an elbow either side of her head, he captured her mouth again and blindly tore the foil. Her arms wound up, she took the condom, rolled him over and proceeded to fit it while he could only stare.

"You need a hand with anything?"

All done, she slid a python grip down his shaft. "Isn't instinct a marvelous thing?"

Instinct? Did she mean practice?

He wished he'd been the first. But he'd given up the chance, and the better part of him didn't regret it. Once she'd been forbidden fruit. Not now. Now nothing was out of bounds.

He flipped her onto her back and growled, "My turn to take charge."

Blood on fire, he eased inside, but only the barest amount. Nibbling her earlobe, he moved, repositioned and tried again.

His curious smile nuzzled into her neck. "Relax. This is fun, remember?"

Her thighs loosened their clamp outside of his.

"I'm relaxed."

Her answer sounded sincere enough. To be fair, she was narrow through the hips, a very slender build. Rubbers were sometimes restrictive. Hell, perhaps unconsciously she was still a little nervous.

It wasn't possible that…hell, she couldn't be…

He drew back slightly and smiled into her eyes. "This

is going to sound completely crazy, but please tell me this isn't your first time."

"I've been with men before." She pressed her lips together. "Just not this far."

A *virgin?*

After the initial shock, he gathered himself. In this day and age, with her looks and worldly experience—not to mention the way she'd rolled on that condom—not likely.

He chuckled. "You're pulling my leg." His smile wavered. "Aren't you?"

"I've had relationships. A few times I came close to going all the way, but I always pulled back. It never felt right. But this feels right." She slid a fingertip over his bottom lip. "*Very* right."

He looked at her for a long, disbelieving moment then exhaled hard. "Well, this is an unexpected turn of events."

"Does it make a difference?"

He lifted his brows. "Not in a bad way, believe me."

Her fingertip trailed around his jaw, down his neck. "Then what are we waiting for?"

He smiled. *What, indeed?*

Running a hand down her side, he offered up his thoughts to a higher plane and maneuvered again. In time, the rhythm increased, the way became smoother and the friction built from shooting sparks to leaping white-blue flames. When she pulled down on his ears to kiss him again, a bone-melting inferno rushed through his body and the pent-up passion of twelve years exploded and broke free.

She cried out when he drove in to the hilt. Then every muscle in her body seemed to clench and she cried out in a different way. Through a haze of physical intensity and a shuddering soul-lifting release, he felt her spasm around him and knew she'd climaxed, too.

Heartbeat booming, Gage dropped his head near her ear and almost uttered the words—the ones he never said. But in time, he swallowed them back down. He'd finally made love to the only woman who'd ever mattered to him. He'd be content with that.

Afterward he held her nestled in one arm, her head resting against his chest, her hand curled beneath her chin.

She looked up at him, her eyelids heavy, her expression dreamy and satisfied. "Will you be here in the morning when I wake up?"

He thought of the fax and the pieces of the Dubai deal that had already hit ground zero. So much money on the line. Years of work at stake. He needed to fly over there. He was a complete fool if he didn't. And yet…

Hell's fire, he couldn't leave her. Not now, after that manipulative message from Leeann. He'd given his word. This time he would stay.

He bundled her closer and dropped a kiss on her brow. "I'll be here."

But thirty minutes later, when she'd fallen asleep, he eased away and quietly moved into the main living room. If he wasn't going to Dubai, Nick sure as hell had to.

After ripping out a fax sheet, he grabbed a pen. About to write, he frowned, tossed the Bic and moved back into the bedroom to dig around in his trouser pocket. When he stood over his desk again, the gold pen in his hand, part of the tension and uncertainty eased from his body.

The fax was almost through when a movement caught his eye. Jenna stood in the bedroom doorway, dressed again in that shirt, one arm stretched lazily above her as she yawned.

Her voice was a sleepy sexy drawl. "Are you coming back to bed?"

The fax beeped. Finished.

Exhaling, he set down his pen and joined her. He gathered the hem of that shirt and dragged it over her head in one fluid motion. "There's a rule I insist you abide by while you're living in my home. No men's shirts."

She half frowned, half smiled. "But I don't wear negligees to bed."

Or panties.

He shut the door. "Perfect."

CHAPTER NINE

A WEEK LATER, Jenna gazed unseeing—barely feeling—past the passenger window of Gage's black Maserati.

The powerful V8 engine hummed around her as, concentrating, Gage navigated the curves and dips of the northbound road. After a recent spring shower, the rural scenery looked lush and fresh. The midmorning sun scattered tiny diamonds across the trees and threw a pail of iridescent green over the gently rolling hills.

Under different circumstances she'd have enjoyed the experience—a leisurely drive with a handsome billionaire, who also happened to be an incredible lover and her husband of three days, no less.

Her engagement ring and matching diamond wedding band shone up from her clasped hands, their brilliance smudged through a blur of tears.

Was she kidding herself? Had marrying Gage really helped her chances of claiming Meg?

Gage reached to squeeze her hand. "Tired? It's been a busy few days. Hours of travel," he flicked over a warm smile, "with a wedding thrown in."

Despite her request that they marry in Australia, as a

safeguard Gage had also lodged the necessary paperwork in New Zealand. With documents in order, they'd flown into Wellington, then on to Mt. Ruapehu. The chateau was a combination of early twentieth century elegance and secluded romantic retreat. In a grand room, decorated with fountains of fragrant lilies and pink satin bows, they'd said their vows, Summer and Nick smiling on.

No one would have guessed they weren't in love. When he'd said I do, even she had believed it—a bittersweet sensation that Jenna tried not to dwell upon. Just as she'd tried not to think about Meg every minute of every day.

Not happening. Even now that heavy, helpless feeling pressed down, crushing her, squeezing the air from her lungs. If only she knew when and how this would end. If only she knew when she would hold her Meg—Amy's baby—again.

Gage seemed to read her mind. "Lance hopes to hear back next week about the petition he lodged for us yesterday with the Family Court."

He'd reassured her of this six times already. Gage's lawyer had filed their petition as a married couple, stating that—given Leeann's intention to leave the country and the age of the child—their case was urgent. Plans were advancing as quickly as possible. Leeann was now fully aware of their objectives. But…

Jenna gazed out the window again. "I just wish Leeann would stop playing her games and let me see her."

An image of Meg's rosebud mouth and big blue eyes was a constant in her mind. She'd heard enough excuses. She was at a point where she wanted to knock down Leeann's door and demand to see her niece. Not wise, but oh-so-tempting.

A few minutes later, Gage turned onto a narrower road. But hadn't she seen a letterbox at the corner? Jenna glanced back over her shoulder. And what was the story with that mile-long brick and iron fence?

She frowned. "This is someone's driveway." A very long driveway at that.

Listening to a blues CD, he tapped a thumb on the steering wheel. "Actually, it's our driveway."

Jenna blinked several times. "Ours?"

"This property is our country retreat," he explained. "Yours, mine and Meg's."

Jenna's jaw unhinged as his words sank in and a sprawling ranch-style home came into view. Timber and dark brick, a triple garage, colorful casual gardens and—

Her breath caught then she closed her eyes tight and dropped her head.

He was trying to keep her hopes up, and have an appropriate address for the judge—acreage where a child could run free and play, rather than a multistory penthouse in the central business district. But seeing an extravagant swing set was too much to bear. Would Meg ever use that bright blue slide, or climb through that candy-red cubby house?

Would Jenna ever become her mother?

The car pulled up on the circular drive directly outside the front door.

She let out a long breath. "I know you're trying to be kind…"

"I'm merely being prepared," he replied, easing out of the car.

Preparing for a dream to come true. Well, the biggest part of her dream anyway—gaining guardianship of Meg. She'd always known Gage wasn't a permanent part of the equation. And she could accept that—even after sharing his bed.

Really, she could.

He helped her out and onto the crushed pebble drive. His mouth hooked up at one side. "Want to have a look around?"

He looked better than incredible in that chambray shirt and pair of deep blue jeans. Although his chest was broader and the fine lines branching from his eyes confirmed he was older, the memories flooded back. Once, when he'd worn jeans every day, she'd fantasized about them owning a home together. She'd envisaged a child as well...maybe two. She'd been so in love with him then.

Her chest lurched.

Don't think about that.

As they walked off, Gage wrapped his arm around her waist. "Looks like we have visitors."

Jenna caught sight of another vehicle, parked on the other side of the garages.

Gage was a mystery in many ways, but he could also be thoughtful. He must have asked Nick and Summer out for the day. Summer had been so supportive in New Zealand and had phoned nearly every day since. The company of that lovely couple could be just what the doctor ordered.

But when two people appeared from around the corner, Jenna's smile slipped and the blood from her head funneled straight down to her toes.

Their visitors weren't Summer and Nick.

Gage's question came in a husky murmur at her ear. "Aren't you going to say hello?"

Dazed, she gaped at him. His expression was warmer than she'd ever seen it and his gray eyes...they were dancing!

Tina—Meg's nanny—stopped before them, the baby, in a soft pink and white dress and booties, asleep in her arms. The tiny matching bonnet had slipped and sat slightly crooked on her crown.

"She should be waking soon." Tina smiled down at Meg, who seemed so much bigger since the last time Jenna had seen her. "Maybe we could go inside. It's starting to get hot out here."

While Jenna struggled with rising tears of joy, and a clashing jumble of emotions—*How long do I have her? How hard will it be to give her back?*—Gage gestured toward the house. "Were you waiting long, Tina? I didn't think we were late."

Jenna's mind hiccupped and caught up. Had Gage arranged this meeting behind Leeann's back? Perhaps he'd bribed Tina to come all the way out here. Which didn't seem to make her a very trustworthy person to leave in charge of a young child.

Gage swung open the door and they stepped into a living room that was...ordinary. Timber and tapestry furniture that looked homey rather than imposing. A stone fireplace built into the far tongue-and-groove wall. A quaint grandfather clock stood ticking in one corner. Scattered rugs on the flagstone floor...a vase of daisies on the table...

She loved it!

Gage curled a knuckle around her cheek. "I think you should hold your niece."

Jenna nodded fiercely, but as soon as Tina laid a

sleeping Meg in her aunt's arms, the thrill of this huge surprise twirled around and hit Jenna high in the stomach.

Her throat felt so thick, she couldn't swallow. Only smile.

"She's so beautiful."

Gage stood close beside her, looking down, too. That knuckle touched Meg's cheek. Her little mouth pouted and sucked in and out, as if she were having a dream about dinner.

Gage grunted—a satisfied sound. "She certainly is cute."

"She is, indeed. And now I'll leave you both alone to enjoy her."

Tina's words snapped Jenna back. Alone? "Where are you going?"

Amy had been gone almost a month. What if Meg didn't recognize her face and cried? The very thought ripped the heart from Jenna's chest, but how could she deny the possibility? She'd rather be in pain herself than see Meg upset.

Gage walked down a hallway. "There's a sunroom down here, Tina, with magazines and cable. An Internet connection too, if you're interested."

Jenna's locked muscles relaxed. Meg's nanny wouldn't be too far away then.

Tina tapped the tote bag slung over her shoulder. "I have a book, thank you." She stepped closer to Jenna. "She'll most likely be uncertain when she wakes to find a…" Her brow pinched. "A different face."

She had only confirmed what Jenna already knew. Leeann, and Tina, had become the people the baby knew and relied upon now.

Jenna gazed down at Meg, so warm and snug in her arms. She nodded. "If she gets upset, I'll have Gage get you."

Tina's smile was appreciative. "Her bag with a written routine is in the front seat of the car."

"I'll get that," Gage offered, returning from having opened a door at the end of that hall. "Make yourself comfortable, Tina. There's a kitchenette in there, too."

Tina had no sooner closed the door behind her than Meg began to stir. Jenna's knees went weak. *Please don't cry, little girl. Please remember me.*

But she settled back to sleep again, curling toward Jenna's breast.

"Surprised?"

Jenna suppressed a laugh. "That's a huge understatement. How did you arrange it?" Her gut pitched. "What will Leeann say?"

"Leeann knows. I contacted her when we arrived back from New Zealand and told her how eager I was to discuss Darley Realty, that I should still be able to make the date we'd arranged for the meeting, but could we get in a nice long visit with Meg beforehand."

Jenna could barely believe her ears. He didn't pull any punches. "And she said yes?"

"Meg is ours until tomorrow lunchtime. It's in writing, so Leeann can't change her story later."

"And Tina?"

His lips twitched. "I have a feeling Tina will enjoy the break—not from Meg but from Leeann. She's staying overnight, too. There's a guest bedroom in that wing."

Slowly waking, Meg stretched an arm and squeaked. Jenna's body tensed. "I've never looked after a baby before."

He chuckled. "Better get used to it."

As the baby moved against Jenna, a sensation of real hope seeped through her. "You really think we have a chance?"

His expression hardened almost imperceptibly. "I normally get what I want, Jenna. I want this for you."

Her eyes misted over; she wanted to ask what else he wanted. But she was scared of the reply. Scared he wouldn't confirm that his needs for the future included them.

Meg blew a bubble and dragged open her eyes. Her lashes swept down again, her flawless brow pinched, then she blinked her eyes fully open.

Jenna held her breath and gently murmured, "Hello, sweetie."

Meg's gaze grew more intense, the corners of her mouth quaked, then she blinked twice more and slowly, slowly smiled.

Jenna choked on a teary laugh.

Gage whispered beside her. "I'm hungry when I wake up. Should we feed her now?"

Jenna carefully sloped the baby up in her arm as Meg seemed to focus more on her. In fact, wouldn't take her eyes off her. "Let's get her bag. Tina mentioned a routine." Guilt knotted in her stomach. "I should have done more research on infants. I just hadn't expected…"

She took in Meg again and relaxed a notch as the warm stir of instinct seemed to take over. "I think a diaper change would be a good idea."

With long strides, Gage headed for the door. "Diapers coming up."

Five minutes later they were in the nursery, Meg on the

changing table, Gage handing over the wipes. He hung further back than Jenna thought entirely necessary.

She hid a grin. "Powder, please."

Meg blew more bubbles, clenched her tiny fist and kicked her heels.

Gage's expression, by contrast, was intense. He rummaged around the baby bag then slapped the powder bottle in Jenna's open palm. "Powder."

Her grin became a laugh. "This isn't an operation."

"Coulda fooled me." Gage gingerly tied the plastic bag that contained the soiled diaper.

Jenna applied the powder then set the new diaper under the baby's bottom. She fixed the tabs, grateful for this day, for Gage's help and his resilience.

She stole a quick glance at him. "I'm proud of you."

He grunted. "Me? Why?"

"I don't know a lot of men who'd be brave enough to tackle that right off the bat." She eyed the diaper bag.

He cocked a brow and held the bag up by one tie. "To be fair to the rest of my gender, it does take courage."

His lopsided grin wrapped around her heart—and squeezed. This exchange was feeling way too comfortable. Too dangerous. *Save that heart of yours, Jenna, and don't get used to it.*

She slipped Meg's bloomers back on then eased her up into her arms. Oh, it felt so good!

She faced Gage. "Want to have a nurse?"

Gage's easy smile shifted enough for a frown line to form between his brows. He ran a hand over Meg's crown. "This is your time. I'm here to assist."

Jenna didn't let her hurt show. After all, what did she expect? If—correction, *when*—the guardianship situation was settled and she and Meg were together without any doubt of separation, Gage would get on with his life. He'd made it clear he didn't want the full-time commitment that went with kids. So it was better that he was wise enough not to get too close now.

Meg grabbed Jenna's finger, her beautiful face glowing as if she truly knew her auntie. Or perhaps it was the memory of her wonderful mother's face that Meg was reacting to.

Jenna bit her inside cheek.

No tears today. This was "happy" time.

"Why don't we get a blanket and sit under a tree," Gage suggested. "She might enjoy the scenery. I read some-where that babies like colors."

Smiling up at her husband, Jenna walked with him out the door. "I think you're right."

They spent the afternoon talking to the baby, feeding the baby, burping then singing to the baby. After six hours, Jenna was bushed. So was Meg.

Tina popped her head out from her room as Jenna was preparing to put Meg down. "Everything going well?"

Gage was folding the picnic blanket. "Absolutely. Thanks, Tina." Whistling, he continued on to the laundry room, not a usual occurrence in a billionaire's day.

Tina joined Jenna and cooed at Meg. "She had a bath before our drive. We'll give her another in the morning." She straightened and smiled at Jenna. "Need any help putting her down?"

Jenna hadn't been sure of Tina when they'd first met, and she'd jumped to the wrong conclusions about possible bribes and lack of responsibility when she'd seen her earlier today. But now Jenna got the best feeling that she and Tina would know and like each other for a long time to come.

She smiled. "I'd like to try to put her down myself. I'll call if I need help."

Tina nodded then pressed a kiss to Meg's brow. Eyes heavy, the baby yawned. "She's ready for a night's sleep. Lay her in the cot, sing her a lullaby. She'll fuss but nod off quickly."

Twenty minutes later, she and Gage stood in the nursery with the nightlight casting slow spinning stars over the ceiling and walls. Meg was still in Jenna's arms, and more than a little fussy. She did *not* want to go down. For the first time all afternoon, Jenna felt her insecurities taking over.

She murmured as she gently rubbed Meg's back. "It's okay, sweetie. Aunt Jenna's here."

Nearby, Gage scrubbed his jaw. "She needs another bottle."

"She's just a little out of sorts in a new environment. I'll put her down again." Surely she'd nod off this time.

But five minutes later, Meg had worked up a steady cry. Her face was red and her poor little mouth was trembling. Jenna had sung and sung, and held her wee hand, while Gage paced up a storm in the background.

He shoveled a hand through his hair and joined her by the cot. "I'll get Tina."

At her wits' end, Jenna was about to give in and agree when a thought struck her. "Let me try something first."

She scooped a whimpering Meg up and handed her to Gage, who reacted by standing stock-still. His voice cracked. "What do you want me to do with her?"

"Hold her a minute."

Jenna straightened the cot blanket then headed for the nightlight while Meg hiccupped and shuddered out a breath. With fumbling fingers, Jenna managed to find the switch and stop the stars from spinning.

She pivoted back to Gage. "Maybe there was too much stimulation—"

Her words trailed off. Just like that, Meg's eyes had shut. No crying. No movement. Her mouth was parted and, free from her rug, her little arm hung over Gage's.

Gage's eyes were round with amazement. He shrugged. "What did I do?"

Jenna wanted to laugh out loud. She threw up her arms. "I have no idea."

But in truth, maybe she did. Despite their past, she always felt safest when she was bundled in Gage's arms. Why should Meg feel any different?

They stood there, simply enjoying watching her sleep. Her cheeks were pink and chubby, a tiny dimple in her chin. Thank heaven she was healthy.

Jenna finally whispered, "Do you want to ease her down onto the mattress?"

"I need to hold her a bit longer. Just to be sure."

Jenna kept her eyes on Gage, who kept his eyes on Meg. She smiled. "I think you're right."

Two hours later, Gage sat in the nursery's comfortable corner lounge, Meg still in his arms. He'd fallen asleep not long after Meg. He'd been up since three that morning; seemed it had been a tiring day all around.

Legs drawn up, chin resting on her knees, Jenna hugged her shins and watched from the cushioned window seat.

She didn't want Meg to fall from Gage's arms. But in her heart Jenna knew that wasn't possible. The baby looked as if she belonged there and perhaps in slumber Meg felt it, too.

Jenna was still drinking in the picture when Gage awoke. His chest inflated then, eyes shooting open, he moved to sit up straight. Immediately he remembered the baby and gingerly settled back down. He gazed at Meg for a long moment before he searched the room.

Feeling all syrupy and warm, Jenna eased up and stretched her back. "I think we can put her down now," she whispered.

Gage took a few moments to push to his feet. Jenna smoothed the sheets then stood back as Gage lowered the baby. Meg didn't move a muscle.

Jenna held her breath as a bone-chilling thought hit her. "Is she breathing?"

Gage's hand zipped down to hover near her nose then drew back. "Definitely breathing."

He threaded an arm around her waist and Jenna leaned in. So warm and big.

"Thank you."

He pulled her close. "My pleasure. Which reminds me…" He angled her around, set his forehead against hers then stole the softest kiss. "Bed for the grown-ups sounds like a good idea."

"A very good idea," she murmured against his lips.

He watched over Meg while she showered. Then she took the watch while he cleaned up. When they finally climbed into bed in the room connected to the nursery, they didn't sleep, didn't make love. Rather they both lay there, staring at the ceiling.

"Do you think she'll wake through the night?" Jenna asked.

Gage crooked an arm to cup a palm under his head. "If she does, we'll hear her."

Of course, he was right. There was nothing to worry about. Nothing at all.

In the dark, Gage rolled over to face her. She could distinguish the outline of his shoulder and the white of his smile in the shadows. "You suit being a mother."

"You suit being a dad."

She felt him stiffen and a shrinking head-tingling sensation dropped through her.

It had slipped out. She knew very well Gage's position. He didn't want to be a father. This situation was temporary…a ruse with good sex thrown in. It was never meant to be, and obviously never *would* be anything else.

Following an interminable silence, he rolled onto his back. "We should get some sleep."

But Jenna lay awake for what seemed like hours. And she could tell by his breathing that Gage did the same—staring at the ceiling and wondering, just like her.

CHAPTER TEN

JENNA woke with a start.

Something—a baby—was squealing.

In a single heartbeat, the day and night before flashed into her brain.

Meg! Something was wrong.

In her pink singlet and matching shorts, she sprang out of bed, tripping over herself to get to the nursery. When she flew in the room, Gage was already there, lifting her niece out of the cot. The squealing, Jenna realized, was a sound of pure delight. With care, Gage swung the baby round on his arm so she sat perched facing Jenna, baby blues wide and twinkling.

Slumping with relief, Jenna pushed her palm against her pounding heart. Then she marched over and spoke softly to Meg. "You scared me, baby."

"It's after seven." Gage jiggled Meg and she giggled. "We've got ourselves a sleeper."

Jenna's heartbeat kicked. He'd never looked more handsome—dark hair mussed, masculine chest bared, his open expression devoid of any thought other than the tiny human being relying on him at this moment. He was so capable. So strong.

To her soul Jenna knew that from this point on, Gage would be the only man to ever kiss or touch her. She'd believed that before they'd met again; now, having given him her virginity, she was certain of it. She was just as sure about herself and Meg needing to be together.

A question formed in her mind before she could tamp it down.

How could he *not* change his mind about family now that he'd been with Meg, even if it had only been for a single day? She hadn't believed it was possible, but after this time spent together, she was even more hooked than before. She only wished now it could be the three of them—not pretending, but for real.

Gage's easy expression shifted as if he realized how he must look. Like a family man. Everything he didn't want long term.

A muscle beat in his jaw as he offered her the baby.

Jenna thought of making some excuse for him to hold her longer and reinforce in his mind how right this baby must feel in his arms. But that wouldn't be fair. All she'd prayed for was an answer to her problem, and hopefully her prayer would be answered by the intervention of the most unlikely person. She must be happy with the solution and not hold out for another miracle.

Gage hadn't said or done anything to indicate that he'd changed his mind. When this was over, he would leave, and he'd take her heart with him. But she would try not to mourn—not this time. That wouldn't be fair on anyone, including Meg.

She took the baby and the day progressed. First a change, then a breakfast bottle, then a bath. Gage stood a little closer than he had the day before, dribbling the washcloth over Meg's round little tummy, laughing when Meg splashed and chirped and squealed.

Over a game of "clap hands," Gage took a video using his cell phone, as well as several photos, some with the baby alone, then with Tina. Finally Tina took a few of the three of them together—Jenna, Gage and Meg. Tina said she'd like a copy.

At eleven o'clock it was time to leave. Time for breaking hearts.

Outside, while Gage locked up and Tina pulled her car around, Jenna held the baby, her lips pressed to Meg's satin-soft brow. Her mind wouldn't work, refusing to go forward and contemplate the next few minutes. She closed her eyes as tears leaked from the corners. Her chest felt as if it had caved in and her spirit had been crushed beneath the weight.

This is where you belong. How can I let you go again? If I don't get you back, how will I bear it?

She simply had to win guardianship. Gage's plan—this pretend marriage—had to work.

"Jenna, it's time."

She needed every ounce of willpower to open her eyes and meet his gaze. Gage's expression was almost impassive, as if he'd turned off his feelings. But when his nostrils flared the barest amount, she was certain this was hard for him, as well.

Because he didn't want to see Jenna hurt? Or because he was hurting too?

Gage put out his hands, palms up. "I'll buckle her in."

Jenna held her breath, felt her eyes go wide, and told herself to just do it.

When the baby left her arms, the air in Jenna's lungs evaporated. It felt as if her soul had been ripped away.

Tina appeared beside her. "I'll take good care of her until next time."

Jenna nodded even as her heart broke open like an empty shell. Yes, there would be a *next time* and maybe soon an *all the time*. She had to stay focused on that or how would she make it through these coming days?

Still, when Tina's car drove off down the crushed pebbled drive, Jenna felt her heart go, too.

Gage wrapped his arms around her, rocking her gently with his chin resting on her crown. "Be brave a while longer."

She swallowed against the anguish stinging her eyes and nose. Then she filled her lungs deeply and looked up into those thoughtful pale gray eyes.

"When this is over," Jenna said, "and Meg's home to stay, we're going to have the biggest damn party ever thrown."

The smile almost reached his eyes.

He tucked her head back under his chin. "You bet we will."

Sitting out on the penthouse's main balcony four days later, Jenna ran her gaze over Sydney's sparkling cityscape and sighed. Would that big party ever be thrown, or was she still just kidding herself?

Of course, nothing could go forward with Meg until after Gage's meeting with Leeann at the end of the week. Patience was needed as well as trust in her husband's judgment. Still, the clawing anticipation of the final outcome kept dragging her down. She was only grateful that, despite his own worries, Gage seemed to be doing his utmost to keep her spirits high.

Gage joined her on the balcony, a carafe of juice in hand to go with lunch. Halfway into his rattan chair, his cell phone sounded. Growling, he set the carafe down heavily enough for the orange juice to splash on the cloth.

Jenna pressed her lips together. Normally he was so cool—effortlessly in charge—yet lately the more his phone rang or that fax beeped, the more edgy he became. The Meg dilemma might be Jenna's sole upset, but she couldn't forget that Gage was an important man with a load of responsibilities, which she couldn't begin to imagine.

She'd heard Dubai mentioned several times and more than wondered whether his negotiations with the hotel consortium he'd spoken of briefly were facing major problems. On numerous occasions after taking a call, he would disappear inside his master suite for an hour at a time. Sometimes she'd hear him yelling. Now that phone was pressed to his ear again.

She gazed down at her meal. She'd be finishing her shelled lobster alone. Or what she could of it. Although it looked better than delicious, she had little appetite these days.

Concentrating on the call, Gage's brow creased. "Yes, I see." An eyebrow flexed. "Is that right?" A smile spread across his face. "That's marvelous. See you then."

Jenna pushed balsamic-dressed lettuce around her plate. "Good news?" *For a change?*

Gage swept up the carafe and filled her glass then his own. "That was my lawyer."

Jenna's ears pricked. "Lance?"

Was he calling about their petition for guardianship? Perhaps there'd been an early date set, or a judge assigned who might be sympathetic toward their case.

"My contractual lawyer, Jenna, not personal."

Hope fading, she set her fork down. "Oh."

"Not just *oh*. He spoke with Darley Realty's financial controller. Mr. Arnold asked that the preliminary documentation be put in order in the event of a buyout going through."

"But we already know Leeann wants you to buy the company. It's no good to her in the state it's in. Anything you offer would be a boon. That doesn't mean at this stage that she's willing to give up Meg for a deal."

His mouth slanted with a mysterious grin. "It tells me she's seriously thinking about it. The afternoon we arrived back from our day in the country with Meg, I took the liberty of pushing our hand."

Jenna stopped breathing. "Go on."

"I made her a verbal offer, an obscene amount of money if she signed two sets of documents. One as the vendor for Darley Realty, the other, a legally binding statement that specifies you and me as the best guardians for Meg. It states all the reasons we've put forward in our petition, and will give permission between the two parties for us to take Meg home immediately."

Jenna's heart hammered a wonderful staccato against her ribs. The sky looked suddenly bluer. Even the sun felt warmer on her skin. "We won't have to go to court?"

"We'll still have a judge sanction the decision. Clearly, if the testamentary guardian relinquishes responsibility to a blood relative—the deceased's own twin—there'll be no objection. At the end of the day the court wants the best for the child." He grinned. "You're the best."

She jumped out of her chair and threw her arms around his neck. "I can't believe it! Maybe you should pinch me."

"The offer is on the table until the day of our meeting. The following day the offer will be halved. The next day I'll tell Leeann to shove the business and we'll win Meg back through the courts."

Jenna shivered. *Ruthless man.* "I'm glad you're on my side."

He drew her down onto his lap. "So am I."

She loved him. It was that simple. She always had and always would. The rebel she'd once known had a good heart, even if it were an incredibly lonely and, in some ways, damaged one. But she wouldn't let her mind wander to places where it might get lost. If she tried to cling to dreams she couldn't hold, she might slip and fall again into that deep dark hole—the one she'd barely been able to claw back out from when he'd left her the last time.

But she had him here and now. For as long as it lasted, she wouldn't waste a minute, not a second. Every tick of the clock was precious, another memory to live on and last for the rest of her life.

She grazed a fingertip over his bottom lip then back again. "Perhaps we should continue our celebration inside."

His fingers threaded up through her hair and brought her head down to his.

He kissed her until she couldn't fathom which way was up and then, as if she weighed no more than a bag full of feathers, he rose to his feet with her slung in his arms. "It just so happens I have a bottle of vintage Bollinger chilling as we speak."

"What? No party balloons?"

He headed for the bedroom. "Not the kind you're thinking."

* * *

They didn't emerge from the bedroom until much later, and only to order in food—club sandwiches, extra fries, and lemon meringue pie with two giant bowls of whipped cream.

Enjoying a sit-down picnic on the living room rug, Gage leant back on one arm, swallowed a mouthful of pie and chuckled.

Jenna's spoon stopped midway to her mouth. "What's funny?"

"A dollop of cream's hanging from your chin."

Jenna brushed her face, felt the cream smear then saw it on her hand.

"I don't have any bibs." He licked his spoon, front then back. "But I'd be happy to feed you, if that'd help."

She grinned. *Smart aleck.*

"You're so sweet," she gushed. "But if one of us needs a bib…" She scooped up a finger full of pie and wiped it down his chest. "I think it might be you."

When he met her gaze again, a look of bedevilment shone in his eyes. "You shouldn't have done that, Jenna. There's an awful lot of cream and meringue here."

He dropped his spoon and collected his bowl with two hands.

Almost repentant, Jenna shrank back. "You wouldn't dare."

His white teeth flashed. "Dare is my middle name."

Jenna shrieked when cream splattered on her shoulder, and again when it hit the rug near her leg. When he fired at her nose, she picked up her own bowl and decided to even the score.

By the time the food fight had lost momentum, pie was pretty much everywhere—arms, legs and an assortment of places in between. As the victor, Gage pinned Jenna down and proceeded to finish his dessert, which meant savoring skin-warmed cream for him and unparalleled pleasure for her.

Finally, feeling satisfied but sticky all over, Jenna shimmied out from beneath him.

He grabbed her arm as she rose to leave. "We're not finished yet."

"I ate, I came, I conquered. Now I need a shower."

"I'm not sure that's how it goes, however," he rubbed a palm over his cream-smeared chest, "I follow your drift."

The moment he jumped up, that blasted fax beeped again. His expression clouded over to almost black; he didn't even think to excuse himself before he strode across to retrieve the message.

Jenna's hands fisted at her sides. *For pity's sake.* Just for once, couldn't they leave him alone? Guess she'd see him later—much later.

She entered her room remembering his comment the day they'd met again—the remark that had established from the get-go that he wasn't a man meant for family. *A child needs a stable home life.* He was right, of course. Any woman who was genuinely married to Gage would need to be endlessly understanding of his commitments, particularly if she had a child begging for her father's severely limited time.

Thinking of Meg again, Jenna entered her private bathroom, which was huge and close to decadent—all shiny green marble and gold-rimmed mirrors. The shower recess was floor-to-ceiling glass on three sides, spacious enough to house hanging baskets of ferns and an assortment of potted palms. Showering was like bathing beneath a secluded waterfall in the jungle.

She adjusted the temperature on the nearest of two nozzles and, stepping under, let the warm, soft spray wash her stickiness away. Her head was back, her hair hanging and wet, when she heard a soft echoing click. She blinked beyond the water running down her face. Gage's long, strong legs stepped past a crow's-nest fern, into the center of the recess.

Hard, hot and naked, he released the second nozzle and its hose from the wall. He found the right temperature and those broad shoulders rotated toward her. "When I make a mess, I clean it up...thoroughly."

While her body tingled at his deep commanding tone, he took both her hands in one of his then waved the spray back and forth over her fingers, her open palms, the sensitive skin of her inner wrists. She could barely believe he'd squared away whatever problem that fax had delivered and was with her again so soon. But she wouldn't look a gift horse in the mouth.

Every minute...every second...

Finished with her hands, he lifted her fingers and kissed each individual gnawed-down tip. So simple an act yet already she was simmering.

She was about to lace her arms around his neck when he frowned. "My job's not finished. Turn around, hands on the wall."

She blinked. "Am I under arrest?"

"Depends on how well you follow orders."

A delicious shiver raced over her skin. Smiling, she stroked his chin and turned around.

The water flowed back and forth on her shoulder

blades, then lower against her back as his thumb pressed skilful circles over tiny hidden knots. As each tension point loosened, her arousal wound tighter, and the flames in her belly leapt high.

His massage reached her hip, and her one ticklish spot. Gasping, she swept back around. "Okay. I'm clean now."

His smile was amusement studded with sin. "You want me to stop?"

"I wish you'd never stop."

They both seemed to stop breathing.

Was she sorry she'd said it? Because she meant every word. What they were enjoying now couldn't last, and yet…if she could make another wish she would ask that they be married in more than name only. She knew it was madness and yet, little by little she was convincing herself that long term wasn't impossible.

As she trembled with anticipation and beating physical need, his eyes narrowed as if he were making a choice. Then his gaze roamed her face, the nozzle hit the floor and his knees bent to bracket the outside of hers.

Noses touching, he cupped her bottom and slowly drew her up so her breasts grazed over the ruts of his stomach then the matted steel of his chest. When her legs scissored around his hips, keeping his eyes on her mouth, he began to shift her weight—right then left, gently up and down. She slipped slightly and, for stability's sake, he pressed her carefully back against the wall.

"Is that too cold?"

She drove her hands through his hair. "What do you think?"

When at last he entered her, an incredible wave of heat and passion rolled all the way through her. It was like a gathering storm, tossing all her emotions together, whipping them high, sending them clashing against one another in a maelstrom of feverish joy. With his mouth on her neck, she clutched onto his shoulders and whispered the words in her mind…

I love you. I love you. I always, always will.

As if those thoughts had cast a spell, the throbbing inside her intensified and spiraled out of control. Unable to hold back, she plunged off the precipice into a glorious white-hot pit; holding her tight, Gage came, too.

While she gave herself over to the irresistible magic, he murmured her name in that deep throaty voice—the same tone she knew so well and adored. And yet…

Something was different.

They'd made love countless times but tonight his embrace felt surer, his words sounded truer. And the feeling…?

As his face buried into her shoulder, Jenna remembered the water raining down around them and the fact that they'd both forgotten protection. Gage didn't seem aware of it even now.

She chewed her lip.

Was it possible—even subconsciously—that Gage was learning to swim?

CHAPTER ELEVEN

GAGE RAPPED his knuckles against his trouser thigh then straightened his royal blue tie and gold cuff links. For the first time in a decade of top-level business negotiations, damn it all, he was nervous.

"Don't worry," he told Jenna, who sat before him in Darley Realty's opulent reception lounge. "This'll all be over in a few minutes."

They'd arrived at these offices precisely on time for their long-awaited appointment with Leeann and her financial controller. His documents had been delivered by courier the day before. All that remained was to get her signature on the dotted lines. Simple.

That woman's self-centered greed would surely reign supreme. He had no doubt Leeann would take the deal— a bundle of money in exchange for Darley Realty and little Meg.

Soon his biggest debt would be repaid.

Soon this all would be over.

He ignored the sharp jab in his gut and tugged on his cuff links again. "After she signs, we'll go straight to collect Meg."

A ragged thumbnail left Jenna's mouth. "I'm glad you're confident. The superstitious part of me doesn't want to jinx today by being too sure."

"Then I'll be sure for us both."

And when Meg was safely back in Jenna's care, he needed to jump on his jet and shoot over to Dubai. Nick had flown over to work the problems through, only to discover that the head honchos wouldn't deal with anyone but Gage Cameron himself. Nick had managed to placate the ruffled feathers, but the fabric of this deal was held together now by the barest of threads. If he didn't get there in the next thirty-six hours, he might as well kiss that billion dollars goodbye. The players had been new to him; this deal had always been somewhat of a gamble, but his gambles always paid off. This would *not* be his first failure. Damned if it would.

When his gaze and thoughts landed back on Jenna, he bit down against a pang of longing. He'd known this would end. More importantly, he'd made certain Jenna had known it too. There was no room for regrets because that only left room for more hurt. He cared too deeply for Jenna to leave her hanging, tied up over someone who couldn't be a partner to what she needed more than air. Her family. Or what remained of it. Better for him to make as clean a break as possible.

Better to be safe. If she knew his deeper reasons, she'd agree.

He cast a look over one shoulder at the doors that would take him to the boardroom. "Sure you don't want to come in?" She'd most likely enjoy watching Leeann sweat. Neither of them owed that woman any favors.

Jenna set her hands in the lap of her white linen suit. "I'll wait here. Hurry back."

When he was ushered in the boardroom moments later, Gage felt his blood pressure rise. What game were they playing? Why the delay?

A squat man in an ill-fitting suit stood at the far end of a gleaming boardroom table. Smiling, he tipped his balding head at Gage. "Mr. Cameron."

"Mr. Arnold." He flung a glance around the empty room. "If Mrs. Darley is held up, I can give her five minutes' grace. I have a full day ahead."

A huge understatement.

"Mrs. Darley regrets she is unable to attend this morning's meeting. She's away on urgent business. Furthermore she apologizes for wasting your time in coming here this morning."

An arctic chill swept up Gage's spine but years of experience and natural acumen meant the flash of doubt didn't show on his face.

"You should remind Mrs. Darley that my current offer is valid only until midnight. This is hardly a time to bluff."

Moving forward, Mr. Arnold smoothed down his comb over. "No games, Mr. Cameron. There's been a rather startling turn of events with regard to Darley Realty and its position. There's also another matter Mrs. Darley wishes for me to discuss with you. It's regarding the child."

When Gage walked back into that reception area, he'd never been more rattled in his life bar once. Not because he'd failed to secure a business deal. Hell, that had nothing to do with the ice freezing the blood in his veins. Today he'd been bargaining in flesh and blood and he'd been arrogant enough to believe he would win.

How could he tell Jenna?

When he caught sight of her, she bounced to her feet, but he was certain his eyes told her everything she needed to know. Where was that poker face now?

Jenna froze. Then the life went from her face, her shoulders sagged and she swayed. He hurried to catch her.

She felt boneless in his arms, and she'd lost all her color. Even her lips had turned white.

"She's keeping Meg, isn't she?" she croaked.

His answer was shards of glass pushed up his throat. "Something's come up. Something I didn't expect."

Hell's fire, he should've been more thorough, should've acted sooner. A week earlier and this could've been wrapped up. Now they would need to rely on a judge.

"We won't talk here." He secured her waist and half carried her past the curious receptionist toward the sliding-glass doors.

In the car, he threw his jacket in the back, dragged loose his tie and, arms straight out, set his hands on the wheel. He didn't start the engine.

"That worthless piece of land in Western Australia," he explained, "apparently isn't so worthless. Global demands for iron ore have never been higher. An overseas conglomerate, which is leasing the iron ore holdings on a neighboring concern, has offered a small fortune to buy your father's land."

She shook her head. "Whatever for? I remember Amy saying there were no mineral deposits to speak of."

"She was right. The iron ore deposits are negligible compared to other pockets in W.A. It's the locality this company is interested in tying up. They want to utilize the property's coastline, and clear passage to it, in order to develop their own shipping port and maximize export capabilities. It seems to be the big thing these days."

Comprehension dawned in her eyes. "So she gets her small fortune and also keeps Meg."

He swallowed the nauseous feeling creeping up the back of his throat. "We won't waste any more time there. Now we need to focus our energies on impressing that judge."

Although it hammered at his brain, he wouldn't think about what he could or couldn't do about the Dubai blowout now. Just as he refused to think about the possibility of them losing in court. It only made sense that Meg should be with them—

He lost his breath.

Not with *them*. With Jenna.

Damn it, he meant *Jenna*.

He clamped his eyes shut and groaned. He had no idea this would hurt so much. All he could see in his mind's eye besides Jenna's tears was baby Meg's beaming little face. The way she'd looked and felt in his arms when she slept. And that was dangerous. He had no right to that kind of warmth.

His hands wrung the wheel. "Want to hear the kicker?"

Staring dazedly ahead, she half nodded.

"Leeann went to the police," he said. "She filed a restraining order against you."

Her face twisted. "What in heaven's name for?"

"Her man Arnold cited an alleged incident at our country home the day Meg visited."

"She's saying I hurt *Meg?*" Jenna spat out a curse. "That's ridiculous. Tina was there. She'll substantiate our—"

"Tina's going to testify against you."

A puff of air left her mouth as if she'd been kicked in the stomach. "I liked Tina. I *trusted* her." Her eyes widened, clouding with worry. "Those two women are going to bring Meg up. Liars and manipulators. What hope does she have?"

Gage knew firsthand how a person's sense of self-worth could suffer as a result of bad parenting. When a kid was old enough to understand the dynamics, the damage was already done. If a person were strong enough—if he had a leg up—he might be able to lift himself out of the bog. But in his experience there would always be something left behind…something missing. Whenever he got too close, that missing part—the slice of his soul that needed its distance—would rattle its cage and howl to be free.

That's when people got hurt.

Some even died.

Jenna's insulted tone brought him back. "What exactly is she accusing me of?"

His hands dropped from the wheel. "Arnold wouldn't expand on that. But he did ramble on about some other cock-and-bull tale—your prior dependency on prescribed drugs, as well as a history of depression. We'll have no problem refuting that in court. They'll only make fools of themselves without any evidence."

"It's true."

She caught him off-guard and he shot her a look. "What's true?"

Jenna's face was expressionless as if she'd given up hope. "When you left without a word I was so down I literally couldn't get out of bed. Amy was away, so Dad asked Leeann to take me to her GP. The doctor explained about stress and brain chemicals and compromised function. He said I might need some help to get back on my feet." Her chest rose and fell on a worn-down sigh. "Antidepressants didn't make the pain go away, but they helped me to keep going. Although I knew it was nothing to be ashamed of, Leeann took pleasure in mentioning it whenever she could until my father told her to stop."

Gage managed to clamp shut his hanging jaw. *My God. I did that to you.*

Didn't matter that he'd been young and thought he'd done the right thing—leaving Jenna before he could get her in trouble, unlike his father who'd screwed up Gage's mother's life by getting her pregnant at seventeen. And, yes, he'd had to escape Leeann's accusations; attempted rape was a serious offence. But if he'd been man enough, he would have found a different way. Right?

Growling, he shook his head at his lap.

Wrong. This revelation about Jenna's illness after he'd left merely proved his point. Fact was that he burned people he got close to…burned them bad.

Gage glanced over at Jenna. She was plowing through her handbag like a dog after a bone.

"I'm going to call Leeann and tell her exactly what I think," she ground out. "If she won't talk to me, I'll go over there and—"

"No, you won't." He took the phone from her.

Her eyes flashed, then she snatched it back and held it from him. Her voice shook and so did her hand. "Don't try to stop me."

For God's sake! "Leeann isn't even in the *state*."

Hearing his voice rise, he tamped down the barrage of emotions hurtling through his overloaded system and set his fraying nerves on a more even keel.

"Leave this to me, Jenna. I'll do whatever it takes to make things right."

The tears brimming in her eyes fell down her cheeks. "How? You know what will happen. In court her attorney will exaggerate those few months I took medication. They'll say I won't make a fit mother. Gage, I need to do something *now*. That baby needs me. *I* need her."

Damn it. "So do I!"

The mind-numbing realization fell upon him like a collapsing building, but he shoved the rubble away. Hell, he'd only met the child twice. He'd held her, played with her. Admittedly some kind of connection had been made, but his goal had always been to have any connection live on through Jenna.

That baby deserved someone a whole lot better than him.

Jenna was gaping at him. Before she could ask, he apologized. "Forgive me. I shouldn't have…shouldn't have raised my voice."

Her tone was calmer but still urgent. "I need to speak with Tina. Maybe if we offered her money, or found out why she's willing to lie…"

He concentrated, his mind hopscotching to various possibilities and solutions. If there was a way, he'd damn well find it.

He fired the engine and threw it into reverse.

As the car veered, Jenna tossed from one side of her seat to the other. She reached for the seat belt. "Where are we going?"

He stepped on the gas and shot out onto the street. "To see justice done."

CHAPTER TWELVE

WHEN the Maserati screeched to a stop outside the property Leeann had moved back into with Meg, and Jenna had once called home, Gage swung open his door.

With one leg out, he said over his shoulder, "Wait here."

Her door was already open. "No way!"

His hot hand snared her arm like a bear trap. "There's a restraining order pending against you. Don't make matters worse."

Jenna tensed. Gage had gone above and beyond the call of duty to try to secure guardianship of Meg. Marrying her, buying her that gorgeous house in the country, he'd even been willing to spend an obscene amount acquiring Darley Realty as an exchange tactic. But she couldn't and *wouldn't* sit back any longer.

She laid her hand over his. "I appreciate everything you've done, but I need to be more than a bystander now. This was my father's house. This is my niece. It's my battle. I need to face Tina, woman to woman, and see if it's not too late to somehow save this situation."

A muscle in his jaw flexed twice before he blinked and slowly released her arm. He shook his head as if to clear it. "I guess this whole guardianship thing has gotten under my skin."

Jenna's smile was wry.

What was the phrase he'd used when all this had started? *Let the games begin.* But this had turned into far more than a game for Gage. He truly cared about Meg and with whom she'd live. He'd been visibly shaken when he'd found out his exchange plan had failed. Later in the car he'd confessed that he'd needed Meg too.

The words burned on her tongue. *I love you. I think you love me, too.* With every passing day, it seemed more and more right that they should stay together—not in a mock marriage but as a real family. A family of three who loved one another, who were there every day and every night to support and to care.

People *did* change when they had a good enough reason. She'd come home, hadn't she?

Why couldn't he?

Gage helped her out of the car then fanned open one side of the iron gates. Ears pricked high, Shadow loped down the long drive. Gage hadn't shut the gate before Shadow jumped up in welcome. After slobbering over Jenna's hand, he sped off into the trees.

Gage brushed down his trousers. "At least someone's happy to see us."

Jenna's smile faded as she surveyed the property and an eerie sensation crept up each vertebra. Leeann had never liked the man her father employed to maintain the grounds. She must have let him go because the lawn was unkempt, the garden lacked water, but the trees unsettled her the most. They seemed to be peering down, judging or, perhaps, pleading with her somehow.

Why did you leave? Why didn't you come home sooner?

Jenna shuddered. No matter what transpired today, she would not return to this place. In a way she was glad her father hadn't left her this house. She didn't need it to remember her family. They would always live on in her heart.

Jenna's adrenaline was pumping by the time they reached the double front doors. Gage grabbed the brass knocker and let it fall three times. After a long tense moment, he tried again then took a few steps back to peer up at the second story.

He shaded his eyes. "Doesn't appear to be anyone home."

She tried to distinguish any movement beyond a heavy drawn curtain. "Tina could be hiding."

"Or she could be out."

Joining Gage, she set her hands on her hips. It was hard to believe that Meg's nanny had betrayed them. She'd had her doubts at first, but Tina had seemed sincere about her responsibilities toward Meg, and anyone who knew Leeann would surely see that woman could only love a child as an object, not a person. Leeann was too self-absorbed to put anyone's feelings before her own.

Shadow reappeared with a heavy stick between his jaws. He wove around Gage, dropped the stick at his feet then corralled Gage closer to the stairs.

Gage ruffled his fur. "Not now, boy."

But Shadow persisted, dropping the stick, running around, picking it up then trotting down the side of the house.

The hair on Jenna's neck stood up and quivered. "He wants us to follow him."

Gage held out his hand. "I just had the same thought."

Shadow trotted off over the lawn toward the hothouse, then to where the pine trees formed a wall that separated this property from the next—from the house where Gage and his mother had once lived. As they passed the foggy walls of the hothouse, Jenna's heart sank. The prize orchids were limp, beyond rescue. Her father would've cried.

Her chest ached when she saw a plant on the hothouse step that she couldn't leave behind a second time. She collected the bonsai and brushed the brittle brown leaves. "Typical of Leeann to dump it out here."

She'd told Gage the story behind the bonsai late one night in bed. Now, as then, he brought her close and pressed a kiss to her temple. "You'll make it well."

She bit down against the ache in her throat. It might be too late for the others but she'd sure as hell save this one.

On the other side of the hedge she heard voices. Gage put his finger to his mouth and they crept closer. Through a hole in the hedge, the same space Gage had crawled through to see Jenna that summer, they saw them... Leeann and a surprise guest.

Leeann's blond hair for once looked disarrayed. She swept it out of her face as she pleaded with the man. "I've told you, we need to be patient."

Gage whispered to Jenna. "So much for being out of state. Obviously this is one meeting she couldn't avoid. Do you know that man?"

Jenna shook her head. "But I'm betting on cold nights he wears a leather jacket."

Gage nodded at the same time the man smashed his beer bottle onto the cracked concrete drive. Jenna and Leeann both jumped.

"I'm *sick* of waiting." The man's voice was low and desperate. "The authorities are still looking into the crash. They've already come around asking me questions. If they find out I reversed the main rotor belt, I can kiss the next twenty-five years goodbye."

Prickling stars rushed over Jenna's scalp. Her vision grew dark before she blinked back to fully comprehend what she'd just heard.

My God. These two had killed her father. Amy and Brad too.

As bile rose at the back of her throat the name came to her. Barry…? Barry Whitmore. She'd read it in the police accident report. This man had been her father's helicopter mechanic. He did all the maintenance work on the *Squirrel,* Darley Realty's six-seater Eurocopter. It seemed Barry's last job hadn't been about upkeep or repairs, but sabotage.

Barry walked a tight circle, his hand at his brow. Sweat stained his khaki collar and under his arms. "I have nightmares where the police break down my door and haul me away."

Placating him, Leeann stroked his stubbled chin. "If they haven't got any evidence now, they never will. When a helicopter suffers hydraulic failure doing 120 knots, nothing and no one lives to tell any tales."

He knocked her hand away, self-disgust hanging on his face. "His daughter wasn't supposed to be there. I felt bad enough about the son-in-law. Hell, that baby's got no parents because of us."

The mole on Leeann's left eyebrow lifted. "And now she has a mother who waited a very long time for the privilege."

Jenna fought the impulse to retch. That's how much Leeann wanted Meg—enough to take away the most precious and irreplaceable things in her life. That wasn't love. That was obsession.

Barry rubbed the back of his neck. "I only wanted to get rid of Darley. It was just a matter of time before he found out I was the one you were seeing. If he'd hit you again," his fingers clenched together, "I'd've killed him with my own hands."

Gage clamped a palm over Jenna's mouth before she could blurt anything out. Leeann had played this man. Her father hadn't hit anyone in his life.

While Barry kept ranting and sweating, Leeann examined the hedge as if she'd heard something.

"We need to get out of here," Barry said with a harried glance toward the road. "You've got that story going about your folks in the States." He grabbed her upper arms, desperate love in his eyes. "We could fly out tonight."

She shucked out of his hold. "You know I can't do that. I need to make sure this W.A. deal goes through. Then we'll be able to go anywhere we want for as long as we want."

Movement beside her caught Jenna's eye. Tears of rage turned into a vengeful smile. Gage had his high-tech cell up and activated. He was recording everything on video! She could've kissed that stupid phone.

Barry wiped a shaky hand down his face. "We committed *murder,* Leeann. Can't you finish this business from somewhere safe, like South America? I did this so we could be together, but not in twin prison cells."

Shadow brushed by Jenna's legs and snarled out a growl. Hearing his growl, Leeann squinted at the hedge and muttered, "Bloody dog." She swooped down on some broken glass and hurled it. "Choke on that, you dumb brute."

Leeann's jaw smacked the dirt when Gage stepped out into plain view.

Barry looked taken aback and raised his fists. "Who the hell are you?"

Gage grinned. "The man who's going to put you both in jail."

Trembling with every conceivable emotion, Jenna joined Gage. "We've recorded your entire conversation, Leeann. All the tragedy you've caused my family…" She swallowed against the raw sting of pain. "At least I'll see you rot in jail for it."

Ready to attack, Barry lunged, but when Gage squared his shoulders and Shadow bared his teeth, the shorter man backed up then scrambled along the side of the weatherboard house.

Wary of the dog, Leeann inched forward, a guilty smile quaking on her lips. "You don't need to go to the police. The baby will be home soon." She held out supplicating hands to Jenna. "Take her. She's yours. And I'll give you everything from the W.A. contract, too." Moisture shimmered in her coward's eyes. "Just give me a day and I'll be out of your lives for good."

Had Leeann conspired with Barry to kill Raphael because she anticipated divorce and the subsequent dent in her financial security? Or had she planned to do away with all of Jenna's family in order to obtain the baby she'd wanted for so long? Most likely it had been a deadly combination of both. Now Leeann was willing to throw Meg away in exchange for her own neck.

She was almost too pathetic to hate.

Almost.

Gage thumbed in a number and pressed the phone to his ear while Jenna held onto his arm.

"You're right about one thing, Leeann. It is time for you to go away," Jenna lifted her chin, "and never ever come back."

An hour later, Jenna sat on the bench holding a sleeping Meg in her arms. Action was starting to die down all around them—police cars driving off, detectives milling around the house—but the baby was content to dream on.

Gazing down, Jenna was swamped by a deluge of emotions: gratitude that the nightmare was over, that Meg would now be safe with her; sadness knowing her sister and father would be alive today if not for two scum-of-the-earth people; love and respect for the man who'd stood by her during this whole ordeal…the man walking toward her now, his gait long and confident, a supportive smile on his handsome face.

Another man stopped his advance. Gage put his hands in his pockets, ready to answer whatever questions this particular officer asked. Jenna sighed. Just a little longer and they could be together—the three of them. After today's events—their actions and confessions—she couldn't imagine Gage leaving her and Meg now.

Beside Jenna, Tina visibly shuddered. She'd arrived with Meg fifteen minutes ago but her face was still pasty with shock.

"I had my suspicions about Mrs. Darley," Tina said in a daze. "I thought she might be seeing someone. When she canceled her flight to Western Australia at the last minute then told me to take the baby out, I had the worst feeling. But it wasn't my business to pry." She cast a look around. "I can't believe it was as bad as all this. That she was a criminal and planned to take Meg away for good." Her brow wrinkled and she pushed the glasses back on her nose. "You believe that I had no idea about that restraining order, don't you? I could see how much you loved this baby. I wouldn't lie in a court and say anything else."

When Tina had arrived, Jenna had taken the sleeping baby from the back car seat and asked Tina straight out about her part in Leeann's allegations against her. The misunderstanding had been cleared up quickly. Seemed Leeann hadn't even lodged a complaint. The story was just a manipulative ploy to gain her time and leverage.

Jenna stroked Meg's dimpled hand and reassured Tina again. "I didn't want to believe the worst. That's why we came here to speak with you about it."

Tina half smiled as she studied Meg. "I know she'll be happy with you. It's so important to have people who truly care."

Jenna thought of her own mother, how she and Amy had had her for too brief a time. But she'd promised herself to hold onto the good memories and bury any regrets concerning her parents. Yes, her father had had his weaknesses; didn't everyone? But she knew he had loved her. She only wished he was alive to tell her now.

She brought herself back. "Does your family come from Sydney, Tina? Do your parents live close by?"

Tina gripped the bench slats. She kept her eyes on Meg. "I lost my parents when I was young. I grew up with a friend of my mother's. A lovely lady. She passed away last year."

Jenna's heart contracted. Meg, Tina as well as herself were all without their parents.

She put her hand over the younger woman's. "We'd love to have you come and stay with us."

Tina's attention kicked up, her eyes wide behind their lenses. "Really?"

"You can help me with all the things I need to learn about—" Jenna's voice broke and she tried again. "About being a mother."

She felt Amy's presence at that moment more powerfully than ever before. Twins shared a certain energy, were bound in ways other people couldn't comprehend. She and her sister had an even stronger bond now—one that Jenna would make her priority all the days of her life.

Gage joined them and Tina stood. "Perhaps I should put the baby in her room. She'll sleep for another hour yet." She blinked down at Jenna. "Unless you want to carry her up."

Jenna pushed to her feet and carefully handed Meg over. "I'll put her down later tonight." She'd dreamed so often of saying those words. Now it wasn't merely tonight, but every night from now on.

Tina took the baby and began to move off. But Gage put up a hand. "Just a minute."

With a pulse leaping in his firm shadowed jaw, he concentrated on Meg for the longest time. Then he lowered his head and gently kissed her brow. "God bless, little one."

As Tina left, Jenna moved forward and set her palms on Gage's shirt. She tugged his loosened tie. "Big day."

"One of the biggest." He brought her near, his linked hands resting low on her back. "You'll be okay now."

A wonderfully warm feeling seeped through her veins. She smiled. "We'll be more than okay."

He glanced behind at the last police car leaving. "They've searched the grounds and neighborhood for signs of dear Barry. No luck so far."

Jenna knew to her bones the authorities would catch him. It was only a matter of time. Putting those two on trial wouldn't bring her family back but at least justice would be served.

"You're staying here the night?"

She nodded. One last night. "Then I thought we could drive out to the country house, reintroduce Meg to that cubby house and slide. She might be a little young for them now, but it won't be long."

His eyes crinkled above a warm but somehow wistful smile, and his hands pressed on her back. "But you know this house will revert back to you, as will Darley Realty. Murderers don't get to benefit from their crimes."

She didn't want to talk about that now. She wanted to go inside and stand with Gage over Meg's cot, as they'd done that night in the country house. Lord, she couldn't believe this was over!

Shivering with the ecstasy of relief, she pushed up on tiptoe to kiss him, but he spoke before their lips could meet.

"Would you like me to look after the negotiations for the W.A. deal? There'll be a delay until the trial ends and Leeann is convicted."

Couldn't he read her eyes? She'd had a belly-full of Darley Realty's twists and turns for one day. Besides, the answer was obvious. "Why wouldn't you handle it?"

His jaw shifted and the brightness in his eyes seemed

to fade. "Then I'll make some initial phone calls on your behalf and have Nick follow it up for you."

Time screeched to a halt then folded in on itself as a horrible dizzy feeling flashed through her. She tried to smile but her quivering mouth didn't want to play. "You're going somewhere?"

His lips thinned. "Dubai. Tomorrow. I may have enough time to salvage some aspect of the deal if I get over there now." His smile looked forced. "No rest for the wicked."

She searched his eyes. "I hear they're busy people."

"You heard right."

All Jenna's energy seemed to drain from her body. Earlier today she'd wanted to confess how she'd felt about him and their future. She'd all but convinced herself that he'd fallen in love with her, perhaps as deeply as she'd fallen back in love with him. Despite his philosophy that children needed a stable home life—a life Gage Cameron the loner tycoon couldn't provide—she'd begun to believe that he'd come around.

That he'd come home to stay.

But it seemed her prayers for one more miracle wouldn't be answered. Gage was pulling away. And there was nothing she could do about it. Nothing she *should* do about it…other than accept and be grateful for the time they'd shared. No regrets—even if it tore her heart out, she had to let him go and do it gracefully. It wasn't only her well-being at stake, but Meg's. That baby deserved her guardian's strength and total commitment, and a whole lot more besides.

Nevertheless, her fingers clung to his shirt as her eyes roamed his face, drinking in every beautifully chiseled feature, burning the image in her mind. Their short time together seemed to be running away from her like rainwater down a pipe.

"Thank you, Gage." Her throat was suddenly thick. "I'll never be able to repay you for all you've done."

His gaze settled on her lips while his heartbeat boomed against her palms. "The books are square. As of this minute, we're even."

Of course, that had been his motivation from the start. Not falling in love. Not staying forever, but rather settling a debt. *And* sampling previously forbidden fruits; to be fair, she'd wanted that too.

His pale eyes glistened in the afternoon sun. A moment longer and his Adam's apple bobbed as he swallowed.

"Jenna...I have to go."

She forced herself to step back and smile.

"I know."

I know.

CHAPTER THIRTEEN

"No messages, Mr. Cameron." The building's desk clerk glanced up from his reception monitor and smiled. "We'll see you back in Sydney soon, I hope."

Gage signed the departure printout with an impatient flourish. "Not for a while."

"Would you like us to make your penthouse available for lease to special clients? I had an inquiry today from New York."

He snapped the pen down. "Tell you what. It's for sale. See what you can get for it."

When he'd left Jenna yesterday, he'd driven straight here. He'd watched cable, downed two scotches, then fallen into bed...and slept not a wink. He'd tossed and turned every other minute of the long, lonely night. He kept feeling her beside him, seeing her lovely face, smelling the perfume of her hair. Every ounce of sanity was needed to persuade himself he'd done the right thing.

This morning he'd dressed feeling like a dog's breakfast—head pounding, tongue glued to the roof of his mouth. His muscles ached as if he'd come down with the flu. He never wanted to see those bedroom walls again.

The concierge strolled up and practically clicked his heels. "Your limousine will arrive shortly, Mr. Cameron. The driver's checked in and your jet is fueled and ready to depart for your journey to the Emirates."

"Very good." Gage popped a mint then dug into his pocket and slapped a large note into the man's hand.

The concierge beamed. "Hope to see you again soon, sir."

Gage scowled. He wished people would stop saying that.

He checked his watch then peered out the twenty-five-foot glass doors to the circular drive and its colorful hedges. He barely noticed the man and his young children trundling into the foyer. Neither did he listen to the conversation the man had with the clerk. He didn't want to even *look* at the man. Or the baby he held. Although he guessed it was a girl.

Roughly Meg's age.

The man spoke to him. "Excuse me."

Gage frowned. "For what?"

The man didn't seem to notice his foul mood. "I need a hand and the boys are too young to hold her. Do you mind? I'll only be a minute." He held out a baby dressed in pink.

Gage counted his heartbeats.

The last time he'd held a baby he'd gotten into a whole pile of trouble—he'd come close to convincing himself that he might be able to cheat the past and pretend to be someone he wasn't.

The man smiled. "She's fast asleep. I'll only be a moment."

The willowy brunette behind the counter raised a hand. "I can hold her." She darted out.

Gage took the baby as the lady reached them.

He grinned. *Too late.*

While the father took care of his business and the disappointed brunette returned to her station, Gage told himself he wouldn't look down. He was a smart man and his smarts told him that to study this child up close could be dangerous.

Beside him, the man apologized: *Just a little longer.*

Gage nodded.

Outside, the stretch limo rolled up and the concierge waved to him.

Uncomfortable, Gage nodded again.

A film of cool sweat erupted around his suddenly too tight collar. He was leaving. For good. Surely one tiny peek couldn't hurt. His eye line trailed down and…Gage grinned.

Not as bad as he'd thought. Nowhere near the tug he'd expected. This baby was cute, but not as cute as Meg. This one's nose was bigger, and she didn't have the cleft in her chin that was more defined whenever Meg was asleep. Her hands were similar though. So tiny, with four dimples delineating each knuckle. Such little nails.

He raised her up then lowered her down.

Pretty much the same weight too.

He studied her face again. Rosebud mouth. Did they all suck like that in their sleep? He frowned. Maybe she was hungry. He wouldn't think about diapers. Diapers he didn't do. Diapers he left to Jenna.

The man was speaking to him. "She's a doll, isn't she?"

Gage nodded. "What's her name?"

"Sarah."

Sarah was a pretty name, but Meg…well, it sounded sweeter.

"Do you have a family?" the man asked.

Gage's insides clenched. The pain—the memories— were so powerful, he almost doubled over.

He handed Sarah back. "No, I don't."

He strode toward the limo, ears and eyes blocked to the man with his family. A young woman passed him on her way to the desk. Sarah's mother? She had that look about her. A look of happiness. Completeness.

What the hell was that like?

The uniformed driver tipped his cap and opened the door. "Shouldn't be any traffic holdups, Mr. Cameron."

Gage strode right past and down the street.

He couldn't get into that car. He needed fresh air and lots of it.

Grabbing his tie, he wound the knot down then ripped the crimson silk completely from his neck and stuffed it into his pocket.

What was wrong with him? He'd accomplished what he'd set out to do. *More.* His debt to Raphael was repaid. Jenna wouldn't have to worry about money for the rest of her life. She had her baby. She was *happy.* Most importantly, she wouldn't have him hanging around screwing with her emotions *or* her life.

He strode across the street, ignoring the pedestrian signal, the beeping horns, the annoyed glares.

God, he wanted her now. Almost enough to convince himself that he could *continue* to make her happy. But that pleasure had come at a cost. It was *pay up now* or *suffer later*. He'd lost count of the number of times they'd made love.

Now it was no longer safe.

He found himself at Darling Harbour. He should get out

of here, as fast and far as those Learjet engines could carry him. But how could he sort out Dubai when his brain felt ready to explode?

At the end of a pier, he stopped to hold his head, clamping the ache, willing it to leave. But still the damning thoughts wheeled in.

All his life he'd wanted to escape…his Leave-it-to-Beaver peers in school, who didn't know how lucky they were…his poor wasted mother, who'd given up caring years before she'd died. Twelve years ago Gage had wanted to escape Jenna too, or rather had wanted her to be free of him. He'd found out yesterday that Jenna had paid dearly for having known him—a crippling bout of depression. Not so long ago, another woman hadn't gotten off that lightly.

Brittany Jackson had been one of his secretaries. On a business weekend away he'd let down his guard, broken his own rule and had slept with the besotted employee. He usually set limits on how long an affair would last. He liked to cut loose before strong attachments could be formed, but Brittany didn't make waves or demands. On top of that, she was discreet. He'd felt comfortable with her…until the day she'd told him she was pregnant.

Completely floored, he'd fallen back in his chair. She'd known his mind. He did *not* want children. They'd always used precautions. What the hell had gone wrong? When she'd cried and run from his Melbourne home, he didn't follow. He had important business to conduct overseas. He'd planned to take her, but now he had to think.

Although they spoke on the phone, he'd stayed overseas

for three weeks—quietly angry at her, but angrier at himself. Although he'd felt trapped, there'd been no doubt in his mind that he'd do the right thing—which also happened to be the worst thing. Money aside, what life would they have? He didn't love this woman. Brittany would grow to resent and perhaps even hate him for his ambivalence. But their child would suffer the most, growing up with a largely absent father and a needy, miserable mother. Hello, *twisted sense of self-worth.* Come on down, *a childhood of shame and rebellion.* Man, didn't that sound familiar.

When he'd finally returned to Sydney and marched into his office with a rock in his pocket and his proposal prepared, his P.A. walked straight in behind and shut the door. Bad news. Over the weekend, one of his secretaries, Brittany Jackson, had been killed in a car accident.

The horror had knocked him senseless. He'd put Brittany and his own child in their graves. If he'd taken her with him, they'd have been married and he'd have become a father. Instead, he'd let them down. Just as he'd let his mother and Jenna down when he'd left. Coming back here, all he'd wanted was to make amends. Atone for past mistakes. Find a little peace.

Gage fell onto his knees.

He didn't deserve happiness. Loner. Mystery man. Who was the enigma behind the mask? Gage knew the answer.

A man who wasn't sure whether to take a blessing and hold it with both hands, or walk away from disaster while there was still time.

Jenna stood outside the pool house. She was peering up at the jet inching its way across the dreary gray sky, taking its passengers to heaven knew where, for heaven knew how long.

The empty ache in her stomach flipped over and she screwed her eyes shut.

Stay strong. This is the last time you'll ever need to get over him. No more heartache, for you or for Meg.

After a long, settling breath, she turned the lock on the pool house door and took in a sweeping view of her childhood home. In the last ten years, she'd been all around the world. So where to now?

Not the country house that Gage had bought. She'd been happy about living there only when she'd fooled herself into thinking that Gage would live there, too. Now the prospect of settling in that house, filled with its bittersweet memories, was perhaps even worse than staying here.

She and Meg needed a fresh start. Somewhere where sad remembrances didn't haunt them and she could give her heart time to mend. Not that the wound would ever completely heal. From the moment she and Gage had locked gazes that summer long ago, she'd belonged to him. Although she would never again know the special magic of his embrace—of his kiss—she belonged to him still. Time and distance could never change that.

But she had what she'd prayed for—Meg safe and sound with her. That should be more than enough.

She pocketed the key.

It was better that Gage had gone. He'd always been a loner, a person who found reasons not to settle down. As much as it pained her, Gage had known best, and he was best shut out of their lives.

She rotated toward the house and collided with what

felt like a solid brick wall. She gazed up into a pair of piercing gray eyes and gasped.

Her mind and heartbeat skidded to a stop. "What are *you* doing here?"

Gage's chest was pumping as if he'd run a marathon. "I needed to see you."

A lock of dark hair had fallen over his brow. Without a tie, his shirt was unbuttoned almost halfway, giving her a tantalizing peek at his chest. That scar on his mouth begged her fingertip to reach out and—

No!

She knocked those dangerous thoughts aside and straightened.

He'd said he needed to see her. Obviously nothing of an intimate nature; yesterday he'd made his final stand on that issue. So, his surprise visit must concern business— her father's company or the W.A. property.

She folded her arms. "I know what I said yesterday, but I'm more than capable of taking care of Darley Realty's concerns from here on." She offered a tight smile. "Thanks again."

She began to circumnavigate the pool on her way to the house.

"This doesn't concern Darley Realty."

Thinking of the jet that had flown overhead, she looked back. "Why aren't you on your way to Dubai? Problems over there were supposed to be urgent."

He joined her. "They are urgent. But nothing compared to this."

A flash of panic raced up her spine. But she knew this couldn't be about Meg; everything was squared away there. She also knew that saying goodbye to Gage yesterday had been painful enough. If she had to go through it again, better to have it over with quickly, like the drop of a guillotine blade.

She set her hands on her hips. "What's this about, Gage?" *Spit it out.*

He took her hands from her hips and held them together in his. "I don't want this to end. What we have is too good to throw away."

Even as the physical contact released within her a surge of desperate longing, she set her jaw. Yesterday, he'd vanished from her life—*again.* From the start, he'd been upfront and she would deal with that…somehow. But now he'd returned, wanting her back in his bed?

It didn't work that way.

"You're suggesting our mock marriage continue?"

"Yes." He frowned and shook his head. "I mean, no."

Her smile was as sad as it was dry. "I know what you mean. You want to be able to fly into Sydney and see that my bedroom door is always open."

"It's far more complicated than that."

She'd never felt more alive—more like a woman— than when she'd been with him. She hadn't thought it possible to feel so whole and new. But having her deepest intimate fantasies come true had also made clear what she'd known all along.

"It's not so complicated, Gage. You told me, remember? You don't grow roots." He didn't do *family.* "What we shared was good, but it was temporary." Now it was over.

"I want us to be more than temporary."

She almost laughed. "You'd like to block off another few weeks in your calendar?"

She flinched at her own shrewish tone, but her sarcasm covered red, raw pain. He was playing with her heart. Damn it, she was worth more than that.

Her eye line dropped. Her fingers were clutching his as though her life depended on it.

Mortified, she stepped back. "You should go."

He planted his feet shoulder-width apart. "I can't."

"Then I will." She walked away, around the pool's edge to avoid a puddle from the morning's rain.

He called after her. "I want to make you happy—make *us* happy."

She said casually, over her shoulder, "And you'll accomplish that how?"

"We should stay married. Really married."

That jolted her back. But of course that scenario would be part of his *what we have is too good to throw away* plan. What did "real" marriage mean to a man like Gage? Commitment or, more likely, convenience? Besides, staying married wouldn't fix things. She was a mother now, with a mother's concerns.

When she turned to face him, the pool's blue width stretched between them. "You said it at the start…marriage isn't the issue. I have a child to consider. I won't put my passions before Meg's well-being. If she comes to look upon you as a father—a father who is constantly saying goodbye—that will leave scars. If I let that happen, I'm no less selfish than Leeann."

Girls needed to depend on their fathers. She knew that better than anyone.

"Jenna, I need to tell you…I've done things in my past I'm not proud of."

Her heart tugged at the open expression on his face,

of whatever secrets he seemed willing to reveal. But there was no need.

"We've all done things we regret." Like leaving her family in a huff and letting pride keep her away far too long. "But there's no need to feel guilty about what's happened these past weeks. You did more than you'd set out to do. I'm grateful for everything. But don't mess it up. It's time to move on."

His voice lowered. "I want us to be a family. A whole family."

Her heart thudded in her chest. It sounded as if he'd really missed them. Heck, maybe today he truly *did* want that family. But what about the sense of desolation she'd suffered when he'd walked away from her yesterday? Did he expect her to fall at his feet without considering the real possibility of a third goodbye?

Her stomach muscles tightened.

Sorry, she just couldn't.

She turned on her heel to leave.

"Jenna, I love you."

Those words stole her breath away. Despite it all, she ached to say them, too. She'd whispered them so often in her mind. But that kind of confession wouldn't change things, other than to leave her more vulnerable.

"If you want me to give up my work," he continued, "I will. I don't care about Dubai. I don't care about money."

Her heart aching, she turned to face him. "It's not making money that you'd miss. It'd be the loss of doing it so well. It's who you are, Gage. If you gave it all up, you'd be itching to find yourself again, by jumping on a jet, making another million, just wanting to escape."

If she said yes to him now and he left her a third time…

Tears blurred her sight.

Damn it, she'd sworn he'd never hurt her again.

His voice reached her over the water. "It wouldn't be like that."

Her heart tore down the middle. "You of all people can't give me that promise."

She only wished he *could* convince her.

As she started to turn from him, her foot slipped on the wet tiles.

One second she was falling face-first toward the water, the next she belly flopped *hard* into the deep end. Jenna opened her mouth to cry out at the same time she landed in the water. Pain radiated through her as she flailed, swallowed water and began to sink.

Only seconds later, she was half aware of being dragged up and breaking the water's surface. She opened her eyes. Gage's strong arms were hoisting her out onto the pool's edge. While she spluttered and coughed, he pulled himself out. Water coursing down his worried face, he knelt and carefully held her in his lap. The pain throbbed worse; she cringed and shut her eyes.

He stood up and swept her into his arms. "I'm getting you to a doctor."

As Gage strode with her toward the house, she gingerly moved her arms and legs. She hadn't hit the side. Nothing felt broken.

When they reached the back patio, she'd stopped coughing and her head wasn't quite so foggy.

"I'm all right," Jenna murmured. "You can put me down."

"I told you, I'm taking you to a doctor."

He gazed down at her, his eyes fiery, his hair swept

back, his hard body not quite trembling as he held her. And then she realized.

Warmth spread through her chest and she smiled. "You're all wet."

He didn't look impressed. "So it seems."

"I thought you'd rather eat razor blades than try to swim."

He'd acted without thinking and had faced his greatest fear when he thought she was in trouble. He said he wanted her to trust him…said he would give up his Fortune 500 lifestyle….

Her mind was still reeling when, sopping wet and cold, he brought his mouth to hers, kissing her with all the fire and honesty she'd lain awake and dreamt of last night. Intense, passionate. Overwhelming and fulfilling.

Panicking, she broke the kiss. "Your cell phone! It'll be ruined, and it has all that footage of Leeann and Barry and—"

He set her feet gently on the ground. "The police already have a copy of the incident and the phone."

He gathered her close. The kiss this time was slow and deep.

She came up for air, dreamy, the fall into the pool almost forgotten, but she needed to ask, "I thought you were certain that you wanted the plane not the anchor."

His brows lifted. "My pen?" She nodded. "My Montblanc is sitting on the bottom of Darling Harbour, or, perhaps, in the belly of some fish."

"Did you drop it?"

"No. I tossed it as far as I could. It flew for a while then sank, a little like you a minute ago." He grinned and held her closer. "You and Meg are what's real to me, nothing else. You're who I am, what I need. Not big contracts signed with gold pens. Not Maseratis or Learjets. I'm nothing without your love. All these years, I was nothing without you."

Jenna gazed up into those incredible eyes, wanting, needing to believe. Her concentration slipped when she heard a distant voice.

"What's going on here?" Tina called out from the far end of the patio. "Do you two often go swimming fully dressed?"

In her nanny's arms, Meg cooed and wriggled.

"Jenna slipped and fell into the pool," Gage explained.

Without another word, Tina disappeared inside. She returned with Meg in one arm and towels under the other. Jenna and Gage gratefully accepted a towel each while Tina asked if Jenna was all right and Jenna assured everyone she really was fine.

After Gage had wiped himself down, he dropped his wet towel, took the last dry one from Tina and held out his arms.

"May I?" He took the baby, sitting her in the towel and gazed down lovingly. "I'm going to be here for you. First words, first steps, first day of school. I'm looking forward to every moment."

Eyes bright and blue, Meg laughed and tried to clap.

Tina laughed too. "Looks like she missed her dad."

Jenna held her breath.

But Gage only smiled. "And I missed her, so much you wouldn't believe."

Tears prickled Jenna's eyes. Could Gage—a professed loner—be a stable father for her baby? Would Amy and Brad have wanted that? More importantly, was that what Meg needed?

He brought Jenna close and brushed his lips against her temple. "I want to be Meg's dad. And I want to be your husband, for real, Jenna. Forever. We deserve this chance. We all deserve some happiness."

Jenna pressed her lips together. They really did deserve happiness, didn't they? Little Meg more than anyone. Perhaps it wasn't wrong to trust one more time, to put her faith in her love and in his.

His tone deepened. "Tell me you love me. Seems I've waited my whole life to hear it."

When, perched between them, Meg placed one hand on his chest and one hand on hers, Jenna felt herself being swept away on the first leg of a beautiful journey. With a smile, she released the last of her fears. "I love you. I've never stopped loving you. I never will."

His eyes glistened as they searched hers. "Then I'm one very happy man."

When their mouths joined above their baby's head, Jenna felt so many powerful forces swirling around them—forming, then sparking and finally melding together to shine more brightly than ever before.

She felt it to her soul.

This union was indeed a match made in heaven. A wonderful heaven on earth.

EPILOGUE

Four years later

AT THE light tap on the door, Jenna set down her nail file and pushed up higher on her family-sized hospital bed. A little weary, but so very happy, she beamed when her husband and excited little girl entered her private maternity suite.

Meg, with her blond pigtails, bounced onto the mattress and crawled over to lie beside her mother. She pressed a big wet kiss on Jenna's cheek.

"I missed you, Mummy."

Gage leant over Meg to give his wife his own kiss, the kind of heart-warming, tender caress that would live on in her memory forever. He smiled into her eyes. "You've never looked more beautiful."

She might have laughed. After giving birth, minus makeup? But the sincerity shining from his eyes sent her fingers curving around his jaw. How she loved this man— so much it sometimes hurt.

Holding her gaze with his, he pressed her palm to his lips then straightened. "These are for you."

From behind his back, he whipped out a bouquet of wildflowers.

Vibrant yellows, soft pinks, striking reds…

"They're beautiful!" Jenna reached for the call button. "I'll have a nurse bring a vase."

His fingers folded over hers. "The nurses have their hands full right now."

"Daddy said there'd be a big surprise when we got here." Meg looked up at her mother and whispered, "I know what the surprise is."

Gage tickled his daughter's ribs. "I'll bet you don't."

On cue, a pair of nurses strolled in, each carrying a cherished bundle.

Meg's hands flew to her mouth at the same time Gage set down the flowers and put out his arms.

His eyes were sparkling—with happiness, wonder, heartfelt thanks—the same gamut of emotions that ignited and twirled through Jenna too. How many moments were there as precious as this? Today must be the happiest of her life.

Gage carefully took the nearest baby. "Which one's this?" He shifted the blanket a smidgeon to look at the face. "Ah, Noah." His smile grew. "What a handsome boy."

The second nurse laid the other twin in Jenna's arms. Jenna inspected the baby's features and grinned. And Isobelle was a gorgeous girl.

Meg's eyebrows sloped, pleading, "Can I hold one?"

"Your little sister or your brother?" Gage asked, indicating with a nudge of his chin that Meg should wriggle back against the pillows.

"Um…that one," she answered, pointing to the bundle in Gage's arms.

Positioned and ready, Meg's eyes widened with amazement as Gage laid a soundly sleeping Noah in her arms. "I can't believe I get *two* babies." When Noah yawned, Meg's sigh went on forever. "I love him," she murmured adoringly. Then she frowned. "But he needs a iron. He's got some wrinkles."

Gage laughed. "That's because he's brand new. He'll fill out soon enough." He tugged one of Meg's pigtail. "You certainly did. Look at you!"

A short time ago Meg had been a baby, too. Both Jenna and Gage had loved and nurtured her; she'd been their whole world. Meg was so comfortable with herself—so sweet yet confident—Jenna knew they'd done a fine job so far.

Jenna tilted closer to Meg. "Why don't you kiss Noah's brow? He'd like that."

Meg pressed her lips to the baby's head. Her small fingers patted the baby blanket as she would her favorite swaddled doll. She couldn't take her eyes off him.

"Can we take them home now?"

Gage stroked Meg's crown. "Not yet, honey. A few more days."

Both babies were a good weight, and there'd been no complications. But, even with Tina's assistance, Jenna needed to regain her strength before tackling the rewarding yet tiring task of caring for newborn twins.

"Are you sure you'll be okay with Meg at home by yourself?" she asked.

Gage pretended to scoff. "We'll have fun."

Meg gave a very grown-up nod. "And the new lady's there to do all the dishes and stuff."

Gage's jaw shifted. "Hey, I can do dishes."

Meg rolled her eyes as if to say, *Well, he tries.*

Gage rounded the bed and sat beside Jenna. "Don't worry about us. Concentrate on building up your strength." His mouth kicked into a playful smile, but his eyes were bright with a deeper emotion. "I'm not surprised you make beautiful babies."

Her gaze ran over the lips she would never grow tired of kissing each morning and every night. "*We* make beautiful babies."

He curled a knuckle around his baby daughter's cheek. "I felt complete before," he murmured, "but *this*…" His shoulders went back. "We'll just have to have more."

Jenna coughed out a laugh. "Can I have a few weeks?"

But of course she wanted more children as much as he did. She'd taken three years to get pregnant. Perhaps the delay was partly due to stress over the trial. Now that her stepmother and Barry Whitmore were serving hard time, Jenna would be happy never to hear their names again.

Gage had been at her side the entire time, except for three days away to save the Dubai deal, which Jenna had insisted on. Then he'd handed over most of his business responsibilities to Nick, who had since married Summer. In his spare time, Gage helped his wife with her directorship of Darley Realty and restored classic cars. His latest work—an Aston Martin DB4 convertible—had sold for an obscene amount at auction.

In four years they'd become so close. He'd told her about that poor woman, Brittany—on top of everything else, no wonder Gage had been terrified to commit. And now little Meg was in Prep—the year of formal schooling before the Big Grade One. She was so bright; Jenna had wondered whether her daughter would somehow work out that her mummy was having twins. Seeing Meg's face now, keeping the surprise had been well worth it.

Gage toyed with Isobelle's tiny hand. "Did you know that 22 percent of twins are left-handed as opposed to 10 percent of nontwins?"

Jenna nodded. "I think you mentioned it." At least a dozen times since they'd learned this would be a multiple birth.

"And the word *twin,*" he went on, "comes from the Greek word *twine,* which means two together."

"Like a tree," Meg offered.

"Sure," he said. "Branches can twine."

"And spread out." Meg spoke to Jenna. "Miss Samuels told us today at school."

Gage smiled mysteriously. "We should show Mummy the special tree you and Miss Samuels made today."

Meg's face lit up. "Can you get it, Daddy?"

Gage retrieved a folded piece of paper from Meg's sequined handbag. He opened it then held the paper up so proudly, it might have been the deeds to a palace. "Meg drew our family tree."

Meg chimed in. "See. There's me and Noah…or Izzybelle. I thought there was one." She tilted her head at the paper. "Here's you and Daddy. Daddy's got a crown coz he comes from kings. And there's my other mummy and dad."

The twist of pain in Jenna's chest was quickly replaced by the warmth of love. She could barely see through her welling tears. Standing to either side of the stick figures that represented herself and Gage were another couple who wore bright yellow halos.

"They're our garjon angels," Meg said earnestly. "Noah

and Izzy's angels now, too." She turned her big blue eyes up at Jenna. "If you're not too tired, Mummy, I want to take a photo of us here for Show and Tell."

Smiling, Jenna cleared the thickness from her throat. "I'm not too tired, sweetheart."

Gage pretimed the camera then set it on the portable meal table at the end of the bed. Sitting beside Meg, he laid his arm along the pillows at their backs and brought his family near.

He winked at Jenna, kissed Meg's crown then smiled into the lens. "Everyone say, *chocolate fudge sundae!*"

The flash went off, but Jenna's smile didn't fade. She wanted this moment to last and last.

Gage nudged her. "Hey, you're off with the fairies. Penny for your thoughts."

She was thinking she'd been given the most priceless gifts in the world—her husband, her family and a loving, stable home where each of them would always belong.

"I was thinking that no one could be happier than I am right now," she admitted.

Gage leant close, and his adoring smile grazed her lips. "No one except me."

* * * * *

The Viking's
Defiant Bride

JOANNA FULFORD

Joanna Fulford has been a compulsive scribbler from the age of seven. Her first passion was horses and every story had one in it somewhere, much to the bemusement of her English teacher, who often found it hard to make the connection between the set topic and the equine world.

Joanna went on to write serials to entertain her friends, each episode more lurid and improbable than the last. Always an avid reader, she developed a love of poetry, drama and the classic novels. History also captured her imagination at school and she went on to study both subjects to postgraduate level.

Other countries and cultures have always exerted a fascination, and she has travelled widely, living and working abroad for many years. Two of these were spent doing Voluntary Service Overseas in Sierra Leone, an experience that she found rewarding on many levels, not least for the friendships made there. What has happened subsequently in that country she can only describe as a tragedy.

Eventually she returned to her roots in England and is now firmly established in the Peak District, where she lives with her husband, Brian. The Peak is an area of outstanding natural beauty, first visited on a camping trip when Joanna was seventeen. The group arrived after dark, so the scenery wasn't revealed until next morning. Looking out of that tent was a jaw-dropping experience and she vowed then to live in Derbyshire one day. It took another thirty years, via many other places, but she made it in the end and has no intention of leaving.

The Reviewers Said:

"Fulford's story of lust and love set in the Dark Ages is reminiscent of Woodiwiss' *The Flame and the Flower.* A suspenseful plot, well-developed characters and a passionate romance combine to keep readers engaged from start to finish. The authentic depiction of the historical setting adds to the enjoyment of this…story."
—*Romantic Times BOOKreviews* on Joanna Fulford's *The Viking's Defiant Bride.*

For my parents and for Brian
who, between them, have supported me
in every way possible.

PROLOGUE

Denmark—865 A.D.

THE only sound in the great hall was the crackle of flames in the hearth. Flickering light from the torches cast a ruddy hue over the assembled warriors who sat stony faced before the implications of the news they had just received. In every heart was burgeoning sorrow and disbelief. All eyes turned to the three brothers at the high table. The sons of Ragnar Lodbrok surveyed the messenger quietly enough, but their eyes spoke of incredulity, of grief and rage.

'Ragnar dead?' Halfdan's voice was grim, his fist clenched on the arm of his chair. 'You are certain of this?'

'Quite certain, my lord.'

Beside Halfdan, at his right hand, Earl Wulfrum was very still, his face expressionless save for the blue eyes, now two chips of ice. Involuntarily, his own hand tightened round the hilt of a wicked-looking dagger in a gesture that mirrored his sword brother's, even as his mind struggled against the knowledge of Ragnar's death. Ragnar the warrior, the war leader, fearless, powerful, respected, a prince among his people; Ragnar the Terrible, whose ships, once sighted, struck terror into the hearts of his enemies; Ragnar, who had been as a father to him, who had found him that day when, a ten-year-old boy, he had stood alone in the smouldering ashes of his home, the bodies of his slain kin all around; Ragnar, whose rough and careless kindness had taken in the son of his oldest friend and raised him as his own, who had given him his first sword, taught him all he knew, and raised him to the warrior caste in turn. And now he was gone, his fire quenched for all time.

Wulfrum revealed nothing of these thoughts, hiding his pain as he had all those years ago. What ill fate was it that he was always spared when those he loved were slain? Too much care and love made a man vulnerable. It was a lesson he had learned early in life, a lesson harshly reinforced now. If you did not love, there could be no hurt. Was it thus, then, that a man must protect himself? His jaw tightened. There would be a reckoning here. The blood feud that killed his kin had had a far bloodier resolution when the boy grew to manhood. How much more then the slaying of Ragnar?

He was drawn from his thoughts by Halfdan, voicing the question that was in his own mind.

'How?'

'As we neared the Northumbrian coast, a fearful storm arose and many of our ships were wrecked. Those of us who reached the shore were attacked by King Ella's soldiers. We were heavily outnumbered and many were slain. Lord Ragnar was taken prisoner. The king ordered his immediate death.' He paused for a moment and took a deep breath. 'He had him thrown alive into a pit of poisonous snakes.'

A collective gasp followed his words as the magnitude and horror of it sank in.

'And how did you come to survive, Sven?' Invarr's voice was cold and his eyes raked the messenger from head to toe, but the man met his gaze and held it.

'We fought our way back to the ship and put to sea. After nightfall we turned back and at first light Bjorn went ashore. He speaks the Saxon tongue and he learned the truth from some in the market place. 'Twas said that before he died Ragnar sang a death song in which he prophesied that his furious sons would avenge him, and then he laughed. They said he died laughing.'

As they listened it seemed to each man there that he could hear the echo of that laughter, and their hearts swelled. Ragnar's courage was legendary. He would make a brave death. That it should not be in battle was a dire misfortune indeed, for he would not win his place in Valhalla and feast in Odin's hall.

'You did not seek to avenge Ragnar?' demanded Hubba.

'To what end? We were a handful against hundreds.'

Hubba's hand went to the axe by his side, but Halfdan shook his head.

'Sven is right. To try to attack Ella under such circumstances would have been madness. Worse, it would have been stupid. Now he will fight another day.'

Hubba glared at him. 'Are you saying that Ragnar died for nothing?'

Wulfrum, silent and intent, waited for the reply, feeling all around him the same curbed rage.

'No. Ragnar shall be avenged and by an army greater than any yet seen.' All eyes were upon Halfdan as he rose to face the assembled throng. 'We shall send a fleet of ships four hundred strong.'

Wulfrum regarded his sword brother with admiration. What he was proposing would be the greatest Viking raid ever known. Almost instantly he corrected himself: not a raid, an invasion.

'Let every man who can wield an axe or sword prepare,' Halfdan continued. 'We shall sweep through Northumbria like flame through tinder. We shall beard Ella in his castle and he shall know the taste of fear. His death shall not be swift, but he will long for it before the end. This I swear by my own blood and by the sacred blood of Odin.'

He drew the blade of his knife across his palm, his gaze meeting those of his brothers. Immediately they followed suit and mingled their blood with his. Then his gaze moved past them and rested on Wulfrum. In it was an invitation, an acknowledgement of friendship and brotherhood. Wulfrum's eyes never left Halfdan's as he unsheathed his dagger and drew the bright blood forth before mingling it with theirs. Bound by the blood oath, their honour was now his honour, their purpose his purpose. Halfdan nodded in approbation, then turned back to the silent watching crowd.

'Who will sail with us to avenge Ragnar Lodbrok?'

A roar of approval shook the rafters and every hand was raised. He looked round the hall, gratified to see resolution in each face. Then he raised his hand for quiet.

'Make ready. Three moons from now the sea dragons sail for England.'

Another roar greeted this.

'A fitting revenge for Ragnar,' Wulfrum observed.

'We shall have more than revenge, brother,' replied Halfdan. 'There will be rich rewards too for those who serve well—land and slaves to work it. And women.'

Wulfrum grinned, knowing whither the conversation tended. 'And the Saxon women are reputed fair, are they not?'

'Aye, they are, and it's high time you took a wife. A man must get sons.'

'True. And when I find a woman who pleases me enough, I shall wed and breed sons aplenty.'

'Your standards are high, but even you might lose your heart to a Saxon beauty.'

'I have never lost my heart to a woman yet. They satisfy a need like food and drink, but they have no power to hold us long.'

'You say so for you have never been in love.'

'No. Nor am I like to be. It is not necessary to fall in love to get sons.' Wulfrum laughed. 'My heart is my own, brother, and I guard it well.'

CHAPTER ONE

Northumbria—867 A.D.

ELGIVA sat on the goatskin rug before the fire, her arms clasped about her knees and her gaze on the flames. It was said that some had the skill to read the future there. Just then she would have given much for such a glimpse to help resolve the chaos of her thoughts. The present dilemma was desperate, but what to do for the best?

She glanced once at her companion, grateful for that comforting presence. To Elgiva, Osgifu had been both mother and confidante. The older woman had entered the service of Lord Egbert as a nursemaid when her husband died. At forty she was comely still, a tall elegant figure, for all that there were lines on her face and white strands in her dark hair. Her grey eyes saw more than other people, for she was known to have the second sight, to see those things hidden from ordinary mortal view. Her skill lay with the runes, not the fire, but the accuracy of her words was sufficient for people to regard her with awe, even fear. Elgiva had never been afraid, only curious. Osgifu's mother had been a Dane, a trader's daughter, who married a Saxon husband. From her she had inherited the gift of the sight and a wealth of stories besides.

When Elgiva was a child, Osgifu had entertained her with tales of the Norse gods: of Thor, who wielded the thunderbolts; of Loki the trickster of Odin; and Fenrir the wolf. Elgiva had listened, enthralled by stories of Jotenheim, the realm of the frost giants, and of the dragon, Nidhoggr, who constantly gnawed at the roots of Yggdrasil, the mighty ash tree connecting earth and heaven. Osgifu had taught her the Danish tongue too, albeit in secret, for she knew Lord Egbert would not have approved. When they were alone, the two of them spoke their secret language and knew their words would be safe from other ears. She alone knew the secrets of Elgiva's heart and it was to her Elgiva turned in times of trouble.

The younger woman sighed and, turning her gaze from the glowing flames in the hearth, looked full at her mentor.

'I don't know what to do, Gifu. Ever since my father's death Ravenswood has slid further and further into chaos. My brother did nothing.' She paused. 'Now he is dead too, and his sons are but babes. The place needs a capable hand.'

She did not add, *a man's hand,* but Osgifu heard the thought. She also acknowledged the truth of it. Lord Osric, concerned only with skill at arms and with hawking and hunting, had taken little interest in the running of his late father's estate, preferring to leave it to his steward, Wilfred. A good man at heart, Wilfred had performed his duties well enough under Lord Egbert's exacting rule, but after, with no master's eye on him, he began to neglect small things, putting off until the morrow what should have been done today. The serfs under his control took their example from him, and Elgiva, on her daily rides, had begun to notice the results. Ravenswood, which had hitherto always looked prosperous, began to take on an air of neglect. Fences were not mended, repairs botched. Weeds grew among the crops and the livestock were not properly tended. The roofs of the barns and storehouses leaked, and she felt sure that the stored grain and fodder within were not as strictly accounted for as they had been. When she had mentioned these things to Osric, he had brushed her aside. The problem grew worse. She had spoken to him again and received short shrift.

'A woman's place is in the house, not meddling in matters that do not concern her.'

'Ravenswood is my concern,' she'd replied, 'as it should be yours.'

'You take too much upon you, Elgiva.' He had eyed her coolly. 'If you had a husband and children of your own, you would have no time to interfere in the affairs of men. You should have been married long since.'

Her brother was right about that and Elgiva knew it. Had Lord Egbert lived, he would have found a bridegroom for her. There had been no shortage of suitors. She had loved her father dearly and he had made no secret of the fact that she was the child of his heart. Her company had been congenial to him for she knew how to make him laugh. A fearless rider, she had often accompanied him on the chase. His death three years earlier had changed everything, and for the worse. Osric, careless, feckless, had become the Thane of Ravenswood. Elgiva, well tutored in domestic matters, saw to it that the household ran smoothly, but she could do nothing about the wider problem. However, their conversation had put Osric in mind of his responsibilities towards his sister.

'I shall find you a husband. These are troubled times and a woman should not be without a protector, even if there is truth in only half the tales we hear of the Viking raids.'

That too was beyond dispute, but she had assumed that he would forget the matter as he did with everything not immediately concerned with his own interests. She had been quite wrong. One day, about a month after the former conversation, he announced that Lord Aylwin had asked for her hand. At first she had not known whether to laugh or cry. A wealthy and respected Saxon lord, wise governor of rich lands, Aylwin was a near neighbour. He had been the friend of her father and, his own wife having died some years earlier, he sought a new bride. At forty he was old enough to be her father and his sons were grown men, but he was still strong and vigorous. Elgiva had baulked. Although she had nothing to say against Aylwin as a man, she knew she could not feel for him what a woman should feel for a husband. In truth, she had never felt it for any man of her acquaintance. However, women of her rank did not marry for love. If both partners respected each other, it was enough. But not for her, she thought, not for her. Osric had not understood.

'Do you know anything against Aylwin?'

'No.'

'You know he is wealthy and of good reputation? A man to be respected?'

'Yes.'

'Then why should you refuse him?'

As Elgiva sought for the words to explain, Osric had pressed his advantage.

'You know Lord Aylwin sought your hand long since.'

'And I said then I did not love his lordship.'

'Love? What has love to do with it? This is an advantageous match.'

'I do not deny it. He is also old enough to be my father.'

'He is in his prime and will make you an attentive husband.'

'I will not consent to such attentions.'

With that she had marched out of the room and there the matter had rested. Osric, for all his faults, still had a certain fondness for his sister and would not force her to a marriage that was distasteful to her. Life had gone on much as before until, a month ago, Osric's horse put its foot in a hole while they were out hunting. Horse and rider fell with force—the former breaking its foreleg and the rider his neck.

The shock had been great and the sorrow also. At a stroke Elgiva found herself alone with all the care of a large estate and two young children. Osric's wife, Cynewise, had died in childbed at the age of twenty. It was a common enough occurrence and, for women, one of the hazards of marriage, but for Elgiva it had been an added shock. She knew that Osric would have married again, in time, for a man might well have several wives in his lifetime. For a woman alone the future looked bleak. When she had told Osgifu that she didn't know what to do, it had been prevarication and they both knew it. She must marry and soon. But Aylwin?

'What do the runes say, Gifu?'

Elgiva knew already what they would say, but she needed to have it confirmed. The runes never lied. Carved out of ash, a tree sacred to Odin, and indelibly marked with ancient esoteric symbols, they would point the way as they had done before. Osgifu regarded her with a steady gaze.

'Ask your question.'

Elgiva drew in a deep breath. 'Shall I marry Aylwin?'

She waited, hands locked together, as Osgifu scanned the rune cast. The silence lengthened and her grey eyes narrowed, a sharp line creasing her brow.

'Well? Shall I marry?'

'Aye, you will be married, but not to Aylwin.'

'Not Aylwin?' Elgiva was puzzled. 'Then who?'

'I do not know the man.'

'What does he look like?'

'I cannot tell. The upper part of his face is hidden behind the plates of his helmet. He wears a shirt of fine mail and in his hand he carries a mighty sword, as sharp as a dragon's tooth.'

'A warrior? A Saxon lord, then. Shall I meet him soon?'

'You will see him soon enough.'

Thereafter she became strangely reticent and all of Elgiva's questions could draw nothing more from her.

The mystery stayed with her but, as the days passed, she knew she could not wait indefinitely for some stranger to ride by and rescue her from all her problems. A woman alone was vulnerable. A woman with wealth and land was doubly so once it became known she had no protector. It was not unknown for such to be married under duress to an ambitious and ruthless lord with a strong retinue and no aversion to the use of force. She shivered. Better to wed a respected man who would treat her well and restore Ravenswood to its former self. It came to her that she must wed Aylwin and soon. Love was all very well in stories of high romance: real life wasn't like that. Her brother had been right. It was an advantageous match. Perhaps, with time, she might come to love Aylwin. Certainly she would make him a dutiful wife and bear his children. Her mind glossed over the details, unwilling to dwell on the matter. Should she be so nice when, every day, girls of thirteen or fourteen were married off to men thrice their age? The question now was how to bring this about. She had refused Aylwin's suit. Could she now go a-begging?

In the event the matter was solved for her when, a few days later, the servants announced the arrival of Lord Aylwin accompanied by a small group of armed men. She received him in the great hall and, having bid him welcome, offered his men refreshment and allowed him to take her to one side. She wished that she had had more warning—she was suddenly aware of her sober-hued gown and her hair braided simply down her back without ribbon or ornament. It was hardly the dress of a woman receiving a suitor. However, Aylwin seemed to find nothing amiss and smiled at her. Of average height, he was stocky and powerfully made for all that the brown hair and beard were grizzled with grey. The expression on the rugged face was both sympathetic and kind, but the eyes spoke of admiration.

For a while they spoke of Osric and he said all that was proper, but it did not take him long to come to the real purpose of his visit.

'Your brother's death leaves you alone and in a most difficult situation, my lady. In these times a woman must have a protector.'

Elgiva heard in his words the echo of her brother's and felt a *frisson* along her spine. Heart beating much faster, she knew what was coming and waited for it.

'I would like to be that man.' He paused, eyeing her with

an unwonted awkwardness. 'I am no longer in the first flush of youth, but I am still in good health and well able to protect you. I can also swear my undying loyalty and devotion.'

Elgiva felt her face grow warmer and for a moment her amber eyes were veiled. Aylwin, mistaking the reason, drew in a deep breath.

'Let me protect you, Elgiva. I do not ask you to love me now, but perhaps in time that may come. Meanwhile, be assured that you will be loved, my lady.'

Hearing an unmistakeable note of sincerity, she looked up swiftly, meeting his gaze.

'Does it surprise you to hear that?'

'I had not thought…that is—' She broke off, floundering.

'Have you any idea how beautiful you are?' he went on. 'From the first day I saw you I wanted you for my wife. My Gundred has been dead these five years and a man grows lonely. I think you are lonely too. May not two such comfort each other?'

Elgiva nodded. 'I think that perhaps they may, my lord.'

For a moment he did not move, the dark eyes intent on her face. 'Then you will marry me?'

'There would be certain conditions.'

'Name them.'

'That the rights of my nephews are protected and that you act as overlord of Ravenswood until they can act for themselves.'

'Agreed. If you wed me, they shall be reared as my own sons.'

'I would also ask for a decent interval of mourning for my brother.'

'It shall be as you ask.'

'Then on midsummer's day I will become your wife.' Elgiva's voice was perfectly level as she gave him the commitment he sought.

Taking her hand, he pressed it to his lips. 'It is an honour I scarce hoped to have.'

'I will try to make you a good wife,' she replied.

The proposed date was three months hence, but if Aylwin had hoped for an earlier wedding, he said nothing. Having got what he wanted he was prepared to give a little ground, knowing it would do his cause no harm.

'Will you pledge your hand to me openly, Elgiva?' he asked then. 'I do not ask for a huge feast—I know it must be repugnant to you in the circumstances—but perhaps a small gathering?'

Elgiva was not surprised by the request. What it meant was a public declaration of intent. It also made clear to all concerned that Elgiva and thus Ravenswood were spoken for, that both lay under the protection of a rich and powerful lord. From the moment their betrothal was announced she was as good as his and no man would touch her. It also meant a respite, time to grow used to the idea of the bargain she had just struck.

'It shall be as you wish, my lord.'

He smiled. 'I am content.'

She had wondered if he would try to kiss her, but to her relief he made no further attempt to touch her. He took his leave not long after that and Elgiva watched him ride away with his men. Then she went in search of Osgifu.

The older woman listened in silence, her face impassive as she took in the news.

'Do you think it was wrong to accept him?' Elgiva asked at length.

'You did what you thought you had to do, child, both for yourself and for Ravenswood.'

'Aylwin will be a good husband and he will restore these lands to their former glory. I cannot bear to see things thus.'

'I know.' Osgifu hesitated. 'But, can you be a wife to him?'

'I must, Gifu. There is no choice now. Surely you see that?'

'Yes.' She put her arms round the girl's shoulders. 'I think you have nothing to fear. It is my view that he will be a doting and most indulgent husband.'

Elgiva nodded and tried to think positive thoughts. Neither of them mentioned the rune cast.

The betrothal feast went as planned, a small and select gathering of neighbours and friends who came together to see the couple pledge to each other. It was in every way a most suitable match and no one thought anything of the discrepancy in the ages of the pair who were soon to marry. It was widely held that Aylwin was a clever and knowing man for at a stroke he doubled his holdings and gained a most beautiful wife into the bargain. Elgiva in her blue gown, embroidered at neck and sleeve, her golden hair braided with matching ribbons, looked very fetching indeed. It was noticed that her prospective groom could hardly keep his eyes off her and was most assiduous in plying her with food and wine, carving choice cuts of meat and serving her with his own hands.

In truth, Elgiva had little appetite but did her best to hide it. Her heart was unwontedly heavy but, unwilling to disappoint her guests with a glum face, she smiled graciously and tried to look as though she were enjoying herself. As she noticed the gaze Aylwin bent upon her, the reality of the situation hit her with force—in three months' time they would be married and he would take her to his bed. She must give herself to him whenever he wished and, eventually, she would bear his children. He had fine sons already, but, if the look in his eye was aught to judge by, he intended to sire more. Elgiva took another sip of wine to steady herself. She had wanted this, had agreed to it of her own free will. Now she must live with the consequences. If he was to be her husband she must get to know him, to learn his likes and dislikes, to discover what would please him. She had no doubt of her ability to run his household efficiently for she had been schooled in domestic duties from childhood. The rules of the bedroom were unknown territory, though familiar to him. She reminded herself sharply that it was not necessary to love for a marriage to work. As long as there was respect. Please, God, she prayed silently, let it be all right.

The feasting done and the hour growing late, the women retired, leaving the hall to the men. Elgiva knew the hard drinking was about to begin and had given orders to the servants to keep the guests plied with ale and mead as long as they wanted it. She was not sorry to make her excuses and bid her future husband a goodnight. He kissed her hand and pressed it warmly. From his flushed face and the hot glow in his eyes it was clear he had had a lot to drink, but his speech was unslurred and his balance still unimpaired.

'Goodnight, Elgiva, and sleep well. Would this were our wedding night that I might share that bed with you.'

She managed a smile. 'In good time, my lord.'

Then she was gone, leaving the hall behind and seeking the sanctuary of the women's bower.

In spite of the late night, Elgiva woke early and for several moments lay still beneath the fur coverlet, enjoying the comfortable warmth of the bed. Though the first grey light of the spring dawn was filtering through the shutters, she could hear no sound of birdsong and the cock had yet to crow. Only Osgifu's gentle snores broke the heavy stillness of the new day. The nurse would not stir for a while yet. Elgiva rose and dressed quickly for the air was chill, pulling the gown over her linen kirtle and sliding her feet into leather shoes. Then, throwing a mantle about her shoulders, she moved to the doorway, pausing once to glance back. Osgifu slept on. For a moment Elgiva watched, her feelings a strange fusion of love and disappointment. She had trusted her. Even now she could hear her words: *The runes never lie.* But the runes had lied, and Osgifu had been wrong. Immediately Elgiva upbraided herself. Why should she be surprised to discover human fallibility? She wasn't a child, for heaven's sake. It was time to face facts and shoulder the responsibilities that fell to her.

Elgiva left the women's bower and made her way through the hall. It was not her most direct route out, but she was hungry and knew there would be a fair chance of finding something to eat without summoning a servant. All about her, men lay snoring on the rushes among the scraps of food, or sprawled on benches and tables among the debris of the feast. After the copious quantities of mead and ale they had drunk she had no fear of waking the sleepers and guessed there would be a few sore heads this morning. She retrieved part of a loaf from the table and broke a piece off. It was growing stale, but it would do for now. Chewing on the bread, she made her way silently among the sleeping forms, wrinkling her nose at air thick with the reek of smoke and spilled ale and male sweat, skirting the hearth where the remaining embers of the fire smouldered in mounds of grey ash. Hearing her approach, two wolfhounds looked up from their slumber, but the low rumbling growl died in their throats as they recognised her. One got to his feet, wagging his tail, shoving his nose into Elgiva's hand. She stroked his wiry head absently and then moved on towards the door, eager to be gone for the confines of the hall were stifling and a sharp reminder of things she wished to forget.

The side door was ajar, a clear indication that she was not the first abroad. Through the gap she could see a man relieving himself in the midden across the way. He had his back to her, but from his dress she guessed him to be one of Lord Aylwin's men. Elgiva seized the moment to slip out and round the end of the hall. From this vantage point she could observe without being seen. Presently, after having answered the call of nature, the man returned whence he came and Elgiva was able to make her way to the stables unnoticed.

Here too, all was quiet, for even the serfs were not stirring yet. They had taken their fill of Ravenswood's bounty the previous evening and there was none to mark her passage along the row of stalls to the one where Mara was tethered. Hearing her approach, the bay mare turned her head and whinnied gently. Elgiva reached for the bridle hanging on the peg and slipped into the stall.

Minutes later she was leading the horse out. Once in the open air, she vaulted astride and headed for the gate. The watchman roused himself and, responding to her greeting, swung the portal open. Elgiva held Mara to a walk as they passed the houses in the hamlet. Here were signs of life: a spiral of smoke from a roof, a dog scratching itself before an open door. She suspected it would be much later before those in the hall roused themselves. Glad to have escaped for a time, Elgiva breathed the cool morning air gratefully, though it could not dispel her sombre mood or the memories that occasioned it. Later she would return and play her part before them all.

Pride and a sense of family honour had led her to spare no expense in the celebration of the betrothal feast. It was, after all, a cause for celebration, an excellent and judicious match. The union would not only unite two great Saxon houses, but would bring advantage to both sides. She had entered into the arrangement of her own volition. Her future husband was a man she could respect. Why, then, in the face of such good fortune, did her heart feel so heavy?

Elgiva was startled out of these sombre thoughts when her horse shied. She tightened her hold on the reins, looking about her, but could see only shadows beneath the trees and curls of mist in the hollows. The wood was locked beneath an eerie silence. The mare snorted uneasily and Elgiva frowned, her gaze taking in the details of the surrounding woodland. The silence stretched out around her, unbroken by any breath of wind, or birdsong or sound of any living thing. Then she discerned movement ahead through the trees where a lone horseman was approaching, bent low over the saddle. Elgiva hesitated, wondering whether the safest course was to flee, but something about the rider's posture gave her pause. He was swaying and for a second she wondered if he were drunk. Just as quickly, she rejected the idea, for as he drew closer she could see he had come far. The horse was lathered, its chest and flanks darkened with sweat, its legs and belly all bespattered with mud. Pulling up, she let the rider approach. Mara whinnied and sidled, but Elgiva kept a firm hold on the rein. The oncoming rider was a man of middle years and, like his horse, all muddied. His face was grey and lined with pain and she could see the side of his tunic was stiff with dried blood. He stared at her as if she had been an apparition and then she recognised him.

'Gunter!'

Her uncle's steward—he must have ridden far. It was a two-day journey and from the look of him he had ridden fast. His horse was all but spent, and he too. Every word cost him effort.

'I bring urgent news for Ravenswood, my lady.'

'We are not far from home. Come, let me take you there.'

He nodded and together they retraced Elgiva's path. As soon as they were within the gates, she summoned help. Grooms came running to take the horses and another helped Gunter into the hall. Men were stirring now and looked up in surprise at their entrance. Elgiva saw Aylwin there with several of his men. He hastened over to her.

'Gunter, my uncle's steward,' she explained. 'He is wounded. I don't know how badly.'

Aylwin took one look at the dark stiffening patch on the man's tunic. 'He has lost much blood. His hurts must be tended.'

Elgiva dispatched a servant for her box of medicines. Another brought a goblet of water and helped raise the injured man a fraction so she could hold it to his lips. He drank greedily, but Elgiva would only allow him a little to begin with. Then she and Osgifu set about dealing with the wound. It was a sword thrust, deep but clean. As far as she could tell it had not pierced any internal organs, though it had bled copiously. Between them they stanched the bleeding and cleansed the wound, before fastening a clean pad over it with long strips of linen cloth. Gunter bore these ministrations in silence, though his face was very pale. Then she allowed him a little more to drink.

'You must rest now and try to recover your strength.'

'Lady, I must speak. My news will wait no longer.'

'Say on then, Gunter. Does it concern my uncle?'

'Aye, my lady, and ill news it is.'

'What of my uncle? Is he sick?'

'Nay, my lady. He is dead with all his kin and his hall is burned. A great Viking war host marches north.'

A deathly silence followed as those present tried to grasp the enormity of the news.

'The rumours are true,' murmured Aylwin.

'Aye, lord. We had little warning of their coming, but even if we had, it would have made no difference for the sheer weight of their numbers. Those Saxons who were not slain were enslaved. I was wounded and left for dead. When I came to, the hall was a blackened ruin and my lord was dead. I found a stray horse and got away under cover of darkness.'

'It was as well you did,' said Elgiva. She glanced at Osgifu, who looked as shaken as the rest.

'You are right, child. We should have had no warning

else. As it is, we must prepare to defend ourselves as best
we may.'

'Truly spoken,' said Gunter, 'for the sons of Ragnar
Lodbrok seek a terrible revenge for their father's death.'

'We had heard of this,' replied Aylwin. 'There were
tales of a great Viking war fleet a year or so ago, but we
had thought the raiders much further south.'

'That is so, lord,' Gunter continued, 'though not by
design. It seems they set sail for Northumbria, but their
ships were blown off course and brought them instead to
the Anglian coast. Since then they have swept through that
kingdom with fire and sword. We heard that they looted
the abbeys at Ely and Crowland and Peterborough. 'Tis
said that at Peterborough Hubba killed eighty monks
himself.'

Startled exclamations greeted this and men looked at
each other in mounting horror.

Gunter drew in a ragged breath. 'They have taken
Mercia too. Now that York has fallen, all of Northumbria
is threatened.'

Aylwin's hand went automatically to the hilt of his
sword. 'What of King Ella?'

'They captured him and acted out their revenge. His
ribs were torn apart and folded backwards to resemble a
spread eagle. Then they threw salt in the wound and left him
to die.'

Elgiva felt her stomach churn. She had heard many
times of the brutality of the Norsemen, but never anything
so barbaric. Beside her Osgifu paled, and she heard several
sharp intakes of breath from those around.

'You must prepare to defend yourselves,' said Gunter.
'The Viking host wintered at York, but the spring thaw

draws them forth again. It is only a matter of time before they come.'

'But surely if Ella is dead they have what they want now,' replied Osgifu. 'They will leave with their plunder as they always do.'

'This time they want more than plunder. Halfdan has let it be known they want land and they plan to take it.'

'Land? Do the pirates mean to stay?'

'It would seem our shores are more fertile than their northern fastness.'

'They will find the price dear.' Aylwin's face was grim. 'My sword is ready, and those of my kin.'

Elgiva could see the determination on the faces all around her and knew a moment of shame that he was ready to fight on her behalf when she had earlier had misgivings about her betrothal to him, putting thoughts of her happiness before Ravenswood. As she looked up he caught her eye and smiled.

'I swear, no harm shall come to you while I live, lady.'

Elgiva began to feel distinctly guilty. 'I thank you, my lord. If it comes to a fight, my family will be much in your debt.'

'They are soon to be my family too,' he replied. 'It is fitting my sword be ready to use in their defence, and in yours.'

Elgiva smiled a little in return, liking him more in that moment than ever before. However, her thoughts were soon distracted for Aylwin had turned away and was already organising the deployment of the men.

'Every man and boy able to hold a weapon must prepare. There can be no knowing how soon the Viking host may march. We shall double our guard and watchers shall be placed at the boundaries to give word of any approaching force. If the Norsemen come, we shall be ready for them.'

He gave his orders and men departed to do his bidding. Elgiva turned to check on Gunter, but he was asleep and Osgifu was with him.

'I will watch over him the while,' she said.

'Will he survive, do you think?'

'He has lost much blood, 'tis true. But he is a strong man and, God willing, he will come through this. What he needs is rest and quiet.'

'I pray God that he may have it.'

'Amen to that, child.'

Elgiva left her and went outside, making her way to the steps leading to the rampart that ran along the inside of the palisade. From there she had an excellent view of the preparations taking place as everywhere men hastened to ready themselves for the defence of Ravenswood. Beyond the hall with its attendant stables and storehouses and the high wooden pale, the countryside lay still. An area of open ground surrounded the pale, and beyond it was pasture and woodland. Usually Elgiva thought of it as a place of peace and solitude, but now those quiet glades held menace. Her eyes scanned the trees, seeking for any sign of movement that might reveal a hidden enemy, but there was nothing to be seen save a few serfs driving their swine to feed. In the little hamlet people went about their business, though looking fearfully about all the while. The knowledge that Lord Aylwin had posted sentinels through the estate offered partial reassurance; at least there would be no surprise attack. Perhaps it was as Osgifu had said: now they had exacted their vengeance on King Ella they would adventure no further. It was a slender hope for the greed of the pirates was legendary. Their periodic raids were a fact of life for the unfortunate coastal dwellers, and the Norsemen had regularly carried off women and live-stock along with any other loot that seized their fancy. Then they had sailed for their northern lands taking their booty with them.

Elgiva shivered to think of the poor souls taken off to a life of slavery in a strange country, of the women who must become unwilling wives or concubines to their new masters. It would be better to fight to the death than submit to such a fate as that. As she glanced away from the distant trees, her gaze fell on the roof of the bower. Within her chamber was the chest where she kept her gowns. Underneath them was the sword her father had given her some years before. He had taught her to use it too, holding that a woman should be schooled in self-defence as well as a man. Elgiva was resolved. If need be, she too, would fight and kill to defend her home.

CHAPTER TWO

THE VIKING attack came within days; the sentinels on Ravenswood's boundaries returned in haste to report the sighting of a marching host hundreds strong. Elgiva had been sewing in the women's bower with Osgifu when the peace was shattered by the wild ringing of the church bell. Her hands paused at their task and for a moment or two she listened before the implications sank in.

'The alarm.'

'Dear Lord, it cannot be.' Osgifu threw down her sewing and hastened to the door, but her companion was before her. Both of them halted in dismay on the threshold; outside was a scene of urgent haste with men running to their posts, buckling on swords as they went. They stopped a man-at-arms who was hurrying to the palisade with a large sheaf of arrows.

'What is it? What's happening?'

'The sentries have reported sighting a large enemy force, my lady,' he replied. 'It is advancing on Ravenswood.'

Osgifu paled, looking in alarm at the armed men running towards the ramparts. 'An enemy force?'

'Aye, the Vikings approach.' He inclined his head to

Elgiva. 'Your pardon, lady, but I dare not stay longer. I must to my post.' With that he was gone.

The two women ran to the hall where Aylwin was barking orders to his men. As they hastened to obey, he turned to Elgiva.

'Go bar yourself in the upper chamber, my lady. It will be far safer. Take Osgifu and the children too.'

Before she had a chance to reply one of Aylwin's men spoke out, throwing a dark glance at Osgifu.

'I've been told that this woman is of Danish blood, my lord. How do we know she can be trusted?'

Elgiva surveyed him with anger. 'Osgifu has served my family faithfully and well for many years. Her loyalty is not in question nor ever has been.'

The man reddened. 'I beg pardon, my lady.'

Aylwin glared at him, then nodded towards the door. The others took the hint and beat a hasty retreat.

'I'm sorry, Elgiva.' Aylwin laid a soothing hand on her arm. 'Such times make men cautious.'

'So it seems.'

With an effort Elgiva forced down her indignation. It would not aid their cause to quarrel among themselves. She turned to Osgifu.

'Fetch Hilda and the children and the women servants. Then go with them to the upper floor.'

If Osgifu had been in any way discomforted by the conversation, it was not evident. Returning Elgiva's gaze, she asked, 'What about you, child?'

'I will come presently, but there is something I must fetch first.'

'Make haste then, my lady,' said Aylwin. With one last warm smile he hurried off to join his men outside.

Elgiva raced back to the bower and, throwing open the chest in the corner, retrieved the sword from the bottom. The familiar weight of the weapon was comforting. At least they should not be completely defenceless if the worst came to the worst. Closing her hand round the scabbard, she slammed the chest shut and went to join the others, barring the stout door behind her as Aylwin had instructed. Then she took up a station by the far window. The shutters were pulled to, but through a broken slat she could see much of the hustle and activity below as men ran to their posts. Aylwin had his plan ready days earlier and each one of his retainers knew where he was supposed to be. Within a short time they were ready, armed to the teeth, and grimly determined to defend their homes and their lives.

The clanging bell had brought the peasants from the fields and the wood to seek the relative safety of the pale. No sooner were they gathered within than the men on the wall called out a warning as the forward ranks of the Viking host appeared. Like an army of sinister wraiths, silent and intent, they emerged from among the trees into the pasture beyond. One of their archers loosed an arrow, killing a Saxon guard where he stood. Then, as though at a signal, a great shout went up from the invaders, splitting the stillness, and they surged forwards as one.

'Merciful heavens,' murmured Aylwin. 'Surely this can be no ordinary raiding party. There are hundreds of them.' By his private reckoning his men would be outnumbered five to one.

Beside him, his armed companion had made a similar calculation. 'This is revenge indeed for their dead chieftain.'

What Aylwin might have said next was lost in a hissing

rain of arrows. It covered the advance of the Viking vanguard that carried ladders to raise against the walls. Swiftly the defenders loosed their own arrows in reply, but each time one of the attackers fell he was immediately replaced and the assault renewed. The Saxons maintained a deadly fire from above, but to right and left the invaders swarmed up the ladders and over the walls. The first were cut down without mercy, but their comrades followed hard on their heels and soon fierce battle was enjoined, filling the air with shouts and the clash of arms.

Peering through the gap in the shutters, Elgiva stared in horror at the scene of carnage below and murmured a prayer. Everywhere she looked the Viking marauders were pouring in over the walls.

'God in heaven, can there be so many?'

Giants they seemed, these fierce warriors, cruel with battle thirst, each face alight with lust for blood and conquest. With sword and axe they cut down all who stood in their way, crying out the name of their war god.

'Odin!'

The cry was repeated from four hundred throats as the Norsemen drove forwards, fearless into the ranks of their foes. The defenders fought bravely but the sheer weight of numbers pushed them back, step by step, the enemy advancing over the bodies of the slain, remorseless, hacking their way on. As the defenders fell back, Elgiva could see another group of the enemy without the palisade, dragging a huge battering ram into position. It was the trunk of a tree, fresh hewn and drawn on a wheeled timber cradle. Under cover of ox-hide shields the marauders rolled the supporting cradle back and forth, building momentum until the end of the trunk crashed against the gate. The stout timbers creaked, but held. Elgiva stared in horrified fascination as with each swing the gate shook. Alive to the danger the nearest Saxon defenders rallied to the gate and swarmed to the rampart inside the palisade, raining arrows and rocks on to the men beneath.

For a little while it seemed that they had met with success; several of the Vikings fell and the momentum of the great ram was lost. It was a brief respite—in moments reinforcements arrived and other warriors stepped up to take the places of their fallen comrades. The assault on the gate began anew. The timbers shuddered and splintered. Amid the clash of arms and shouts of men a thunderous crack announced the breach, followed by a roar of triumph from the invading horde who poured through the gap like a tide beneath their black-raven banner.

Helpless, Elgiva could only watch as the Saxon defence crumbled and her retainers were beaten back towards the great hall. Beside them Aylwin and his men fought on, shoulder to shoulder, returning the enemy blow for blow. Half a dozen more men fell under Aylwin's sword while all around him the group of defenders grew smaller and more desperate, redoubling their efforts, hacking and thrusting and parrying, each man determined to sell his life dear. Tireless they seemed, yet one by one they fell. Aylwin fought on, laying about him with a will, his sword smoking and bloody as it rose and fell, slashing and cutting until the bodies were piled before him. And then its edge struck the blade of a huge war axe. The sword shivered and Aylwin was left undefended. He hurled the sundered hilt at the foe in a last act of defiance before the enemy blade cut him down.

Elgiva's hand flew to her lips, stifling her cry, and she

closed her eyes a moment, forcing back tears. Weakness would not help Aylwin now, or any of the survivors who would depend on her. Striving to regain some measure of self-control she turned from the window, sombrely regarding the other occupants of the room. Seeing that stony expression, Hilda let out a terrified sob as she cowered, clutching the baby, Pybba, to her breast. The nursemaid was but six and ten years old and plainly terrified. Osgifu stood beside her, pale but silent, her arm about the three-year-old Ulric, who clutched her skirt and bit a trembling lip. Around them the women servants sobbed.

In the hall below were gathered a handful of men left for their defence. Violent banging on the barred outer doors announced the invaders' intent and the great timbers shuddered. Elgiva knew it could only be a matter of time before they broke through for above the din she heard the sinister thunk of axes against timber. A woman screamed. Minutes later the door gave way amid a roar of voices and the clash of weapons as the defenders tried to stem the tide of invaders. Shouts and shrieks filled the hall. More invaders poured in through the shattered doorway. Several made for the stairway in pursuit of plunder. Elgiva heard the heavy footfalls and men's voices. Someone tried the chamber door and found it barred. Then she heard a man's voice.

'Break it down!'

There followed the fearsome sound of axes in wood. Hilda let out a stifled sob of terror. The baby began to cry and in desperation she tried to quiet it, while little Ulric looked on, wide-eyed with fright. Elgiva looked from them to the door, which shook under the assault. In another minute the first blades were visible through a hole in the timber, a hole that grew larger with each blow. A few more moments and they would be through. With beating heart she backed away to the far side of the room, watching the splintering wood in helpless horror, struggling to control her growing fear. With her back to the wall, she closed her hand round the hilt of the sword and, taking a deep breath, drew the blade from the sheath.

As she did so the door burst asunder and the first three men fell into the room, followed by half a dozen more. Their greedy gaze fell immediately on the cowering group in front of them and they strode forwards, seizing upon the women servants. One man grabbed hold of Hilda, who clutched the baby in one arm and the terrified Ulric in the other. Osgifu strove to come between, but a heavy blow sent her reeling back into the wall. She hit her head and fell, stunned. Hilda shrieked, struggling wildly against the hands that held her, her screams mingling with those of the baby.

Outraged to see such treatment meted out to the weak and helpless, Elgiva stepped forwards.

'Leave them alone! Let them go!'

It proved a futile protest, but the words drew attention from a different quarter and Elgiva found herself confronting another armed man. Tall and well made, fair of hair and beard, he might have been handsome save for the thin cruel lips drawn back in an indulgent sneer.

'Well now, what have we here?'

Her face blazed with loathing and contempt and her hand tightened round the hilt of the sword.

'Viking scum! You would make war on women and helpless infants! Come, try your luck here! I'll slit your belly and spill your yellow guts for you!'

All eyes turned towards Elgiva, registering surprise, and then, on seeing the sword, amusement.

'Have a care, Sweyn,' called one of his companions in mocking tones. 'That one is a regular fire eater.'

Sweyn bared his teeth in a smile, his cold grey gaze speculative. 'A warrior maid, no less. One of Odin's daughters, perhaps, and fluent in our tongue. That will be convenient when I give her instructions in bed.'

Appreciative grins greeted the words and the speaker turned away for a moment to share the joke with his companions. Elgiva darted in for the attack. From the corner of his eye he saw the flashing blade aimed at him and leapt aside. The thrust that should have pierced his heart merely gashed his arm. Incredulous, he clapped his free hand to the wound, staring at the dripping blood, amid roars of laughter from the rest. Undeterred, Elgiva laid on with a will and for several moments Sweyn was forced to defend himself most dexterously before the onslaught, being driven back several paces. However, very soon greater strength and skill began to tell and then it was Elgiva who was forced back step by step until she came up hard against the far wall. A heavy blow beneath the hilt numbed her hand and wrist and with a gasp of pain she dropped the sword, only to find the Viking's blade at her throat.

'Beg for mercy, vixen!'

Elgiva spat at him. She knew he would kill her now, but she would not give him the satisfaction of seeing her fear, of hearing her plead. Lifting her chin, she let her gaze travel the length of the bloody sword until it met that of the man who held it. The tip of the sword pierced the skin and she felt the warm trickle of blood. With pounding heart she waited for the final thrust. For a long moment there was silence. Then the blade was lowered a fraction and for a fleeting second there was something like admiration in his eyes.

'No,' he said softly, 'I will not kill you. What a waste that would be.'

'You speak true, Sweyn!' called a voice from the assembled group behind. 'Take her to your bed. I wager you'll never have a livelier piece.'

Another shout of laughter went up. Elgiva felt her cheeks flame as she heard Sweyn laugh, saw his hot gaze strip her.

'I'd rather be dead.'

'You're not going to die,' he replied. 'Not yet.'

He sheathed the sword and, stepping close, seized her by the waist, bringing his mouth down hard on hers amid shouts of encouragement from the watching men.

Elgiva struggled in furious revulsion, but to no avail. In desperation she bit down on his lip. With a cry of pain and outrage, he released her abruptly, his hand moving to his mouth where the blood welled. Giving him no time to recover, Elgiva brought her knee up hard. Instinct made him move, though he still caught a glancing blow. She heard a grunt of pain and he reeled backwards while his companions redoubled their mirth. Elgiva didn't wait to see how badly she had hurt him, but turned and fled across the room. Hilda was still struggling in the arms of the young man who had first seized her, but, hampered by the baby, could do little. The crying Ulric was standing beside the still figure of Osgifu. Elgiva reached him and flung her arms around him.

Across the room Sweyn staggered to his feet. Seeing the movement, Elgiva looked up and, as her gaze met his, she saw the murderous rage in his eyes. He crossed the intervening space and with a crash flung open the shutters. The room flooded with light. Then he tore Ulric from her arms and raised him aloft. Realising his intent, Elgiva screamed.

'No!'

Sweyn's lips twisted in a chilling smile.

Then a much louder voice sounded above all. 'Hold!' There was no mistaking the tone of cold command. 'Enough! Put the child down, Sweyn.'

Elgiva, very pale, tore her gaze from the man by the window and risked a glance at the speaker. She had a brief impression of a tall, dark-haired warrior in a mail shirt. His face was concealed behind the plates of his helmet, but it was clear that all the intruders knew him and that he had authority with them for the room fell silent. His blue gaze locked with that of the other man. Frantic, she looked back across the room at Sweyn. For one hideous moment it seemed as though he would follow his intent, but then, to her unspeakable relief, he slowly lowered Ulric to the floor. Bewildered, the little boy ran to Elgiva, who held him close. Ignoring them, Sweyn confronted the other man.

'Did we not swear to avenge Ragnar with fire and sword?'

'Aye, man to man. Do men make war on babes?'

'A mewling Saxon brat. What does it signify?'

At this casual dismissal of helpless innocence Elgiva, sickened, thought her heart might burst with rage. She missed the casual glance that the dark warrior threw her way before his gaze locked again with Sweyn's.

'Slaves are valuable, no matter what their age, and we

have need of them. There will be no more killing here this day.' The tone was calm, but no one missed the inflexion of iron beneath.

Sweyn shrugged. 'Whatever you say, Wulfrum.' He turned back to Elgiva. 'Even so, I have a reckoning to settle with this one.'

Elgiva struggled to her feet and, thrusting Ulric towards one of the serving women, backed away. Sweyn came on. She turned and fled for the door.

She never reached it for in her blind flight she hurtled headlong into the warrior who had spoken before, stumbling against him, her hands slamming into chain mail as she tried frantically to push him aside. He stood like a rock. Strong hands closed round her arms, bringing her flight to a dead stop.

'Not so fast.'

The voice was low and even, the tone amused. Elgiva's gaze, currently level with a broad chest, travelled upwards, took in a powerful jaw and strong sensual mouth, parted now in a smile. She twisted in his hold, but her efforts made no impression except that, if anything, his smile widened.

'I'll take the wench, Wulfrum.' Elgiva's pursuer halted a few feet away. 'I'll teach the Saxon bitch to mend her ways and that right soon.'

He took another step forwards and Elgiva spun round, shrinking back involuntarily against Wulfrum for the expression in the other's eyes was terrifying.

'By Odin's blood, it looked to me as if she was teaching you a thing or two, Sweyn,' said a warrior, who stepped forwards to stand beside Wulfrum.

Amid the mirth and jests that greeted the remark Elgiva

looked round and then froze. The speaker was a fearsome figure, a giant of a man all bedaubed with blood, and a good head taller than any present. Grey mingled with the brown of his hair and beard, and his weathered face was seamed with lines, but his dark eyes were cool and shrewd. In one fist he held a great bloodstained axe.

'Ironfist is right!' called another. 'She's too hot for you, Sweyn!'

Sweyn glared. 'We'll see.'

'You are careless with your captives,' said Wulfrum. 'You let the wench escape. I caught her. She is mine now.'

Elgiva looked up in alarm, but Wulfrum's gaze was fixed on Sweyn. One hand rested on the hilt of his sword, the other on her shoulder.

'True enough,' said Olaf Ironfist. 'We all saw it.'

Murmurs of agreement greeted his words.

'Nay, Wulfrum. I say she is mine.'

'Not so. You let her get away.'

'Wulfrum speaks true,' said another.

A chorus of agreement greeted this. Sweyn darted angry looks to left and right, but could find no support. Elgiva held her breath, praying that he would not prevail, quailing to think of the revenge he would take. It was in her mind to run but, as if he read her thoughts, Wulfrum tightened his hold a fraction.

'Take the bitch, then,' replied Sweyn. ''Tis but a wench after all.'

'Aye, and there are plenty more,' said a voice from the doorway.

All heads turned in the direction of the speaker and the men fell silent, parting to let Lord Halfdan enter. Although only of average height, he was powerfully made and, like

Wulfrum, carried with him an aura of authority. When he reached the group around his sword brother, he took in the scene at a glance.

'There are women and slaves aplenty in England and land enough for all.' His voice carried without effort across the room. 'Therefore there is no reason to quarrel.' He bent his gaze upon Elgiva, scrutinising her. 'A comely wench, Wulfrum. She will fetch a good price in the slave market, unless of course you plan to keep her.'

'I do intend to, my lord.'

'Well then, keep her close.'

'I shall, my lord.'

'Put the matter beyond dispute.' He glanced across the room at Sweyn. 'It seems to me she would make a fine Viking bride.'

'Never in a thousand years!'

The words were out before she could stop them and Elgiva felt her throat dry as both men turned their attention towards her. Wulfrum laughed and his arm closed about her, ignoring the resistance it encountered.

'A spirited piece,' said Halfdan, 'and impudent too. She must learn who her master is.'

'I will never acknowledge any Viking as my master!'

'Oh, I think you will—eventually.' He smiled down at her.

Elgiva's stomach churned.

'She will learn,' said Wulfrum.

'From you?' Her tone was blatant disdain. 'I think not.'

'Aye, from me.' He took another look at the face turned up to his and all former reservations about marriage evaporated like mist in the sun as he made his decision. 'For, by all the gods, I will have you to wife.'

'I will never agree to that.'

'You have no choice, my beauty. You belong to me now.'

'No!'

'Oh, yes. Unless you would prefer to go with Sweyn?'

She swallowed hard, every fibre of her being wanting to spurn him, but when she looked upon the alternative, her heart was filled with loathing and contempt.

'Well?'

'I will not go with a coward and a child slayer!'

Wulfrum looked from Elgiva to Sweyn. 'The girl has chosen.'

'Then I wish you joy of her,' replied the other. The cool tone was at variance with the expression in his eyes.

It had no effect on Wulfrum. 'I shall find joy enough, I have no doubt.'

'Then it is settled.' Halfdan turned back to Wulfrum. 'You have done good service under the black-raven banner. From henceforth this hall and these lands shall be yours. The slaves too, to do with as you will.'

'You are generous, lord.'

'Aye, to those who serve me well.' He glanced at Elgiva. 'As for the girl, take her—she is a worthy prize.'

'Indeed she is.'

Elgiva glared at them. The Viking chief threw her a mocking smile.

'Your fate is clear, wench, and you had best submit.' He turned to the assembled warriors. 'Go down to the hall. Summon the others. I would speak to all.'

The men turned and began to troop out of the chamber, one carrying the screaming Hilda under his arm.

'No!' Elgiva fought the hold on her. 'Take your filthy hands off her!'

On the floor Osgifu began to stir. Wanting to go to her, Elgiva strove harder.

'Come,' said Wulfrum.

'I will not. Let *go* of me, you pirate scum.'

For answer she was thrown over a broad shoulder and, regardless of violent struggle and loud protest, was carried from the room. Only when they reached the hall did he set her down, but a strong arm about her waist prevented any chance of escape. Breathless and furious, Elgiva threw him a venomous glance and wished in vain for a sword to disembowel him with. Undismayed, Wulfrum grinned. Then his gaze moved on from her across the hall and she became aware that Halfdan was speaking.

'Tonight we shall feast in celebration of our victory. We shall rest here long enough to bury the dead and tend our wounded. Then we push on until all Northumbria is ours.'

A rousing cheer tore from the throats of the assembled men. He held up his fist for silence.

'Before we leave we shall witness the joining of Earl Wulfrum and this fair Saxon maid in marriage. She will bear him fine sons who shall inherit this land after him. Let it be known that the Norsemen are here to stay.'

Another cheer shook the rafters. Elgiva closed her eyes and took a deep breath, trying to steady herself, determined to stifle the wail of terror rising in her throat. When she opened them again, it was to see Wulfrum watching her. Under that cool gaze her resolve stiffened.

'If I am to take a wife, I would have a name to lay to her,' he said.

For a moment she was tempted to refuse, but then common sense came to the fore. If she did not tell him, he might well beat it out of her.

'I am Elgiva, daughter of Egbert, and sister to Osric, late the thane of this manor.'

'Elgiva. The name is pleasing—as pleasing as the outward form.'

She felt herself grow warm beneath that keen scrutiny. Wulfrum smiled and removed his helmet. The face beneath might have been chiselled from rock, so strong were the planes of cheek and brow and jaw, the latter accentuated by a beard close trimmed and dark as the hair that fell over his shoulders. The eyes regarding her now were the startling blue of a summer sky. She saw their expression change and he reached out a hand, lightly touching the cut on her neck.

'You are hurt?'

'No. 'Tis merely a legacy of your brave friend, Sweyn.'

He ignored the gibe. 'How is it that you speak our tongue so well, Elgiva?'

'I was tutored in it by my nurse. Her mother was a Dane.'

'It is an advantage I had not thought to find.'

'An advantage indeed, for now I can call you the loathsome reptile you are and have you understand.'

Wulfrum was not so easily goaded. If anything, his enjoyment grew.

'You could say it in your own language if you wished.'

Hearing him speak the words in fluent Saxon, she was temporarily at a loss.

'I have learned much in my travels,' he explained.

Letting his hand drop a little, he brushed the top of her gown. Elgiva instinctively took a step back. The smile widened.

'Soon you will beg me to touch you, lady.'

'That I never will.'

'You say so now—you have yet to share my bed. May I say I look forward to it?'

Hot colour flooded her face and neck, but before she could reply Ironfist appeared beside them. He glanced down at her for a moment and then took her chin in one huge hand, turning her face to his.

'By all the gods, not bad.' He let his hand slide to her arm, encircling it easily. Then he looked at Wulfrum and grinned. 'She's a little slender for my taste, but to each his own.'

Elgiva glowered. Did these Viking clods think her a prize horse to be mauled thus?

'I'm glad you approve,' replied Wulfrum.

'Thor's beard, 'tis high time you took a wife. A man must breed sons.'

'I intend to.'

'I'll cut out your liver first!'

Both men looked down at her in silence for perhaps the length of two heartbeats. Then they laughed out loud.

'I do believe she'd try,' said Ironfist. 'You'll have trouble with this one, believe me. Are you equal to the challenge?'

'Trust me,' replied Wulfrum. He turned her to face him. 'Come, Elgiva. Let us seal our betrothal.'

Before she could anticipate him she found herself being forcibly kissed, drawn hard against him, held in strong arms and kept there at his pleasure in an embrace that left her breathless. No man had ever kissed her like that, a kiss that was both knowing and disturbingly assured. When he released her, the warmth of his mouth lingered on her lips. Her eyes blazed as she hit him, the crack ringing loud.

There was a sharp intake of breath from others nearby and heads turned to watch the developments with keen interest. Not a man there but expected to see the mutinous wench laid at Wulfrum's feet with one blow of his fist. To their surprise he merely grinned.

'I suppose I deserved that.'

'You said it,' replied Ironfist.

Elgiva launched a second blow, but Wulfrum caught her wrist and held it. 'Now that's no way to behave towards your future husband.'

'I will never take you as my husband.'

'You will, Elgiva, believe me, and that soon enough.'

Before she could reply Lord Halfdan drew near.

'Come, that's enough romantic dalliance, Wulfrum. You can deal with the wench later. There is work to be done.'

'As you say, my lord.'

'Take her back to the upper chamber and put a guard on the door. Then join me outside.'

Wulfrum nodded and turned to Elgiva, ignoring her attempts to pull free.

'Don't you dare touch me!'

He raised an eyebrow and threw Olaf a speaking look. The hand round her wrist tightened and he strode to the stairs, drawing her after. Resistance was futile for his grip was like a vice. When they reached the upper chamber, he pushed her inside.

'Until later, Elgiva.'

Then he left her, pausing only to issue instructions to the guards outside the door. Breathless and shaking, she watched him go.

When she was satisfied that he really had gone, she

turned and looked fearfully at the scene before her. The
two children were still there, apparently unharmed and
being comforted by frightened servants. With enormous
relief Elgiva saw one of the latter help Osgifu to her feet.
The older woman was still dazed. Her lip was cut and a
dark bruise was already showing down her cheek.
Hastening forwards Elgiva guided her to a chair before
pouring a little water into a basin and gently bathing the
cut lip. Osgifu sat very still throughout, though her hands
trembled slightly in her lap. As she had no access to her
medicine chest, there was relatively little that Elgiva could
do for she had no arnica or salve to hand. The best she
could manage was a cool compress on the bruised area of
the face.

For some time neither woman spoke, each trying to
come to terms with the terrible events that had shattered
the peaceful course of their lives and changed it for ever.
Eventually it was Osgifu who spoke first.

'Are you all right, child? They did not hurt you?'

'No, I am quite well.'

'Thank God for it. And the children?'

'Both well too.' Elgiva cast a glance at the open window
and shuddered. If Sweyn had had his will, both her
nephews would be dead, impaled on the spears of the
horde beneath. It had been prevented. Remembering
Wulfrum's ringing command, she could only be thankful
he had appeared on the scene when he did. Seemingly he
had no taste for the slaughter of babes, either. He had kept
her out of Sweyn's clutches too. She knew that if he had
not, the other would have exacted a terrible revenge for she
had bested him and caused him to lose face before his
comrades. It was not a thing he was likely to forgive. There

could be no forgetting the expression in the cruel grey eyes.

Unable to read her mind, Osgifu guessed accurately enough the thoughts passing through it. She had been stunned for a short time, then disorientated, lying still until she could be sure of her bearings. None of the invaders had paid any further attention to her and she had heard much of the conversation in the room, listening with mounting concern for Elgiva. The girl turned to her now.

'Did you hear?'

'Aye, enough.'

Before they could speak further, Ulric broke free of the woman who had been holding him and came to them. Elgiva scooped him up and sat him on her knee, holding him close, speaking words of reassurance. The tears that had risen in her eyes unbidden were swiftly quelled. A show of weakness would not help anyone, least of all herself. If she hoped to survive the ordeals that lay ahead, she would need every ounce of courage she possessed. The trouble was that she had never felt so afraid in her life.

CHAPTER THREE

WULFRUM rejoined Halfdan and Olaf Ironfist outside. His men were already moving among the bodies of the slain, collecting weapons and armour along with any valuables they might find. The fighting had been fierce while it lasted—the Saxons had put up a brave defence even though they were heavily outnumbered. He admired courage and it had been shown here this day. Their leaders had fallen and many besides, but a goodly number had been taken prisoner. They stood roped together under heavy guard. From their sullen expressions he knew them unbowed, though they feared for their lives even now. It was well. It meant they would do nothing foolish. He had no intention of shedding any more blood for he would need able hands to work these lands in future. However, it would not hurt his cause to leave them in doubt a while longer.

Wulfrum turned away from the prisoners and met the keen gaze of his sword brother. Halfdan lowered his voice.

'Hold this place well, brother. Lying as it does on the road to the north, it is of strategic importance to us.'

'You may depend on it.'

'I know it.' Halfdan clapped him on the shoulder. 'I could think of no better hands to leave it in. Even so, it will keep you busy. The place seems to be strangely neglected.'

Wulfrum glanced around. 'It looks to have seen more prosperous days, but they will come again, I promise you.'

'Why would any man worthy of the name allow his holdings to fall into such disrepair?'

'I know not.'

'Unless of course there was no man in view,' said Halfdan, his tone thoughtful.

'Perhaps, yet the Saxons were organised and fought valiantly. It suggests a leader, does it not?'

'Belike he fell in the fighting, then.'

'Most likely. The Saxon losses were heavy. I shall make enquiries.'

Before further conjecture was possible they were interrupted by the approach of two of their fellow Danes, dragging a captive with them. The man's hands were bound before him and his face beneath a layer of grime was ashen. From the shaven crown and long robe Wulfrum recognised one of the Christian priests. He glanced once at Halfdan and then watched in silence as the trio came to a halt before them.

'Look what we found, my lord.' The guard's lip curled as he glanced at the prisoner. 'The craven swine was hiding in the barn.'

'Hiding, eh?' Halfdan's expression mirrored the guard's as he looked the priest over. 'Scarcely surprising, I suppose. He's a poor specimen by the look of him. Must be fifty if he's a day.' He turned to Wulfrum. 'What do you want to do with him? Shall we have him spitted and roasted like an ox? Or shall we flay him and nail his hide to the door of his accursed church?'

'Beg pardon, my lord,' said the guard, 'but we burnt the church down.'

Halfdan followed his gaze towards a distant plume of thick dark smoke. 'Ah, yes, so we did. Pity. We'll spit him, then.'

Grinning, the men moved to obey.

Wulfrum held up a hand. 'No, not yet. He may prove to be of use.' He fixed his gaze on the trembling form. 'How are you called, priest?'

'Father Willibald, my lord.'

Halfdan stared at the earl in disbelief. 'You want this shaven ass?'

'Aye, I do.'

'Very well, as you will. Put him with the others, then.'

With ill-concealed disappointment the guards dragged the priest away.

Halfdan watched them a moment before turning back to his companion.

'Have some of your men search the forest hereabouts. 'Tis likely some of the serfs have taken refuge there. We should not lose valuable slaves thus. Besides, if left on the loose, they may foment trouble later.'

Wulfrum nodded for it had been his thought also. 'It shall be done, my lord. If any are hiding, they will be found and brought back.'

'Meantime, let the injured be carried into the hall and treated. There must be those among the Saxon women versed in the knowledge of healing. They must be identified and put to work.'

'It should be easy enough. I'll wager that priest will know.'

Wulfrum was right. Two minutes was all he needed to elicit the relevant information. Hearing the names, he hid a smile. It seemed that his beautiful future bride had other talents to her credit. He strode back to the hall and collared one of his men.

'Have the guards bring the Lady Elgiva down here,' he ordered. 'And the woman called Osgifu.'

Wulfrum seated himself casually on the edge of the long table and waited. A few minutes later the guards reappeared, ushering the two women in front of them. They came to a halt a few feet away, eyeing him warily.

'I'm told you have skill in healing,' he said without preamble. 'You will help to tend the injured.'

He saw the flash of defiance in Elgiva's eyes, but he was not alone; her companion put a gentle hand on her arm and the two exchanged looks. Then the older woman spoke.

'We will do so, lord.' She paused. 'I will need my things.'

'Fetch them.' Wulfrum turned to one of the guards. 'Go with her.' Then he turned his attention back to Elgiva, who was regarding him with a distinctly hostile gaze. He let his glance travel the length of her and saw her bridle in an instant. 'Do not think of trying any tricks, Elgiva.'

'Do you think I would harm injured men? I have a greater regard for human life.'

'Then give them all tending.'

'Does that include Saxon, as well as Dane?'

'Of course. Slaves are of value to me too.'

'A pity, then, that you have slain so many.'

'The fortunes of war.' He paused, smiling faintly. 'They could always have surrendered.'

'To a life of slavery? You cannot seriously think so.'

'I don't. I merely offer it as a possibility.'

The amber eyes blazed, but her anger appeared to leave him unmoved. A few moments later Osgifu returned with the box that held her herbs and potions. She eyed Wulfrum and hesitated.

'Well?' he asked.

'I will need hot water and clean cloths too,' she said, 'and some help to bring pallets for the injured.'

He glanced at the guard standing nearby. 'Arrange it.'

The man nodded and went with Osgifu to do his bidding. Wulfrum turned back to Elgiva, who had made no move to obey. He raised an eyebrow and saw her chin come up. She lingered a moment more and then, in her own good time, turned away. Had she seen the glint in his eyes she might have made more haste for an instant later the flat of Wulfrum's sword caught her hard across the buttocks. With a gasp of indignation, she spun round.

'Defy me again, wench, and you go across my knee.'

The words were quietly spoken, but, looking at that imperturbable expression, Elgiva was left in no doubt he meant it. She was also aware of several grinning faces around them from those who had witnessed the little scene, no doubt hoping for further entertainment at her expense. For a moment she hesitated, caught between anger and indecision. Then Wulfrum stood up and took a pace towards her. Elgiva fled.

The afternoon was wearing on when the Viking hunters returned with some dozen bound captives, those who had fled when defeat became inevitable. Some were wounded, all dirty and dishevelled. Wulfrum surveyed them for a moment and then turned to Ceolnoth, who had formed one of the hunting party.

'These were all you found?'

'Aye, my lord.'

'Very well. Keep them apart from the rest. I'll deal with them later. Meanwhile, take some of the women to the kitchens. They can start preparing the food. Lord Halfdan and his earls will be hungry tonight. See to it.'

'Yes, lord.'

Ceolnoth swung down off his horse and moved towards the captive women, who eyed him with fear. Enlisting the aid of a warrior companion, he cut half a dozen free, including the girl, Hilda. Wulfrum noted the young man's gaze lingered far longer on her than on the rest, and he smiled to himself. It seemed he was not the only one to have an eye for a comely Saxon wench. He watched as the women were taken off towards the hall. Then his gaze went to the upper storey of the building and in his mind's eye he saw again the chamber where he had first met Elgiva. It was a fine room. Henceforth it would be his, as would she. Their union would set the seal of his ownership on these lands and these people. Whether they liked it or not, the Danes were here to stay.

He had no doubt as to Elgiva's mind on the matter. In truth, she was a spirited piece as Lord Halfdan had said, and brave too. Her defiance of Sweyn demonstrated that beyond doubt. Not that he blamed the man for wanting her. She was a rare beauty and it must have cost him a pang to lose her so soon. Wulfrum had not forgotten the look in his eyes when the girl had spurned him, nor again when Wulfrum claimed her for his own. If Ironfist and the others had not been there, Sweyn might have disputed the matter further. Even if he had, Wulfrum knew he would have fought to keep her for, from the moment he set eyes on the wench, he knew he wanted her for himself. Wanted her and intended to have her. Halfdan had seen it too. It was why he had urged Wulfrum to take her to wife and settle the matter once and for all. Wulfrum knew that a week ago he would have dismissed the suggestion out of hand. Today he had embraced it. After all, he was five and twenty and should have taken a bride long since. He would have if he'd ever found one he wanted. It had seemed a hopeless quest. That situation had just changed. Besides, he could think of many a worse fate to befall a man. Recalling the kiss he had stolen from Elgiva earlier, he grinned. If looks could kill, he knew he'd be a dead man now. Too bad—he was determined that kiss would be the first of many. Let her fight him tooth and nail; it would avail her naught. She would yield in the end. He would strip away her defences as he intended to strip away her clothes.

'My lord?'

Jolted back to the present, Wulfrum focused his attention on the man before him.

'Well?'

'Lord Halfdan requests your presence in the hall.'

'I will come.'

When he returned, he made his report and then looked about him with curiosity. He could see that the Saxon healers had not been idle. They had organised matters so that those men who had been badly injured had been lifted onto makeshift pallets and, having been tended, were watched over now by some of the serfs. Elgiva and her companion continued on to see to the walking wounded, of whom there was a goodly number.

'Those women know what they are about,' observed Halfdan, noting the direction of Wulfrum's gaze. 'It is useful to have experienced healers to call on. They will serve you well.'

He turned aside then to speak to one of his men, leaving Wulfrum free to observe. Across the hall he could see Elgiva with her latest patient, bandaging his arm. It seemed that Halfdan was right—she worked with assurance, her hands moving swiftly and competently about their task. From her hands he let his gaze travel on across the graceful curves of her figure, from the swelling bosom and narrow waist to the gently flaring hips. A thick golden braid hung down her back, though several tendrils of hair had escaped to curl about her neck and cheek. Just then her profile was towards him and he missed nothing of the delicate bone structure beneath that flawless skin. She was lovely, a prize indeed. As if sensing herself watched, she turned her head and looked round, perceiving him immediately. He saw the dainty chin tilt upwards before she looked away, and smiled to himself. She was safe enough for now; there were many more wounds to stanch and bind and he had still many matters to attend to, including a trip to the Danish encampment.

'After that, my lady,' he murmured, 'we shall see.'

Elgiva and Osgifu worked on. It was late in the day when the last of the wounded were carried in. Among them was Aylwin, his face waxen beneath the dirt and gore. He had taken a deep sword thrust in the side and his tunic was dark with blood, yet a faint pulse testified that he lived. Swiftly they cut away the tunic and the shirt beneath. The wound gaped, wide and ugly, but it looked clean. Several superficial cuts marked his arms and livid bruises attested to the ferocity of the fighting. Elgiva set to work to stanch the bleeding. As she did so a shadow fell across them and she glanced up. Her heart skipped a beat to see Halfdan standing there. He surveyed the injured man a moment and then the pile of discarded clothing. Even soiled, it could never pass for the garb of a peasant.

'Who is he?'

Elgiva felt her throat dry. Then she heard Osgifu speak. 'This is Lord Aylwin.'

'A Saxon lord.' Halfdan looked from her to Elgiva. 'Your father, perhaps?'

'No. My father is dead.'

'Ah, your husband, then?' His hand moved to his sword hilt.

Elgiva bit back a cry of alarm, her mind racing. If Halfdan's earl intended to marry her as he had said, then she could not have a husband living. If he thought that the case, he would rectify the matter.

'He is not my husband, but I am betrothed to him.'

The Viking relaxed his grip on the sword and he laughed. 'Not any more.'

As she watched him walk away Elgiva let out the breath she had unconsciously been holding. Exchanging a brief glance with Osgifu, she set to work again with trembling hands to stanch the wound and bind it. She wondered if Aylwin would last the night and thought it unlikely. It might be better if he did die. The alternative was a life of slavery beneath the Viking yoke, something he would never submit to. Nor would he suffer another man to take his betrothed without a fight. Elgiva swallowed hard. Aylwin had been allowed to live for now, but for how much longer?

She and Osgifu worked until all had been attended to. The sun was going down before they finished and both women were exceedingly weary. Elgiva wondered if she would ever get the stink of blood and death from her nostrils. Every part of her ached from the effort of bending or stretching and her gown was soiled with blood and dirt. She retired with Osgifu to the women's bower and, having assured herself that the children were safe in the hands of one of the older women, she turned her attention to herself, bathing her hands and face in an attempt to cleanse away the memory of the past hours.

'Oh, Gifu, so many good men slain.'

The battle today had been a rout in the end despite all the Saxons had been able to do. No one could have withstood the invaders for long. Now they were the masters here and every last Saxon soul who survived was in their power. One taste of it was enough to strike terror into the heart.

'Aye, yet not all our warriors fell in the battle. The Vikings have already sent men out to search for fugitives, but they will not find them all.'

'I fear it will be too late to be of help here.' Elgiva met her gaze, unaware of the desperation in her own eyes as, unbidden, the memory of a man's face intruded into her thoughts, a strong, chiselled face and disconcerting blue eyes. She forced it down and strove against rising panic. She would not wed the Viking.

Osgifu broke into her thoughts. 'The forest is large and there are many places of concealment.'

'Aye, there are for those who know its secrets.'

Elgiva moved away as, through the haze of fear and desperation, the germ of an idea formed in her mind. She knew the forest paths well for, with Osgifu, she was used to spending time there, gathering the plants she needed for her medicines. She could not wait to see if Aylwin survived, if there would ever be a Saxon uprising. All that would take time, and time was the one thing she didn't have. Elgiva found suddenly that she was shivering with delayed reaction and the atmosphere seemed stifling. She moved to the doorway.

The place seemed quieter now—the evening meal was preparing in the hall and beyond the palisade the majority of the Viking host had encamped for the duration. The smoke from their cooking fires was already rising into the evening air. The women's bower was situated behind the hall where over the years various rooms had been added according to need. Looking around now, Elgiva could see the bodies of the slain lying where they had fallen and beyond them a few of Halfdan's men moving around outside stables and barn. However, there seemed to be no one at the gate just then and the broken timbers hung wide. Not far away the forest beckoned. Elgiva bit her lip. If she could somehow reach the gate without being spotted, there might be a chance of reaching the trees. The Viking encampment lay in the opposite direction and, while it would mean skirting the edge of the village, she could be fairly certain no Saxon would give her away. Once in the forest she would stand a reasonable chance of eluding pursuit. What she would do then she had no clear idea, but it seemed to her that there must be Saxons who had escaped the Viking host. If there were enough of them, they might return by stealth and put the invaders to the sword in their turn. Failing that, she might be able to find help elsewhere in those lands where the Danes held no sway. Anything was better than remaining here to become the bride of a conqueror.

Looking round the room, she saw the empty bucket and with it the idea. A trip to the well would serve as a plausible excuse for leaving the bower. She made for the door.

'What are you doing?' Osgifu looked at her in concern.

'I can't stay here, Gifu.'

'Elgiva, think.'

'I have thought. I will not do what they want.'

'If you run, they will find you and bring you back. These men are ruthless. Who knows what punishment they may inflict?'

'It cannot be worse than what they're already planning.'

'Don't do it, I beg you.'

'I will not stay here to be married off to a Viking warlord. I must get help. You said yourself that some of our men have fled into the forest. I will find them.'

'Elgiva, wait!'

The words fell on empty air for Elgiva was already heading for the well. Picking her way among the bodies all around, she tried to ignore the rising stench and darted covert glances all about her, fearing at every moment to hear someone raise the alarm. However, no one did challenge her and she reached the well a short time later. Putting down the bucket, she took another furtive look around but could still see no one at the gate. Summoning all her courage, Elgiva made towards it at a steady pace, not wishing to draw eyes her way by careless haste. At every step her heart hammered; she expected at each moment to

hear the shouted challenge and the sound of pursuit. It
never came and she reached the shattered entry. Cautiously
she walked through the gateway and looked about her. The
way was clear. Picking up her skirts, she ran, sprinting
across the open ground betwixt her and the edge of the
trees, ignoring everything but the need to escape and put
as much distance as possible between herself and
Ravenswood. Focused on her goal, she did not see the
horseman approaching fast at an oblique angle to cut off
her route.

By the time she heard the thudding hoofbeats, he was
much closer. One horrified glance over her shoulder
revealed the approaching danger in a brief impression of
a great black horse and the warrior who rode it. Elgiva
summoned every remaining vestige of energy and put on
a last desperate spurt. The trees were no more than a
hundred yards away now. If she could but reach them, she
would have a chance of escape. Behind her the hoofbeats
sounded louder, thudding in her ears like the sound of her
own heartbeat as she willed herself on. It was a vain effort.
The rider leaned down and a strong arm reached out and
swept her off her feet. Elgiva shrieked as she was thrown
face down over the front of the saddle, held firmly across
the rider's knees. For some further distance every bone in
her body was jarred before the horseman reined to a halt.
Fury and fright vied for supremacy as she fought to
recover her breath. Then she heard a familiar voice.

'Whither away, Elgiva?'

Her stomach lurched. Wulfrum! Frantically she strove
to push herself upright, but a firm hand between her shoulders kept her where she was, his well-trained mount
standing like a rock the while.

'Let go of me, you clod. You Danish oaf.'

'Clod? Danish oaf? These are grave insults indeed.' Wulfrum regarded his struggling captive with a keen eye. 'It seems to me that you need to learn better manners.'

'You have the nerve to lecture me about manners, barbarian?'

'I think you were not attending to me earlier, wench, for I warned you what would happen if you defied me again.'

Suddenly she did recall the words and her face grew hotter as she divined his meaning and realised the extreme vulnerability of her present position.

'You wouldn't dare.'

'Is that so?'

The flat of his hand came down hard, eliciting a yelp of indignation and further futile struggles.

'Let me go, you bastard! You swine! Let me go!'

It was an unfortunate choice of words for half a dozen sharp whacks ensued. Elgiva yelled in rage but bit back any further insults, knowing he would avenge himself if she uttered them.

'You're not going anywhere,' was the pleasant rejoinder. 'You belong to me now and I will hold what is mine.'

Fuming, she forgot her former resolve in the face of this breathtaking arrogance. 'I will never belong to you, you loathsome Viking filth.'

That last was a mistake—the hand descended several times more and much harder. Elgiva gasped.

'Anything more?' he asked. 'I can keep this up indefinitely if you can.'

Indeed there were plenty more things she could have

found to say, chiefly concerning his lowly birth, probable ancestry and certain destination in the hereafter, but with a monumental effort she forced them back. Only a very small exhalation of breath escaped, a sound that reminded him of an infuriated kitten. Wulfrum waited a moment, but there was nothing more. His lips curved in a sardonic smile; touching his horse with his heels, he let it move forwards at a walk. Elgiva gritted her teeth in helpless fury as they headed back towards Ravenswood and a dreadful suspicion grew that his retribution wasn't over yet.

In this she was right. Wulfrum took his time about the return journey, knowing full well the helpless ire of his captive and her present discomfort. He had been visiting the Viking encampment earlier and was returning when he caught sight of the running figure heading for the forest. He had recognised her at once and knew a bid for freedom when he saw it. He also knew she must not be allowed to get away. How she had got so far was a mystery, one for which the guards would get a roasting later. As for Elgiva, she would discover that it did not pay to disobey him. Right now he knew she was smarting, as much from the humiliation as from his hand. It had been most tempting to put all his strength behind it and beat her soundly, but he had resisted the notion and tempered the punishment. As it was, she would think twice before crossing him again. Like all the Saxons she would learn that rebellion came at a price.

In consequence Elgiva was held across the saddle bow all the way back to the outer door of the women's bower. If she had thought then he would let her slide from the saddle and slink indoors, she was mistaken for Wulfrum dismounted first and dragged her off the horse after.

Tucking her under one arm, he carried her inside in another casual and humiliating demonstration of superior strength. When at last he set her down she was hot and breathless and, to Wulfrum's eyes, most attractively dishevelled, for the golden mane had escaped its braid and fell in tumbled curls about her shoulders.

Furious, Elgiva glared up at him, wishing anew for a sword to cut the arrogant brute down to size. However, he was very big and to her cost she knew his strength. She hated to think what other retribution he might take if she angered him further for she was uncomfortably aware of the bed on the far side of the room and of the dimming light and of his dangerous proximity.

It was not hard to discern some of her thought but, far from being perturbed in any way, Wulfrum smiled, thinking that anger heightened her beauty for those wonderful eyes held a distinctly militant light. He was sorely tempted to take her in his arms and kiss her again, but he suspected that if he did, he would not be able to stop there. Better to let her think about what had happened, to understand the futility of attempting to escape him. She was no fool and the lesson would be well learned. Besides, time was on his side now.

For the space of several heartbeats they faced each other thus. Then, to her inexpressible relief, he moved towards the door, pausing when he reached it.

'You will remain here until I say otherwise. I should perhaps point out that there will be a guard outside from now on.'

He left her then, closing the door behind him. Weak with relief, Elgiva collapsed against it, listening with thumping heart to the muffled hoof falls as he rode away.

CHAPTER FOUR

IN THE DAYS following an atmosphere of deep gloom hung over Ravenswood along with the stench of death and corruption. Carrion birds flapped among the bodies or perched in readiness on the palisade as the demoralised Saxons, with an air of bitter resignation, went about the business of digging graves. Since the church had been burned and the priest taken prisoner there was little chance that he might bless the graves, a grievous lack that added to the pain of loss. The living had perforce to be content with murmured prayers and the laying of flowers.

Osgifu and Elgiva helped with the laying out of the dead, working in silence and in grief for the lives snuffed out so soon. Aylwin lived yet, though he was much weakened from loss of blood. The Vikings kept a close watch, but they made no move to harm him. Elgiva did what she could for him, but there were many others requiring her attention too, and her time was spent in tending the wounded, changing dressings, applying salves and balms, dispensing the medicines that dulled pain. Some men were beyond help and died; others like Aylwin clung desperately to life. His troubled gaze followed Elgiva as she moved among her patients, an attention that had not gone unnoticed.

Waiting until Elgiva was not by, Wulfrum made his way towards the pallet where the Saxon lay, regarding him dispassionately. He made no attempt to sit, thus putting the other at an added disadvantage by compelling him to look up at his visitor. At first neither man spoke. Then Wulfrum broke the silence.

'Your wound heals?'

'It heals.'

'Elgiva is skilled.'

At the mention of her name, the older man's eyes narrowed and his hand clenched at his side.

'What is it you wish to say?'

'That I know of your former betrothal to her…' Wulfrum paused '…a betrothal you would now do well to forget.'

'Elgiva is mine.'

'Not so. She belongs to me, as does this hall and these lands, and I shall take her to wife.'

'By God, you shall not!' The injured man started up, then winced as his wound protested.

Watching him fall back upon the pallet, Wulfrum raised an eyebrow. 'Indeed? And how will you prevent it?'

Aylwin remained silent, knowing too well the futility of any reply he might make. More than anything he wanted to be left alone, but his tormentor lingered still.

'You should have wed her when you had the chance.'

'Would that I had.' Aylwin regarded him with hatred. 'But she asked me to observe a decent period of mourning for her brother. I would not expect you to understand, Viking.'

Wulfrum laughed. 'I think I understand. The lady was not so keen as you to marry.'

Aylwin reddened for the words had touched a nerve. The same thought had occurred to him too.

'You should be thankful—if you had married her, you would be dead now,' the other went on, 'for I would still have taken her from you. As it is, your claims on her are void and you had best accept it.'

'Never!' The word exploded between them.

Wulfrum smiled and, throwing the Saxon one last contemptuous look, walked away.

Two days later Aylwin disappeared. At first no one thought it significant. A man so badly wounded could not have gone far. However, an exhaustive search revealed nothing. Elgiva heard the news with deep concern. Even if he escaped as far as the forest, Aylwin's weakened condition made him ill suited to such rough living and, without careful tending, he might well die. Angered that so prestigious a prisoner had slipped through their hands, the Vikings questioned everyone who had contact with him, including Elgiva and Osgifu.

Seeing their captors so disturbed, Elgiva knew only intense satisfaction. When Wulfrum questioned her, she was able to say with perfect truth that she knew nothing of the matter. However, she was unable to hide her feelings with complete success, a fact that he did not fail to note.

'He could not have gone far alone. He must have had help.'

'That is possible, lord,' she replied.

'Who was it?'

'I don't know.'

'But you wouldn't tell me if you did know.'

'No.'

It was a reply that was both honest and impudent in equal measure. With an effort, he curbed the urge to seize and shake her soundly. For all that air of quiet calm, the vixen was enjoying this. He didn't think for a moment that she was personally responsible for Aylwin's escape—she was under guard in the women's bower at night—but her relief when they failed to find him had been quite evident. Perhaps she wasn't as indifferent to the Saxon as he had first believed. The thought did nothing to improve his temper and he dismissed her before he did something he might later regret.

Relieved to be out of that unnerving presence, Elgiva returned to her work among the injured, conscious the while of the brooding blue gaze that watched her every move. The Viking would not find Aylwin now, she was sure of it. If he died, his friends would bury him in secret: if he lived, they would get him away to a place of greater safety—somewhere the Danes held no sway. The thought filled her with fierce pleasure and only with difficulty could she hide her elation. She might not have loved Aylwin, but she did rejoice in his freedom.

Unwilling to dwell too long on the chances of her former betrothed, Elgiva put her mind to more immediately pressing matters. Chief of these was the welfare of her nephews. After their recent treatment at the hands of the invaders she kept a watchful eye on them. Pybba was too young to know how near he could have been to death but, for some days after the coming of the Vikings, Ulric clung to Hilda, his nursemaid, staring wide-eyed and silent from behind her skirts if any of the men appeared. Elgiva, touched by his vulnerability, would take him on her knee and sing to him and he would snuggle against her, seeking her warmth and gentleness. With her and Hilda he knew he was safe.

In spite of her other responsibilities Elgiva spent time each day with the children. She also kept an eye on Hilda for the girl had suffered at the hands of the conquerors. In particular the young man called Ceolnoth sought her out as a companion for his bed. All her struggles and protests had availed her nothing. Elgiva knew there was nothing she could say to soothe that hurt and the girl's strained expression was a cruel reminder of the fate she too might have suffered had their positions been reversed.

Thus far Wulfrum had not intruded into the nursery. It was women's work and he was content to leave it so, and since he had become Lord of Ravenswood none of his men had laid a hand on any child, noble or base. However, one morning as he took a short cut through the rear of the hall, he was arrested by the sound of women's laughter and the playful squealing of a child. Moving towards the source of the noise, he paused in the doorway. Elgiva was kneeling on the floor. In front of her the oldest child was lying on the rug, laughing and giggling as she tickled his ribs. Across the room the girl Hilda watched and smiled from her place beside the baby's crib. It was a scene of innocent delight so different from anything he had known that Wulfrum was drawn and held in spite of himself. This was an Elgiva he had never seen, laughing and relaxed as though without a care in the world. The children were her nephews, but she tended them as though they were her own, with a gentle and loving hand. Watching, he smiled unawares as a new dimension opened up before him. One day he would have sons. His gaze warmed as it rested on his future wife. It would be good to have children with Elgiva. His smile grew rueful. One day.

Though he made no movement or sound, some instinct warned the occupants of the room that they were not alone. It was Hilda who saw him first. Her smile faded and a look of fear replaced it. Elgiva looked up and followed the direction of her gaze. Then she too froze. The child stared at him wide-eyed. In a moment the atmosphere in the room changed and became tense. He saw Elgiva rise and draw the child close.

'My lord?' The tone was anxious, even wary.

He surveyed her for a moment in silence, wanting to speak, but not knowing what to say. Then, 'The children are well?'

'They are well,' she replied.

'Good.' He paused, then glanced at the toddler. 'The boy is afraid.'

'Has he no cause?'

'None.' He met and held her gaze for a moment. 'He shall not be harmed if I have power to prevent it. Please believe that.'

Elgiva stared at him in surprise, but said nothing for her heart was unaccountably full. His expression and his words had seemed sincere. His former actions too had prevented harm coming to the children. He was their enemy but, perversely, in that moment she wanted to trust him in this.

Unable to follow her thought and seeing she remained silent, Wulfrum felt suddenly awkward. What did he expect her to say? That she believed him? Trusted the children to his care? Aware of how ridiculous a notion that was, he turned abruptly away. Trust could not be commanded, it had to be earned; thus far, he could see he had done little to earn hers.

As he left the hall, the memory of the scene stayed with him. It stayed throughout the morning as he supervised the work of the serfs. He could not forget the fear of Hilda and the child when they saw him or Elgiva's wariness. What did they take him for? Then he remembered Sweyn and what he had been about to do before he was stopped. Wulfrum sighed. True enough, the child had cause to be afraid and the women too. It would not be easy to overcome it, either, but Sweyn would soon be gone and then they might learn there was nothing to fear from him or his men. While he lived no harm should come to them. He was their lord and their protection was his responsibility. For the first time he began to feel its weight.

It had taken several days to bury the dead for goodly numbers had fallen on both sides, but eventually it was done. Elgiva stood by the Saxon graves a while and said her own silent prayers since Father Willibald had not been permitted to officiate at the burials or to say a mass for the souls of the dead. To her surprise Earl Wulfrum had raised no objection to her attending the funerals or made any attempt to interfere. In any case, his men were taking care of their own dead. A few of the Viking warriors stood at a distance watching the events with a careful eye, their presence a reminder of the new order.

A cold breeze stirred the branches of the forest trees around and Elgiva shivered, drawing her mantle closer, fighting down the fear in the pit of her stomach. Like a leaf swept along on the current of a stream, she had no control over the events that would shape her future. Everything she had known and loved was gone as though in a past life. True enough, she thought, she had been someone else then. And now? Now she was a prisoner like all the rest, little better than a slave. Not quite, she amended. Ever since Wulfrum had announced his intention to marry, his men had regarded her as his domain. She had not been troubled or molested in any way, though they looked their fill whenever she appeared. Neither had a hand been raised to Osgifu, who came and went to her mistress's bower without hindrance. To the best of her knowledge, the earl's promise that there should be no more killing had been kept; now most of the Saxons serfs had been put to work, albeit under the watchful eyes of their conquerors. Only the fugitives rounded up in the forest remained chained and under guard. Rumours abounded as to their eventual fate, though Elgiva had been cautiously optimistic.

'Surely he will not kill them—he has need of them to work the land and tend the stock.'

Osgifu had been more sceptical. 'He doesn't need to kill them to make an example of them.'

However, a day went by and another and nothing happened, but each time the Saxons had looked at the prisoners they had felt only deep disquiet for the reputation of the Danes went before them and had been well earned. Since their coming all the certainties of life had vanished, leaving only a dread of tomorrow.

Recalling that conversation with Osgifu, Elgiva wondered if her optimism had not been misplaced. She drew in a deep breath. Whatever the Danes decided, the prisoners would have no choice but to obey. Like the rest she had been kept under guard but she had been grateful for her relative isolation, not wishing to have any greater contact with the conquerors than was absolutely necessary. Now, outdoors again, she was restless, and her gaze went beyond the burying ground to the forest. Its quiet glades and green solitudes beckoned, inviting and forbidden, particularly after the confinement of the bower. It recalled happier days when she had accompanied her father and brother on the chase; recalled the sheer exhilaration of the gallop, the power of the horse beneath her. Thinking of the game little mare in the stables, Elgiva knew that was something else forbidden to her now.

Forcing down her resentment and her anger, she laid her flowers on the graves. All around her groups of people began to disperse, mostly in silence, and sorrow hung heavy in the air. Elgiva followed, wrapped in her own thoughts. Then she became aware that two of the Saxons had been keeping pace with her and glanced up to see Leofwine, the smith, and Elfric, his son. The smith shot her a swift glance.

'My lady, we must speak with you.'

Elgiva nodded discreetly, aware that she was watched. 'What is it, Leofwine?'

'My lady, there are men hiding in the forest, in the cave by the old dolmen stones.'

Elgiva caught her breath. 'How many?'

'Two.'

'They must get away. Why do they linger?'

'One is hurt, lady. My brother, Hunfirth. He has a bad wound in his side and an arrow lodged in his shoulder. Our cousin, Brekka, got him away after the battle and hid him in the cave. I urged him to save himself, but he will not leave Hunfirth in such sore case. We have kept them supplied with food, but I fear my brother will die unless he can get proper tending.'

Elgiva bit her lip. She was watched day and night and so was Osgifu. If they tried to get out, they would likely lead the earl's men straight to the hiding place. Yet they could not stand by and let men die.

'I will think of something, Leofwine, I promise. When I do, I will send word with Osgifu.'

'God bless you, my lady.'

'I think we all have need of blessing,' she replied.

He nodded and walked away, unwilling to draw any unnecessary attention. Elgiva continued on. Her path led through the hamlet, or what was left of it. The smell of charred wood lingered still and everywhere was evidence of destruction in the piles of ash and blackened skeletons of burned-out dwellings. Hard by stood the sombre ruins of the church. At intervals dark patches stained the turf, marking the places where men had fallen and died. Where once a thriving village had stood, all around was a scene of desolation and death. Now it looked as though more men would die. Suddenly she was determined that it must be prevented. She must speak to Osgifu as soon as possible.

She came at length to the hall where the shattered portal still hung askew, another painful symbol of defeat, and hurried on. It was safer by far to walk round than through for more of Wulfrum's men were about and she had no wish to draw their attention. Every thought of the Viking marauders was anathema. By day Halfdan sent out groups of men to hunt for fugitive Saxons to return to their new master and for game, for such a large force must be fed, the men demanding meat to supplement what they had stolen on their passage through the countryside. By night they feasted. The great hall rang with the sound of their laughter and jesting over flowing mead horns. Then the female serfs faced another fear as the thoughts of the men turned from fighting to other things. She shuddered, the chill of one realising all too well that she lived on borrowed time.

Hastening towards the bower, so engrossed in thought, she failed to notice the man standing nearby. She was almost on him before she saw him and stopped short with a sharp intake of breath when she recognised the cruel predatory smile. Sweyn's gaze travelled over her appreciatively. Elgiva regarded him with coldness and said no word, but as she made to pass him, he blocked her way.

'Not so fast, wench.'

He lifted a hand towards her, but she stepped out of reach, her eyes raking him with scorn.

'Get out of my way.'

His thin lips twisted in a smile, but it never reached his eyes. 'Still high and mighty, Elgiva?'

'Let me pass.'

'We have some unfinished business, you and I.'

Elgiva's heart beat faster but she lifted her chin and stared him down.

'You and I have no business of any kind.'

'You think so?'

She tried again to pass him, but this time he held her arm to prevent it. His fingers dug into her flesh as he drew her closer. Wincing, Elgiva shrank back. His grip tightened and he smiled.

'Afraid, my lady?'

'You flatter yourself.'

'Do I so?'

'Let go of me, oaf.'

'You heard the lady,' said a voice behind them.

Both of them turned in surprise to see an imposing figure standing there, a grizzled giant carrying an axe. He surveyed them calmly enough, but his expression was utterly uncompromising. Elgiva had not thought ever to be thankful for the presence of a Viking, but now she breathed a sigh of relief. However, Sweyn was unwilling to give up his prey so easily.

'Mind your own business, Ironfist.'

'This is my business. The woman belongs to Wulfrum. Now let her go.'

For a few moments his steady gaze held that of Sweyn. The cold eyes spoke of anger, but he released his hold on her arm.

'You should return to your bower, lady,' said Ironfist.

Elgiva wasn't about to argue. Throwing him a brief glance, she hastened away, aware that both men watched her departure. She had scarcely taken a dozen paces when another familiar figure hove into sight. Startled, she checked mid-stride, unable to go forwards or back.

Wulfrum surveyed her in surprise, noting her evident unease, and then glanced over her shoulder towards Ironfist and Sweyn, now some yards distant. The berserker threw him a mocking smile and then turned and strolled away. The giant watched him go.

Wulfrum frowned and his gaze returned to the girl, looking closer now. 'Are you all right, Elgiva? Has Sweyn been bothering you?'

Her face, pale before, turned a warmer shade. 'No.'

'You're a poor liar, my lady. What happened?'

'It was nothing. Hot air.'

'Did he lay hands on you?'

Elgiva forced herself to meet his eye. The last thing she needed now was a confrontation between Wulfrum and Sweyn. 'Ironfist dealt with it, my lord.'

'Did he so?'

'Please…it was nothing.'

'I'll decide that.'

'Hasn't there been enough strife already?' The words came out with unwonted force. She drew a deep breath. 'I beg you, let there be no more of it.'

He heard the distress in her voice, but it was the power of those amber eyes that arrested him most. In them he read anxiety and distrust. Did she fear that he might lay the blame at her door? Knowing what Sweyn was capable of and knowing of Elgiva's detestation of him, Wulfrum did not think for a moment that she would have anything to do with the man. Whatever had occurred had shaken her, but it was clear she didn't want him to pursue the matter and that to do so would add to her distress. He was loath to do that. Rather he wanted to say something to alleviate it, but the situation was new to him and he found himself at a loss. Better to let the matter lie, at least as far as she was concerned. He could always speak to Ironfist later.

'It is not safe to be abroad. Go back to the bower, Elgiva, and stay there.'

For all it was a command, the tone was gentler than she had expected and surprise rendered her silent, merely inclining her head in acknowledgement of his words. Then she walked away. With a wry smile he watched her go, well aware of the alacrity with which she left. He would have liked to find a reason to detain her and it was in his mind to call her back, but if he did she would obey only because she must. It was clear she took no pleasure in his company. But, then, why should she? He sighed, wondering why it should matter. It never had before.

Glad to be out of that unsettling presence, Elgiva let out the breath she had been holding. Wulfrum had been quite gentle on this occasion but he was still a conqueror, a fact that must not be forgotten. As for the other, she could still feel the imprint of Sweyn's fingers on her flesh. Chilling to think what might have happened if Ironfist hadn't appeared on the scene. She recalled his words: *The woman belongs to Wulfrum.* The thought occurred then that Ironfist hadn't come along by chance. The earl guarded what was his. She had no doubt he would fight to keep it too, fight and kill. Shivering now, she hurried back to the sanctuary of the bower and closed the door, wanting to shut out the Viking presence at least for a while.

A few minutes later Osgifu appeared and Elgiva explained what Leofwine had told her. The older woman heard her with mounting concern.

'Somehow we must help those men. There have been enough deaths here.'

It was exactly what had been going through Elgiva's mind. 'How are we to get out though? The earl's guards are vigilant.'

Men had been posted outside the women's bower, as well as at the gate to Ravenswood and at intervals along the palisade. No one now could come or go undetected.

'In truth, I don't know.'

'There must be a way.'

Elgiva was thinking hard. The plan had better be a good one. She had no desire to lead Wulfrum's men to the fugitives or to be caught and dragged ignominiously before him to face another interrogation.

Osgifu broke into her thoughts. 'A simple disguise might serve.'

'A disguise? How? Surely the guards would never fall for it.'

'They might, if it were done subtly. People generally see what they wish to see. The guards are no different in that respect, I think.'

'What is in your mind?'

Osgifu explained. Elgiva listened and smiled. It was a simple idea but for that reason it might just work.

'I will speak with Hilda,' Osgifu went on. 'We'll need her help. In the meantime let us hope Wulfrum doesn't decide to visit the women's bower. That would be more than a bit inconvenient. He's not a man to cross.'

'What the earl doesn't know won't hurt him.'

'True.' Osgifu donned her old grey mantle and pulled up the hood. 'Happily this weather suits our purpose.'

The spring had been cool and showery and it had been raining intermittently all day. It was a perfect reason to wear a hood and one drawn forwards over the face as now. Elgiva watched her leave and then set about gathering up those things they would most likely need.

A short time later Osgifu returned with Hilda also clad in a grey mantle with the hood drawn up. She doffed the outer garment and helped Elgiva to put it on.

'God send you can help Hunfirth, my lady.'

'Amen to that.' Elgiva slipped the leather bag containing her things beneath her cloak. It was small enough to escape detection. Then she drew up her hood. Even a cursory glance would not mistake Hilda's tawny locks for her own gold ones. Pulling the cloth forwards to hide her face, Elgiva nodded to her companions.

Osgifu turned to Hilda. 'You must wait here till we return.'

'I shall. The children will be safe enough meanwhile. I've left them with Acca.'

It was a happy choice. Acca might be getting on in years, but she was kind and a most trustworthy servant besides.

Elgiva smiled. 'It is well.'

'My lady, you must use this chance to get away.' Hilda regarded her earnestly. 'Get far away into the forest where the conquerors will never be able to find you.'

'And leave you to their tender mercies in my place?'

'It does not matter.'

'It matters to me, Hilda. We have seen what cruelties they practise and I would not have anyone suffer at their hands again.' Elgiva squeezed the girl's arm. 'I will give what help I can to Hunfirth and return as soon as may be. Do you stay here meanwhile?'

Hilda nodded. Then, with swift-beating heart, Elgiva followed Osgifu from the bower. The guard outside glanced their way, but made no move to stop them, having seen two identically dressed women go in before. They walked away, resisting the temptation to hurry, and made for the gate. It was open to allow the normal traffic in and out and, though the guards kept an eye on those who came and went, they saw nothing suspicious in two more servant women going about their business.

Only when they were past these first obstacles did Elgiva breathe more easily. However, they could not afford complacency, for the Vikings kept a presence in the village too. At the smithy Elfric joined them and from there they followed the path that led towards the woodland. The rain had slackened a little, but the chill was penetrating and for that reason most people had sought shelter. Elgiva took a covert look around but could see no sign of any Danes. Belike they were within doors too. Fortunately the smithy was on the edge of the village; from there it was but a short distance to the trees. As they walked they looked about the while to ascertain that they were not followed.

In spite of the potential danger Elgiva felt her heart lift to be in the open air again, to breathe the welcome scent of damp earth and leaf mould, to see on every bough the glad new leaf appearing, wreathing the branches in a mist of green. The forest held a promise of freedom. She knew its secret places, knew she could hide herself there with ease and, equally, knew she never would. Her word was given and she would not break it. Thus with unerring steps she made her way along the familiar paths towards her goal.

It was perhaps a matter of half a league to the ancient dolmens, three great monoliths topped by another, stained and weathered, greened with moss and lichen, and so old none could say how they came there. A little further on was a rocky outcrop in the trees, where lay the cave they sought.

As they neared the place they slowed and she heard

Elfric whistle softly twice. At his signal a man emerged from the cave, a drawn sword in his hand. When he saw who it was, he lowered the weapon.

'Elfric. God be thanked.'

Elgiva recognised the speaker, the man called Brekka who had been one of her brother's retainers. He turned to her now and inclined his head respectfully.

'My lady, you take a great risk in coming here, but I thank you and Osgifu too. Hunfirth is in a poor way. I have done what I can for him, but it is little enough.'

They followed him through the narrow entrance into the wider cave beyond. In the dim light they could see the injured man lying on the hard earth floor. Elgiva knelt beside her companion and they made a careful examination of their patient. She knew Hunfirth by sight, but her heart misgave her as she looked at the man's pallor and heard his ragged shallow breathing. An examination of his wounds did nothing to restore her confidence. Apart from a deep sword thrust to his side, there was the arrow lodged in his shoulder and the signs were that the wound was already festering.

'This arrow must come out or he has no chance,' said Osgifu. 'Even then the outcome is doubtful given how much blood he has already lost.'

'He will die if you do not treat him,' replied Brekka.

Osgifu nodded. 'That is so.' She took the leather bag from beneath her cloak and began to get out her things.

It took some time to perform the task, given the limitations of the place and the basic nature of the equipment they had been able to bring, but eventually it was done. The patient had lost consciousness long since. In her heart Elgiva doubted whether he would survive the night. She turned to Brekka.

'If Hunfirth dies, you must not linger here.'

He shook his head. 'If it comes to that, my lady, I shall seek the other Saxon fugitives and join with them.'

'Enough blood has been spilt. I beg you to save yourself.'

'If I do, it will only be to fight another day.'

Seeing it was useless to argue, she and Osgifu gathered their things and prepared to leave. Outside the air was colder and the grey sky darkening. Elgiva realised then how much time they had spent in the cave. It was imperative now to get back before they were missed. They said their farewells to Brekka and retraced their steps, coming at last to the edge of the trees. Elfric looked around to check that the coast was clear. He need not have worried: it had begun to rain again and the place seemed deserted. In a little while it would be dark.

They reached the smithy, expecting to see Leofwine waiting there. However, the lean-to was dark with no sign of the smith. Elgiva frowned, feeling suddenly uneasy. It was too quiet. Something of this had occurred to her companions too and she could sense their nervousness.

'Go, my lady,' said Elfric. 'It is not safe to linger here.'

She was about to reply when a muted sound stopped the words, the sinister scrape of metal on stone. Before she could utter any warning, half-a-dozen dark shapes detached themselves from the shadows of the building and in moments the three of them were surrounded by armed men. Elgiva drew in a sharp breath as she recognised Ironfist. Taking a firm hold on her arm, he turned to his companions.

'Take those two and chain them with the others.'

Elfric and Osgifu were hustled away. With beating heart Elgiva looked up at her captor, but the giant's face was impassive as he drew her inexorably with him. Instead of following the rest, he peeled off at a tangent towards the women's bower. When they reached it, he shoved open the door and pushed her inside. In the dim light she could see the tall dark-clad figure before the fire. On hearing them enter, the figure turned round. Elgiva's mouth dried. Wulfrum!

'Good evening, my lady. I have been looking forward to your return for some time. Perhaps you would care to tell me where you have been.'

For a moment they regarded each other in silence, but even in the firelight she could see the anger in his face. She paled, heart thumping hard against her ribs, but she was thinking fast. How had he found out? What unlucky chance had led him here? There was no way of knowing what information he had already extracted from Leofwine and Hilda, but some instinct warned her not to lie to him, that to do so would make matters worse. Behind her she was aware of Ironfist's bulk blocking the door, cutting off all possibility of escape. She took a deep breath.

'Osgifu and I went to help a wounded man.'

'What man? Where?'

'Leofwine's brother, Hunfirth. He was wounded in the battle for Ravenswood and he took refuge in the forest.'

'How many are with him?'

'Just one.'

'Where are they?'

'Where we left them.'

'Don't test my patience further, Elgiva. Where are they?'

'I cannot tell you that.'

'Cannot or will not?'

'These are my people. I will not betray them.'

'You'll tell me,' he replied.

For the first time she noticed the coiled whip at his side and felt her legs tremble beneath her. Wielded properly, the lash could cut a groove in solid wood. She had seen what it could do to human flesh. He could not really be intending to use it. Her eyes sought for any clue in his expression that might suggest otherwise, but they found none. Then she remembered his response the day she had tried to run and a faint sheen of perspiration broke out on her forehead despite the cold without. The Viking knew how to punish and wouldn't hesitate, either. Elgiva bit her lip, clenching her fists at her sides to stop them from trembling. Come what may, she could not betray Hunfirth and Brekka. Let the warlord do his worst—she would never tell him. Her chin lifted and she met his gaze.

'I am a healer, lord. It is my part to save men, not to destroy them. Leofwine asked for my help and I gave it willingly. As I gave it to your men too. As I would to any human being who needed it. If that is a crime, I am sorry for it.'

'No, that is not a crime. Disobeying my orders is.'

'I was not aware you had given any orders about letting wounded men die.'

'Don't try to twist my words, wench.'

'I had no thought of doing so, lord.'

'It seems you have plenty of willing accomplices too.'

'Leofwine sought to aid his brother. Osgifu and Hilda helped me because I asked it. They are not to blame. If your anger must fall on anyone, let it fall on me.'

Wulfrum's gaze burned into her own, but Elgiva did not flinch. Inwardly she thought he might kill her.

'You may live to regret those words.'

'I beg you, lord, do not hurt them. They could not have done other than they did.'

'They show a reckless loyalty to you, that's for sure.'

'Loyalty is not a crime, either.'

Wulfrum's jaw clenched even as he admired the breathtaking audacity of the reply. He had to admit the little vixen did not want for courage. Even though she knew her present peril full well, she had answered him calmly enough and he had discerned no trace of fear in the unwavering amber eyes. She hadn't lied to him, either, although she was undoubtedly smart enough to realise he would have learned the truth long since from her confederates. By rights he should thrash her now along with all the others in this latest exploit. He was still tempted.

When he had visited the bower earlier and found her gone, his anger had known no bounds. Hilda, on the receiving end of it, had very soon told him the plan, a tale corroborated in part by the guards. Then Ironfist had remembered seeing her speaking with the smith earlier that day, on her return from the Saxon funerals. Wulfrum had gone to the smithy with half-a-dozen men and, in a very short time, had all the information he wanted from Leofwine. He had been able to believe the tale about the injured man, but certainly not the part about Elgiva's intention to return. She had got out of Ravenswood with a head start and would surely make good her escape. Yet both Hilda and Leofwine evidently had complete faith in her word. Even with his anger at white heat it gave him pause. Against his better judgement he had not ordered immediate pursuit, but instead had waited. In the meantime he had had the two Saxon miscreants chained with the dogs in the kennel where they could do no more mischief and could think at leisure of their probable fate.

Unable to follow his thought, Elgiva quaked.

'We will test that loyalty,' he said. 'We shall try how far it will go under the lash. I think it will not be long before your friends tell me what I wish to know.'

Elgiva's colour ebbed and tears welled in her eyes. 'Please don't hurt them. They have done nothing….'

'Then tell me where the fugitives are.'

'I cannot. You must know that.'

He took a step closer. Elgiva swallowed hard, but remained still, aware of Ironfist just behind.

'This is the last time I shall ask you. Where are they, Elgiva?'

Seeing she remained silent, Wulfrum looked beyond her to Ironfist.

'Go to the hall and find out,' he said, handing the giant the whip.

'Consider it done, lord.'

With sinking heart Elgiva heard Ironfist leave and then she was alone with Wulfrum, who regarded her with that in his face which made her heart thump unpleasantly hard.

'Please don't do this,' she said then.

'If you were truly concerned for the welfare of others you would have considered the consequences of disobedience.'

'Then punish me, not them.'

The amber eyes glistened with unshed tears. He wondered if she would weep and doubted it somehow. He had cause to know her courage and her pride.

'Believe me, Elgiva, you will learn to obey me.' He paused. 'The lives of your accomplices will be forfeit if you attempt to leave Ravenswood again without my knowledge. There will be no other warning.'

Her face was very pale, but she faced him, dread vying with resentment, choosing her words with care. 'Then you do not propose to kill them?'

'Not this time, but their future well-being depends on you.'

'I understand.'

'Do you?' He drew closer. 'I hope so.'

It took every bit of self-control for her not to take a step backwards. He towered over her, seeming even larger in the confined space. His expression sent a chill through her.

'In the meantime you will be confined to the women's bower until further notice.'

The implications began to dawn. 'But what of the injured? And Ulric and Pybba?'

'You should have thought of that earlier,' he replied.

'But, my lord, I—'

'I have said. You will do as you're told.' His keen gaze saw the glint of anger in her eyes before they were veiled. 'Otherwise I shall thrash you to within an inch of your life.'

Her hands clenched with helpless ire, but she knew it would avail her nothing to argue. In his present mood he might well carry out the threat and she knew already the weight of his hand.

'How long must I remain here?'

'For as long as it pleases me.'

Elgiva fought the temptation to tell him the thoughts uppermost in her mind. However, it did not need a seer to read them for anger was writ large on her face.

He lifted an eyebrow and regarded her with a speculative eye. 'Perhaps I should take your clothes too, just to make sure.'

Elgiva's face registered an interesting variety of emotions. Wulfrum smiled, watching a wonderful rosy blush rise from her neck to her cheeks. Then he waited. Seeing that smile, she knew beyond doubt that the knave was enjoying this. It was in her mind to call him every kind of scurvy rogue in creation, but she bit back the words that rose to her lips—in truth, she dared offer no more provocation, knowing now he would do just what he threatened. The brute had no shame.

As a matter of fact, Wulfrum had himself well in hand. The idea of Elgiva without her clothes was a heady one, but he put it aside, for now. His time would come. In the meantime he would leave her to think about the folly of wilful disobedience. He strolled to the door.

'I'll bid you a good evening, my lady.'

Elgiva glared after the departing figure and saw the door close after him. There followed muffled words as he spoke to the guards outside, and then silence. For some minutes she paced the floor in helpless fury and frustration. Her heart was filled with dread to think of the possible fate of her companions, but she dared not try to find out. She had been so preoccupied with helping Hunfirth and Brekka that she had put others at risk. Pacing the floor, she tried to think. When she had calmed a little she realised she need not fear for Ulric and Pybba. They would be safe enough for surely Wulfrum would not punish the helpless for her fault. Wulfrum again! Everything came back to Wulfrum. Could she trust him in this regard? She had to hope so. Throwing herself on to the bed in helpless ire, she felt the awful truth sink in. She was exactly where he intended her to be and she would be there at his pleasure. Elgiva punched the mattress hard, unsure whether she was angrier with him or herself.

CHAPTER FIVE

SHE HAD plenty of time to think of all the things she would like to do to Wulfrum in the days that followed. A guard brought her food and drink and emptied the slop bucket, but other than that she saw no one. As time passed the bower seemed to grow smaller and incarceration chafed her spirit. With growing anxiety, she pondered the fate of Osgifu and the others, praying that they were unhurt. Had Leofwine led the Vikings to the hidden cave? Had they captured Hunfirth and Brekka? Was Aylwin still alive? Were her nephews being cared for? Tormented by the lack of news, she could not settle to anything and paced the floor, inwardly cursing Wulfrum and all his fellow Vikings. She had no regrets about trying to help Hunfirth. It had been the right thing to do. If only she could be certain that her people had not suffered as a result. The enforced idleness was as bad as the lack of knowledge. Wulfrum knew it too, of that she had no doubt.

'Damn him!'

The very thought of the man was enough to stir her anger again. He knew how to punish. Yet in her heart she knew this was but a small taste of his power. Had he chosen to, he could have flogged her until the flesh hung

in ribbons from her back. She shivered. In truth, she had
been surprised that he had not, surprised and mightily
relieved too. He held all their lives in his grip now and they
were his to do with as he pleased. Why had he stayed his
hand? He could have made an example of her, of all of
them. Perhaps he already had. Perhaps he had lied to her
when he said he would not kill her companions, and
Osgifu and Hilda were hanging from a tree even now
along with Leofwine and Elfric. Perhaps her incarceration
was but a prelude to something far worse. The uncertainty
was what she hated most, as of course he knew she would.

'Damn him!' she said for perhaps the hundredth time.

Her imprisonment was running into its third day when the
door opened to admit Osgifu. Elgiva leapt up, staring at
her in disbelief. Then she was running across the intervening space and they were hugging each other fiercely.

'Oh, Gifu. Are you all right? I've been imagining all
kinds of terrible things. Did they hurt you?'

'No. I am quite well.'

'What of Hilda and the others?'

'Well, too.'

'And the children?'

'Both fine.'

Elgiva closed her eyes and gave silent thanks to God.
The relief was so intense she found herself shaking.

'What of you, child? Has he hurt you?'

'No. Things are as you see.' She glanced with distaste
around her prison. 'But I am not hurt.'

'Thank heaven. When you were taken away that night,
we feared the worst. No one has set eyes on you since and
rumours are rife.'

'How did you get in here?'

'The guards let me pass, on Lord Wulfrum's orders.'

'When did he release you?'

'The very next day.'

'What!'

'It's true. At dawn he and his men came for Leofwine and took him away. Hilda and I thought we'd never see him alive again. As for Elfric's fears, you can imagine.'

Elgiva could, only too well. 'What happened?'

'A few hours later the Vikings returned. Leofwine had taken them to the cave, but when they arrived, all they found was Hunfirth's body. It was cold. He must have died in the night. Brekka was gone.'

Elgiva digested the news.

'Where will he go, do you think?'

'South, probably, to try to reach Wessex or somewhere the Danes do not hold sway.'

'I wish him God speed.'

'And I.'

'Will the Vikings try to find him?'

'I don't think so. From what Leofwine said, they showed no interest in pursuit. They brought Hunfirth's body back for burial too.'

'Wulfrum let Leofwine bury his brother?'

'Yes. And he freed the rest of us. He sent me straight back to tending the remaining wounded from the battle.' Osgifu shook her head. 'I thought we were dead for sure that night we were caught returning from the forest. He is a strange one.'

'Strange indeed,' replied Elgiva, turning the story over in her mind. Wulfrum had shown mercy to an extent she could never have imagined.

'We thought you were dead at first. Then we learned you were shut up in this room. I begged to be allowed to see you but he refused, until now.'

'Oh, Gifu. I've been so afraid. I thought I would never see you again.'

Elgiva's tears spilled over now and ran down her cheeks. Then Osgifu's comforting arms were round her.

'Don't cry, child. You have been so brave. Your strength has given us all the will to go on.'

'I was terrified, Gifu.'

'No one would ever have known it.'

'I thought he would kill us all.'

'The Viking respects courage and you have shown that in good measure.' Osgifu smiled. 'I think it is why he has not exercised his power as he might have done. In truth, I expected a very different outcome to the events of the past few days. You must have made quite an impression.'

'I've paid for it since.' Elgiva dashed her tears away with the back of her hand. 'He has let me sweat in here, not knowing anything. He knew it would be almost as bad as a flogging.'

'The man is cunning.'

'He's a devious swine. I would give much to tell him so.'

Osgifu looked at her in surprise. 'Have you not seen him then since he locked you up?'

'No, only his guards. He means to teach me a lesson, you see.'

'Surely he will free you soon.'

Elgiva sighed, wishing rather than believing it might be so. The knowledge that he had freed the others long since made her continued punishment all the more pointed. This was not about helping an injured man, it was about defiance. He did not need to beat her bloody to let her know his power. A more subtle demonstration had worked just as well. Elgiva gritted her teeth.

'How I hate that man!'

'He has made his point. He can't keep you locked up much longer.'

However, it seemed Osgifu's prediction was wide of the mark for that day passed and the next and still Wulfrum made no move to release her or even to speak with her. Elgiva could only feel thankful for his continued absence. Though it was most irksome to be confined, it was infinitely preferable to the plan originally proposed for her future. Perhaps he had changed his mind now. Indeed, it looked as if he had forgotten all about her. She prayed it might be so.

The hope was short-lived for the following day he did come to the women's bower. Hearing the door open, Elgiva assumed it was Osgifu, but turned to see Wulfrum standing there. For several moments they faced each other in silence. He surveyed her critically. She was a little paler than usual but he put that down to her enforced stay within doors. Otherwise he could detect no ill effects from the experience. She was as beautiful as he remembered and, from the look in those glorious eyes, quite unrepentant. He was amused. Shutting Elgiva up might have restricted her freedom, but it had not cowed her spirit for her chin lifted in a manner that was becoming familiar to him. Would she plead with him now to set her free? He suspected not. Pleading was not something that came readily to her, at least not for herself, however eloquent she might be on behalf of others. If he knew anything about her, it was that she would cut out her own tongue before asking any favour of him. She was proud and she was brave and he was becoming hourly more reconciled to the thought of their wedding. Far from having changed his mind, she would have been unnerved to learn that recent events had but confirmed him in the decision. Unable to follow his thoughts, Elgiva grew restive under that keen scrutiny and it was she who broke the silence.

'There was something you wished to speak of, lord?'

'Indeed. I have had no chance before now, being occupied with other matters.'

'Such as the burial of the slain?'

He heard the ironic tone, but let it go. 'That was a part of it,' he acknowledged. 'However, 'tis done, and now other things take precedence.'

Elgiva threw him a cool quizzical look but ventured no comment and remained where she was, watching him cross the floor towards her. She had forgotten how tall he was, how powerful a presence.

'It is of our marriage I speak,' he said.

Some of the colour faded from her cheeks.

'Never tell me you had forgotten, my lady. Or perhaps you were hoping I had?'

She bit her lip but said nothing, for it was a most accurate shot.

'I regret to disappoint you, Elgiva. You and I wed on the morrow.'

The words hit her like a blow, but she recovered fast enough. 'I will not.'

'Your consent would be better. More dignified.'

'Do you intend to use force, then?'

'If I have to,' he returned mildly.

Amber eyes glared into cool blue, Elgiva the while much tempted to hit him and remove some of that infuriating self-assurance. Then she reflected that it wouldn't even dent the surface. His arrogance was as impenetrable as his armour.

'Do you think I would stoop to wed a Viking thief? I would rather die.'

Wulfrum held his temper. 'You are overproud, my lady, and pride goes before a fall.'

He drew closer. Elgiva took a step back and then could have kicked herself for it, seeing the mocking expression reassert itself. His gaze swept her from head to foot and he frowned.

'I would see you in something more festive for our wedding.'

She had donned her plainest gown in token of mourning and the sober brown shade was unadorned save for the girdle that rode her waist. Evidently it found little favour with him. Bridling under that keen scrutiny, Elgiva wondered if he thought she would don her finery in his honour. If so, he was sorely mistaken. She would not make herself attractive for him. Then she became aware that Wulfrum was looking beyond her to the chest by the far wall. Without further ado he crossed the room and threw back the lid, revealing the garments within. Seething, she watched as he lifted them out one by one, surveying them critically before tossing each one aside on the bed. Blue, green and mauve followed in swift succession until he came to the gold gown with the embroidered neck and sleeves.

'You will wear this on the morrow.'

'I am in mourning and therefore cannot.'

'Tomorrow you become the wife of an earl and you should be dressed as befits your rank.'

'I cannot forget the slain so soon.'

'I do not expect it,' he replied, 'but I shall expect you to wear this gown.'

'I won't.'

The blue gaze never left her but there was no shade of humour in it now.

'You will wear it, Elgiva, if I have to dress you myself.'

It was on the tip of her tongue to say that he wouldn't dare, but a second's reflection stopped the words there. She knew with certainty that he would make good the threat. Forcing back her fury, she returned his gaze.

'Is there anything else?'

'Aye, there is.'

Wulfrum drew her close. Elgiva stiffened. Amusement returned as he looked down into her face.

'You can fight me all you like, lady, but you will kiss me.'

'Why, you arrogant, conceited—'

The words were lost as his mouth closed over hers. Elgiva struggled, but there was no chance of escape and he took the kiss in his own good time.

'Let go of me! How dare you treat me like this?'

'I shall not let you go. As to what I dare…'

Elgiva's cheeks turned a deeper shade of pink for the warmth and the nearness of the man, the faint scent of leather and musk. Out of the corner of her eye she was more than ever aware of the bed, now strewn with her gowns. If he chose to force the issue she would never be able to hold him off, being well aware he was using only minimal effort to restrain her now.

He kissed her again, the pressure of his mouth forcing hers open. Thereafter the kiss grew gentle and lingering. Elgiva shivered, but her hands ceased to push him away. The thought returned: no man had ever kissed her like this. No man had ever caused that unsettling flicker of warmth deep inside her, either. When he eventually drew back, she saw him smile; all at once her response appalled her. This man was an enemy. That she should have yielded to his kiss made her sick with self-loathing. Worse, what had left her shattered was clearly a source of amusement to him.

'Please...'

'What would you have of me, lady?' His lips brushed her hair, her ear, her cheek.

In desperation Elgiva tore away from him. 'Nothing! I want nothing from you! I want no part of you. I loathe you.'

Wulfrum regarded her steadily but made no attempt to hold her. 'Now I had a very different impression a moment ago.'

'You imagined it, then.'

'You deceive yourself, Elgiva.'

'I do not.'

'Shall I prove it to you?'

'No! Get out!'

He laughed out loud. Dry mouthed and with beating heart, she watched him cross to the door.

'Until tomorrow, then, lady. I feel sure you will understand when I say you will remain confined until then.'

Incensed, Elgiva watched him go, looking round for something to throw. There was nothing immediately to hand. The nearest item was a wooden stool some feet away. By the time she had grabbed it he was gone, but she flung it anyway and with all the force she could muster. It hit the door with a crash that reverberated through the bower, but as the noise faded she could hear the unmistakable sound of his laughter.

Seeing Wulfrum enter the hall, Ironfist looked up quizzically. Halfdan followed his gaze and grinned.

'And how is the fair Saxon?' he demanded. 'Burning with impatience for her wedding day?'

Wulfrum returned him a wry smile. 'Burning with impatience to stick a sword in my guts.'

'Aye, she has spirit, that one,' said Ironfist.

'Spirit and beauty,' replied Halfdan. 'It will take some taming but you will bend her to your will—in time.'

He glanced across the hall to where Sweyn sat with a group of men and his tone grew more serious.

'Keep her close, Wulfrum. Sweyn is still smarting from losing her.'

'Then he should have taken more care. She is mine and I will guard her well.'

'See you do.' Halfdan threw another glance across the hall. 'There is no point in inviting trouble. When I leave, I will take Sweyn with me. We shall see if the lure of land and gold will turn his mind to other things.'

'It is a good plan,' said Ironfist.

Halfdan grinned. 'He will find Saxon maids aplenty to keep him occupied and turn his thoughts from this one.'

'Let us hope so.'

'You doubt it?'

'Some women are not easily forgotten.'

'Never tell me you're soft on the wench too?'

Ironfist threw him a speaking look. 'I am long past such foolishness, but I can see straight. The girl is fair. She draws men's eyes as a flame draws moths.'

'It is no crime to look, eh, Wulfrum?'

'No, my lord. They may look their fill.'

'But no touching?'

'Ordinarily I am not one to quarrel over a wench or two,' said Wulfrum, 'but this one I share with no man.'

Elgiva looked with loathing at the gold gown and every fibre of her being rebelled.

'How can I do this, Gifu? How can I wed that barbarian?'

'I think you have no choice.'

'There must be some way out of this.'

Elgiva paced the floor, cudgelling her brains for some means to prevent the disaster looming on the morrow. Osgifu's grey eyes were resigned.

'There is none.'

Something in the tone gave Elgiva pause and she stopped pacing, regarding her keenly. Her heart began to beat a little harder and she remembered an earlier conversation.

'Was this what you saw in the runes?' Seeing Osgifu remain silent, Elgiva swallowed hard. 'Was it? Answer me.'

'Yes.'

'It cannot be true. It cannot be.' Elgiva's eyes filled with tears. 'I will not wed the Viking. He will not take me as he has taken these lands. I must get away somehow, tonight, and go somewhere he will not find me.'

'There is nowhere to run, child. The Danish marauders are everywhere, and renegade Saxons too,' Osgifu replied. 'It is too perilous for a woman to be abroad unprotected. Even if you did escape, Wulfrum would send out men and dogs and he would find you. I think you would discover then the full weight of his wrath.'

Elgiva swallowed hard. It was the truth. She dreaded to think what Wulfrum might do if she tried it and yet the alternative seemed every way as bad.

'I cannot just submit! Shall I wed an enemy of my people? A pirate?'

'You have no choice but to submit. If you do not, he will use force.'

It was so precisely an echo of what Wulfrum had said that Elgiva shivered.

'Yes, and not against me, against those I should protect.'

'He said so?'

'As good as. He let it be known any disobedience on my part would result in others bearing the brunt of his anger.'

'He is clever and devious.'

'You said it.'

'I think they truly mean to stay this time,' Osgifu continued, 'not just to plunder and kill. They want the land.'

'Our land. Land they have no right to, that they slew Saxon people to get.'

'Aye, and will slay more to keep if they have to.'

Elgiva felt a sudden pang of guilt. Aylwin had been prepared to lay down his life for her and hers, but she had held him lightly. He had deserved better. In all likelihood he was dead of his wounds and lying in an unmarked woodland grave. Hot tears pricked her eyelids as the memories returned unbidden. She would have married Aylwin and tried to make him a good wife as her duty dictated. Now he was a fugitive and she was the prize of a conqueror.

In her mind's eye she could see Wulfrum's face again, with those piercing blue eyes and the mocking smile. The very thought was enough to stoke the fires of her anger. Did he really have the arrogance to think she would give herself to him? Then she remembered how big he was and how strong. He could take her whenever he wished. It occurred to her that he could already have done so, yet he had stayed his hand. Did he think that by making her his wife he would earn her gratitude? That she would submit meekly and tamely in his bed? Elgiva clenched her fists. She would see him in hell first, along with his entire accursed race.

'Do not torment yourself, child.' Osgifu's voice broke into her train of thought. 'It will serve no purpose.'

'I could not offer Aylwin my heart, Gifu. Yet he defended Ravenswood with his life.'

'He was a good man. Whether Wulfrum is another only time will tell.'

Elgiva stopped in her tracks. 'Wulfrum is a Viking, a pirate, a marauder. How can he be a good man?'

'I know not, but it seems to me that he is not like that other, Sweyn.'

Elgiva knew it was true. There was a streak of cruelty in the man that she had not found in Wulfrum or in his giant companion.

'Sweyn is evil,' she replied. 'Evil and brutal.'

'He desires you, it is plain.'

'I'd slit my own throat first.'

'As the wife of Wulfrum you will be beyond his reach. That one has the ear of Halfdan. Aye, and his favour too, as he has granted him the gift of land.'

'Stolen land.'

'But who is there now to make them give it back?'

Elgiva sighed, knowing the answer. For years Northumbria's rulers had been involved in petty disputes, Osbert north of the Tees and Ella in the south, each vying for the crown. The kingdom was ill prepared to withstand invasion, a situation the Vikings had exploited to the full. Now Osbert and Ella were dead and, since Mercia and East Anglia had fallen, there was nothing to stop the invading army. Northumbria was as good as theirs. They would never yield it up, nor would they return to their cold northern shores. Halfdan and his brothers would take what they wanted and reward their faithful earls with lands and serfs to work it. The Viking horde was there to stay.

'There is no escape, is there?' she said at last.

'No.'

'I'd rather be dead.'

'Then who would protect your people from the vengeance of the Vikings?' demanded Osgifu.

'It will make no difference to them whether I live or die.'

'It will make all the difference. As Wulfrum's wife you will have great influence.'

'I will have no influence.'

'Then you are not the woman I took you for.'

Elgiva stared at her, but Osgifu's gaze remained steadfast.

'The man is clearly besotted. You must use your power over him.'

'Besotted?' Elgiva gave a hollow laugh. 'Hardly.'

'I have seen the way he looks at you.'

'He looks at me with lust, that is all.'

'Then why does he take you to wife? He could have had you the day the Vikings took this place and then kept you as a concubine or handed you over to his men for a plaything. Instead he offers you a place of honour at his side.'

'Honour? You call it an honour?'

'In his view, aye. By doing so, he puts you beyond reach of all others, beyond danger. Consider the alternative.'

Elgiva lapsed into a confused and angry silence. Seeing it, the older woman pressed her point.

'This situation is not of your choosing or of your making, but you can turn it to advantage. You have beauty and wit. Use them.'

'You overestimate my powers, Gifu. Wulfrum will do as he wills.'

'A beautiful woman can make a man do as *she* wills. A clever one can make him think it was his idea.'

In spite of herself, Elgiva smiled. 'Truly you are cunning.'

'A woman must be cunning to survive. You will survive because you are strong. Aye, and brave too. You will do what must be done.'

Elgiva knew she was right. Now that Osric was dead and Aylwin a fugitive, it was her place to protect her people in so far as it lay within her power to do so. Just then she did not believe that amounted to much.

'And by that you mean I must marry Wulfrum on the morrow?'

'There is no other choice,' replied Osgifu.

CHAPTER SIX

THE CEREMONY was held outdoors in a forest glade hard by, the better to accommodate the number who would attend. Even if the church had been intact it could not have held so many. In the midst Father Willibald waited in resigned reluctance, surrounded by the warrior host. Unaware of the priest's discomfiture, the warriors talked and jested among themselves until the arrival of Wulfrum with Olaf Ironfist and Lord Halfdan. A cheer went up and the jesting increased. Wulfrum smiled, letting it wash over him, and cast a swift glance around. The priest, looking up at the three of them, swallowed hard and tried to conceal his nervousness. His gaze moved past them to the assembled Saxons whose presence the earl had likewise commanded, seeing in their expressions his own doubt and fear. Of the Lady Elgiva there was no sign.

'And the bride, my lord?' he asked diffidently.

'She is coming,' replied Wulfrum.

An imposing figure, he was dressed in a scarlet tunic of fine wool over blue leggings. A cloak of dyed red wool, embroidered at front and hem, was thrown over his shoulders and fastened by a silver dragon brooch. His shoes were made of good leather and by his side he wore a fine sword.

Halfdan and Ironfist were also attired in their best to do honour to their friend. They glanced once at Father Willibald and then ignored him, a state of affairs that suited him perfectly.

The minutes passed with still no sign of the bride and Halfdan exchanged glances with Ironfist, though he said nothing. Wulfrum felt a twinge of unease, but forced it down. It was, after all, a woman's privilege to keep her groom waiting on her wedding day. It occurred to him that Elgiva might consider flight, but, if so, she would soon have found it impossible: Ravenswood was well guarded and by his own men. A cat could not slip out unnoticed. No, this marriage would take place as planned. It was an important symbol, announcing that the Norsemen were there to stay and that they would ally themselves with Saxon blood. He knew too that if he intended to rule these people, it would be far better to show them that their lady was held in a position of respect. To see her demeaned as his whore would have added to existing resentments. In many ways it was a political move, though, if he were honest, not entirely. He did not deceive himself that Elgiva entertained any tender feelings on his account; given the chance, she might well drive a sword into his heart.

'Where is the wench? What keeps her?' demanded Halfdan.

Distracted from his thoughts, Wulfrum frowned. The assembled crowd was growing restless. If Elgiva was playing some petulant female trick, he would return to the hall and drag her forth himself. The flicker of doubt grew into a spark of annoyance. Would she dare to humiliate him before his men, before his overlord? By Odin's beard, if she tried it—

He never finished the thought, aware suddenly that the conversation around him had stopped and all eyes were drawn to the far edge of the glade. He turned and looked, then looked again, and all anger died in an instant. Elgiva, attended by Hilda and Osgifu, moved across the greensward towards him. For a moment he wondered if she were real or some sprite from the forest. Glancing sunlight caught her in its rays, enfolding her in a halo of light. Clad in the golden gown with her golden hair loose about her shoulders and restrained only by a circlet of flowers, she seemed some ethereal being, so graceful in her movements that she might have floated above the earth rather than walked on it.

'Thor's thunderbolts,' muttered Olaf Ironfist, 'but she is fair.'

Beside him Halfdan nodded. 'I'm starting to wonder if I wasn't too hasty in letting Wulfrum have the wench.'

Wulfrum forgot his anger and his doubt and felt in his heart the first stirring of pride that this Saxon maid was to be his wife, along with the knowledge that every man present wanted to be in his shoes.

Elgiva walked with unhurried step across the glade with head held high, looking neither to left nor right, giving no sign that she was aware of the attention focused on her. When she reached Wulfrum's side, she made a brief and graceful curtsy, meeting his gaze for a fleeting moment before he took her hand.

'You shine like the sun, my lady.'

There was no mistaking the admiration in his eyes, but Elgiva returned it with coolness.

'You are all kindness, lord.'

If he noted the ironic tone he gave no sign and led her forwards to the waiting priest. She concealed her surprise to see Father Willibald there, knowing that many of the Vikings had yet to embrace the Christian faith and worshipped their old gods. She realised she had no idea of Wulfrum's beliefs. Part of her had expected to endure a pagan ceremony, something that could never have been regarded as binding by the Saxon population. Had Wulfrum known that? One moment's reflection assured her that he had. This marriage was intended to be binding in every way. Her heart pounded. There was to be no escape.

The ceremony went without the least hitch. Contrary to all her hopes there was no timely interruption, no divine intervention, and no Saxon army to save her at the last moment. The words were spoken, the rings exchanged and the air was split by a rousing cheer from the assembled crowd as Wulfrum took his bride in his arms and sealed the moment with a kiss. Elgiva permitted that embrace but did not respond.

Wulfrum's lips brushed her hair as he whispered, 'You will kiss me, Elgiva. I shall hold you thus until you do.'

She knew it was no idle threat and had perforce to yield to a much longer and more intimate embrace. The roar of approval from the gathered crowd echoed through the forest and flocks of birds rose startled into the air. Wulfrum drew back a little and looked into her face, now a deeper shade of pink, and he smiled. Elgiva laid a hand on his breast.

'My lord, there is something I would ask.'

'Ask, my lady. I will refuse you nothing if it be reasonable and within my power to grant it.'

'It is that the graves of the Saxon slain should be blessed by the priest.'

He regarded her in silence and then nodded. 'Very well, it shall be done.'

Elgiva let out the breath she had been holding. It was a conciliatory gesture that would please her people and she suspected he knew it. It was part of the role he played, for all he was a Viking warlord and their conqueror still. She had no time for further reflection because Wulfrum's men pulled him away from her and she saw him raised shoulder high. Then strong arms swung her off her feet.

'By the breath of Odin, 'tis a woodland fairy after all!' exclaimed Halfdan.

'How so?' demanded Olaf Ironfist.

'See for yourself.'

He tossed her lightly to Ironfist, who caught her with ease.

'By the breath of Odin, you're right.'

Ironfist laughed and threw her up to sit on his shoulder, an arm about her knees, supporting her feet in one huge hand. Then, surrounded by the cheering throng, he carried her along beside her lord, back towards the hall for the feast. Elgiva was set on her feet before the door with Wulfrum beside her. He took her hand and led her across the stepped threshold to another rousing cheer. The bride had not stumbled and the auspices were good.

The feasting lasted all day and into the night, with songs and jests and tests of strength while the mead horns over-flowed. Many a health was drunk to the newly-wed couple, along with toasts to the gods. Elgiva watched it all with a growing sense of detachment, aided in part by the amount she had drunk. It was little enough in comparison to the men all around her, but, taken on a stomach almost empty, it went to her head quickly and added to a growing sense of unreality. From time to time she felt herself being watched and would look up to see Wulfrum's gaze resting on her. From the number of times his horn was replenished she had hopes he might drink himself insensible before the night was out, but to her growing dismay the mead seemed not to touch him. To be sure he laughed and joked with his men, but the blue eyes remained watchful for all that.

Elgiva felt only increasing panic and a desire to slip away and run. It was impossible. She would be caught very quickly and returned to her husband. Her husband! It was inconceivable that she wore his ring, symbol of the eternal bond between them, a bond that would be sealed this night when he took her to his bed. Her jaw tightened. If he thought she would yield up her body, as well, Wulfrum was much mistaken. A decidedly militant light appeared for a moment in the amber eyes before being swiftly veiled. When she looked up again it was to see Sweyn watching her from across the hall, a fleering smile on his lips. Elgiva returned the stare for a moment or two and then looked away. He was the least of her worries now. Besides, in a day or two he would be gone and she would never see him more. With any luck he would perish in the fighting to come.

These thoughts were interrupted by Osgifu, who now approached her chair. Behind her were Hilda and some of the other women.

'Come, my lady. It is time.'

Elgiva's stomach lurched and she closed her eyes to steady herself. The women would lead her to the bedchamber and prepare her for the arrival of her husband. *That's what I'll never stand,* she thought. *I'll never give myself to him.* Her fingers brushed the hilt of her belt knife and its touch reassured her. There was another way. She opened her eyes to see Wulfrum watching her and the sight of his mocking smile stiffened her spine like nothing else could. With every bit of self-possession remaining, she rose from the table, following her women to the stairs, accompanied by a loud cheer from the assembled throng.

When they reached the chamber the silence was almost deafening; the usual laughter and jesting that should have accompanied the bridal preparations were absent. The women said nothing and their demeanour was anything but joyful. Elgiva stood like a rock while they removed her girdle and unlaced her gown, drawing it off, and leaving her in her kirtle. Someone poured water into a basin so that she could bathe her hands and face. Then Osgifu removed the flowers from her hair and combed it out across her shoulders. Finally she was ready. At the side of the room the great bed waited. The women looked from it to her. Elgiva remained where she was.

'My lady, you must—'

'I must nothing. Now leave me.'

The women exchanged uncertain glances, but Osgifu ushered them to the door. As it opened to allow their departure, it also admitted a great wave of noise from the hall below, a mighty cheer from the warrior host as Halfdan and half-a-dozen others hoisted Wulfrum on to their shoulders and carried him to the staircase led by Olaf Ironfist with a lighted torch. When they reached the chamber they set their burden down with much laughter and many a ribald jest. Then their attention moved from Wulfrum to his bride, their eyes burning with lust as they feasted them on the woman before them. The thin kirtle did little to conceal the lines of her body, a form whose hinted curves seemed made for a man's touch. Mentally each gaze stripped the fabric away, leaving her naked save for the mane of gold hair that flowed down her back. Elgiva forced herself to remain still, to fight down the terror knotting her gut. A sheen of perspiration started on her skin. She knew now how a cornered deer felt before a pack of wolves.

As if he had divined her thought, Halfdan spoke. 'Oho, beware, my lady! Here's a wolf will gobble you up!'

''Tis a tender morsel,' agreed Ironfist, grinning.

'We shall look to see the proof of his feasting.' Halfdan clapped Wulfrum on the shoulder.

Elgiva felt her heartbeat quicken, but before anyone could say more Wulfrum turned towards them.

'The wolf feasts tonight, but he will do so at his leisure and in private.' He nodded to the door.

With mock grumbling and some final crude injunctions the men turned and began to troop out. Those too slow to suit him were forcibly ejected. Weak with relief to see them go, Elgiva watched him bar the door. However, the relief was short lived, for now he turned and all his attention was on her.

'I am not minded to be disturbed this night,' he said, 'no matter what the pretext.'

Elgiva said nothing, her gut knotting further as he divested himself of his cloak and unbuckled his sword belt. Then the tunic joined the cloak. One look at those broad shoulders gave her little hope of holding him off by force. The lamplight gleamed softly on his silver arm rings and revealed the lines of old scars on his flesh, several on his upper arms and a deeper one across his ribs. Seeing that she did not move, Wulfrum smiled.

'That kirtle becomes you well, my lady, but I am curious to know what lies beneath.'

'So the wolf can feast?'

'Something like that.'

'I am not minded to satisfy your curiosity, Viking.'

'Say you so?'

'Do you think I would give myself to one who has slaughtered my kin and enslaved my people?'

'Slaughtered? It seems to me that the menfolk of this hall put up a strong resistance. They died honourably with swords in their hands as men should. As for the serfs, they will work these lands as they did before, albeit for a new master.' He paused. 'And you, my lady, you too will yield.'

Elgiva felt warm colour flood her face but her eyes met and held his. 'I will never yield.' She took a deep breath. 'I will not lie with you.'

'You will lie with me tonight and every night.' He drew closer, pausing only when he was within arm's reach. 'Now, take off that kirtle.'

Elgiva's eyes flashed and he saw her chin come up. He raised an eyebrow.

'Must I do it for you?'

She bit back defiant words. He would do as he threatened and she had no way to stop him. Her eyes sought for some means of escape, but the window was shuttered fast and the door barred. Worse, she would have to pass him to reach it.

'I'm waiting, Elgiva.'

'How I hate you!'

'It will make our marriage the more interesting. Take off the kirtle.'

'I will not.'

Wulfrum bent on her such a look that she quaked. As she retreated, her leg brushed the edge of the chair where her gown and girdle lay discarded. She remembered the knife and, turning, grabbed it, drawing it from the sheath and bringing it up in front of her. Wulfrum saw the glint of the blade and grabbed her wrist, arresting the progress of the point. For a few moments it wavered between them. He increased his grip and heard her gasp. The blade clattered to the floor.

'For you or for me?' he demanded.

'For me.'

'You will not escape me so, Elgiva. You belong to me now and I will keep safe what is mine.'

'I am not yours, Viking!'

'Not yet,' he agreed.

Before she guessed his intent, he lifted her bodily off the floor and strode to the bed, tossing her on to the furs. Elgiva scrambled away, retreating until her back was to the wall, watching in horrified fascination as he unfastened his leggings and let them fall. Then he came on. She drew in a sharp breath. Having had a brother, she was no stranger to the male body, but every inch of that lithe and muscled form spoke of a warrior's strength. Struggling to her feet, she launched herself off the end of the bed and then uttered a shriek of despair as Wulfrum's arm locked fast about her waist. With insulting ease he tossed her down on to the fur coverlet. Strong hands grabbed the hem of her kirtle, ripping it upwards in one fluid movement.

The thin fabric parted to the neck. Elgiva twisted away and struggled to her knees. For a moment they faced each other and her cheeks flamed as the Viking's insolent gaze raked her from head to toe. Then he grinned and the glint in those blue eyes became dangerous.

Again she backed away and again her back met the wall. Wulfrum came on, seizing her arms, drawing her towards him. Somehow she got a hand free and hit him hard across the cheek twice. He laughed, catching her wrist before she could get in a third blow, and flung her backwards. Elgiva turned her head and bit him, the nails of her free hand raking his shoulder, raising scarlet welts on his flesh. It was a brief victory; in seconds he had hold of both her wrists and imprisoned them above her head. Cursing him, Elgiva writhed and kicked out, but he held her easily now, forcing her down into the furs with the weight of his body. With a sense of panic she felt the hardness of his manhood against her.

'You bastard! You cur! Let *go* of me!'

'No, my lady, I shall not do that.' His hand travelled down to her waist, over the curve of her hip, down her thigh in a long lingering caress. He felt her kick out again, try to raise her knee, and laughed softly.

'None of your tricks will work, Elgiva.'

'Give me a sword and I'll geld you like a steer!'

'Then I should fail in my duty as a husband, and I do not mean to fail.'

Before she could reply his mouth closed over hers in a kiss that was burning and insistent while his hand continued its exploration of her body. Elgiva tasted the sweet mead on his breath, breathed in the musky scent of his skin as he took the kiss at leisure. Then he drew back a little, letting his gaze travel the length of her, taking in every curve of breast and waist and thigh, the long slim legs and dainty feet. In the lamplight her flesh seemed golden.

'Truly, lady, you are beautiful.'

Elgiva's angry reply was lost in a thunderous banging that shook the chamber door and her heart leapt in terror to hear Halfdan's voice.

'Come, Wulfrum! Have you done your duty to your wife?'

'Odin's sacred ravens,' bellowed Ironfist, 'he's had long enough to do it half a dozen times!'

A roar of agreement followed from those without the door. Wulfrum grinned as he looked into Elgiva's bewildered face.

'They seek proof of our union, my lady.'

For a moment her mind was blank. Then, as she recalled the earlier banter, her cheeks flamed. The banging continued and the voices without became more insistent. The door shook on its hinges. A little more and the entire Viking war host would be witness to their wedding night. Elgiva swallowed hard and closed her eyes. Suddenly she felt Wulfrum's weight shift and the hold slackened on her wrists. When she looked again, it was to see him retrieve the fallen knife. In horrified fascination she saw him draw the blade across his arm and then the welling beads of blood as he gathered up the torn kirtle and opened it out before wiping the cloth across the wound.

Throwing a speaking look at his wife, he crossed the room and unbarred the door, opening it sufficiently to thrust the garment out to the waiting hands. For a moment there was silence, then a rousing cheer. Without waiting for more, Wulfrum slammed and barred the door again, letting out a long breath. Then he looked at Elgiva, who was kneeling on the bed, golden hair spilling wildly round her shoulders and over the pelt she was using to shield her nakedness. Her amber eyes were wide, her face ashen. Presently the noise outside diminished and retreating footsteps announced the departure of the intruders. Elgiva drew a ragged breath. They were going. Once again she became aware of Wulfrum. For a long moment their eyes met and she saw him smile. Then he became aware of the blood trickling down his arm and crossed to the basin to retrieve a cloth. She took a deep breath.

'You'd better let me bind that.'

'It's a scratch, no more.'

Elgiva tucked the fur around her and quit the bed to join him at the basin. She poured a little water and, taking the cloth from him, wiped away the blood. As he had said, the cut was not deep, but it bled profusely nevertheless.

Wulfrum watched with quiet amusement, but stood quite still while she bathed the wound and stanched the bleeding enough for her to bind it. He said nothing while she worked, but his eyes never left her. Elgiva kept her eyes on the improvised bandage, hoping he would not notice how her hands shook. When she had finished, he glanced at her handiwork and nodded.

'It is well.' He turned her to face him. 'Now, where were we?'

Elgiva shivered as his fingers brushed her shoulders and strayed across the tops of her breast, ill concealed by the fur pelt. Then his hand closed about her arm and he drew her back to the bed. This time she did not struggle, knowing there was little point. She knew his strength and hers could never match it. She lay beside him, felt him undo the pelt and then his weight as he leaned across her. He would take her now. It was his right. Elgiva closed her eyes and turned her head away. It would soon be over.

Wulfrum's lips seeking hers brushed her cheek instead. He could feel the tension in her body, even though she no longer fought him. Her face was turned away from his, but there was no mistaking the expression of fear and reluctance. He frowned.

'Look at me, Elgiva.'

Slowly she turned towards him and he could see tears welling in her eyes. It was the first time he had ever seen her afraid. Even when Sweyn wanted to kill her she had radiated courage. Now it seemed her store was exhausted. He was not altogether surprised, given the events of the past few days. She had shown greater resilience and determination than any woman he had ever known. With a gentle hand he smoothed the hair from her face.

'You need not be afraid of me, Elgiva. I will not hurt you.'

She remained silent, but the amber eyes registered confusion. He thought ruefully that, had it not been for Lord Halfdan's untimely interruption, he would have taken her. Ironic that his men had prevented the very deed they applauded. It was a good thing they were drunk enough to accept the proof he gave them. Even if they had been sober, it would have been inconceivable to them that he could be in bed with a beautiful naked woman and not possess her immediately and by any necessary means. Looking at the body lying next to his, he thought they had a point.

Seeing Wulfrum's smile Elgiva felt her confusion grow for she could not fathom his thought. Was he trying to lull her into a sense of false security, only to pounce when her defences were down? It would be just like him. He had no shame. Like all his vile race, he took what he wanted without regard to others. He had married her because he willed it, because she was as much a prize as these lands and this hall. As a captive her views had not been considered. The only choice had been to wed him or take Sweyn. Thinking of her likely treatment at those hands, Elgiva shuddered. She might not have survived the revenge he would have exacted. This marriage to Wulfrum had saved her from that fate. In his arms lay her safety. His men would not touch her and Halfdan's were leaving on the morrow, Sweyn with them. She would not be sorry to see them go. They would find other lands to conquer, other plunder to seize, other captives to take, but Wulfrum would not be with them. He was here and here to stay and nothing now could ever be the same.

Fatigue washed over her, along with the soporific effects of the mead, and Elgiva felt her eyelids grow heavy. She fought it. She must not relax her guard. However, pressed close to Wulfrum, the warmth of his flesh beneath the coverlets added to her drowsiness and her tired body relaxed of its own volition. Her eyelids drooped again, fluttered once and then closed.

Wulfrum glanced down, stroking back wisps of golden hair from her cheek. She stirred slightly, but did not wake, unaware of the gaze that drank in every line of her face. Truly, he thought, she was beautiful. And she was his, nominally anyway. The rest would come. She would yield as he knew she must. A body like that was made for lovemaking. Lightly he stroked the warm skin of her breasts, tracing a path down the curve of her waist and the gentle flare of her hip, breathing in her scent. It was powerfully erotic. However, he resisted the temptation to wake her. After all, he had time enough now.

CHAPTER SEVEN

ELGIVA awoke to broad daylight. For a few confused seconds she could not remember where she was. Then memory flooded back and with it shame. Beside her lay the man who was her husband now. Wulfrum slept on and for a moment or two she watched. He was lying on his back, one arm thrown behind his head in an attitude that seemed both abandoned and vulnerable. Her gaze travelled from the dark tousled hair to his face, exploring its chiselled lines, then moving on to the lips and chin and thence to his naked torso where the marks of her nails showed a harsh red. The welts looked painful, but she felt no remorse. It occurred to her as she watched him sleep that anyone with a blade could kill him where he lay, driving the point between his ribs and thrusting it in to the hilt. It would be no more than he deserved. Even as the thought formed itself, she rejected it—she could never kill a man in cold blood. Besides, had he not spared her from dire humiliation last night? Aye, and rape too. Why had he? It was his right to take her and yet he had waived that right. Truly the man was an enigma: on the one hand, a fearsome warrior, and, on the other, capable of tenderness and compassion. He intrigued even while he repelled.

Throwing the coverlet aside, she eased herself to the edge of the bed but was stopped short. Her hair was partly trapped beneath the weight of his body. With great care she eased it away. Wulfrum stirred, but did not wake. Elgiva drew in a deep breath as the strands came free. Cautiously she climbed out of bed, glancing around for her kirtle. Then she remembered what had become of it and her cheeks grew hot. Seizing a pelt from the bed, she wrapped it around herself and tiptoed to the window, peeping through a crack in the shutter. Nothing stirred, either in the courtyard or the meadow beyond the palisade where the majority of Halfdan's force was encamped. No doubt many would feel like death this morning after the vast quantities of mead and ale they had consumed. She turned back into the room, thinking to retrieve her gown. It would not be so comfortable without the kirtle beneath, but there was no alternative unless she wished to leave the chamber clad only in a wolf pelt. The rest of her garments were in the chest in her bower.

Looking round the room, she saw the clothing that Wulfrum had discarded the previous night and with it his sword. Elgiva moved towards it, her bare feet making no sound on the wooden floor. With care she lifted the heavy blade from its resting place and studied the hilt in curiosity. It was made of iron, gilded, and bound with copper wire, the pommel set with red jasper. Closing her hand round the hilt, she drew the blade part way from its scabbard. It was a fine weapon and beautifully wrought— a true melding of iron and steel. Where the hammer had fallen on the metal, it had left wondrous patterns like wreaths of frozen breath, fantastic shapes that seemed to change with the light. Down the centre were hammered grooves to channel the blood. She had no need to try the edge of the blade to know it was keen. She would have wagered too, that it was finely balanced. In truth, it was a warrior's weapon.

'Were you planning to use that, Elgiva?'

She spun round to see Wulfrum watching her from the bed. Recovering her self-possession, she slid the blade back into the scabbard.

'No. You are more use to me alive. All the same, it is a beautiful sword.'

'It is called Dragon Tooth.'

'An apt name.' Elgiva laid the weapon back where she had found it.

'So it is,' he agreed. 'It was wrought by a smith of great renown among my people. He made it for Lord Ragnar, and he gave it to me.'

'A handsome gift. He must have favoured you highly.'

'He was like a father to me.'

Elgiva looked at the sheathed blade and thence at Wulfrum. The blue gaze that met hers was implacable. Elgiva shivered. Suddenly a lot of things had become clearer.

'And when King Ella slew Ragnar, you sought to avenge his death.'

'Of course. I swore the blood oath along with his sons. With my sword brothers. It was a matter of honour.'

'A matter of honour to slay King Ella, perhaps,' replied Elgiva, 'but to slaughter the innocent too?'

'Kings are not as ordinary men. The decisions they make fall on all their subjects for good or ill. When Ella threw Ragnar into the snake pit, he not only murdered a great warrior he added grave injury to that insult—a warrior must die with a sword in his hand or he cannot enter Valhalla. Ella denied him that right and in so doing he sealed his own fate and that of his kingdom.'

Elgiva bit her lip, knowing there was more than a grain of truth in his words. Besides, for years Northumbria's rulers had been involved in petty disputes. Had they only joined forces, the Vikings might have been repelled. As it was, the land was overrun and its people conquered. Guessing the trend of her thoughts, Wulfrum frowned.

'There is no use repining. What's done is done.'

'Indeed, but do not expect a conquered people to enjoy their situation.'

'I do not, but I expect to be obeyed.' Wulfrum's voice was quiet, but every word carried weight. 'The conquered must bend to the yoke.'

'Aye, my lord, for who would dare do other?' The tone dripped sarcasm.

'I think you are not conquered, lady.'

Elgiva glared at him. Undismayed, he let his gaze travel over her appreciatively. The pelt she had wrapped about her left her arms and shoulders bare and stopped short mid-thigh, revealing a shapely pair of legs, and he was reminded of those other more intimate places beneath. He resisted the temptation.

'Come, do not deny it.'

'Whatever you say, my lord.'

'The man who would be your lord, Elgiva. Only I think another stands between.'

Genuinely puzzled, she could only stare at him.

'Don't pretend you don't understand. I refer to your former betrothed.'

'Aylwin?'

'He.'

'How can he stand between, my lord? He is gone.'

'And yet you have not forgotten him.'

'No. How could I?'

'Then you were fond of him.'

'He was a good man. I respected him.'

'More than that, I think.'

Elgiva began to feel uneasy, wondering at the tenor of his questions.

'He was a friend of my father's. Since his death, Lord Aylwin considered it his duty to help our family.'

'Indeed. And what of your brother?'

'He died in a hunting accident two months ago.'

'And yet the neglect I see around this estate goes back further.'

'Osric had no interest in anything save his hawks and his hounds.' She hesitated. 'You have seen how things are at Ravenswood. I could not bear to see it so neglected. The only way to change things was to marry a man who would restore the place to what it was when my father was alive.'

He heard the sadness in her voice and understood. He too knew what it was to lose a father. Yet her brother must have been a wastrel indeed, to let so fair an estate fall into rack and ruin. In that moment he had an insight into her predicament and knew it would have been hard on a woman alone.

'So after your brother's death you were left alone.'

'Save for Osric's sons,' she replied. 'The children whom Sweyn would have murdered.' The contempt was clear, but he could understand it.

'Did your brother make no attempt to find a husband for you?'

'No.' She did not qualify it, hoping yet to keep the conversation away from Aylwin. 'I told you, he had no interest in the matter.'

'Very remiss of him.'

Elgiva felt her blood race, more than ever aware of that searching blue gaze. Why should he care about her relationship with Aylwin?

'A woman alone would find herself in an unenviable position,' he went on. 'Particularly a beautiful woman with wealth and land.'

'I did not choose the circumstances.'

'No. What woman would?' He paused. 'You would seem to have been fortunate in your friends.'

'As you say, lord.'

'But this Aylwin was much more than a friend, was he not?' The blue gaze grew warmer. 'You loved him, didn't you?'

He saw the momentary flicker of surprise on her face and knew a moment's triumph. His guess had been right, then. Her reluctance for him stemmed from her love for another.

'Some marriages are made for love, my lord,' she replied, 'but precious few.'

The irony was pointed and his jaw tightened in response.

'True,' he replied. 'And yet that has never been grounds for a wife to deny her husband.'

'You think I denied you because I loved Aylwin?' Elgiva wanted to laugh, but it caught in her throat like a sob.

'Is it not so?'

She shook her head, unable and unwilling to explain. Wulfrum smiled grimly.

'Then let us put it to the test.'

Without warning, he scooped her up and carried her to the bed, spilling her on to the coverlet and pinning her there with the weight of his body, clamping her wrists in strong hands. For a moment he was silent and Elgiva remained quite still, waiting, praying, striving to keep her breathing even, to ignore the pleasurable warmth along the length of her skin. It seemed as if every part of their bodies touched. If he pressed his advantage now, she could not stop him. For a fleeting second she wasn't even sure she would try. Appalled, she pulled herself up abruptly. He was the enemy. There could be no warmth between them.

Unable to follow the thoughts behind the smooth brow, Wulfrum frowned. For all that they afforded pleasure, women were subtle and devious creatures, not to be trusted like men. Elgiva's golden beauty made her more dangerous than most. He knew that she had told him some of the truth, but he was not naïve enough to think she had told him everything. However, it answered some of the questions that had been puzzling him in the past few days. He would discover the rest by and by. In the meantime he was in a highly desirable position.

Elgiva saw his expression change and tensed beneath him, putting up a token resistance to the kiss he took next. His mouth on hers was gentle, but it would not be denied, forcing hers open, demanding her response. It seemed to go on for a long time. Then he drew back a little, looking into her face.

'Give yourself to me, Elgiva.' The tone was more a plea than a demand, his voice husky with desire. Her body tensed further. Seeing her expression, he masked disappointment with mockery. 'No? I thought not.'

She met his gaze and tried to ignore the dangerous thumping of her heart.

'I will never give myself to you.'

The blue eyes burned. 'Did you give yourself to Aylwin?'

For a moment she was thrown. If she hadn't known better, she would have thought he was jealous. It was tempting to lie, to tell him she had belonged to his enemy, but somehow she couldn't quite bring herself to do it.

'No.'

'He was a laggard, then.'

'He showed restraint out of respect. I cannot expect you to understand.'

'I understand, all right—you didn't want to bed him.'

Her cheeks grew warm, partly for the accuracy of that shot and partly for the assurance with which it was delivered.

'Come, admit it.'

'I admit nothing except that I loathe you,' she retorted.

If she expected him to become enraged, she was mistaken.

'No, you don't.' He smiled and reached out, taking a lock of her hair between his fingers, testing its softness. 'And you will come.'

Her jaw tightened. Did this arrogant barbarian think she would fall into his arms just because he willed it?

'You are thinking you will never do that, isn't it so?'

The blush on her cheeks was sufficient answer and his smile widened.

'Never is a long time, Elgiva, and time is all on my side.'

Then she felt his weight shift and she was no longer

pinned. In trembling relief she massaged her bruised wrists and watched him leave the bed to cross the floor and retrieve her gown. Then he tossed it to her. She caught it awkwardly.

'Put it on.' He saw the fleeting expression of surprise in the amber eyes. 'Yes, I'm letting you go—for now.'

Nothing loath, Elgiva rose and struggled into the gown, conscious the while of his watchful gaze, but she could think of nothing to say. Then, having dressed, she moved to the door. It was still closed and the wooden bar heavy and awkward. As she struggled to lift it, Wulfrum moved. Two large hands covered hers. Elgiva froze. Had he changed his mind? She looked up at him to find out. The mocking smile was back, but he lifted the heavy bar. Weak with relief, Elgiva swallowed hard. However, he held the door closed a moment longer.

'I will give instruction for your things to be moved in here.'

'I have my own bower.'

'Henceforth you will share this room with me,' he replied. 'Love me or loathe me, you will discover how real this marriage is going to be.' The tone was soft enough, but utterly implacable. Unable to withstand his gaze longer, Elgiva looked away. Wulfrum smiled. Then, to her unspeakable relief, he opened the door and let her pass.

Elgiva made her way back to her bower and sank weak-kneed and shaking on to her bed. The tears she had been holding back spilled over and fell unchecked, all the fears and tensions of the last week pouring out in great racking sobs. She cried for the loss of her kin and her home and for the knowledge of a past life that could never be

regained. She cried for a long time. Osgifu, peeping in unnoticed, saw her and retreated again to let her have her cry
out. The grieving was long overdue.

When it was over, she brought hot water and helped her
mistress wash away the scent of the bedroom. Then she
helped her to dress again in a clean kirtle and the blue
gown. She combed out the golden hair and braided it
down Elgiva's back in a neat and sober plait. When she
was done, it seemed to her that no trace remained of the
frightened girl at the end of her tether and that in her place
was a poised and lovely woman.

By now life was stirring in the hall and Elgiva had no
wish to meet any of the Viking war band. She slipped out
and, after checking that the coast was clear, went to the
stables where her bay mare was stalled. Hearing her
footstep, the horse whinnied softly, turning her elegant
head to look at the approaching figure. Her soft muzzle
snuffled the proffered palm and Elgiva wished she could
have found an apple to bring. She stroked the glossy neck
and looked the animal over with an expert eye, but to her
relief the horse was unscathed by recent events. A look
around the stables made it clear they all were. It was
evident the Vikings held livestock too dear for indiscrimi-
nate slaughter. The mare's bridle still hung on the peg at
the stall's entrance and for a moment Elgiva was swept
with longing to get out of Ravenswood, to ride away from
everyone and everything. Another moment's reflection
assured her it would never be permitted. She might be
Wulfrum's wife now, but she was a captive for all that and
would not be allowed out of sight. The war band would
leave soon and Ravenswood would be in Wulfrum's

hands, as would she. He would certainly never permit her to ride and so provide the means for her escape. Elgiva sighed. The horse was a symbol of the freedom she had lost and would never have again. Ravenswood was no longer her home, it was her prison and she shackled irrevocably to her gaoler. Nothing could change that now except death. In that bleak moment it seemed in many ways preferable to the future that awaited her. Then she remembered Osgifu's words and knew she could not abandon her people. That dark future beneath the Viking heel was theirs too; somehow she and they must dredge up whatever remained of courage and resilience and find the means to face it. The old days were over. Sad at heart, she gave the horse a final pat and reluctantly quit the stall.

As she left the stables, she became aware of other people all moving in solemn procession towards the burying ground. For a moment her heart misgave her and she wondered who else was dead. Then she remembered. Wulfrum had promised that the Saxon graves might be blessed. Fear was overlaid by relief and a measure of surprise. He had kept his word. Though his men were everywhere in evidence, they made no attempt to interfere. She noticed Sweyn in the background. He gave her a sardonic smile. Elgiva ignored it and looked away, focusing her mind instead on the priest and the words of the blessing.

Standing in the midst of the crowd, she became aware of the man next to her. He seemed familiar, but it was hard to see his face for he wore a hood that concealed his features in its shadow. Then he turned just for a moment and she started. Brekka!

She stared at him aghast. 'What are you doing here?'

'I had to speak with you, my lady.'

'Why?'

'Lord Aylwin sent me.'

Elgiva paled and for a moment thought she might faint. With a severe effort she regained her self-control.

'Aylwin lives?'

'Aye, he lives.'

'Where is he?'

'In the forest with those of our warriors who survived the battle.'

'Is he well?'

'Well enough, though his wounds are not completely healed.' Brekka paused. 'He bade me tell you to be of good cheer and to say that he will come for you.'

Elgiva drew in a sharp breath. 'Brekka, he must not. The Vikings will kill him if they catch him.'

'They will not catch him. When he is recovered, he will gather a force to retake Ravenswood.'

She stared at him in consternation. 'It is madness. It will but lead to more bloodshed.'

'That is unavoidable, my lady.'

'Tell him he must not do this thing. Tell him to get away, far away—Wessex, perhaps. Anywhere the Vikings hold no sway.'

'I will tell him what you say, my lady, but I think he will not heed it.'

After that they spoke no more, being unwilling to draw the attention of the Viking guards. However, Elgiva's mind was in turmoil. Aylwin was alive. He had survived against all the odds. The news made her glad and at the same time much disquieted. He would not lightly relinquish what had been his, but this plan was madness. He had too few men.

Surely he must see that. She prayed he would heed her message and go before Wulfrum found out. She shivered, not wanting to contemplate the thought. She was married to the Viking earl and he would keep her. He had made that plain enough. Plain too, what would happen if she disobeyed him again. If he thought for a moment that she plotted his overthrow with her former betrothed, his wrath would be terrible indeed. She had meant it when she said there had been enough bloodshed. Pray God Aylwin saw sense. She could not speak of this to Wulfrum—to do so would be to betray her own people. However, it sat ill with her to deceive him, though she could not have said precisely why.

Halfdan's war band left the next day and Sweyn with them. Elgiva watched him go with a certain sense of relief, for soon he would be far away and she would never see him more. Besides, there were other things on her mind quite apart from Aylwin—Wulfrum had let it be known that he would decide on the fate of the Saxon prisoners taken in the forest. Suddenly she wondered if her optimism had not been misplaced. Would he really kill them, or exact some other fearful penalty? There was no way of knowing.

At midday the prisoners were dragged in their chains to stand before him on the greensward outside the great hall. Having been chained in the open for several days, prey to the elements and fed on scraps, all were filthy and ragged and fearful now for their lives. Wulfrum had given them time to ponder their fate, time for their defiance to leach away. Now he had their full attention. He surveyed them

keenly, flanked by two of his most trusted warriors, Ida
and Ceolnoth. Behind him the rest of his men waited in
silence, flanking the fearful Saxon villagers who had been
rounded up to watch the punishment. Off to one side stood
a brazier full of hot coals in which irons were heating.
Beside it was a large wooden block where stood Olaf
Ironfist, leaning on the handle of a great axe. From time
to time the prisoners eyed him with distinct unease.

Elgiva slipped out of the bower and along the side of
the hall unnoticed, coming to a halt on the leading fringe
of the Danish group. She could see her husband quite
clearly, but his face was impassive and it was impossible
to tell what was in his mind. Then he turned and said
something to Ida. As he did so, she saw him look beyond
the man to the place where she was standing. Her heart
beat faster. Would he command her to leave, tell her this
was men's business, that she had no place or right here?
However, Wulfrum said nothing, turning back to the prisoners. Elgiva moved closer. Then she heard him speak
again, this time to Ironfist.

'These are all the men who were taken in the forest?'

'Aye, my lord. Cowardly dogs all that fled after the
battle.'

'Indeed.' Wulfrum let his eyes rest on them. 'They will
learn that there is no escape. This land and its people
belong to me now and I will guard well what is mine.'

Elgiva shivered, recalling how he had used the words
to her on another occasion. Their import was the same, but
the tone was grimmer by far.

'The penalty is clear enough for slaves who run: the
loss of a foot or the cutting of the hamstrings.'

The prisoners shifted in their chains, looking with horrified understanding at the brazier and the guards who flanked it, then at Ironfist. Elgiva drew in a sharp breath, shooting a fearful glance at Wulfrum as the implications sank in. Surely he could not really be going to do this. It was inconceivable. With thumping heart she moved forwards. For a moment his glance flicked towards her but the handsome face remained stern and he made no other acknowledgement of her presence.

'Bring forwards the first prisoner.'

Elgiva watched appalled as the guards moved to obey, seizing the nearest man, a serf called Drem, who, panic stricken, began to struggle. Several heavy cuffs about the head subdued him while they unfastened the length of chain that joined him to the others. Then he was dragged forwards and thrown at Wulfrum's feet. The earl glanced down a moment and then turned to Elgiva.

'Well, my lady, what is it to be? Shall we hack off a foot or have the varlet hamstrung?'

'Have mercy, lord, I beg you.' Elgiva fought back tears. 'Do not maim these men.'

'It is the standard punishment. They tried to escape.'

'Surely there can be no blame in that. The battle was lost, the place overrun. Who could think of aught at such a time beyond the need to survive?'

Wulfrum's face was expressionless as he looked down into hers. For the hundredth time, Elgiva found herself wishing she might know what he was thinking. Seeing he did not immediately brush her aside, she pressed her case.

'You said the slaughter was over, my lord. That you had need of every able-bodied man available. Does it make sense to cripple these? Spare them, and they will serve you well.'

At her feet Drem hung on her words, ashen faced. Then both of them turned to Wulfrum, though in truth he saw only one. Elgiva was trembling now, her beautiful eyes pleading.

'Show mercy, lord.'

'Leniency may encourage further transgressions. Would you have me show weakness to these people?'

'Mercy is not weakness. All here know you are the lord of this domain and its people and that your will is law. The matter is now beyond dispute. What purpose will be served by fuelling their hatred and their fear? Give them this chance, I beg you.'

Wulfrum appeared to meditate the matter. Beside him Elgiva bit her lip, heart pounding in her breast. Would he heed her at all? The wretch at her feet closed his eyes.

'Very well, then. Since it is your wish I show mercy, it shall be so.' He turned to the guards. 'Henceforth these prisoners shall wear the iron collar of the slave as a reminder of where their duty lies. In addition, each man will receive ten lashes. Carry out the punishment.'

Elgiva let out the breath she had been holding. All around her she heard a similar exhalation and the tension eased as the watching Saxons gave silent thanks for the deliverance of the prisoners. A flogging was a painful reminder of the new order, but Wulfrum had let them off lightly and everyone knew it. The first glimmer of hope awakened in their hearts that perhaps the worst was truly over. In silence they watched as each of the prisoners was forced to kneel by the wooden block while the iron collar was fastened around his neck and then closed with a hot rivet. Elgiva had no desire to witness their humiliation and would have quitted the scene then, but Wulfrum's hand closed round her arm.

'You will stay, my lady, and watch the sentence carried out.'

Swallowing hard, she looked up at him, but his expression permitted no further parley and she knew she must obey. Her heart filled with pity for the men beneath the lash, but she also knew that Wulfrum had shown great forbearance in this punishment. Even so, as the strokes were counted, Elgiva had to bite her lip to fight down the nausea she felt. Only with an effort could she prevent herself from flinching at each blow. However, she knew it was nothing to the way she would have been feeling now if he had followed his first thought.

Eventually it was over and the gathered crowd began to disperse. Elgiva would have left then, but Wulfrum held her beside him, seemingly in no hurry to let her go, watching his men break off into smaller groups while the serfs returned to their allotted tasks. From the buzz of conversation it seemed that recent events were much under discussion. Elgiva turned to look at her husband.

'Thank you for sparing those men.'

'No thanks are necessary,' he replied. 'I have need of them and now they will all live to serve me well.'

Elgiva caught the gleam in his eye and a suspicion began to form in her mind.

'You never had any intention of doing anything other than flogging them, did you?'

'No.' Wulfrum smiled. 'But it was important that they believed otherwise.'

Elgiva stared at him as the extent of the plan became apparent. 'You knew I would plead for them too, didn't you?'

'I thought you would try to intercede,' he acknowledged, 'and you did. Most eloquently, I might add.'

For a moment she was speechless before the sheer brazen effrontery of the man. Then anger replaced disbelief and she hit him hard.

'You let me think you were really going to maim those men. You let me make a fool of myself.'

Wulfrum caught her wrist before she could deal a second blow.

'No, you didn't make a fool of yourself. Anything but.'

'I believed you back there.' Elgiva tried in vain to disengage herself from his hold. 'I really believed you.'

'Yes, I know. I needed you to believe it.'

'So you used me to make yourself look magnanimous.'

'No, I used you to resolve a dilemma. Believe me, I am grateful.'

'Oh, good.'

Wulfrum smiled down into the amber eyes, thinking how very attractive she was when she was angry. 'Come, now, admit that this was better than the alternative.'

Elgiva was silent, but under her ire she knew he was right. He was also detestably arrogant and high-handed and much too close for comfort. The silence stretched between them.

'Admit it.'

'All right, the way it worked out was better,' she conceded. 'Let's just say I don't approve the means.'

'Then for that I am sorry.'

Elgiva wondered if she had heard aright, but there was no trace of mockery in his face or his tone.

'I must govern these people, Elgiva, and they must learn to obey me. In that way only lies their peace. The sooner they learn it, the better.'

He let her go then and she watched him walk away, turning over his words in her mind. Knowledge of the stratagem still rankled, however, and she felt foolish to have been so easily deceived. In truth, she had played her part to perfection. He must have enjoyed it enormously. Elgiva kicked a loose stone at her feet. Men! They were devious and ruthless in the pursuit of their goals, and Wulfrum was no exception. In future, he would not find her so easy a dupe. She had to admit his apology had sounded sincere enough, but then so had everything else. It was impossible to tell whether he meant it or merely wished to placate her.

She began to walk back to the bower, her annoyance still simmering. Part of it was directed at herself for having fallen so easily for a ruse. Surely she should be able to read him better. He was her husband, after all, and yet it seemed to her now that she knew nothing about him. On the other hand, he seemed able to read her with uncanny precision. He could read a situation too, and manipulate it for his own ends. The man was insufferable. Worse, he was right—on this occasion, at least. The matter had fallen out better than she or anyone else could have devised. Except that he had devised it, of course.

'Hateful brute!'

Elgiva sent another stone scudding out of her path. He was an arrant knave, a domineering, overbearing rogue. However, he was not cruel. Sweyn would have punished the prisoners with the utmost rigour and would have enjoyed doing it. She shivered. Wulfrum was the lesser of two evils, although bad enough. Glancing across the intervening space betwixt herself and the barn, she saw him there speaking with some of his men. By chance he glanced round and she saw him smile. Disconcerted, Elgiva returned him a cool look and kept on walking.

CHAPTER EIGHT

As Wulfrum's men began to set about the necessary repair work, Elgiva experienced mixed feelings. More than anything she wanted to see Ravenswood prosper again, but could never have foreseen the circumstances in which it might happen. That Wulfrum was a strong and capable leader was in no doubt. His word was obeyed without question and he supervised the work with a critical eye. Nor was he above getting involved when occasion demanded it. Gradually, life began to move into a routine as a sense of order and purpose were established.

Wulfrum too noted this with satisfaction. He determined that Ravenswood would be prosperous again and bent his energies to that end. Slackness and mediocrity had no place in his scheme of things and he oversaw the ongoing work with a keen and critical eye. The Saxon workforce might resent his presence, but they were quick to recognise a master who would not be trifled with and bent themselves to their tasks accordingly. They discovered also that he was fair. While he would not tolerate poor workmanship of any kind, he was ready to praise when praise was merited. Nor did he punish lightly. However, a culprit got only one warning. The message was not lost on the rest. Moreover, no one knew where he would be at any given time and he tended to appear when least expected.

One morning, having left Ida to supervise the serfs clearing a ditch, Wulfrum decided to see how the repairs on the root store were progressing. Heading that way, he had barely taken a dozen strides when a movement near the women's bower caught his eye and he saw a small child running from the doorway. He recognised Ulric. Wulfrum grinned, expecting to see an anxious Hilda appear in pursuit at any moment. Even so, he kept his eye on the boy, following his erratic progress, only to see him stumble on a stone a moment later and fall hard. For a second there was silence. Then the air was rent by howling.

Wulfrum sprinted across the intervening space and picked the child up. A swift inspection revealed little actual damage. The tears were more about fright than pain. Lifting Ulric into his arms, he held him close and spoke as he might to soothe a timid horse, letting him understand he had nothing to fear. Eventually the tears abated and the sobs quieted to shuddering breaths. Wulfrum ruffled the child's hair and smiled. Very shyly Ulric smiled back.

Elgiva watched in silence from the doorway. She had seen her nephew run from the nursery and, as Hilda had been busy changing Pybba's soiled underclout, she had offered to go in pursuit. Her surprise could not have been greater to discover Wulfrum there first. The readiness and ease with which he comforted the child moved her to no small degree. She could never have believed a man so physically powerful could be capable of such gentleness. It was an altogether different side to him and one which drew her in spite of herself.

Sensing a presence nearby, Wulfrum turned and she saw him smile. 'Were you looking for the boy by any chance?'

'Yes.' She drew closer, looking the child over, but he seemed none the worse for his mishap.

Wulfrum noted her expression. 'He's not hurt, are you, lad?'

Ulric burbled a reply and smiled.

His large mentor grinned. 'I'll take that as a no.'

Elgiva found herself smiling too. 'Hilda will be relieved. Ulric ran off when her back was turned.' She paused. 'Thank you for taking care of him.'

For a moment Wulfrum was thrown by the warmth of that smile. To cover it he looked away and surveyed the child instead.

'How old is he?'

'Three.'

'A fine boy. Like his brother. A man would be proud of such strong healthy sons.'

'And yet my brother showed little enough interest in them.' Elgiva bit her lip. 'Do you think me disloyal for saying it?'

'No. But you are not as your brother, I think. These little ones mean a great deal to you.'

'Yes, of course. I am their aunt, after all.'

'It is more than that,' he replied. 'You like children.'

'Yes.'

'That's good.'

The tone was light enough, but Elgiva sensed more

beneath, and a suggestion that brought sudden warmth to her neck and face. Just then, however, Hilda appeared on the scene, holding Pybba in her arms. Seeing Ulric's present situation, she checked uncertainly. Wulfrum glanced at her and then handed the child to Elgiva.

'I'll leave him in your capable hands.'

With that Wulfrum took his leave. Elgiva watched him go. The man continued to surprise. Just when she thought she understood his character, some new facet was revealed. Clearly he liked children and would not suffer them to be hurt or abused. Had he not saved her nephews from Sweyn? And now he had shown unlooked-for kindness to Ulric. Then she recalled the latter part of the conversation and was jarred by the unspoken implication. Once she had wanted children. Had she married Aylwin she would have borne his sons without complaint. Wulfrum was another matter—he was her husband, but how could she bear his seed without compromising everything she held dear? Elgiva took a last look at his retreating figure before turning abruptly away.

Having spent some time at the root store and found everything progressing as he would wish, Wulfrum returned to the hall. There he found the two healers embarked on their morning round of the injured. His glance slid over Osgifu and came to rest on Elgiva. She was changing a dressing, her whole attention on the task as her hands moving surely and gently about their work. Occasionally she spoke quiet words to her patient. It was Harald, one of his own men. A youth of seventeen, Harald had received an arrow in the shoulder in the battle for Ravenswood and then contracted a fever afterwards. For some days his life had swayed in the balance and it was only thanks to the skilled care he received that he survived at all. Now it seemed he was recovering, for he was able to speak to his nurse. Wulfrum saw her smile. He could not hear the words she spoke in reply, but, from the expression on the young man's face, they were having a most powerful effect. Wulfrum's eyes narrowed.

Before he had time for further thought, Ironfist appeared. One look at the giant's expression was sufficient indication of bad news.

'What is it, Olaf?'

'Half the work party for the barn roof failed to turn up this morning. Their companions said they'd gone down with the flux.'

'And have they?'

'It's true, my lord. I've just come from the village. They're sick, all right.'

Wulfrum frowned. 'Is it known what caused this? Tainted meat, perhaps?'

'No, lord. It seems only a few had eaten meat. The rest had bread and pottage.'

'We must find out. I've seen what the flux can do to entire armies. Somehow this must be checked—I can't afford to lose the better part of the work force.'

'I know not how it may be done,' replied Ironfist, 'but we have with us those who may.'

Wulfrum followed the other man's gaze to the other side of the hall. Elgiva was still with Harald. The young man never took his eyes off her. It occurred to Wulfrum for the first time that Harald was a good-looking youngster and well made withal. He had, besides, a most winning smile. It drew the like from Elgiva. The earl frowned. Leaving Ironfist, he crossed the intervening space until he stood by the pallet bed. His wife glanced up in surprise.

'My lord?'

'I would speak with you and Osgifu when you have finished here.'

The tone, though quiet, was distinctly cool and two women exchanged glances.

'As you will, my lord,' replied Osgifu.

Elgiva's hands continued with their task on the bandage. Wulfrum looked down at Harald.

'You are recovering well, I see.'

'Indeed I am, my lord. Thanks to this lady.' Harald's eyes spoke his admiration louder than words. Wulfrum saw Elgiva smile again in response and his jaw tightened.

'I hope it will not be long before you're on your feet again.'

'I hope so too, my lord.' Harald threw another fond look at Elgiva. As she fastened the cloth strip into place, her hands rested a moment on his breast.

'I'm glad to hear it,' replied Wulfrum.

At last Elgiva got to her feet and he took her arm, leading her aside. Osgifu followed them. As Wulfrum explained the situation they listened in silence, though Elgiva exchanged a troubled glance with her companion. It was Osgifu who spoke.

'I would need to see the sick for myself, lord.'

'You may go into the village. Ironfist will accompany you.'

Elgiva looked up at him. 'May I go with her?'

'No. You will remain here and prepare whatever medicines are necessary.'

'But I may be able to help.'

'Even so.'

'But—.'

'I have said.'

She bit her lip, but remained silent, watching the other two depart. Then she turned away.

'Stay!'

Elgiva paused. 'Lord?'

For a moment the amber eyes met his and he caught a glimpse of anger there and something else besides that said more plainly than words what she thought of his decision. Wulfrum concealed the smile that would otherwise have risen to his lips.

'You will tend to your duties here.'

'Whatever you say, lord.' The tone was cool and level, but it carried a nuance of criticism that did not escape him.

'Osgifu will assess what needs to be done.'

'Indeed she will, and right well too. But if this is an epidemic, it will require more than one pair of hands to deal with it.'

'If it is an epidemic.'

For a moment she was silent before the amber eyes met his own. 'You still think I might run away, don't you?'

'The thought had occurred to me.'

'Do you think I would leave my people when they are sick and dying?'

'It did not stop you before.'

He saw the colour rush to her cheeks, but she held his gaze. 'That was a moment of madness I regret. Besides, I had a much better chance to run afterwards, but I did not take it.'

'Because you knew I would find you eventually.'

'Because I would not leave my people to the tender mercies of the Vikings.'

'But they are at my mercy, are they not? You included.' Wulfrum watched the colour deepen in her face to a most attractive shade of pink.

'Then let me help them.'

'You are helping them.' Wulfrum gestured to the men she had just left. 'Saxon and Dane alike have much to thank you for.'

'That is not what I meant and you know it.'

'Nevertheless, it is where your duty lies at present and where it will remain.'

The tone was casual enough, but Elgiva could not miss the note of iron beneath. With an effort she forced back the protest that sprang to her lips and held on to her temper, aware of his eyes on her the while.

'Then I shall return to my duties, lord.'

'When I give you leave,' he replied.

Elgiva stopped, every line of her body rigid. Wulfrum waited, wondering if she would yield to the impulse to hit him, for he correctly divined it was in her mind. The provocation had been great—and deliberate. Would she rise to the bait? In a part of his mind he hoped she might.

The silence stretched out, but Elgiva said nothing, forcing herself to remain still under that penetrating blue gaze. The bastard was enjoying this. He would enjoy it even more if she tried to defy him now, but she wasn't about to give him an excuse to touch her. She saw his smile widen. The urge to hit him grew stronger, but she controlled it.

'You may return to your work, Elgiva.'

Her chin lifted. Throwing him a most expressive look,

she turned on her heel and strode away. Wulfrum watched her go. He wasn't sure his decision to keep her here was the right one, but time would tell. Meanwhile, she would remain where he could see her.

Elgiva initially headed for the women's bower where she paced the floor for some minutes in impotent ire, her pride in complete revolt. It seemed his arrogance knew no bounds. After a while, though, when her temper cooled a little, her thoughts went next to Osgifu. If the problem in the village was the flux, then they would need something to reduce fever, a soothing tea to calm the stomach and a tincture of white clay to bind the gut. She might as well get on with the preparations now. Even if the Viking would not let her go outside the pale, she could still do something useful. Thus she went to the still room where she and Osgifu kept their herbs and dried them for their potions and salves. After making up the fire and setting some water to heat, she selected a jar of willow bark. Then she began to prepare an infusion.

After three hours' work she had prepared a goodly supply of medicines for Osgifu. It was a satisfying job in many ways and a soothing one; she could forget about everything else and concentrate only on what she was doing. She was so absorbed that she didn't hear the door open.

Wulfrum paused on the threshold, looking round. It was the first time he had been in this place, but his eye took in the neat arrangements of pots and jars and the bundles of herbs hanging from the beams. The scent of the herbs was pleasant and filled the room with their fragrance. He identified mint and thyme and sweet lavender, perfumes he had come to associate with Elgiva. She was standing by her work bench across the room, for a moment or two unaware of his presence. He smiled and stepped into the room.

Elgiva heard the movement and looked up.

'My lord?'

He glanced at the jars of cooling liquid. 'You have been busy.'

'Yes, Osgifu will need these medicines tomorrow.'

Elgiva strove to keep her tone level, but for all her outward air of calm her heart was beating faster. Suddenly the room seemed much smaller too.

'Your skills have already proved most useful,' he said.

'I'm glad you think so, my lord.'

'What other hidden talents do you possess, Elgiva?'

For a moment she met his gaze, but as always his expression was hard to read. Even so it was disturbing. She bit her lip and turned away, busying herself again with her task. Wulfrum watched. Under that dark gaze Elgiva grew warm. Although he had remained quite still, he seemed to emanate dangerous strength. The air was charged with it, charged too with the memory of their earlier disagreement. Unwilling to provoke his anger by alluding to it, Elgiva remained silent.

Wulfrum had a shrewd idea as to her thoughts and knew he couldn't entirely blame her. When he refused her permission to go to the village, it wasn't because he feared she might attempt to escape—it had been an excuse. Just as this visit to the still room was an excuse. Looking at her now, he knew why he had come. Advancing with slow deliberation, he came to stand beside her. To cover her confusion, she turned away, but his arms slid round her waist and prevented it. She felt him nuzzle her hair and then the warmth of his lips on her neck. Elgiva's blood raced even as her mind rebelled. Then, without warning, she was tipped back into the crook of his arm and his mouth was on hers. Intent initially on stealing a kiss, Wulfrum had not reckoned with the powerful effect of the scents on her clothes and skin. The kiss grew more passionate and all of Elgiva's resistance availed her nothing. Only when he eventually drew back and looked into her face did he seem to recollect himself.

'Was that another demonstration of power?' she demanded then.

'You know it wasn't.'

The words were quietly spoken and she knew them for truth—if he had really chosen to demonstrate his power over her he would have pursued the matter to its conclusion. He surveyed her keenly.

'Whom do you fight, Elgiva? Me or yourself?'

'You flatter yourself.'

'Do I?'

Her cheeks burned as indignation mounted, but for the first time she was lost for words. Wulfrum returned a slow infuriating smile that only added to her discomfiture.

'*Do I?*' he repeated.

Though he held her but lightly now, she could feel his hands through the stuff of her gown. It seemed that where they touched her flesh burned.

'Believe what you like,' she retorted.

'I believe you want me as much as I want you.'

'You are mistaken.'

'Shall we put that to the test?'

'No!'

'Are you afraid I might be right?'

'I have no such fear. Now let me go.'

To her surprise and relief his hold slackened. His expression then was compounded of amusement and frustration and something more, something harder to define.

'All right, Elgiva, I'll let you go—for now.'

Watching him move away, she let out the breath she had been holding.

'Until later, my lady.'

Then he let himself out and she was alone. It was some time before she could compose herself sufficiently to finish her work.

Osgifu and Ironfist did not return until late afternoon. Elgiva had been watching for them from the door of the bower and hurried to the hall, anxious to hear what Osgifu had to say. When she arrived, Wulfrum was already there. After their earlier encounter she had wondered how to face him again, but he merely glanced round, inclining his head in acknowledgement of her presence, before turning his attention to Ironfist.

'How goes it, Olaf?'

'Not good. We've had the first fatality already: a child of six. Many more will die unless we can discover the cause.'

Elgiva listened in mounting concern. Catching Osgifu's eye, she saw her own sadness mirrored there. In any outbreak of sickness the old and the young were the most vulnerable. She thought of Ulric and Pybba and her sense of helplessness increased.

'There must be a common link somewhere,' she said. 'Something we're overlooking.'

As the others turned to look at her Elgiva reddened, realising she had been thinking out loud. She half-expected Wulfrum to be annoyed by her interruption, but he made no comment, merely giving her a searching look.

'Osgifu has suggested that latrines should be dug to take the waste,' Olaf went on. 'I think she's got a point. The place stinks.'

Wulfrum nodded. 'I'll get Ida to organise a work detail in the morning. This thing must be stopped somehow.'

Having expected him to reject the idea out of hand Elgiva was unable to conceal her surprise and with it pleasure that he should be willing to listen. If only he would let her accompany Osgifu on the morrow. However, after his previous reaction, she didn't dare raise the topic.

Osgifu had no such reservations. Meeting Wulfrum's eye squarely, she spoke up with calm assurance. 'My lord, there are more people sick now than I can tend. I need help.'

Beside her Ironfist nodded. 'She speaks the truth, lord.'

Wulfrum looked from one to the other and then at his wife.

'Very well, you may go with her tomorrow, but you will be accompanied at all times.' He gave Ironfist a meaning-ful look.

Elgiva inclined her head in token of acceptance. 'As you will, my lord.'

The dulcet tone didn't deceive him for a moment, any more than the lowered eyes and meek expression. The vixen had never done anything meekly in her life. She was enjoying this retraction and he knew it. If he'd been alone with her, he'd have...

Before that seductive thought could finish itself, Ida hove into view and Wulfrum's mind was recalled to present business. Summoning the newcomer, the earl took him aside along with Ironfist and soon the three were deep in conversation.

Osgifu turned to Elgiva and smiled. 'It will be a happiness to have you with me again, child.'

'It will be a happiness for me too,' returned Elgiva. 'In the meantime, I have prepared some medicines.'

'In good time. We're going to need them.'

The words were prophetic—half an hour later Ceolnoth appeared with the news that two of the Danes had fallen ill. It struck a sombre note with the rest and the meal that night was taken in an unwontedly quiet atmosphere.

Elgiva slipped away as soon as she could and went to check on her nephews. They were asleep and, according to Hilda, both had been quite well before she put them to bed. Reassured, Elgiva returned to the chamber she shared with Wulfrum. It was her habit to retire first and often she was asleep before he returned. This evening, therefore, she was surprised and not a little dismayed to see him there already and clearly preparing to retire. He had stripped off his tunic and shirt and her startled gaze fell on the silver arm rings and the muscles beneath, muscles whose strength she already knew.

'Are the children well?' he asked.

Elgiva stared at him in surprise, wondering how he could have known her errand.

'Quite well, my lord.'

'I'm glad to hear it. I would not have them succumb.'

He sounded sincere and she was touched in spite of herself. It behoved her to make an effort in turn.

'Thank you for allowing me to go with Osgifu tomorrow.'

Wulfrum unfastened his breeches. 'It was what you wanted, wasn't it?'

'Yes. I know I can be of help.' Elgiva turned away, removing her girdle and laying it aside, keenly aware of the naked form just feet away.

'So I think.'

Her hands paused on the laces of her gown and she looked up, half-expecting to see mockery in his expression, but it was conspicuous by its absence. For the second time she was taken aback. If he knew it, Wulfrum gave no sign, but merely climbed into bed.

'If we could just discover the cause, it would be something,' he said.

Elgiva unlaced her gown and drew it off, laying it with the girdle. 'I was thinking about that. If food is not the common link among the sick, could it be the water?'

She unfastened her hair and shook it loose. It fell in shining waves across her shoulders as she reached for the comb. Wulfrum propped himself on one elbow, watching. With an effort he dragged his thoughts back to the question.

'How so?' he replied. 'The villagers draw their water from the stream, my men from the well by the hall.'

'Is it possible your men might have drunk from the stream too?'

'It's a thought. I shall question them tomorrow.'

Elgiva nodded. 'It might be a good idea, my lord.'

She resumed her task, taking her time over it, aware the while of Wulfrum's gaze. His face gave no clue as to the thoughts behind but the memory of the afternoon was still keen, his parting words in particular: *I'll let you go— for now.*

Eventually she could delay no longer and, with reluctance, laid aside the comb. Then she blew out the lamp and joined him, hurriedly drawing the pelts up under her chin. With thumping heart she felt his weight shift and her body tensed. Then she realised he had but stretched out beside her; she could feel his warmth beneath the furs. She swallowed hard, waiting, every nerve alive to him, every fibre of her being keyed to fight. The outcome could be in no doubt, but there would be no tame submission.

For some time she remained thus, straining to catch the least sound or movement that might signal danger, but none came. Wulfrum made no attempt to touch her. She could detect no trace of his earlier behaviour in his manner this evening. It was almost as if the incident had never happened, except that memory would not be denied. Almost she could still feel the searing passion of that embrace and with it resurgent anger. No man, even her betrothed, had ever dared to kiss her like that. Her fingers brushed her lips. Would Aylwin *ever* have kissed her thus? Somehow she doubted it. That thought led to others that were infinitely more disturbing and with them the mocking echo of another voice: *Whom do you fight? Me or yourself?*

The two women set out early for the village. Wulfrum watched them leave, noting with some interest that it was Ironfist who carried the heavy basket of potions. His gaze followed them until they were out of sight. Then his mind began to turn over what Elgiva had said earlier about the water supply. He went to find the two Danes who had fallen sick. Both were feverish and stricken with cramps, but had sense enough to be able to answer his questions. After hearing their replies, he went to saddle his horse.

Wulfrum rode slowly, skirting the village, and came to the stream from which the peasants drew their water. There was nothing in the clear flowing depths to indicate aught amiss. He knew it had its source in the hills some miles away and that it joined the river further on. Turning the horse's head, he rode upstream, as close to the bank as he could, keeping his eyes peeled. He had not gone a league before he saw it, the remains of a dead sheep lodged among boulders on the stream bed. It seemed Elgiva had been right. He dismounted and waded into the water. It wasn't deep, but it was cold and the rotting carcase was foul. Almost gagging on the stench, he dragged it out on to the bank and then staggered away, retching. It took him several minutes to get his breath; the stink of putrefaction seemed to lodge in his throat. No wonder people were sick. He thought it surprising more of them hadn't died. Reaching for the reins, he remounted his horse and headed back towards the village.

Elgiva emerged from the peasant hut into the pale sunshine, drawing in a welcome breath of fresh air. Ironfist straightened, pushing his shoulders away from the door frame he had been leaning on.

'Whither next, lady?' he enquired.

Elgiva was about to reply, but the words died in her throat as she recognised the approaching rider. Her mind raced to try to discover the reason for his presence. Had he come to drag her back to the hall? Was he angry about something? He didn't look angry, but that was no guarantee of anything. He reined in before the hut. Just then Osgifu emerged from a neighbouring dwelling and, seeing the others, came over to join them. Wulfrum glanced at her a moment before turning to his wife.

'It seems you were right, my lady,' he said.

'Lord?'

'The village water supply had become contaminated.'

'How, my lord?' asked Osgifu.

'A dead sheep further upstream. It was truly rotten. 'Tis no wonder so many here fell ill.'

'You went to check,' said Elgiva, regarding him with open curiosity.

'Yes. After what you said, it seemed the logical thing to do. You were right about my men too; they told me that the last time they were in the village they also drank from the stream.'

Osgifu shook her head. 'Well, I'm blessed! At least we know now. I'll pass the word that all water is to be drawn fresh and the old discarded.'

Wulfrum dismounted and came to stand by his wife.

'I think the epidemic is as good as over.'

'I think so too.' She paused. 'Thanks to your timely dis-covery, lord.'

'It was you made me think of it,' he returned.

'At least no one else will fall sick, though some are in poor enough case.'

'If anyone can help them, I think it will be you.'

She looked up in surprise, but there was no trace of a smile on his face now.

'I will do my best.'

'I know.'

The intensity of his gaze was disconcerting and Elgiva felt her pulse quicken. He extended a hand towards her.

'Will you return with me now, Elgiva?'

She hesitated and it was Osgifu who spoke. 'You go,

my lady. There is little left to do here. I can finish off. Besides, you look tired.'

Wulfrum seized his opportunity. 'She is right. You have done everything possible. Come.'

The tone was gentle, but firm. He intended to be obeyed and Elgiva knew it would be pointless to argue. She watched him remount and then nod to Ironfist. With no more effort than if she had been made of thistledown the giant lifted her on to the crupper. Then he looked at Wulfrum.

'Have no fear, my lord, I'll see Osgifu safe home.'

Wulfrum nodded and then turned the horse's head. For a while they rode in silence, he holding his mount to a walk. Having achieved her company, he had no intention of losing it again too soon. Almost he could feel the tension in the figure at his back, though her hands rode but lightly on his waist, just enough to steady herself. If he had been composed of burning coals she could not have touched him with greater caution. Thinking of his earlier suspicions, he was conscious of a twinge of guilt. It had been churlish when, clearly, her desire had only been to help. Mentally he strove to find the right words but, being unused to baring his thoughts to a woman, found they did not come easily.

'Where did you learn such skill in healing?' he asked.

'From my mother while she lived, and then from Osgifu.'

'They taught you well.' He paused. Then, 'I owe you much, Elgiva, and I thank you.'

Caught off balance by the remark, Elgiva stared for a moment at the broad shoulders in front of her. 'You owe me nothing,' she replied. 'These are my people and their welfare is my concern.'

'They are fortunate then.'

Again she listened for a note of mockery, but heard none. Like his actions this morning, it took her aback. She would not have expected him to take so close an interest in the matter. He could have sent one of his men to investigate the water supply, but he had not. In spite of his earlier opposition, he had listened and acted on her words. It was, she acknowledged, quite an admission and one she could not have envisaged him making even yesterday. Who could have expected so proud a man to unbend so far? It seemed to call for a reciprocal gesture.

'You did your part too, my lord.'

Wulfrum could detect no irony in her voice and was surprised, being well aware how cutting her tongue could be. And yet perversely the same tongue could disarm him in a moment. It had never occurred to him before that a woman might be an ally, much less a friend. Yet these last few days had shown how valuable a woman's allegiance might be. A man might achieve much with such a one at his side. The idea was disturbing and welcome at once. Yet how to tell her his thought? Again, such words did not come readily; if he said the wrong thing, the fragile truce would be broken. Worse, she might laugh in his face. If she did, he could hardly blame her, given their brief history together. It was probably better to say nothing.

Elgiva had no clue as to his thought, but sensed a change. The tension between them had lightened, at least for now. Uncertain how it had come about, she was unwilling to do anything to change it and kept her own counsel. Thus they returned home in what she might, under other circumstances, have described as companionable silence.

* * *

Over the next few days the condition of many of the villagers improved and Osgifu was sufficiently encouraged to voice the opinion that they had turned a corner. Responding to treatment, their patients began to shake off the ill effects they had suffered. More were able to leave their beds and get about again. The fever left them weaker than before, but they were out of danger at least.

In the hall the number of patients had diminished also, until only a dozen or so of the worst cases were left. For all that young Harald would have left his bed, Osgifu refused to allow it.

'If you want to tear that shoulder anew, by all means get up.'

'I have lain here three weeks already.'

'If you know what is good for you, lad, you'll remain a week more.'

He threw her a belligerent look that left her quite unmoved. She turned to Elgiva.

'You speak to him. See if you cannot talk some sense into that hot head.'

Elgiva regarded the young man with an understanding smile, but her tone was firm. 'Osgifu is right. You must remain abed a little longer.'

He sighed then and acquiesced. 'Your wish is my command, lady.'

'Have a care what you promise.'

Harald's expression grew earnest and he carried her hand to his lips. 'I would perform whatever you asked of me, my lady.'

Elgiva laughed. 'I will remember that, Harald. You may have cause to regret your words.'

'Never.'

She extricated her hand and gathered up her things, preparing to move on. As she did so, she looked up and saw Wulfrum watching them from the other side of the hall, his expression flinty. Elgiva noted it with some surprise. Surely a young man's infatuation for his nurse would not make the noble earl jealous? Yet he seemed much out of humour. She ought not to have been amused. Forcing back a smile, she continued with her round.

Across the room Wulfrum's gaze followed his wife's movements among her remaining patients. He saw their expressions as they looked at her, saw their eyes light, saw them smile. A few exchanged pleasantries with her. He saw her smile and reply with a kind word for all. His gaze went back to Harald. Quite clearly the young man was besotted. Wulfrum sighed. Who wasn't? It seemed half his men were in love with his wife. In that moment he felt ashamed of his ill humour. How was it with him that he should respond thus because a callow youth made eyes at her? Elgiva was his. None would dispute it. Harald was young and brave and had ever served his overlord with commitment and loyalty. He might imagine himself head over heels in love, but his was not a treacherous nature. Wulfrum had no reason to suspect him, or Elgiva, either. What she did now she did at his command, and, thanks to her and Osgifu, many lived who might otherwise have died. He had much to thank her for, not look for offence where there was none. In truth, no woman had ever caused the sensation he had felt a few moments ago when he saw Harald take her hand. Wulfrum shook his head. He had thought himself the conqueror here. Now he wasn't so sure. With a final glance across the room he turned and quit the hall, seeking fresh air to cool his head.

CHAPTER NINE

ELGIVA looked round the still room with mounting concern. Tending the sick and injured in such numbers had severely depleted the current stock of medicines and used up most of the dried herbs that she and Osgifu needed for their salves and potions. If they did not replenish supplies very soon, there would be none left at all. The older woman had been thinking on similar lines.

'You must speak to Wulfrum,' she said.

'To what end? He will not let us go into the forest to gather plants.'

'He said he wouldn't let you go to the village too, didn't he?' replied Osgifu. 'But you went in the end.'

'That was different. People were sick.'

'People will be sick again and when it happens we must be prepared.'

Elgiva knew Osgifu was right. With some trepidation she decided to approach her husband on the matter, though she was doubtful of the outcome. Now she deeply regretted her previous attempt to escape. It had been madness, a moment of folly born of desperation and fear, but he would remember it and perhaps count her words suspect

now. On the other hand, he had indeed let her go to the
village. Besides which, the atmosphere had been less tense
of late. Would he listen? With some reluctance she left
Osgifu and went to seek him out.

She found him in the yard, supervising repairs to the
gate where the carpenter and his team were already busy.
Elgiva hesitated; she could see Olaf Ironfist there, as well,
along with Ida and Ceolnoth and some of the others. They
looked up as she approached and the conversation stopped.
Under their speculative regard Elgiva's self-conscious-
ness increased. Had the need been less urgent, her courage
might have failed. As it was she waited, wondering if
Wulfrum would be angry that she interrupted them.
However, when he turned and saw her, he smiled.

'What would you, my lady?'

'A word, my lord, if the moment is convenient.' She
looked round at his companions. 'I can come back later
if…'

'No. There is nothing pressing. Come.'

He left them and took her arm.

'What is it, Elgiva?'

She explained, searching his face for clues as to his
likely response. He heard her in silence and then nodded.

'Go and gather what you need. Osgifu may go with
you.'

For a moment she wondered if she had misheard, then
managed to stammer out her thanks.

'There is no need to thank me,' he replied. 'Rather I
should thank you. The injured made good progress under
your care. Now I have seen your skill I would be the last
to do anything to hinder it.'

Elgiva felt herself redden under his praise. 'The plants

should be picked with the dew on them, close to dawn.'
She paused. 'We would go tomorrow, if you have no objection. The matter is urgent now.'

'As you will.'

She smiled, unable to think of anything else to say, all
too aware of his closeness. She felt sure that he would
return to his men now, being bored with women's affairs,
but to her surprise he did not. Retaining his hold on her
arm, he drew her away.

'The repairs on the gate will be finished in a day or
two,' he said. 'After that the men will restore the doors to
the mead hall.'

Thinking of the shattered timbers, Elgiva knew there
was a goodly amount of work involved. Already men were
busy in the saw pit, while in the village the serfs had
begun the necessary rebuilding of the houses that had
been destroyed by Halfdan's war band. Others had
returned to tend the fields under the watchful eyes of their
Viking masters.

As Wulfrum talked, they strolled on and came presently to the stables. It was quiet within and fragrant with
hay and horses. Aside from the beasts it was deserted.
Recalling the last time they had been alone in a place like
this, Elgiva began to doubt the wisdom of remaining.
Wulfrum glanced down at her.

'Why are you afraid?'

'I'm not.'

'Then why are you trembling?'

She bit her lip, unable to think of anything to say.

'Do you think I might throw you down on a pile of
hay?' He let his gaze travel the length of her. 'Not such a
bad idea, now I think of it.'

Her chin came up at once. 'Try it and I'll spit you with that pitchfork!'

'That's better,' he returned. 'But you needn't worry— I am too fearful of my life to do any such thing, although you do make it a tempting risk.'

He turned her to face him, his hands riding her waist. Elgiva caught her breath, suddenly aware of the quiet barn, the absence of people, the large pile of hay in the corner and his proximity. Over the sweet smell of hay and straw she could detect the musky scent of the man, sensual, alluring and dangerous. Would he kiss her again, and, if he did, what then? Appalled by the direction of her thoughts and in the cause of self-preservation, she stepped aside, out of his hold, into the stall where the bay mare was standing. Wulfrum smiled and followed her, moving to the horse's head, letting her breathe in his scent and accept him. Then he patted the glossy neck and ran an experienced hand over her shoulder and back.

'A beautiful animal,' he said, 'but finely made. Not up to a man's weight. A lady's mount, I think.'

Elgiva said nothing.

'Yours?'

'Yes. She was a present from my father.'

'A generous gift.'

'Yes.'

'She will breed fine foals,' he observed.

Elgiva's jaw tightened, but she remained silent. What was there to say? The mare belonged to him now, just like everything else around here. He could do with her as he liked. He could do with them both as he liked. Had he not shown her as much in the still room? A wave of resentment

welled up and she turned away. Wulfrum frowned, sensing
the change in her mood.

'Elgiva?'

He reached out a hand towards her, but she ducked
under the horse's neck and thence out of the stall, running
for the door. She heard Wulfrum call after her, but she did
not stop. He stared in surprise after her departing figure
and shook his head, unable to account for the sudden
dramatic change in her mood.

'Now what in Odin's name was that about?' he
wondered aloud.

The mare snorted and stamped a hoof. Wulfrum shook
his head, bemused. Women were unpredictable creatures
at the best of times, like horses. They needed careful
handling, but they needed to know their master. Perhaps
he should have taken Elgiva that first night, should have
demanded her submission. It had been a novel experience
for a woman to resist him tooth and nail. Initially he had
found it exciting, until he had seen the look on her face,
a look of fear and revulsion. It had stopped him in his
tracks. He had never forced a woman and would not force
this one, although he wanted her more than any woman
he had ever met. Thus he had played a waiting game. Now
he wasn't sure how much longer he could endure it. Night
after night he lay beside her, listening in the darkness to
the sound of her soft breathing or in the dawn light
watching her sleep. It took all his will power not to touch
her, to lay claim to what was his by right. So many times
he had been on the point of using force, but each time he
rejected it. She must come to him. Only then would she
be truly his. So many times he had imagined that moment,
tried to visualise the circumstances when she would give

herself to him, willingly and without reserve. Wulfrum permitted himself a wry smile. He was not naïve enough to think it would be easy or soon, but it was a challenge and he had ever enjoyed those. A wild spirit was more worth the winning. Giving the mare a last affectionate slap on the rump, he made his way out of the stable.

Elgiva hurried back to the hall, angry with herself for having let him upset her. What was the use? Ravenswood belonged to him now and everything in it, and the sooner she accepted it the better. All the same, the knowledge rankled. Worse, because of her foolish behaviour, he might rethink his permission to let her gather herbs on the morrow.

That evening, as he spoke and laughed with his men, she watched him to see whether he seemed angry, but could detect no sign of it. On the contrary, the atmosphere seemed good humoured with the conversation turning on weapons and hunting. The forest abounded with game and the Vikings were wont to take advantage of it to supplement the food at table. Now it seemed there were plans afoot for a boar hunt. Elgiva, who had been standing in the background overseeing the serving of the food, listened and felt sad, thinking of all the times she had accompanied her father and brother on the hunt, recalling the thrill and speed of the chase. She could ride as well as any man and, for all the little mare was finely made, she was swift and had stamina enough to hold her own against the larger mounts. However, all that was of no import now. She would never be allowed to ride the horse again and Mara would be used to breed fine foals.

'Elgiva, what are you doing there?' Wulfrum's voice broke into her thoughts.

Drawn from her reverie with a guilty start, she threw a swift glance over the table to see what he lacked.

'Come, my lady, that is work for the servants. You will sit beside me.'

'My lord, it is my place to serve you with food and drink.'

'Your place is where I say it is.'

The tone brooked no argument and, with reluctance, she left off what she had been doing and seated herself in the chair beside him. Wulfrum nodded his approval while beside him Olaf Ironfist watched impassively. The other men exchanged glances before addressing themselves again to their meat and the conversation resumed. Elgiva assumed a manner of outward composure, aware the while of Wulfrum's eyes on her.

'From now on you will sit with me at table.'

'As you wish, my lord.'

'I do wish it, and my name is Wulfrum.'

'As you wish, Wulfrum.'

He nodded and, taking up a platter, served her meat and bread himself. For a while they ate in silence, Elgiva paying close attention to the food and trying to appear unconcerned by her husband's scrutiny. Then he called for more ale, waiting while a serf hastened to fill his cup.

'About your proposed excursion tomorrow,' he said.

'Yes?' She felt her heart leap. Was he about to change his mind?

'Olaf will accompany you.' He threw his companion a meaningful look.

Although relieved that he had not reneged on his promise, she couldn't hide an ironic smile.

'I will make no attempt to escape.'

'No, for I would find you soon enough and you know it,' he replied. 'But the forest may hold unseen dangers, for the times are uncertain. It is like to be so until the Danes have consolidated their rule in Northumbria.'

Elgiva said nothing, feeling a familiar surge of resentment. He spoke as if it was but a foregone conclusion. The trouble was, she suspected he was right. The Danes wanted this land, so much better than their own, and, having won it, intended to keep it. Looking round the hall at the assembled men, she knew it for truth. All of them were warriors, armed and trained, living for the thrill of battle and the taking of plunder. These owed their allegiance to Wulfrum as he owed his to Halfdan, and they would serve him well. Already she could see the respect in which they held him. Wulfrum wore his power lightly, but his word was law with them. They would give short shrift to any man who crossed that line, or any woman if it came to it. They treated her with due deference because she was his wife, but they watched her too, as Olaf Ironfist would watch her tomorrow. What Wulfrum had said about possible danger was true, but he was taking no chances on her slipping away into the forest, either. Not that she had intended to. To run would be to leave her people to the mercy of the Vikings.

Her thoughts were distracted by a shriek of protest and she looked up to see Hilda struggling in the hold of one of Wulfrum's men. It was Ceolnoth. The young man seemed intent she should sit on his knee and she equally intent that she should not. A loud slap rang out as her hand met his cheek, a gesture greeted by a roar of laughter from his companions. Elgiva looked at Wulfrum, but he did not

seem minded to interfere. Ceolnoth got up with a glint in
his eye and, before Hilda could flee, swung her into his
arms and strode to the door with her. Her yells and protests
were drowned in laughter.

Elgiva turned to her husband. 'Will you do nothing?'

'What would you have me do?'

'Stop your men molesting helpless women.'

'Helpless? Now that is not how I would describe you.'

'You know what I mean. Hilda is not a whore. Nor does
she deserve to be treated as one.'

'She is comely and it is plain that Ceolnoth warms to
her. Shall I forbid him what I mean to enjoy with my own
wife?' He noted with satisfaction the hot colour that
flooded her face, the spark of anger in her eyes, and knew
she read the message aright.

Elgiva refused the bait. 'She is not his wife,' she
retorted.

'No, but she soon will be. Evidently his passion for the
wench has grown. He spoke to me this morning, seeking
my permission to take her to wife, and I have nothing to
say against it. He will wed her as soon as may be.'

'And what of Hilda's views on the matter? Did you seek
to discover those too?'

He raised an eyebrow, for her tone was hot though the
words were quietly spoken.

'I do not consult the wishes of servants,' he replied.
'Hilda will wed Ceolnoth and there's an end. He is a good
man and will make her a fine husband.' He cast a compre-
hensive glance around the hall. 'Would that matters might
be so simply arranged for all my men. However, there are
not enough women to go around.'

That was undeniably true. Ceolnoth had made his interest

in Hilda plain from the first. It seemed his desire had not abated and now the girl's fate was sealed, like her own. Sensing something of her mood, Wulfrum eyed her shrewdly.

'Is it not better for a woman to be a wife and hold a respected position thus?' he demanded. 'Would you prefer that I handed her over to my men to have her in common?'

'I would not wish that on any woman,' she replied. 'Nor would I wish any woman to be compelled to wed a man she does not—'

Elgiva broke off, blushing and inwardly cursed her hot temper. Again, Wulfrum raised an eyebrow.

'Does not love?' he finished.

'Care for, I was going to say.'

'You did not care for me, but you are my wife.'

'I had no choice.'

'True. But tell me, Elgiva, have you not grown to love me since?' The tone was mocking and her cheeks coloured a deeper shade.

'No.'

Wulfrum laughed out loud, causing several interested looks to come their way.

'You will.'

'You delude yourself, lord.'

'Do I?'

He let his gaze dwell on the lovely profile now turned towards him, drinking in every flawless line, and then move on to her neck and the swelling bosom beneath her gown. Mentally he stripped the cloth away. Aware of that penetrating gaze, Elgiva felt her face grow warm. Wulfrum saw it and grinned, enjoying her discomfiture. Presently she turned towards him, the amber eyes bright with anger.

'Must you stare at me like that?'

'What man would not stare?' He traced a hand down her sleeve. Elgiva forced herself to sit still, though it seemed that her skin burned beneath the cloth.

'Besides,' he continued, 'I think it does not displease you as much as you pretend.'

She fought the urge to hit him, as much for the accuracy of the comment as for its confounded self-assurance.

'Belief is free, my lord. If you choose to delude yourself, I cannot prevent it.'

'I think it is you who delude yourself, Elgiva.' The blue eyes were no longer smiling, and before she could think up a fitting retort he had leaned across his chair and kissed her full on the mouth. Taken thus by surprise and unable to move, she was forced to endure it, incensed alike by the treatment and the dawning knowledge that he was right. Wulfrum released her then, meeting her gaze with an expression that revealed not a shred of remorse. Crimson with embarrassment, Elgiva strove to regain her composure, keenly aware of the sudden heat in her blood and the amused stares they were receiving from all quarters of the room. She kept her voice low, though the tone throbbed with anger and indignation.

'This is mere sport to you, isn't it?'

His brow creased. 'Is that what you think?'

'I don't know what to think.'

'Then know that I do not sport with you, nor ever have.'

'Then what was that?'

'Don't you know? Didn't Aylwin kiss you like that?'

Elgiva stared at him, wondering what Aylwin had to do with it.

'Well, didn't he?' he demanded.

Her blush deepened. 'Certainly not. He always showed respect.'

Wulfrum let out a guffaw of delighted laughter. More heads turned their way. Elgiva rose from her seat and surveyed her husband with rage.

'You're impossible!'

Far from being grieved by the accusation, he only laughed the louder and made no move to stop her as she flung away from him and marched off towards the stairs.

Elgiva woke with the early light next morning and eased herself from the bed, throwing a baleful glare at Wulfrum as she did so. However, he slumbered on unaware. He must have retired very late for she had not heard him at all. Unwilling to disturb him in case it provoked another conversation like the last, she gathered up her clothes and dressed in haste before slipping away. Osgifu was waiting for her with a basket and with few words the two of them made their way to the gate where stood Ironfist, armed with sword and axe. Instructing the guard to let them through, he followed the two women to the forest.

The sun was high when they returned with laden baskets. The rest of the morning was devoted to tying bundles of herbs for drying, or steeping them in hot water, or grinding them to mix with goose grease to make salves. The room was filled with the smell of their potions, a scent that Elgiva associated with healing and well-being. Part of a woman's role in the household was to know what nostrums to use in the treatment of all ailments from a fever to a cut, from a boil to the toothache. It was a role that Elgiva enjoyed. Each season brought its own flowers for harvest. She knew them all and the places where they grew.

As she worked, it occurred to her that she wielded considerable power—not all plants possessed solely healing properties. Three or four grains of digitalis would provide relief from heart pain; eleven grains would kill. A few nightshade berries mixed in a stew would achieve the same end, as would the leaf or pounded root of monk's hood. She banished the thought, smiling in self-mockery. The chances of killing all the invaders were remote and those who survived would soon discover what had befallen their comrades and would exact a terrible revenge. If Halfdan thought one of his favoured earls had been a prey to treachery, he would be merciless. Besides, she knew it was one thing to think about taking life and quite another to do it. The Danes might hold life cheap, but she could not. Poison was a coward's weapon in any case. She might detest the invaders, but she could not murder in cold blood. Her part was to save life, not destroy it.

She was interrupted in these thoughts by Hilda, who burst through the door, wild-eyed and breathless.

'Help me, my lady! I beg you.'

'What is it?' Elgiva turned, and wiping her hands on her apron, went to comfort the girl. Hilda threw herself into her mistress's arms and clung to her, sobbing. Osgifu frowned, lowering the pestle she had been using.

'What ails thee, child? Are you hurt?'

Hilda shook her head, but before she could say any more half a dozen men appeared in the doorway, led by Ceolnoth. He spied Hilda and grinned.

'Come, my bird.'

He stepped forwards and took hold of Hilda's wrist, drawing her away from Elgiva. Hilda shrieked and struggled, but he held her without effort.

'What is the meaning of this?' demanded Elgiva. 'You have no right to hurt one of my servants.'

''Tis not hurt I intend, my lady,' replied Ceolnoth. 'I would have her to wife.'

Osgifu glared at him. 'You cannot wed without Lord Wulfrum's permission.'

'He has given it. The girl is mine.'

'Yours, Viking?'

Brandishing the pestle again, she took a step closer, but Elgiva laid a restraining hand on her arm.

'He speaks true, Gifu. Lord Wulfrum has given his consent.'

Osgifu stared as outrage gave way to shock. 'Is this so?'

'Yes.'

'My lady speaks the truth,' said Ceolnoth with a grin.

Hilda burst into tears.

'Can you do nothing, my lady?' demanded Osgifu.

'I tried, Gifu, but Wulfrum's mind is made up. If there were women enough to go around, he would marry them all to his warriors.' Elgiva turned to Ceolnoth. 'Go, wait outside. Hilda will be out directly, but first I would speak with her.'

He frowned and, for a moment, she thought he would refuse. However, one glance round the room assured him that the girl wasn't going anywhere since there was but one door and a small window.

'Very well, my lady. But don't keep her too long. I grow impatient for my bride.'

With loud laughter the warriors left the room and

Osgifu closed the door behind them. Elgiva turned to Hilda.

'You know there is nought I can do to change this, Hilda.'

'I do not wish to wed him.'

Elgiva looked to Osgifu and the older woman stepped forwards.

'Hilda, listen to me. You have no choice but to wed Ceolnoth, unless to become the plaything of all the rest.'

Hilda drew in a ragged breath and stared at her in horror.

'Gifu is right,' said Elgiva. 'We are none of us free to choose, unless it is to take the lesser of two evils. As the wife of Ceolnoth, his companions will not touch you.'

'He has already forced the girl,' replied Osgifu. ''Tis no wonder she is not minded to have him.'

Hilda drew a deep breath, and dashed away her tears with the back of her hand. 'He has taken me against my will and mayhap I already carry his child in my belly. Must I breed a bastard too, and let it suffer the world's scorn?' She paused. 'I know you can do nothing, my lady, for you are in as sore case yourself. 'Tis just that I am so afraid.'

She began to cry again and Elgiva held her close to comfort her.

'I was too, Hilda.'

'You were never afraid, my lady. I was watching the day you wed Lord Wulfrum, the way you looked about with such calm, facing down all those men. All their eyes could not make you quail.'

'Not so, Hilda. I wanted to run away so far and so fast they would never find me. If I did not, it was because I knew I would never succeed, and I would not give them the satisfaction of seeing my fear. And so I am Earl Wulfrum's wife for good or for ill. There is naught to be done but make the best of it.'

Hilda heard her in wondering silence and then took another ragged breath. 'As I must do with Ceolnoth.'

At that moment a heavy fist pounded on the door.

'Will you come out, wench, or must I come in?'

Osgifu strode across the room, pestle in hand, and put her face close to the wood. 'She'll come when she's ready, Viking.'

'She'll come out now, old woman, or I'll know the reason why.'

'You come in here and I'll brain you, you charmless oaf!'

Further heavy pounding shook the door. Osgifu started back. Elgiva bade Hilda bathe her eyes in cool water from the bowl on the table and then went to the door and opened it. Ceolnoth, startled, lowered a clenched fist.

'Lady?'

'Hilda is coming. Be patient a few moments more.'

The quiet tone was courteous enough, but it bore a command too, and Ceolnoth hesitated. Though he would have liked to push her aside and drag Hilda out by main force, he dared not; he knew well that Lord Wulfrum would not take kindly to any man laying violent hands on his wife. Therefore he swallowed his anger and let his hands fall to his sides. Elgiva remained in the doorway, blocking his path. A few moments later Hilda joined her on the threshold.

'I am ready,' she said.

Elgiva stood aside and let her pass. The girl had regained her composure now, though her eyes bore signs of weeping still. For a moment she and Ceolnoth faced each other in silence. Then he smiled and offered his arm. After a brief hesitation Hilda took it and they walked together through the gathered group of warriors to the waiting priest. Elgiva removed her apron and tossed it aside and then, with Osgifu beside her, followed on.

The ceremony was brief enough and through it she recalled her own wedding day and the terror in her heart. For all she might have fooled the onlookers, she knew it would have taken only a small thing to make her run. Suddenly she became aware of someone beside her, and she looked up to see Wulfrum. He put an arm round her shoulders and drew her close. Still smarting, Elgiva tensed and tried to pull away. The arm tightened. Together they stood thus in uneasy proximity until the brief ceremony was over. Ceolnoth's friends clapped him on the back and gathered round the pair. However, seeing Wulfrum, they fell back a little. He moved among them, his arm still round his wife, drawing her with him to congratulate the newly-wed couple.

'Live long, Ceolnoth. Live long, Hilda.' He took off one of his silver arm rings and gave it to Ceolnoth. 'Wear this in recognition of your service to me. In addition, I will give you one hide of good land. There you may build a home and raise fine sons.'

A rousing cheer greeted his words.

'You are generous, lord,' replied Ceolnoth. 'My wife and I thank you.'

A shocked Hilda stammered out her thanks. Clearly she had not been expecting anything like this. Neither had Elgiva and she looked at her husband in surprise.

'This night we shall feast to celebrate your union,' said

Wulfrum. 'Mayhap in future we shall celebrate many more.'

Another cheer followed this and then conversation broke out in different groups. Elgiva looked at Ceolnoth and Hilda and then threw a quizzical glance at Wulfrum.

'Thank you,' she said. 'It was a generous gift.'

'It is fitting I should reward those who serve me well,' he replied. 'Besides, land gives a man a stake in the place and ties him to it, ensuring his loyalty and that of his kin.'

'And providing for his wife.'

'Yes, that too. One day many of these men will have wives and when they wed they shall have land to farm. There is plenty for all and it is good land, rich and fertile.'

Saxon land, thought Elgiva, but she kept the thought to herself. With this gift he had ensured a good future for Hilda, as well as for her husband. It might yet turn out well. Certainly the matter had been settled more advantageously than she could have hoped yesterday.

Wulfrum sensed a slight softening of her mood. Her body no longer tensed against his arm and, though they regarded him appraisingly, the angry spark was missing from the amber eyes. Now that he was close he could detect the sweet smell of herbs and beneath it the warm scent of her flesh, subtle and arousing. He bent his head and let his lips brush hers. Taken by surprise, Elgiva did not fight. The kiss grew more insistent and her heartbeat quickened as pleasurable warmth swept through her. When he straightened she was pink-cheeked with confusion. Casting a swift glance around her, she could see their embrace had not gone unnoticed.

'My lord, your men…'

'Let them watch.'

He kissed her again, slowly, felt her lips yield to the pressure of his and tasted the sweetness of her mouth. Gods, how he wanted her, wanted to throw her down and make love to her till she begged for mercy, but he knew he couldn't. The damned place was a little too public for that and Elgiva far too shy of him anyway. Reluctantly he drew back, his gaze searching her face. There was a strange expression in those amber eyes, one that he couldn't quite fathom. What was she thinking? He would have given gold to know. Controlling himself with an effort, Wulfrum slackened his hold.

Elgiva turned away in confusion, shocked by her own reaction to his kiss. The first had been stolen, the second had not. She should have felt disgust, but she had not. On the contrary, what she had felt was stealthy and growing warmth. Almost she had wanted him to kiss her again. The realisation burned as his former words returned to haunt her: *You will come.* Humiliated by the memory and by her weakness, she detached herself from his arm and turned away.

'What are you afraid of, Elgiva?'

'Nothing.' The assertion was belied by the rosy blush on her neck and cheeks.

'Liar.'

'It is the truth.'

'Is it?' He drew closer and she saw him smile.

'I…it's the herbs. I was but part way through my work when Hilda came in. I must go and finish it. I don't want the plants to spoil.'

The smile widened, telling more than words of his scepticism and his enjoyment of her evident confusion. However, he made no further move to hold her and she turned and walked away, trying to gather her scattered wits, determined to put as much distance between them as possible and aware the whole time that Wulfrum watched her retreat. And it was a retreat. She acknowledged it to herself. Another few minutes and he would have kissed her again and she would have let him. Recalling the dangerous power of his kisses, Elgiva shivered. She would not allow him to manipulate her again. He wanted her surrender and meant to have it, to conquer her as finally as he had conquered Ravenswood. It was a challenge to him, nothing more, and she would not yield herself up as a prize. Women meant nothing to Wulfrum other than as a pleasing diversion, a distraction, and it seemed she was his latest amusement. To her horror Elgiva felt hot tears prick her eyelids and she hastened into the storeroom before anyone could notice.

Later, when she had calmed down, she cursed herself for her stupidity in seeming to give the incident too much significance. Certainly Wulfrum made no mention of it when they met that evening in the hall, and, if he was angry, he gave no sign. He greeted her with courtesy as she took her place beside him and to her eye appeared quite unruffled by an experience that had shaken her to the core. It seemed to her that it was the practised ease of a man completely familiar with women who took what he wanted and moved on. He might be her husband, but it was foolish to think she could ever mean more to him than any other woman. The only difference was that she belonged to him. He could take her whenever he chose. When she returned his kiss, he must surely have scented victory. Her own weakness appalled her. Had she so little resolution after all, that a man could conquer with a kiss? Elgiva bit her lip. She could still feel the warmth of his mouth on hers. What a fool she was. He would never regard her as anything other than a trophy.

CHAPTER TEN

As THE DAYS passed the brooding atmosphere lightened in the warm sunshine and, as the threat of death and destruction receded, the people in the village began to go more freely about their business again. Now the work was in full swing, for, apart from all the necessary repairs, there were crops and livestock to be tended and the work had to be supervised. Since the steward had been one of those killed in the fighting when the war band struck, Wulfrum needed to find another and soon. He decided to consult Elgiva.

'Whom shall I appoint?' he asked. 'Who seems to you to be the best candidate?'

Recovering from her surprise she gave her answer without hesitation. 'Gurth. He's got a good head on his shoulders and he's hard-working. I know my father always considered him to be reliable and honest too.'

Accordingly Gurth was summoned to appear before Wulfrum in the great hall. A short, stocky individual of middle years, with grey in his hair and beard, Gurth was, nevertheless, an impressive figure, for he had about him an air of quiet assurance. He stood calmly enough before Wulfrum, though he eyed his men with some inner unease, clearly wondering what he could have done to draw such unwelcome attention. He glanced once at Elgiva, though her face gave no clue as to the reason for his presence here, and then listened carefully as Wulfrum spoke. As he heard the words, Gurth could ill conceal his surprise and pleasure.

'I need a man I can trust,' said Wulfrum. 'My wife seems to think you are that man.'

'The lady honours me,' replied Gurth.

'Will you serve me in the office of steward?'

All eyes were on Gurth and, in the brief silence that followed, he was aware of the intentness of their gaze. It was possibly coincidence that several of Wulfrum's men rested their hands on their sword hilts. However, Gurth was no fool and this was a considerable promotion. It didn't take him long to make up his mind.

'I will, my lord.'

Wulfrum smiled. 'It is well. You will commence your duties immediately and you will answer directly to me. Tomorrow early we will ride out. I want to know every detail of this estate down to the last cow and chicken, the last sack of oats and sheaf of hay.'

'It shall be as you wish, my lord.'

There being little else to say, Gurth was dismissed shortly afterwards. He made his bow and left the hall.

'I think he is a good choice,' said Wulfrum as the man disappeared from view.

'Well, if he isn't, I'll spill his tripes for him,' replied Ironfist.

Seeing Elgiva's startled look, Wulfrum concealed a grin. 'You need have no fear, my lady. If he serves me well, Gurth will thrive.'

'He will serve you well,' she replied.

'Good, for I would have this estate restored to order.'

'I also. As it used to be when my father was alive.'

'I promise you it will be so again.'

Elgiva believed him. Already the signs of his rule were everywhere in building and repair work. It gladdened her heart to see it. More than that, it pleased her to know he had asked for her advice and acted on it.

'Gurth will be a real asset,' she said. Then, throwing her husband a sideways glance, 'Would you really have Olaf kill if him if he were not?'

'Of course. I will have no truck with treachery or incompetence. Olaf here will keep an eye on the man, and he does not suffer fools gladly.'

'Gurth is no fool.'

'I'm glad to hear it. In that case he may live.'

Wulfrum caught Ironfist's eye and the two of them laughed out loud. Realising too late they had been teasing her, Elgiva glared at them.

'Why, you…' Words failed her.

Wulfrum's amusement increased. Elgiva shook her head, annoyed with herself for falling into the trap, and annoyed with him too. Then the funny side of it struck her and she began to laugh, albeit unwillingly. Wulfrum stared at her in surprise and his own laughter faded a little—he had not thought her beauty could be improved. Seeing her now, he knew he had been wrong. Feeling the intensity of that look, Elgiva felt suddenly self-conscious and her own amusement ebbed. It was definitely time to leave.

'My lord, I fear I am no match for you today. With your leave, I have matters to attend to.'

Disappointed, he nodded. 'As you will, my lady.'

She nodded to Ironfist and then crossed the hall and made her escape, knowing as she did so that every step was observed.

In fact, Elgiva had not lied when she said there was work to be done and she determined to turn her attention to it now, returning with swift steps to the bower. She entered and heard the door shut behind her. A man, garbed in the manner of a serf, stood in the shadow behind. Elgiva caught her breath.

'Who are you? What do you want?'

'Do you not know me, Elgiva?' He lowered his hood and she found herself staring at Aylwin.

'You.'

'Did I not promise I would come?'

Elgiva swallowed hard. 'My lord, you must not be found here. The Vikings would show no mercy.'

'Brekka keeps watch. He will warn if any approach.' Aylwin smiled. 'But danger or no, I had to see you.' He surveyed her critically. 'You look well, Elgiva.'

'I am well enough,' she replied. 'And you, my lord? Are your wounds healed?'

'Aye, for the most part.'

'Then I beg you to go. Leave this place while still you may.'

'And abandon you?'

'You must. I am Wulfrum's wife now.'

His brows drew together. 'The Viking may have forced you to wed him, but your captivity will be over very soon.'

'What do you mean?'

'I shall not tamely give up what belongs to me.'

She shook her head. 'I do not belong to you any more, Aylwin.' Even as she said it, she knew she never had.

'You will be mine again, Elgiva. I swear it. I will free you from the accursed Viking's yoke.' He took her by the shoulders and looked into her face. 'I have dreamed of this moment for so long and yet now I am here with you I can scarce believe it.'

Appalled by the tenderness in his voice and the almost fanatical light in his eye, Elgiva trembled. As Aylwin drew her to him, she turned her head aside so his lips only grazed her cheek.

'My lord, you must not.' She took a step back.

His hands dropped to his sides and he frowned. 'What is it, Elgiva? What is wrong?'

'Don't you see? I can never be yours. Wulfrum will never let me go. Even if you were to steal me away, he would find us, no matter how long it took, and his vengeance would be terrible.'

'I will find a way.'

In desperation, it was she who now gripped his arms. 'There is none. You must believe that.'

For a moment he was silent. 'No way?' he asked. 'Or is it rather that you do not wish to leave the handsome earl?'

'That isn't fair, Aylwin. I did not choose my fate. It was forced on me and I cannot change it.'

'You mean, you would not.'

'Ravenswood is my home. I will not abandon it or its people.'

'A noble sentiment and a convenient one.' His gaze bored into her. 'You hide behind it to avoid the truth.'

'No.'

'Aye. How long did it take the Viking to win your heart? Or is it the pleasures of his bed that draw you?'

Elgiva's cheeks grew hot, but she kept a hold on her temper.

'Insulting me will not change anything, my lord. For good or ill Wulfrum is my husband now and my first loyalty is to him.'

His lip curled. 'I had not thought you so faithless, Elgiva, or so treacherous.'

The words stung and brought tears to her eyes. To conceal her hurt, she turned away from him. Aylwin moved towards the door. As he reached it, he paused.

'I see it was a mistake to come here.'

'Just go, my lord, while you may.'

'I'll go.' His voice was soft and bitter. 'But I'll be back. And with an army to rout these Danish scum once and for all. Then I will slay your husband with my own hands.'

Elgiva heard the door open and close. Then she was alone. Heart pounding, she leaned against the wooden planks in trembling relief. For some minutes she remained thus as the enormity of the situation was borne upon her. Then, unable to bear the close confinement of the room any longer, she quit the place and went out into the fresh air. She needed space to think. Without conscious choice her feet turned towards the burying ground.

How long she remained there she had no idea. All she could see was Aylwin's face as he turned from her in disgust. She had betrayed him and sided with the enemy. Yet what else could she have done? Made him false promises? She did not love him and never would, but she wanted him safe all the same. If he continued on his present course, it could only end in disaster for all concerned.

A footfall behind roused her from the reverie with a start and she looked round to see Wulfrum approaching. Did he know? Had he seen? Her heart thundered in her breast. Only with an effort did she force an outward semblance of calm. If he had seen anything at all, or even suspected, then Aylwin and Brekka would be prisoners now.

Wulfrum halted a few feet away, his gaze taking in her evident agitation.

'Your pardon, I have startled you,' he said. 'You looked so rapt in your thoughts I did not wish to intrude.'

She took a deep breath. 'Was there something you wished to speak of, my lord?'

The tone was courteous enough, but there was a tension beneath that Wulfrum caught immediately. He excused it. Given the place, it was perhaps only natural under the circumstances.

'Nothing of importance,' he replied.

By tacit consent they walked back to the hall together, but he was aware that she had withdrawn from him somehow.

'What is it, Elgiva?'

'Nothing,' she replied. 'Or nothing that can be helped.'

'Grief is not soon healed,' he acknowledged. 'Nor can one set a time on it.'

Elgiva threw him a searching look, wondering what he might know of grief or loss. Surely that was what the Vikings inflicted on others. They walked on in silence for a little way.

'But life goes on,' he continued, 'and the living must learn to deal with their loss.'

'I cannot forget.'

'No, but you can move on. Besides, what is the alternative—to brood continually over the past until we grow old and withered?'

'You are an optimist.'

'No, I am a realist.'

'The Danes have made the reality we live in now,' replied Elgiva.

There was an unaccustomed bitterness in her tone and he eyed her shrewdly.

'You still feel anger in your heart, do you not?'

'Yes.'

'So would I, but destiny is a strange thing.'

'It was not destiny brought the Norsemen here,' she replied. 'It was a thirst for revenge, revenge and greed.' She turned to face him. 'That's all the Danes know, isn't it? Killing and destruction and the use of force.'

Wulfrum's gaze met and held her own. 'That is past.'

'Is it? I think that memory is not so soon erased.'

'No, it is not.'

'How would you know?'

His expression altered and for a moment she saw both pain and anger in the blue eyes. 'I discovered it early.'

'How so?'

'As a result of a blood feud. One night his enemies came to my father's hall and surrounded it. Then they set it alight and waited for those inside to come out. When they did, they were cut down. None escaped.'

'But you—'

'I wasn't there. I had gone with one of the men to a neighbour's farm to deliver some things for my father. It being winter, the days were short and we remained overnight. When we returned next day, we found the hall a smoking ruin and my family slain.'

Elgiva had heard of such things, though never till now from one who had experienced them, and she felt pity in her heart for the frightened and bewildered boy he must have been on that terrible day.

'How old were you?'

'Ten.'

'That is young to be cast adrift on the world.'

'Aye, but I was fortunate.'

Suddenly she remembered the words he had spoken that fateful morning when she had examined the sword, Dragon Tooth.

'It was Ragnar who took you in, wasn't it?'

'Yes, my father was one of his closest friends. He sheltered me, brought me up. From him I learned the warrior code—in fact, just about everything I know. When I grew to manhood, I avenged my family and slew those responsible for their deaths, all still living anyway. I slew them with the sword Ragnar gave me. Then I took back the title that was mine.'

'And when Ragnar was killed, you came to avenge his death.'

'That's right. As I told you, it was a matter of honour.'

As she listened it seemed to Elgiva that many things had become clear. In her mind's eye she could see the small boy standing alone amid the ruins of his home and the bodies of the slain. She could imagine him growing up, passing from childhood to manhood, learning the skills of the warrior, his rage becoming a cold, implacable thing, biding his time until his family should be avenged. It was not hard to see why he should have felt such love and loyalty for a man who was the sworn enemy of her people.

Wulfrum watched her closely, wondering why he had

told her. It hadn't been his intention, but somehow it had come out anyway. Perhaps it had needed to. At least now she knew who he was, knew something of the events that had shaped his life.

'I'm sick of bloodshed and fighting, Elgiva.'

'What do you want, then?'

'To build something worthwhile.'

'Out of the ashes?'

'Aye, why not?' He paused. 'You and I together.'

'I? Am I not your chattel?'

'You are far more than that and you know it.' He drew her closer. 'Let there be no more secrets between us.'

There was no trace of mockery in his face or his voice. Bending his head, he kissed her very gently. Elgiva closed her eyes. No more secrets. How she wished it were true. But how could she make such a promise and keep it? Could she tell him that she was consorting with rebels? If he ever discovered the truth, his goodwill would evaporate on the spot. Worse, there would be a dire retribution. Even if he let her live, his trust would be gone for good. Then what would remain? She shivered.

Wulfrum glanced down at her.

'Don't be afraid, Elgiva. All will be well.'

Sick at heart, she wished she could believe it.

Later she told Osgifu about Aylwin. The older woman heard her in appalled silence.

'Aylwin should never have come. God send the Danes do not find out.'

'God send Aylwin has more sense than to lead a revolt. He and his followers would be slaughtered to a man.'

'True enough.' She paused. 'What will you do now?'

'Nothing.'

Elgiva sighed. If she spoke, she betrayed her people. If she kept silence, she betrayed her husband. Torn between two loyalties, she dreaded the time when she must be with Wulfrum again, acting a part now, pretending that all was well, knowing it was a lie. He was perceptive and intuitive, and, if the act was not convincing, would know immediately that something was amiss. He was her husband and he had in some measure given her his trust. The knowledge that she betrayed it was like a knife in her heart. She could never have imagined it would cut so deeply.

If Wulfrum noted aught amiss in her manner, he said nothing. Indeed, with the warm weather his days were busy anyway. Under his governance Ravenswood began once again to show signs of its former prosperity. The buildings were restored to a proper state of repair, the fences mended, the land well tended. The crops ripened in the fields and the first hay crop was cut. Under proper tending young lambs grew strong and new calves grazed beside their mothers in the pastures. Even the fruit crop would be good, for the branches of the orchard trees were laden. The air was filled with the drone of bees moving among the flowers and the hives. Beyond it all, the forest stretched in a rolling canopy of unbroken green.

The fine weather drew Elgiva out of doors and she and Osgifu did much of their work in the sunshine before the open door of the women's bower. Several times they went out to gather plants. Wulfrum made no objection to these small excursions, though each time one of his men was never far behind. To Elgiva it was a salutary reminder of the order of things, yet she gave no sign that she found the presence of the guards irksome, and it would have been futile to protest. Instead, she gave her full attention to the task, returning at length with Osgifu to prepare the balms and potions for which they were renowned. Never by word or look did she give any indication that the forest held more significance than its healing flowers and plants.

However, the knowledge of deceit weighed heavy on her and Elgiva found it harder to sleep. She would lie awake in the sultry darkness, her mind racing, listening to the sound of Wulfrum's breathing, her skin damp with perspiration from his nearness, part of her wanting him to reach out for her and part of her fearing that he might, every nerve alive to his presence. For all manner of reasons the bed was too hot and eventually, after tossing and turning, she would doze for an hour or two and then waken unrefreshed.

Invariably Elgiva woke early with the sun and, one morning, unable to stay any longer in the stifling heat of the room, she left Wulfrum sleeping and dressed quietly. Then she slipped from the chamber and left the hall, heading for the unguarded postern gate. It was always barred, but that presented little obstacle. Thence the way was clear to the forest. The place she sought was not far off, but it was secluded and there the river flowed over a rocky outcrop into a wide pool beneath. The thought of the cool clear water was more than ever appealing and, at this hour, she could be certain of being undisturbed.

The early morning air was fresh and clear, smelling of damp earth for the dew was yet on the grass. It wet the hem of her gown as she passed and soaked into her shoes. Elgiva smiled, making her way unerringly through the trees to the river. It was narrow and swift flowing, and she followed it a little way before coming at length to the pool. Looking cautiously around to ensure she was alone, she slipped off her clothes and waded into the clear water. It was cold enough at first to make her gasp, but its freshness was delightful after the heat within doors, and, taking a deep breath, she plunged in.

Wulfrum woke early and stretched, yawning prodigiously. For all it was early, the heat in the room was already mounting. He rolled over and reached out a hand for Elgiva. The bed was empty. The knowledge brought him to instant wakefulness. A swift glance around the room revealed that her clothes were missing and the door unbarred. In moments he was out of bed and dressing swiftly before making his way down to the hall. Men sprawled on benches and floor, oblivious to his presence. Of his wife there was no sign. Wulfrum strode to the door and looked about, but found no sign of life or movement. Then he noted the unbarred postern and his jaw tightened. He ran to the stable to saddle Firedrake.

A few minutes later he was mounted and heading out on the track that led to the forest. He had guessed immediately which way Elgiva would go and, sure enough, as he left the hall behind and came into open ground, he found her trail in the wet grass. She had said nothing about wishing to collect plants and none of his men was in attendance. It was a matter he fully intended to take up with the vixen when he found her. Holding the horse to a walk, he followed the trail to the river. There he reined in and, studying the ground, found the print of a shoe in the soft earth, a small foot, undoubtedly a woman's. Certain now that Elgiva had come this way, he frowned, wondering what she was up to. Even after all these weeks she still had the power to surprise and unsettle. Unpredictability was, he reflected, all part of her considerable charm. He let the horse follow at a gentle pace until the dense growth made riding impractical and he was forced to dismount and continue on foot. The narrow path continued on a little way beyond and presently he saw a rocky outcrop and a waterfall with a pool below where a woman was swimming. Wulfrum grinned and moved forwards to a vantage point where he could watch unseen.

It was some time before Elgiva turned for the bank. However, the sun was getting higher and she knew she should return to the hall before her absence was discovered. Wulfrum might take it amiss that she had gone out without one of his men in attendance but, with luck, she would be back before he woke. She waded ashore and was reaching for her kirtle when some sixth sense warned her of another presence. Her head jerked up and with a gasp of outrage she found herself staring at Wulfrum.

'You!'

He grinned, unrepentant. 'I.'

'What are you doing here?'

'Looking for you.'

'How long have you been there?'

'Long enough.' Long enough, he thought, to look his fill at that wonderful body. Despite the kirtle she was holding so close, an agreeable amount was still on view and he was unashamedly making the most if it.

A dark suspicion began to form in her mind. 'You've been watching me?'

'Yes.'

Unable to think of any immediate or suitable reply, she eyed him warily, only too aware of her present state of undress and that his eyes missed nothing. He surveyed her thus for some moments before getting to his feet. Before he had taken two paces Elgiva was struggling hastily into her kirtle, throwing her wet hair back over her shoulders. Wulfrum grinned. He drew closer, making her aware again of the remoteness of the place and that they were quite alone.

'I missed you when I woke.'

'It was hot. I couldn't sleep.'

'And you managed to get past my guards once more.'

'I...I thought there could be no danger here.'

'You will not do it again, Elgiva.' The words were quietly spoken, but there was no mistaking the implacable tone.

'Did you think I had fled, my lord?'

'No. I trust you more than that. But the times are uncertain and the place remote and I would not have you in danger.'

Elgiva was caught unawares, as much by the sincerity in his voice as by the words themselves. The knowledge of her deceit returned with force. However, there was no time for deeper reflection, for his arms were round her and then his mouth closed over hers. As he kissed her, the familiar stealthy flame flickered into being deep within her. She shivered a *frisson* that was partly the residual chill of the water and partly fear—not of him, but of herself.

Wulfrum felt her shiver and looked down into her face. However, he could not fathom the expression he saw there. Did she fear him still? He wanted her now, wanted her with every fibre of his being, but he sensed a deep-seated unease behind her reluctance. Drawing back, he bent to retrieve her gown. Elgiva put it on quickly but her wet hair became entangled with the lacing and her cold fingers fumbled the task. Wulfrum's disquieting smile didn't help in the least. He watched her struggle for a while. Then she felt his hands on her shoulders turning her gently round. He untangled her hair and laced the gown himself. Then he held out his hand.

'Come, my lady.'

For a fraction of a second he saw her hesitate before placing her fingers in his. Then, together, they retraced their steps along the path to where his horse was tethered. Wulfrum turned her to face him.

'Ride with me.'

'There's no need. I can walk back.'

'It wasn't a request.'

The expression in those blue eyes admitted of no argument. He laced his hands and bent to receive her foot, sending her lightly into the saddle. Then he mounted behind her. For some time neither one spoke and the only sounds were the faint footfalls of the hooves on the turf and the creak of saddle leather. Elgiva's face was much warmer now, partly because the sun was higher in the sky, but chiefly because Wulfrum's arm was round her, holding her close, and she was annoyed to find that she liked it. Liked the warmth and the strength of him and the scent of musk and leather she had come to associate with him. Now they evoked other more disturbing thoughts: thoughts of his kiss, thoughts of fear and desire. She had tried so hard to hate him, but knew now that she did not.

Once he glanced down at her and she saw him smile. Her colour deepened, but still she said nothing. To be close to him thus and know she gave succour to those who intended his death turned the knife in her breast. If she had thought there was the remotest chance of escaping the high saddle, she would have taken it, but the arm that held her was as unyielding as oak. His face was dangerously close to hers now and the blue eyes alight with amusement.

'You're enjoying this, aren't you?' she demanded, striving for the bantering tone that would lull suspicion.

'Yes, very much,' was the unruffled reply. 'Aren't you?'

Elgiva remained silent. Wulfrum did not press her for a reply, but his smile widened. It had not escaped her either that his horse was being held to a slow walk and it was taking a mighty long time to get home.

It was a good half an hour later when he reined in by the stables. Elgiva breathed more easily and some of her self-command returned, for now he would lower her to the ground and she could make good her escape. She was quite wrong; he dismounted first, lifting her down after him and, retaining his hold on her waist, drew her into a more intimate embrace, a long, lingering kiss that set every nerve alight.

Wulfrum felt her response, felt her melt against him, and his passion woke in reply. He crushed her to him, hungry for her. The warmth of her flesh beneath her gown recalled the sight of her naked, pressed beneath him on the furs of their bed. He wanted her so badly it hurt. In that moment he would have sworn she wanted him, but then, just as soon, he felt her body tense and she turned her head aside. He looked into her face, saw the anguish there.

'What is it, Elgiva? What's wrong?'

'Nothing. I…'

'There is. Tell me.'

His lips nuzzled her hair, her neck, her throat. Elgiva closed her eyes, every part of her alive to his touch, every part of her wanting it to go on and knowing it must not. It took every ounce of her will to step away.

'Please, Wulfrum. Let me go.'

He wanted to deny her, to test her resistance, to carry her to their chamber and continue where they had left off, but he underestimated the power of the amber eyes that spoke more eloquently than words of some inner distress.

'Why, Elgiva? What are you afraid of?'

She shook her head, unable to frame the words to explain. He saw only her reluctance and his heart sank. In any other woman he would have suspected caprice, some game to whet his appetite, but he sensed this was something more. How he wished she would tell him, but he would not force her confidence any more than he would force her compliance. He let his hands fall from her waist.

'Go, then, if you must.'

The look of relief on her face was quite apparent and once he might have found it amusing. His hand tightened over the rein as he watched her walk away. Then he led the stallion into the stable. He unsaddled the horse and brushed it down himself, for in truth he required some space from his men and the public life of the hall. The mechanical task of grooming was soothing and busied his hands, though his mind was elsewhere. The early morning encounter with his wife had unsettled him more than he would ever have thought possible. When he had married Elgiva, he had taken a bride of good family and much wealth. That he had found her most desirable was an added bonus. The advantages of the match were obvious, at least for himself. He had never considered her feelings in the matter. He had forced her compliance in almost every way. It had never occurred to him then that he might find himself in the position he was in now, that what had begun as physical desire would turn into something much stronger and infinitely more disturbing. He did not deceive himself as to the feelings Elgiva had for him; she was physically attracted to him, but she continued to fight it— he was still the enemy. Once he had desired only her physical surrender. Now he wanted far more than that. The irony was not lost on him.

Having seen to the needs of his horse, Wulfrum left the stable, thinking to make his way back to the hall. However, a glimpse of blue gown caught his eye and he saw Elgiva standing by the gate to the paddock where Mara was turned out to graze. Since the coming of the war band she had not been permitted to ride, but still lost no opportunity to spend a few moments with the horse. Evidently the feeling was reciprocated for the mare had walked across to greet her, standing close to the fence while Elgiva stroked her nose. He heard her speak to the animal, but did not catch the words because the distance was too great. She remained there for several minutes more before moving with evident reluctance towards the women's bower. The mare watched her go and whinnied softly. Elgiva gave her a fleeting smile and turned to look over her shoulder once before continuing on her way. She did not see Wulfrum, being evidently preoccupied with her own thoughts, but he could see her clearly. The mask of poise and serenity that she wore in public had slipped for the moment and all he could see now was the deep unhappiness that lay beneath. It hit him with the force of a blow.

CHAPTER ELEVEN

ELGIVA was rudely awakened the following morning by a lusty whack delivered by a strong hand across her bare buttocks. With a yelp of protest, she started up to see Wulfrum standing over her. He was already dressed in leather leggings and tunic, belted at the waist where a wicked-looking knife was sheathed.

'Get up, wench. 'Tis broad daylight already and I would hunt.'

'Your pardon, my lord. I had not realised it was so late.'

Elgiva scrambled from bed under his appraising gaze. Then she pulled on a kirtle and raked her nails through her hair, trying to bring about some semblance of order. Wulfrum grinned and strolled to the door.

'Make ready, Elgiva. I am not intending to wait.'

Abandoning the failed attempt to tame her hair into a braid, she slid her feet into shoes and reached for her gown.

'Shall I fetch you some food, my lord?'

'One of the servants can do that. Ready yourself.'

'My lord?'

'For the hunt. You are coming with me.'

Elgiva stared at him in stunned amazement and then her face was lit by a dazzling smile. 'Do you mean it?'

'I have said. Besides, that puny mare in the stable needs exercise and she is not up to a man's weight. Make haste now.'

Elgiva needed no second bidding. Summoning Osgifu, she went to the chest where her clothes were stored and drew out leggings, shirt and leather tunic, the clothes she had worn when she hunted with her father. She had not thought to wear them again and her heart beat faster at the thought of a long ride in the fresh air. It was with difficulty that she could sit still long enough for Osgifu to comb and braid her hair. When it was done, she hurried down to the courtyard where Wulfrum waited with his men. Her mare was saddled and ready. Seeing his wife, Wulfrum smiled faintly, running his eye over her costume, but he made no comment, swinging himself into Firedrake's saddle. The black tossed its head and sidled, eager to be off, but Wulfrum held him in while Elgiva mounted. The little mare seemed tiny among the larger mounts of the men, but she knew the horse would hold her own. Sensing her rider's excitement, Mara gave a half-rear for she too scented open country and freedom. Elgiva laughed and patted the glossy neck.

Once beyond the gate the riders set off a steady pace, holding their horses in, not wishing to tire them before the chase. The mare pranced and bucked to feel turf under her hooves. Wulfrum said nothing, but watched as Elgiva brought her under control, her hand gentle on the rein. He knew the animal was fresh for she had not been ridden these last weeks, but her antics seemed not to worry her rider in the least. He heard Elgiva speak softly and saw the spirited little horse drop her head and settle into her stride. He smiled to himself. His wife could ride, no question.

They rode further into the forest, following a well-worn path wide enough for two horses to walk abreast. Beside them walked serfs with Wulfrum's boarhounds, huge and powerful beasts hungry for the chase. It was early yet, but the sunlight dappled the ground with shade and the grassy verges were bright with wild flowers. All around them the trees were full of birdsong and every branch alive with new green leaves. Elgiva breathed deeply and smiled, feeling the tension flow from her, enjoying the clean air and the movement of the horse beneath her. Beside her Wulfrum rode in silence, seemingly wrapped in private thought, but Elgiva did not mind. From time to time she cast a covert glance at him, noting well how easily he controlled the powerful horse, how his body moved with the animal's rhythm as though he were part of it. She wondered where he had learned to ride, who had taught him. It occurred to her there were still many things she did not know about the man who was her husband.

Presently they came to a place where the spoor was clear and the hounds were loosed. The riders followed, turning into the trees. It was ancient woodland, where the branches of oaks and beech met overhead in a green vault that shut out most of the sun save for occasional dappled patches of light. Then the hounds found the scent and the hunters were away. Elgiva touched Mara with her heels and felt the mare shift from a standing start to a canter. Leaning forwards, she guided their course through the trees, ducking low boughs and weaving to avoid the branches that slashed at them. The horse stayed for nothing, leaping the fallen logs in her path, the flying hooves thudding over the carpet of leaf mould beneath the great trees. Once Elgiva thought she glimpsed the hounds, running swift and silent ahead of her. Around her she could hear the voices of the men calling, urging their horses on to greater speed.

The boar had been following a direct line, but now veered away down a steep, open slope. This last was largely covered by dense blackthorn. The pig plunged into the thicket where it was much harder for the riders to follow. Elgiva drew rein, thinking fast. If they followed into the thicket, she and Mara would be scratched to ribbons, for she knew the place of old. Her father's men had once brought down a boar nearby. The slope ended in a stream with more woodland beyond, and she guessed the quarry would make for it, trying to throw the hounds off the scent. She knew a path that skirted the slope and came out by the stream further on. Turning Mara's head, she touched the horse with her heels once more, cantering off on a tangent. Out of the corner of her eye she saw Wulfrum's stallion and grinned. Thus far he had not let her out of his sight. They would see now whether his mount was the equal of hers for speed and stamina. Elgiva held to her course, hoping her guess had been right. Off to her right she could hear the men shouting and picked up curses on the wind. It seemed they had found the blackthorn. As the path curved, she glimpsed the stream and then the dogs. She was right. Her grin widened triumphantly. As she neared the place she saw other riders breaking from the thicket, urging their mounts across the stream. Elgiva slowed Mara a little and splashed through after them. The hounds were milling round, trying to pick up the scent again. A few moments later Wulfrum drew up beside her, grinning broadly.

'You know the land well, my lady.'

'I have ridden over it many times. My father hunted here very often and I with him.'

'So I see.' Wulfrum couched the great boar spear and sat back in his saddle, observing her. 'You follow your own path.'

'Where it is a better path, lord.'

He glanced at his men and the scratches they sported on face and hand, even on the tough leather hunting clothes, and he laughed.

'In this case it was a better path. I have no love for blackthorn.'

'Nor I.'

Just then the hounds picked up the trail again and the hunters pressed on. Elgiva urged the mare on and felt the little horse leap forwards to a gallop, hurtling down the narrow path, twisting and turning through the trees. Elgiva bent low over her neck to avoid the branches that clawed at her, thankful for the protection of her stout clothing. As they raced through the green gloom beneath the tree canopy, she thought she could see a pool of light up ahead and headed towards it. Before her lay a clearing, a grassy glade, edged by great trees and, between, dense thickets. Somewhere to her right she could hear the sounds of the other horses but she could no longer see them. Glancing left, she could see nothing there, either. That look was a mistake for she failed to see the low bough until she was almost on it. Swift reflexes saved her and she ducked, throwing herself low along the near side of her mount, and the branch that would otherwise have smashed into her body caught her right knee instead. It lifted her out of the saddle, pitching her clear off the horse. She landed hard and for a few dazed seconds lay still, fighting to regain her breath while the branches spun crazily overhead. Eventually, when her breathing steadied, she sat up cautiously to ascertain that there was no serious damage. All seemed well enough. However, when she managed to get back on her feet, she was immediately aware of the protest from her knee. She glanced at it ruefully. No doubt it would sport a magnificent bruise on the morrow. Still, it could have been much worse and there was naught to do but thank fortune for a lucky escape.

Her horse was grazing some yards away and Elgiva began to hobble in that direction. She was only feet away when Mara suddenly threw up her head and snorted. Elgiva spoke quietly to calm her, but the mare did not respond, staring instead across the clearing to the edge of the thicket. Following the horse's gaze, Elgiva looked to see what was spooking her. Then she froze. There, part shadowed by undergrowth, stood a huge boar. The red eyes glinted with menace and its tusks gouged out great chunks of turf as it tossed its head this way and that. With trembling hand she reached for the trailing reins, but Mara bolted, shouldering her violently aside. Elgiva lost her balance and fell backwards. Attracted by the movement of the fleeing horse, the boar made a short charge in that direction. Elgiva screamed. The boar stopped short, sensing another quarry. Then it turned towards her, sniffing the air. She screamed again, edging away, an icy knot of fear in her gut. If it reached her, the creature would rend her limb from limb. She had no spear, no weapon save one small belt knife, worse than useless against such a foe. She was dry-throated with terror as her eyes scanned the nearest tree, but even if she could have got that far the branches were too high to reach. The boar moved forwards a few paces and pawed the ground, sending dirt flying. Elgiva swallowed hard.

Then there came another sound, the thud of galloping hooves, and a great black horse hurtled into her line of vision. It came to a sliding stop on its haunches just a few yards away. Then she heard a familiar voice.

'Don't move, Elgiva. As you value your life.'

With leaping heart she saw Wulfrum dismount, the great spear already in his hand. Then he moved across the clearing, all his attention on the animal in front of him. The boar discovered a new enemy and turned in his direction. Without warning it charged. Elgiva's hand flew to her mouth, stifling a cry of terror as in slow motion she saw Wulfrum drop into a crouch to brace the end of the spear in the turf, but the pig was upon him. She saw him throw himself to one side and watched in horror as the animal hurtled past, one of its tusks tearing a great rent in the sleeve of his hunting tunic. He rolled up on to one knee in an instant, bracing the spear fast as the boar spun round like lightning, coming at him again, squealing with rage. Ashen faced, Elgiva watched the great beast hurl itself on to the spear point, hearing its fury and pain as it charged full to the cross piece, burying the barb deep in its breast. Hot blood sprayed over Wulfrum's arms and chest, dyeing his leather gauntlets and tunic as he wrestled with the enraged creature, vicious and deadly even in its final moments. The squealing and the struggle went on for what seemed a horribly long time until at length the brute rolled over in its death throes. Almost rigid with fright, Elgiva watched the struggle between man and beast, hardly daring to breathe until the great boar lay still. Wulfrum got to his feet, breathing hard.

'Are you all right?'

Elgiva nodded, fighting faintness, unable to speak. He drew her to her feet and then his arms were around her and he was holding her. He could feel her shaking.

'It's over. The beast is dead.'

Weak with relief, Elgiva took refuge in that close embrace and closed her eyes, feeling the fierce pounding of her heart and the sickness in her stomach from her brush with death. She was aware that he was speaking to her softly, as he might to a child, quieting her fear. It was his gentleness that brought the water welling into her eyes and then caused it to spill over as all the tension of the past weeks found its outlet. Wulfrum realised then that he had never seen her cry. Through every trial her courage had borne her triumphant, but even courage has its limits. He heard in her sobs the stresses she never spoke of, the fear and the hurt that she kept hidden, and his arms tightened about her. For some moments they remained thus until, gradually, as the terror subsided and the sobbing ceased, some of her colour returned. Wulfrum smiled.

'It's all right,' he said. 'You're safe now.'

Elgiva looked into his face. 'Oh, Wulfrum. If you hadn't come…'

'I would never let harm come to you.'

He spoke as if it were an everyday occurrence to slay a boar single-handed, but she knew he had put his life on the line for her.

'Thank you,' she said. It sounded so inadequate to her ears but he heard the sincerity in those simple words.

For a moment neither one moved. Then, very gently, her hands reached up and drew his face down to hers and she kissed him full on the lips. In stunned surprise he stared into the amber eyes, not quite daring to believe what he saw there. Elgiva kissed him again. Then his arms closed around her, crushing her to him, his mouth seeking hers in a lingering passionate embrace that encountered no resistance. Rather he felt her arms around his neck, her soft mouth yielding to his as she pressed closer. He had dreamed of this so often that even now he was unsure whether he woke or slept.

Just then he heard voices and several horsemen appeared through the trees. With a rueful smile Wulfrum slackened his hold on Elgiva. She returned the smile and reluctantly let her hands slide from his shoulders. As they did so they encountered torn leather and the stickiness of blood. She glanced down, frowning.

'Wulfrum, you're hurt!'

'It is slight. The beast caught me with his tusk on that first rush.'

'Let me see.'

He extended the arm to reveal a ragged gash. It wasn't deep, but it had bled copiously, staining the shirt and the leather tunic.

'That must be cleaned and bound when we return,' she said, 'lest it should fester.'

Wulfrum didn't argue, for in truth the wound was beginning to ache. Looking at it, Elgiva was reminded again of how much he had risked for her sake and what she might have lost.

Further reflection was denied her by the approach of the oncoming riders. The huntsmen halted a few feet away, led by Olaf Ironfist. He looked at the waiting pair and then at the dead beast.

'By Odin's beard, a fine boar,' he observed. 'He must have put up a worthy struggle.'

'Worthy enough,' acknowledged Wulfrum with a wry grin.

The two men exchanged a few words about the transportation of the dead pig, then, having seen the instructions carried out, Ironfist went to retrieve the horses now grazing quietly a few yards off. Wulfrum turned to Elgiva.

'Come, my lady, it grows late. We should return.'

It was a considerable relief when Ravenswood came into view half an hour later. As soon as they had dismounted Elgiva drew Wulfrum aside and led him indoors, calling to the servants to fetch hot water and cloths. Once in their chamber, she helped him unfasten his belt and remove the leather tunic. The shirt sleeve beneath was soaked in blood. With great care she removed that garment too, her practised gaze assessing the damage.

'You were lucky, my lord,' she said then. 'It isn't deep, but it does need cleaning.'

Wulfrum vouchsafed no comment, but seated himself as she prepared the things she would need. He had seen her tend others so many times but had little thought he would one day be the subject of her ministrations. He watched as she worked, her expression intent on the task, her small, deft hands cleaning the blood away from the wound, moving gently across his skin. The ride had brought the fresh colour to her cheeks and loosened tendrils of hair from her braid to form a halo round her face, a face whose contours were so familiar to him now he could summon them with his eyes shut. He could remember all too clearly the touch of those lips on his, the taste of her mouth, the subtle erotic scent of her flesh.

Elgiva broke into his thoughts. 'A boar's tusks are dirty, my lord. This cut must be washed with wine, but…I'm afraid it will hurt.'

'I'll live.'

The level tone suggested indifference, but the sudden sharp intake of breath as wine met torn flesh told a different tale.

'I'm sorry,' she said.

Wulfrum set his jaw against the pain and made no reply, but the sudden pallor of his cheek spoke louder than words. Unwilling to prolong the agony, she worked fast and, having sluiced the wound clean, prepared a poultice of herbs. These too would help prevent infection. Having slathered the mixture over the gash, she bound it firmly.

'That should stay on for three days. Then I'll change it.'

'As you will.' Wulfrum flexed his hand. 'It eases already.'

Seeing some of his natural colour returning, she smiled. 'I'm glad.'

He looked up and met her gaze. 'Thank you.'

'It was the least I could do.'

He rose from his chair and took her hand in his, pressing it to his lips. Every fibre of her being thrilled to that touch, for the memory of the earlier scene in the forest was etched on her consciousness. Supremely aware of his nearness, of his warmth, of his scent, she knew only that she wanted him. If he kissed her now… Closing her eyes a moment to steady herself, she felt him release her hand. Then he moved past her to the door. Elgiva bit her lip. She heard the door close and then the soft thud as the bar dropped into place. For a second its significance escaped her. Then she was very still, hardly able to breathe, hardly daring to hope—until she felt his hands on her shoulders.

'I would thank you properly, Elgiva.'

Very gently he turned her to face him and then his arms slid around her waist and shoulders. For a brief moment he looked into the face tilted up to his before his mouth closed on hers. He felt her quiver, felt her mouth open beneath his, tasting again its honey sweetness on his tongue. Elgiva shivered, but not with fear, her body surrendering to the embrace, relaxing against him, answering his kiss with her own. She felt his hands move to her waist, felt him unbuckle her belt and heard it fall before he turned his attention to her tunic, unlacing the fastenings and sliding the garment down over her shoulders. The shirt followed a moment later. Then he loosened her hair from its braid, running his fingers through its silky length, twisting a hank around his hand to draw her head back. A longer, deeper kiss ensued. He bent and slid an arm under her knees, carrying her to the bed. There he drew off the rest of her clothing before removing his own.

His love-making was tender and passionate, he controlling his desire in order to increase hers. He had waited too long to spoil this with haste. So he prolonged the exploration of her body, whose beauty he already knew, and, paradoxically, knew not, relearning the curves of breast and waist and hip, stroking, caressing and arousing, by turns both tender and insistent. Elgiva's pulse leapt, her flesh burning beneath that knowing touch, every sense alive to the lithe power of the body pressed so close against her own. Wulfrum moved lower, exploring the warm hollows of throat and collarbone and thence to her breast, lingering there, teasing the nipple to tautness, sending a thrill of pleasure along her flesh. She felt his knee move between her thighs, felt the answering slick warmth. Deep within, the sensation intensified, growing, mounting until it seemed that blood became fire. Every last defence overcome, she knew only that she wanted him. Her breathing quickened. She felt his weight shift and then the hardness of him as he entered her. The pressure increased and there was a moment of exquisite pain. Then it was past and he moved deeper in a slow rhythm that stoked the fire laid down before. Elgiva gasped, closing her legs round him, drawing him into her, yielding all of herself, moving with him as the rhythm became stronger, building to its shuddering climax. She heard Wulfrum cry out, felt the surge of energy between them in a moment of heart-stopping delight.

For a while afterwards neither one spoke, too shaken by the intensity of the experience to find the words. She felt his arm draw her close, holding her in the hollow of his shoulder. Beneath her hand she could feel his heartbeat and the sheen of sweat along his skin. He glanced down and smiled.

'I've wanted to do that from the first, but I never imagined it would be so perfect.'

She looked into his face but saw only truth there.

'I was afraid,' she replied. 'First of you, and then of myself.'

'You have no cause to be afraid, Elgiva. I would never hurt you.'

He propped himself on one elbow and looked into her face, tracing a finger lightly along her cheekbone to her lips and chin and throat as if he would memorise every part of her. Even now he could scarcely believe what had happened. While he knew her nature to be passionate, its depths had astonished and delighted him. Never in his wildest dreams had he imagined such a magnificent surrender, and he had dreamed of it often. Yet even as the knowledge sank in, he found other thoughts intruding, thoughts he could never have imagined before he met her. Elgiva had yielded her body, but what of her heart? It had never mattered before. Women had satisfied a need. While he had ever treated them with gentleness, their thoughts and feelings were of no interest. This was different.

Unable to fathom his thought, Elgiva had yet to own to surprise. She heard that men were brutal or indifferent after making love. Wulfrum was neither. He had been gentle too, more than she could have hoped or imagined. For all that, his handling of her spoke of a man experienced with women. They held no secrets for him. Was she just another woman to him? Even at the height of their passion he had not said he loved her. Why should he? She was his wife, married by force out of political necessity. He had not prosecuted his right before because he had no need to. As he had said, time was all on his side. A consummate strategist, he had intended to have her submission and he had won. And yet it had not seemed like defeat. What manner of man was he, this enemy who could make surrender taste so sweet? More than that he had shown her what lay in her own heart. Wulfrum might have died today in the forest. A few short months ago the notion would have been most pleasing, but somehow a shift had taken place—there was no trace left of the hatred she had once felt. It had been replaced by something far worse. She could no longer evade the awful truth that she did care for him. It was bad enough that he was the enemy of her people, a conqueror, who had taken her as a prize of war. Now, in spite of her best efforts, he was stealing her heart, as well, and her case was perilous indeed, for who knew what was in Wulfrum's mind, or in his heart?

CHAPTER TWELVE

'HE saved your life?' Osgifu stared at her. 'How so?'

The two women had taken their sewing outside and were enjoying the sunshine by the door of the bower. It was peaceful there and private too; a place conducive to confidential conversation. As Elgiva summarised the events that had taken place on the hunt, the older woman listened with rapt attention.

'It would seem we owe him much,' she observed when the tale was concluded.

'He took the matter so lightly, Gifu, as though it was a perfectly normal thing to do, and yet he risked his life for me.'

Osgifu smiled. 'Men always make light of such things.'

'Do they?'

'Of course. They prefer to say little and hide their feelings for fear of showing too much.'

Before Elgiva had time to ponder the words, she heard a footstep and looked round, thinking to see Hilda or one of the other servants. Her heart missed a beat to discover Wulfrum in the doorway. For a moment he said nothing, taking in the quiet domestic scene. Then he smiled.

'I thought I might find you here.'

Elgiva laid aside her sewing and rose from her stool. 'Was there something you needed, my lord?'

'Will you bear me company awhile?' He glanced at her companion. 'I'm sure Osgifu can spare you.'

The servant inclined her head and hid a smile. Elgiva, knowing her well, was not deceived, though she could not see the occasion for this hidden amusement. She had no chance to dwell on it, though, with Wulfrum so close by. He offered her his good arm and, rather diffidently, she took it.

For a little while they walked in silence. Elgiva glanced up at him, wondering why he had sought her out. They seemed to be heading for the stables.

'I thought you might like to check on Mara,' he said.

Elgiva looked up in surprise. Any opportunity to visit her horse was welcome. How had he known? He did not enlighten her on the point, but stood aside to let her enter the building. Then together they made their way along the stalls until they came to Mara's. The horse turned her head and whinnied as Elgiva approached.

'Here. She might appreciate this.' Wulfrum produced a withered apple from inside his tunic. 'It is from last year's store, but I don't suppose she'll mind too much.'

He was right. The mare crunched the fruit with obvious enjoyment. As she stroked the glossy neck, Elgiva regarded her husband out of the corner of her eye. This was the hidden side of him once more, the one she had glimpsed when he was with Ulric. He liked children and he liked horses too. Glancing across the stable, she could see his stallion tethered nearby. At seventeen hands, the powerful horse took some riding, but with Wulfrum's hand on the rein the black was meek enough. She wondered at their partnership, for it was clear he had trained the animal himself.

'How long have you had Firedrake?'

'Two years.' He grinned. 'He was a handful at first, wild and mighty contrary.' He glanced down at Elgiva, thinking that, in some ways, the two were perhaps not so very different except, of course, that the stallion now obeyed his every command.

'He's a beautiful animal,' she acknowledged.

'So is the mare. Your father chose well.'

For a moment Elgiva remained silent, her eyes on the horse, stroking the velvety muzzle. Recalling the last time they had been in the stables and had spoken thus, Wulfrum could only wince. He seemed to recall his words then had been more than a little tactless.

'Do you still intend to breed her?' she asked at length.

'Not without your consent. After all, she is your horse.'

Her surprise was evident, for he saw warm colour rise in her cheeks, but the look in her eyes said more. It was a moment or two before she could speak.

'Thank you, Wulfrum. She means a great deal to me.'

'I know.'

Elgiva's heart was suddenly beating much faster, but her pleasure at his words was great. More, he had shown a true regard for her feelings. She laid a hand on his sleeve.

'Mara means a great deal, but it means even more to me to hear you say that.'

Wulfrum knew a deep inner glow, but, not knowing quite what to say, he smiled and remained silent.

Having left the horses, they walked a while and came to the orchard. It was a fine day and enjoyable to stroll in the dappled shade beneath the trees. For some time they did not speak, being content to share the quiet and the moment. Presently Wulfrum stopped and spread his cloak on the grass.

'Sit and rest a while, Elgiva. It is most pleasant out here.'

She sat down to join him, very aware of his nearness, of the lithe strength of the man. Her eyes drank in the powerful line of his jaw, the blades of his cheekbones, the sensual curve of his mouth, remembering its pressure against her own. Shocked by the direction of her thoughts, Elgiva looked away.

If he was aware of her confusion, he gave no sign. Indeed, Wulfrum's thoughts were on the scene around him, on the land, his land. Here in this rich earth was wealth indeed, a place where a man could set down roots and belong. He thought back to the country of his birth, of the farm where he had been a boy. Back then it had seemed very fine, but he had had nothing like this to compare it with. It seemed to him that in England a man could put a stick in the ground and it would grow and thrive. Back there the land yielded a living far more grudgingly. He thought of it as back there rather than home. This was his home now, the place he intended to stay, and the place where his sons would be raised—one day. He glanced at Elgiva. It was a strange fate that had brought him to this place, to her. The two were inextricably bound up. In some ways she was this place for him and always would be.

Unable to follow his thought, she surveyed him closely. 'Is there something on your mind, Wulfrum?'

'I was thinking of the strangeness of destiny and how it brought me here.'

Elgiva remembered the evening in the bower when she had asked Osgifu to cast the runes. It was but a few months since, but already it seemed a long time ago. In her mind she heard the voice saying, *The runes never lie.*

Wulfrum stretched out beside her, hands behind his head, looking up through the leafy branches to the sky beyond. Watching him, Elgiva felt the truth of his words: it was a strange destiny that brought him here, a destiny with its beginnings in an ancient feud. So many lives, yet all were strangely linked. Osgifu had long ago told her of the Nornir, the three old women who spun the threads of fate. It had seemed then like just another fabulous tale. Now she wasn't so sure. Wulfrum had told her something of his past. It was as if a corner of that mysterious web had been lifted, allowing her a tantalising glimpse of the man she had married. He had learned early to conceal his thoughts, to use his head and not his heart. Though he had not said so, she knew his life must have been hard, but he had survived and become strong, a man whom other men would follow. They trusted him, respected him, and obeyed him. It made her want to know more.

'Was it in Lord Ragnar's hall that you met Olaf Ironfist?'

'Aye. He and I go back a long way. He saved my life.'

'Tell me.'

There was a note in her voice he had not heard before, curiosity and something else that was harder to define. Withal there was an earnestness in those amber eyes that would not be resisted.

'We were hunting wolves and had a beast at bay. It was a fearsome creature, weighing full as much as a man, and savage with hunger. I came upon it first and, being young and foolish, thought to take it on armed merely with a belt knife.'

Elgiva laughed out loud. 'Never! What happened?'

'The beast attacked and I gashed it with the knife, which only made it madder. It went for my throat. I managed to hold it off for a little while, but my strength was waning and I knew I was going to die. Fortunately for me, Olaf appeared and grappled with the creature. He throttled it with his bare hands.'

'How old were you then?'

'Three and ten.'

'It is surprising you lived to manhood.'

'But for Olaf I might not have. He was five and twenty back then, and already well known for his feats of strength. I have seen him kill a bull with his bare hands. I can see him now, standing over the body of the dead wolf; how he laughed when he saw that belt knife. Then Ragnar arrived on the scene and of course he had to be let in on the joke. I swear, I thought the two of them would die laughing.' Wulfrum smiled, remembering it. 'It took me a while to live that one down.'

'And you and Olaf became friends.'

'Yes. He mistook my stupidity for courage, you see. But, like Ragnar, he taught me much, and we have stood together in the shield wall many times. He is a brave warrior and a good friend. There is no man I'd rather have at my back in a fight.'

'I believe it. Truly Olaf Ironfist is well named.'

'Indeed he is.'

They lapsed into companionable silence, Elgiva pondering the things he had told her and keen to hear more. Even so, she would not press him. Confidence could not be forced. If he wanted to tell her about the past, he would do it in his own time. Once, not so long ago, such a conversation would have been unthinkable. She could never have envisaged then that she would discover so much—or that she would wish to.

For a long time they stayed together beneath the tree, soaking up the afternoon warmth, neither one in any hurry to move, both knowing that something important had changed and fearing to do anything that might break the fragile balance that had been established. The sun was setting before they eventually started back to the hall.

Preparations for the evening meal were well underway and the hall already lively with talk and laughter when they entered. Many eyes turned in their direction and several knowing smiles appeared on the faces of the observers. Elgiva knew what they were thinking: two lovers returning from a cosy tryst. It wasn't altogether wide of the mark either. Somewhat embarrassed, she glanced up at her husband. However, he seemed not in the least discomposed and paused to exchange greetings with some of his men. She would have slipped away but his hand on her arm forbade it.

'Stay, Elgiva.'

'Whatever you say, Wulfrum.' The tone was demure enough, but he was undeceived. She saw him laugh.

'I'd like to think so, but I'm not so naïve.'

Later that evening, when they retired to their chamber, he made love to her again. Again he was gentle and patient, wanting her to enjoy the experience as much as he did. He found her willing, even eager now, responding to his passion with warmth and he lost himself in her, forgetting the past and all the brutality of the world. Nothing existed for him then but her. And afterwards, when they lay in drowsy slumber, he dreamed of the future they would carve out together. He had heard it said that behind every successful man was a strong woman. He had not believed it until now. With Elgiva at his side he felt invincible, that anything was possible. No other woman had ever made him feel that way, think that way. He couldn't even remember what those women looked like now, but it didn't matter. He knew he had found the one he sought, a woman to cherish and to trust.

As Wulfrum continued to familiarise himself with the land and its people, he found increasing pride in this rich and fertile domain with its warm, dark soil and fields of growing crops. Under his hand, Ravenswood had begun to resemble its former self. Elgiva watched too, and knew her husband a capable ruler of men. The Norsemen might be warriors and of fearsome appearance, but they also worked hard, and gradually the Saxons began to view their presence, if not with gladness, at least with a grudging acceptance.

From time to time they received news from further afield. Halfdan had established his rule in York and his war bands had roamed far and wide through Northumbria. Much more of the kingdom was now within their hold. It was not welcome news to Saxon ears, but there was naught to be done about it. They heard that the southern kingdom of Wessex stood out against the Danes, and some secretly hoped that the resistance would spread. Others prayed it would not, being tired of slaughter and destruction. From time to time pockets of rebellion flared up across

Northumbria, but these were dealt with ruthlessly. The Danes would not tolerate any such infraction and the perpetrators were hunted down and killed.

Elgiva shivered when she heard these tales, praying that as she had heard nothing of Aylwin for a while he had abandoned his former plans and gone to safety. It seemed to her that she had seen enough bloodshed and killing to last a lifetime. War meant waste and destruction, a ravaged land that could not support the people. Peace meant a future for all. It came at a price, but there was nothing to be done about that, either. It was futile to try to live in the past. They must make the best of now. Accordingly she set her shoulder to the wheel and, when not accompanying Wulfrum, turned her skilled attention to the household affairs.

Wulfrum observed more than he ever said, but he found no fault with her management of domestic affairs. Food was well prepared and appeared on the table to order; the serfs knew their tasks and obeyed her; the hall was well kept. It was a comfortable place and one that men, hungry and tired, looked forward to returning to. He noticed how his men would greet her now when they returned from work, sometimes with a jest, but always within the bounds of decorum. They knew that if one of them got a cut or a splinter she would tend it, and came to have a respect for her skill with herbs and potions. It occurred to Wulfrum that his marriage to Elgiva had been more than a shrewd move: it was a decision that pleased him more with every passing day. More than ever he looked forward each night to the time when he would be alone with her and she would share his bed. He knew other men envied him his good fortune. He saw them follow her with their eyes.

Elgiva never returned such looks or showed she was aware of them, never once gave him cause to doubt her. How should she? In her was only goodness and sincerity. He was proud that she was his wife and he trusted her.

Towards the end of July the watchman announced the approach of a group of horsemen. It was a warm day and Elgiva was sitting with Osgifu outside her bower, mending one of Wulfrum's shirts while Ulric played nearby. They heard the sentinel's warning shout and then, soon after, the arrival of the horses. Leaving Ulric in Osgifu's care, Elgiva went to see who the newcomers were. When she entered the hall, she saw a dozen men, all Danes, and all with the dust and sweat of travel upon them. They were already being received by Wulfrum. Elgiva, standing apart, listened as he welcomed them and, catching his eye, gave quiet instructions to the serfs to fetch ale and food. When she turned back to the guests, she realised that one of their number was watching her with interest. With a feeling of dismay she found herself looking straight at Sweyn. He smiled and bowed. Elgiva acknowledged him with the barest inclination of the head and then turned her attention back to the rest, for the man called Torvald was speaking to Wulfrum.

'We carry messages from Lord Halfdan to his brothers, and also for you, my lord.'

Wulfrum nodded. 'I thank you. But first wash off the dust of travel, and then sit and eat. You've had a long ride.'

The men were only too glad to obey and, having sluiced their faces and necks with cool water, disposed themselves around the table. As they ate they spoke of matters in York and elsewhere. Elgiva listened with close interest. It was as she had suspected. The Danes increased their hold on their new kingdom daily. They put down rebellion with ruthless efficiency and brought Northumbria under their yoke.

'There are still pockets of resistance,' Torvald continued, 'and bands of rebels who hide out in the forest. We have reason to believe one of them may be Aylwin.'

Elgiva froze at the mention of that name, but the men paid no heed.

'Since the forest is hard by, my lord, it might be as well to double your guard around the place until such time as the troublemakers can be flushed out.'

'I shall do so, Torvald, and I thank you for the warning.'

'It is but a matter of time before they are caught and destroyed.'

'I think so too. I will have my men search the area immediately. If any rebels are in hiding hereabouts, they will be found.' Wulfrum exchanged glances with Olaf Ironfist and missed his wife's expression. 'Take some men out tomorrow and see what you can discover.'

'I will, my lord. And if we find any renegades?'

'Then you will either kill or capture them.'

Ironfist nodded and looked at Ida, who grinned in obvious anticipation.

'What news more?' demanded Wulfrum.

'Lord Halfdan holds a council in the autumn,' said Torvald. 'It is his will that all his earls should attend.'

Wulfrum regarded the speaker and nodded. 'I will do so.'

Elgiva caught the look that passed between him and Olaf Ironfist, though the latter said nothing, only listened attentively to the conversation. She noted he also looked once at Sweyn, though it was but a fleeting glance and probably not significant. The man's presence caused her deep uneasiness and she longed to see him ride on. Having thought never to see him again, it was a disagreeable surprise to find him here in the flesh.

She said as much to Osgifu a little later.

'Disagreeable indeed,' replied Osgifu. 'Worse, he is alive and well. The gods have not heard my prayers on that score.'

'Fortunately they ride on tomorrow.'

'Good riddance.' Then, 'What news did the riders bring from York?'

She listened with close attention while Elgiva summarised what she had heard.

'I must get a message to Aylwin, warn him.'

'You cannot risk venturing out there.'

'Not personally, but it should still be possible to get a message through.'

'How?'

'Through Leofwine. Can you let him know what is afoot and bid him find Brekka if he can? I know the rebels move their camp often.' She paused. 'It is the last thing I can do for Aylwin. Let us pray that he heeds the warning.'

'Let us hope so. Let us hope also that Wulfrum never finds out that his plan has been betrayed.'

'This is not done to betray Wulfrum, but to prevent more blood from being shed.'

'He would not see it that way.'

'I know it,' replied Elgiva, 'but I cannot just let Aylwin and the others be slaughtered.'

After Osgifu departed for the village, Elgiva paced the

floor in an agony of suspense and inner turmoil. It seemed to her then that every turn of events mired her deeper in deception. She needed something to do to take her mind off it all and keep her away from their visitors. It was politic to keep her distance until the men should have gone. As always there was spinning to do, enough to last until the evening meal when she would have the safety of numbers about her.

She occupied herself thus until the late afternoon. Then, feeling the need of fresh air, Elgiva went out, heading away from the bower and the hall towards the paddock. The day was fine and warm and scented with flowers and cut grass. Glossy horses grazed beyond the fence, cropping the lush turf. However, being preoccupied, she devoted little attention to them. Had the message reached the rebel group? It was all she could do and little enough. Recalling their last meeting, Elgiva sighed. Aylwin's words still stung. What made it worse was that much of what he had said had the ring of truth. She would not undo her marriage to Wulfrum, would not be Aylwin's bride instead. He was a good and respected man, but she knew that she had never felt for him what she felt for Wulfrum. Aylwin's look did not send a pleasurable shiver along her spine, nor did his touch burn. His kiss would never set her heart aflame. She could never return the feeling he had for her. She wondered why it should be that one man could inspire passion and another not, no matter how worthy. Wulfrum was her lord and there could be no other.

Elgiva walked slowly from the paddock towards the orchard and sat down in a pool of dappled shade. It was pleasant out of doors and for the time she began to relax, to let the sweet air and the sunshine soothe her. She did not hear the man's approach, for the turf silenced his steps, and was not aware of his presence until his shadow fell across her face.

'Aylwin!' For a moment she was numb with shock. 'Are you insane?'

'I had to see you again, Elgiva.'

'In heaven's name, why?' She looked round, scanning the place with anxious eyes. 'If you are found here…'

'I had to thank you.'

'For what?'

'For the warning and the information…' he paused, searching for the words '…and to say how much I regret what occurred at our last meeting. I can see now that the words were harsh. You don't know how often I have wished them unsaid.'

Elgiva shook her head. 'Let's not quarrel about the past.'

'You are generous.' He gave her a wry smile. 'And brave too. You took a risk to send that message.'

'All the more reason for you to heed it and take your men away from here before it is too late.' The amber eyes were earnest as they met and held his gaze. 'Ravenswood is of strategic importance to the Vikings. They will not suffer a Saxon challenge.'

'There are many kinds of challenge, Elgiva. I am not so foolish as to think we could meet them in open battle yet. They are too numerous, but more men will join us. Our intelligence improves apace. We are in communication with other rebel groups. In the meantime, we shall use what means we have to harry the foe and then melt back into the forest.'

'Give it up, I beg you. It can only end in more deaths.'

'I told you, Elgiva, I will not give up what is mine.' He bent a meaningful look upon her. 'But I was wrong to doubt you. Come away with me now. The forest has many secret places. The Viking will never find you.'

'Wulfrum would find me,' she replied. 'I am his wife.'

'You were mine before you were his.' His hand closed round her wrist. 'I know you fear his wrath and rightly so, but I will never let him harm you.'

'His wrath would not fall on me alone, Aylwin, but on others too.'

'That is a price I am willing to pay.'

'But I am not.' She tried to disengage her hold, but his grip tightened. 'You must understand that.'

His gaze hardened. 'Still you make excuses to remain with him.'

'Aylwin, please! This is a futile argument. You must go before someone sees you here.'

He let out a ragged breath and she saw some of the tension leave him. The grip on her wrist slackened a little.

'I'm sorry, Elgiva. I did not come here to quarrel with you. I shall go—for now. But know this: one day soon I shall kill the Viking and free you.'

'You cannot.'

'Lord Halfdan has shown me the way, Elgiva.'

'What do you mean?'

'Be ignorant of the knowledge until you can applaud the deed. Suffice it to say that Wulfrum must ride for York in the autumn. The waiting is almost over.' Aylwin smiled and released his hold. 'Meanwhile I must go.'

'Stay. Will you not tell me what you intend?'

He shook his head. 'Farewell, Elgiva.'

'Aylwin, wait!'

But he was gone, running swiftly through the trees. Elgiva watched until he was out of sight, her heart thumping with fear and horror at his words. Automatically she massaged her wrist, feeling yet the imprint of those strong fingers. She was left in no doubt now that he had meant every word. He would not go. Anxiously her gaze scanned the quiet orchard, but she was alone. The nearest men were raking hay two fields away, too far to have seen or heard anything. She drew in a deep breath. Aylwin had taken a foolish risk to come here. His words had disturbed her much and she understood now how far she had underestimated the strength of his feeling for her. Ironically her warning had had the opposite effect from the one she had intended.

She was so preoccupied in thought that she failed to see the man at the orchard's edge until she was almost upon him. Then her heart missed a beat. Sweyn! He smiled at her, the cool grey eyes missing no detail of her appearance.

'Well met, Elgiva. It seems married life agrees with you.'

'As you say, Sweyn.' She tried to step around him, but he blocked her path.

'I have missed you, my lady.'

'Really?'

'I can't get you out of my mind.'

'Try harder.'

'You are still cold, Elgiva.'

'I am not like to be different.'

'Not toward me, perhaps,' he agreed, 'but what of the man you were with just now? He didn't look much like Wulfrum to me.'

Elgiva forced herself to meet that mocking gaze. 'Hardly,' she replied. 'It was one of the serfs.'

'Indeed?'

'I do not think I need explain myself to you.'

'But would your husband feel the same if he knew?'

'Why don't you ask him and find out?' The words were uttered with far more confidence than she felt. 'Though, of course, he might wonder then how it was that *you* sought out his wife for a private conversation.'

He frowned and she saw the shot go home. 'It is nothing to me if you lower yourself to converse with peasants.'

'It was ever the custom to treat our people well,' she replied. 'You should try it some time.'

She would have swept on, but he seized her arm, detaining her.

'I would treat you well, Elgiva, if you gave me the chance.'

Incredulous, she could only stare at him. Then, recovering herself, 'Let go of me, Sweyn. I am Wulfrum's wife and he would not take kindly to having another man lay hands on me.'

'Do you think I fear Wulfrum?'

'No,' she replied, 'but I have seen enough bloodshed to last me a lifetime. Even the sight of yours has no appeal. Now let me go.'

For an instant she saw something like admiration in his eyes. Then he loosed his hold. With intense relief Elgiva walked away, conscious of his gaze at every step.

She returned to the chamber she shared with Wulfrum, and lay down on the bed, trying to order her scattered thoughts. The experience had left her feeling shaken and she needed to be calm when Wulfrum returned, lest he suspect something untoward. She had no wish to see

Sweyn again before he left, and no wish to play the hostess to his companions, either. Somehow she must avoid the evening meal without arousing suspicion. Elgiva closed her eyes and tried to think.

Some time later she awoke with a start to see Wulfrum looking down at her in concern.

'Are you well, Elgiva?'

She struggled up on to one elbow, feeling groggy and disorientated.

'A headache, that is all.'

Her pallor was genuine enough and Wulfrum frowned, sitting down on the edge of the bed to scrutinise her better. His hand felt her forehead for fever, but if anything it felt cooler than usual. He pushed her gently back and covered her with a pelt.

'Stay here and rest,' he said. 'I will send Osgifu to you.'

'There is no need. I am sure a little sleep will serve.'

Wulfrum frowned, but did not press the point. 'As you wish.'

He bent over her and brushed her cheek with his lips, a caress that was both gentle and caring. Elgiva wanted to put her arms around his neck, wanted to feel his arms around her, but she was afraid that he would suspect something. Unhappily she watched him move to the door, saw him pause and look back with concern in his eyes. Then he smiled.

'Rest, my lady.'

With that he was gone. Elgiva felt tears pricking her eyelids and forced them back, feeling both relief that he had suspected nothing and guilt that she had lied to him, if only by omission. If Wulfrum ever found out about her meetings with Aylwin, his anger would know no bounds. As for Sweyn, she could only pray he would not attach any real significance to what he had seen. Aylwin had been garbed as a peasant and from a distance the disguise protected him well. Her story was credible. Elgiva sighed. She felt as though she were caught in a web of deceit. Yet what else could she do? To speak would betray Aylwin—not to speak betrayed Wulfrum. For that was how he would interpret her silence. Once she would not have cared, but now she knew his good opinion of her was important. More than that, he was important. He never spoke of his innermost feelings, but his behaviour towards her spoke of regard and warmth. She wanted to think that she had his heart as he had hers. It was the reason she had not wanted to see him fight Sweyn. Though she knew well his prowess in battle, what if, in defeating his enemy, he were to be fatally injured? Or what if, through some evil trick, Sweyn were to emerge the victor? The idea was chilling. She would rather be dead than fall into his clutches again. Better to remain silent and let the matter rest. Sweyn would be gone on the morrow.

Elgiva unfastened her gown and slipped out of it, laying it aside over a chair. Then she bathed her face and hands and unfastened her hair to comb it out. The familiar rituals were soothing and some of her former mood began to lift. From the hall below she could hear the muted sounds of men's voices, their laughter. Wulfrum would play the host well. In her mind's eye she could see him there among his men and for the first time was thankful for their presence. The thought of Olaf Ironfist was a distinct comfort tonight. With him at his back Wulfrum would be safe from treachery. Elgiva smiled to herself and, finishing her grooming, slipped off her kirtle and returned to bed drawing the coverlet over her.

She did not hear Wulfrum return or see him bend over her. Her face was peaceful, untroubled, and he noted with relief that some of the healthy colour had returned. Golden hair spilled across her shoulders, taking on a soft, resinous sheen in the lamplight. He lifted a stray tress and his fingers brushed her naked shoulder. His eyes followed it along the curve of her arm to her wrists. There they stopped. Wulfrum frowned, looking closer. His frown deepened as he looked at the dark bruises encircling its slenderness. Five prints left on her skin, the prints of a man's fingers.

He straightened, looking at the sleeping figure of his wife, tempted to rouse her now and demand to know how they came there. He controlled himself. It was late. There would be time enough to speak to her on the morrow. He undressed and blew out the lamp before climbing into bed beside her. Elgiva stirred in her sleep, but did not wake; for a long time he lay there in the darkness pondering what he had seen. Someone had left those marks on her, someone with a strong hand. Grim faced, he turned over the possibilities. His men wouldn't touch her. He had seen their growing respect for her; besides, he trusted them. They would not lay hands on his woman. He thought of the Saxon serfs and knew it wasn't one of them. Elgiva was their lady. In any case, it was more than their lives were worth and they knew it. Well, come what may, he would know the truth on the morrow.

Elgiva woke with the light and stretched lazily, pushing her hair out of her eyes. She felt Wulfrum's warmth beside her and smiled. She had not heard him come to bed. It wasn't until she turned her head that she saw he too was awake, propped on one elbow and regarding her intently. His expression was grim and her heart beat just a little faster as she tried to remember what day it was. Had he wished to rise early to hunt? Should she have risen and brought food? She started up in concern.

'Wulfrum, I…'

A strong hand pushed her back on to the bed and held her there.

'There is no matter pressing, Elgiva. Save one.'

She looked at him in confusion. 'What is it?'

'These.' He slid his hand down her arm to her wrist.

Elgiva stared in dismay at the dark bruises there and the memory of their creator returned.

'I…I must have hit my wrist yesterday, though I cannot say I recall doing it.'

Wulfrum's blue gaze burned. 'You play me for a fool, Elgiva. Do you think I don't know the difference between an ordinary bruise and those left by fingers? A man left those marks and I would know his name.'

Elgiva swallowed and tried to rise, but his hand forbade it.

'You are mistaken—'

'Don't lie to me, Elgiva.' His voice was harsh now. 'Who was it?'

'Wulfrum, it is of no consequence.'

'I will decide that.'

'It was a foolish matter, not worth the mentioning.'

Her reluctance to speak caused Wulfrum's frown to deepen as another thought occurred to him.

'Whom do you protect, Elgiva? A lover?'

'What!' Elgiva's heart thumped unpleasantly hard. Did he really think she would be capable of it? Did he trust her so little after all? 'You cannot seriously think so, for you have had me well guarded, my lord. Would I carry on an illicit affair for the amusement of your men? Were it so, you would know of it by now, I think.'

Wulfrum saw the anger in her eyes and knew she spoke the truth. However, it still did not explain those marks and he was determined to discover their cause.

'Then tell me truth, or, by all the gods, I will beat it out of you.'

Elgiva pushed his hand away and struggled to her knees, eyes blazing.

'I will not be cowed by a Viking bully! You are no better than Sweyn, for I see you learned your manners in the same sty!'

'Sweyn! Was it he who did this?'

'Aye. It seems he has not forgotten how you kept me from him.'

Wulfrum's brow darkened further. 'Did he force himself on you?'

'No, he only grabbed hold of me for a moment.' It was a partial truth only, but Elgiva knew it could not be helped.

'Why didn't you tell me, Elgiva?'

'Because I didn't want you to fight him.'

'Have you so little faith in my prowess as a swordsman?'

'No, but Sweyn is treacherous, and I was afraid you would—' Her voice quavered and she broke off, turning away. Wulfrum took her shoulders and turned her back.

'Afraid I would what?' he demanded.

Tears started in her eyes. 'That you would be hurt or killed, even.'

'Not likely. Sweyn isn't that good.' He paused as the import of her words sank in. 'Would it matter to you then if I had been?'

'Of course it would.'

'Why?'

When she remained silent, he took her chin in his hand and tilted her face to his. 'Look at me, Elgiva.' Reluctantly, she met his gaze, but he persisted. 'Why?'

Elgiva felt herself blushing. Wulfrum grinned.

'Come, my lady, I await your answer.'

'Because you are my husband and I owe my loyalty to you.'

'Don't prevaricate.'

She saw his grin widen and grew hotter. 'Because if you were dead, I might fall into Sweyn's clutches.'

He chuckled. 'He would get more than he bargained for, then. However, our guests left early, at first light. Sweyn is gone.'

'Gone?'

'Aye, but he will pay for his insults in good time. Meanwhile, you have nothing to fear from him.'

The tone was mild and threw Elgiva off her guard. A powerful arm tipped her backwards and she found herself pinned beneath him.

'Wulfrum?'

'You still haven't answered my question, Elgiva.'

'I have. At least all the answer you're going to get.'

'Is that right?'

'Wulfrum, let me go.'

'No.'

She tried to push him away, but her efforts left him unmoved, except perhaps to deepen his amusement. Then he took a kiss.

'Answer the question.'

'I will not.'

He kissed her again and for longer this time and there was a dangerous glint in his eye.

'What did you call me just now? A Viking bully, was it not?'

Elgiva struggled in vain. 'If the cap fits…'

'Oh, it does, my lady, as you are going to discover.'

CHAPTER THIRTEEN

MINDFUL of what he had been told by Torvald, Wulfrum sent out various patrols to test the truth of the rumours about raiders and outlaws. Having established peace at Ravenswood, he had no intention of having it destroyed by neglect. Therefore, Ironfist and his companions rode out into the forest and made a thorough search of the surrounding area, but found no sign of the rebel band Torvald had spoken of. He reported back to Wulfrum.

'We found evidence of an old camp, but the rebels were long gone.'

'All the same, we will increase the patrols on the boundaries and post extra guards until we know more.'

'You fear a surprise attack?'

'I fear nothing, but I will not be caught napping. See to it, Olaf.'

Ironfist nodded and went off to deal with the matter.

Elgiva, who had been listening carefully to the exchange, felt both guilt and relief. Aylwin *had* thought better of it and heeded the warning after all. Surely now the rebels would not attack Ravenswood. It was a question she put to Wulfrum.

'If they do, it will be the last mistake they ever make,' he replied. Then, seeing her worried look, he smiled. 'Have no fear, Elgiva. No harm shall befall Ravenswood while I have breath.'

'You guard well what is yours,' she replied.

Wulfrum laughed then. 'Just so, my lady. Therefore, no harm shall befall you, either.'

Elgiva regarded him quizzically. Was he merely guarding her along with the rest of the property? Somehow she did not think so; his behaviour to her of late had been more markedly gentle, or mostly anyway. Recalling that recent scene in their chamber and the confession he had extracted, she felt her face grow rather warmer.

'Meanwhile,' he went on, 'you and Osgifu will not go out to collect herbs again until we know more.'

She did not argue for she could see the reason behind the words. Besides, thanks to their former efforts she and Osgifu had replenished many of the plant supplies they needed. The forest was no longer the sanctuary it had seemed. Once she had thought that, being a Saxon, she would never come to harm at the hands of her fellows. Now she wasn't so sure. Would they consider her to be treacherous, a turncoat? It was not a pleasant thought.

Wulfrum was as good as his word and posted men at strategic points around Ravenswood to forestall any attempt to attack his holding. However, as the days passed, there was no sign of the raiders.

'It is most like they have moved on,' said Ida when a week had gone by with no trace of the enemy.

'Perhaps,' replied Wulfrum. 'However, we shall maintain our vigilance until we can be certain.'

* * *

Elgiva hoped that Ida was right. However, two days later one of the men reported the loss of two sheep from the flock. Tracks were found leading into the forest but a thorough search again revealed nothing. The guards were increased and men took it in turns to patrol the boundaries, but still no trace was found either of the livestock or the thieves. Shortly after that a steer was taken.

'How are they getting through our defences?' demanded Wulfrum when the news was brought to him. 'This place is so tightly guarded now that even a mouse would find difficulty in stealing anything.'

'Maybe they aren't,' said Ironfist.

'You think someone in Ravenswood is giving them aid?'

'It is a possibility.'

'As you say. It is strange how the raiders know the exact moment and place to strike.' Wulfrum's expression grew hard. 'If you are right and there is a traitor in our midst, we shall discover him soon enough and he will rue the day.'

Elgiva heard the words with misgivings, her mind running through the names of all the people she knew, but she could not think that one of them had been responsible. And yet she had to acknowledge that there were many who only tolerated the new order because they had to. After all, someone had helped Aylwin to escape in the first place. Would they join in secret confederacy with the outlaws to strike back at the Danes? She realised that she did not know the answer. The woodland was large and there were many hiding places in its heart, places hard to find unless you knew them. There were caves too, some big enough to shelter a considerable number of men. However, it was all surmise on her part. She had no real proof.

Meanwhile the summer days grew sultry with a sticky heat that made every exertion uncomfortable. Elgiva thought longingly of the forest pool, but she would not disobey Wulfrum and venture out there. The brooding air foretold a coming storm, although some rain would be welcome now for the land lay listless beneath a metallic sky. Elgiva laid aside her sewing and rose from her stool, unable to bear the confinement within doors. Her head ached and her clothes stuck to her and every movement seemed to bring beads of perspiration to her face. She walked towards the orchard, thinking to find some respite from the heat. Indeed, it was a little cooler there and she sank gratefully on the grass beneath the leafy canopy. All around the ripening fruit was swelling on the branches, sure sign that the coming harvest would be plentiful. Soon the corn harvest would begin and the barns and granaries would fill. The first hay crop was already gathered in. In a few more weeks the first leaves would begin to change colour. The year turned and all their lives with it. Who could have foreseen in the previous winter what would befall them in the spring? Already it seemed like a past life.

At the evening meal Elgiva found herself watching Wulfrum, listening as he spoke and laughed with his men. He was relaxed, leaning back in his chair, his hand toying with his ale horn. From time to time he glanced her way and smiled and her heart would leap. She knew that later they would retire to their chamber and he would make love to her once more and she would yield. *You'll come*. He had said that long ago. Had his knowledge of other women fuelled his confidence? She knew there had been others; his skill as a lover could only have been born of practice. What had they been like, his other women, the ones before her? Had he loved any of them? Was there one he remembered with more fondness than the others? He never spoke of them. Did it mean he had forgotten? Elgiva forced the thoughts to the back of her mind, angry with herself for even entertaining them. What did it matter? It was in the past. She was his wife now, a relationship made real every night they retired to bed.

On this evening Elgiva excused herself early from the table and went before him to their chamber. She undressed to the thin kirtle and went to stand by the window to find relief from the heat. A breeze had sprung up and in the west the clouds had begun to mass like the vanguard of a great celestial host labouring up. Distant flashes of lightning preceded its arrival and the air was pungent with promised rain. Elgiva leaned back against the wooden frame, watching the storm approach, feeling the wind lift strands of hair from her neck as it cooled her skin. She had not bothered to light a lamp, for although it grew late some light yet lingered in the sky.

She stood for some time, watching the display in the heavens, fascinated by its power. The storm rolled nearer. Soon it would be overhead, for the thunderclaps followed each other in quick succession. A brilliant flash of light illuminated the whole area around the hall and with it a dark figure running towards the stables. Elgiva frowned, staring into the twilight shadows. Perhaps it had been one of Wulfrum's men hastening to take shelter before the rain came. The man paused and looked round. The next light-

ning flash lit him plainly for a split second. Drem! Elgiva
started. It couldn't have been. He had no business there,
wasn't even a groom. Another flash of lightning lit the
scene, but this time she saw no one. Even so an uneasy
feeling prickled between her shoulder blades like an itch
she couldn't reach. She remained by the window a few
moments more, her eyes scanning the area, but she could
see no sign of the man again. It wouldn't have been Drem,
only someone who looked a bit like him. After all, she had
only seen him for an instant. Most likely it *had* been one
of the guards seeking temporary shelter, for in truth the
storm would be fearsome when it really hit them.

She closed her eyes, suddenly aware that her earlier
headache had gone as if somehow the release of tension
in the skies had found its parallel in her. Just then the
breeze brought with it a whiff of smoke and she heard a
horse neigh. Elgiva opened her eyes, scanning the ground
in her view. Her gaze was arrested by flickering light in
the thatch of the stable roof. For a moment she froze
before her mind grasped the significance. Suspicion
became certainty. Grabbing her mantle from the top of the
clothes chest, she threw it about her shoulders and ran
from the room, heading for the hall. At the head of the
stairs she paused.

'Fire! The stable is on fire! Make haste!'

All conversation stopped and fifty pairs of eyes looked up
in astonishment to see the apparition on the staircase, a wild-
eyed figure with golden hair tumbling across her shoulders
and clad loosely in a cloak that revealed only a kirtle beneath.
For perhaps the space of a few seconds they stared before
the import of her words began to sink in. Elgiva had by then
reached the bottom of the stairs and turned to Wulfrum.

'My lord, quickly! The stable is ablaze!'

Wulfrum leapt to his feet, but she was ahead of him, making for the door. Behind her she could hear shouting and running feet as men sprang into action. Elgiva raced for the stable, ignoring everything save the need to get Mara and the other horses out. She could hear restless hooves and whinnying now and the smell of smoke was stronger. In the darkness beyond the door flickering flames lit the far end where a pile of hay was already ablaze beneath the burning roof. Elgiva darted forwards, feeling smoke sting her eyes, coughing on the thick fumes. Mara's stall was towards the far end and already the little mare was snorting and rolling her eyes in fear. Elgiva went to the horse's head and unfastened the halter rope, speaking gently to try to calm the frightened animal. However, when she tried to back the horse out, it refused to budge. All around the smoke thickened and the sinister crackling of the flames grew louder. Fragments of burning thatch fell about them and she heard Firedrake scream with terror, his hooves drumming on the side of the stall as he fought the rope that held him. Then other horses took up his cry, their panic spreading. Shouting voices sounded from the entrance way and flaring torches showed men freeing the animals nearest the door. In desperation Elgiva pulled on Mara's halter rope, but still the horse wouldn't stir.

'Elgiva, give me your cloak.'

She heard Wulfrum's voice beside her. She tore off the cloak and watched him use it to cover the horse's eyes. Then, speaking softly, he coaxed the mare out of the stall and led her to the door with Elgiva stumbling after. Outside a line of men had formed a chain from the well to pass buckets of water in an attempt to douse the fire while the others tried to get the remaining animals out. Fortunately most of the horses had been turned out, the nights being fine and warm.

'Get the mare away from here.' Wulfrum removed the cloak from Mara's eyes and shoved the halter rope at a serf. Then he soaked the cloak in the trough before turning to Elgiva. 'Wait here.'

She saw him throw the wet cloak over his head before plunging back into the chaos of the stable. Elgiva watched through stinging eyes the smoke swirl through the thatch on the roof. The fire was louder now, the flames brighter. Smoke billowed from the open doorway as from the gateway to hell, while above them the storm rumbled on. Tight-throated with fear, she looked in horror as the moments passed and Wulfrum did not return. Visualising the stallion's panic and his flying hooves, Elgiva's heart pounded. What if Wulfrum were hurt and couldn't get out? What if he were overcome by smoke? He would die in there, a horrible lingering death. It couldn't happen. It must not happen. She began to run back towards the stable, but a strong arm caught and held her. She heard Ida's voice.

'You cannot go back in there, lady. It's too late now.'

'Wulfrum's in there. Let me go.'

Elgiva struggled hard, but the arm did not yield. Tears coursed down her face as she watched the thick smoke and the leaping flames. Surely nothing could live in there now. In her mind's eye she saw Wulfrum overcome by smoke, lying helpless on the floor as the blaze licked closer. Desperate now, she fought to free herself.

'I must go back. Wulfrum!'

Ida held on for grim death, ignoring her tears and pleas

for he dared not let her go. He knew enough about her now to realise she would run straight back into the flames if he did. His gaze moved beyond her to the burning building, willing Wulfrum to come out. Seconds passed and the roar of the flames grew louder. Ida stared in horror at the smoke billowing through the open doorway.

Then, through the choking fog, came Wulfrum leading Firedrake. He was coughing hard and his clothes were singed and blackened, but he was alive. The horse was frightened, but otherwise seemed none the worse for his brush with death. Elgiva slumped, weak with relief.

'He's alive! Oh, Wulfrum!'

Freed from Ida's hold, she ran to him, watching anxiously as he struggled for breath.

'Are you all right?'

He nodded, unable to speak for the bitter fumes in his throat. His gullet felt raw. It was some moments before he could draw breath again. Elgiva shut her eyes, trying to stop her tears. She thought she had really lost him. Then her arms were around him, holding him close. Wulfrum glanced down in surprise, but before he could say anything Ironfist appeared beside them.

'All the horses are out, my lord, but we can't save the stable.'

'Let it burn, then. We'll risk no more lives tonight.'

The heat was fierce now and they retreated to a safer distance, watching the flames lick into the night sky. The supporting roof timbers sagged at one end and then collapsed in a wave of heat and smoke. Elgiva shuddered, thinking of what might have happened if they had come too late to save the horses. A stable could always be rebuilt.

Suddenly a mighty clap of thunder shook the earth and the first drops of rain began to fall, and then more until, with a roar, the clouds opened and poured their stored burden on the earth beneath while jagged lightning streaked the sky, illuminating the human drama for a brief moment. Then it was absorbed again into the gathering gloom as the rain intensified to a deluge. Elgiva gasped, soaked in seconds, staring in disbelief at the curtain of rain sweeping across the land, a curtain so dense it shut out all view. Then she became aware of Wulfrum smiling down at her.

'Come.'

Together they staggered back towards the hall, heads down against the deluge. Elgiva stumbled and would have fallen but for the strong arm about her waist; at length they reached shelter. It seemed a haven of peace and light after the nightmare darkness outside. Gasping, Elgiva wiped the water from her eyes and face and wrung out her hair. Like herself, Wulfrum was drenched, his dark locks plastered to his head and shoulders, his clothing hanging in sodden folds. Then she became aware he was regarding her with a most keen interest, a broad grin splitting his face. Following his gaze down, Elgiva realised with a shock that her kirtle had become transparent with the water and clung tight, revealing every detail of her body. She felt her face grow warm.

'We had better get you upstairs, my lady, before my men return. Otherwise I couldn't answer for the consequences.'

She nodded, but already she could hear voices without and at any moment now men would be coming through the door. It was also some distance to the stairs. Appalled at the implications, Elgiva ran. In much amusement Wulfrum watched her go. She just reached the top of the staircase before Ironfist and Ida entered the hall, followed by the rest.

'Fenrir's fangs, what a night!' The giant shook water from his hair and beard. Water streamed from his clothing. A large pool formed on the floor at his feet.

'It might have been a lot worse if the fire had spread to the barn and the byre,' replied Ida. 'As it is, the rain will quench the flames. We'll probably have to rebuild the stable all the same.'

'How in the name of all the gods did the fire start anyway?'

'Could have been a lightning strike.'

'Not likely. We'd have heard it. It would have blown the roof apart. Although the thatch was burning, it was still more or less intact when we first got out there.'

Ida frowned. 'That's right, now you mention it. Belike the fire began within—an overset lamp, perhaps.'

'Perhaps. I'll question the grooms tomorrow. If any of them has been careless, I'll wear his guts for garters.'

Wulfrum called for ale. He knew he needed some and, after being choked by smoke and fumes, his men would need to rinse their throats too. As he suspected, it was a suggestion that found instant favour. He joined them in a horn or two and thanked them for their efforts in rescuing the horses. As Wulfrum thought of Firedrake and the others burning to death his anger revived, for he held the beasts in great affection. Had Elgiva not sounded the alarm when she did, they might have come too late to save them. He recalled her racing to the burning stable and how his heart had leapt almost into his mouth when he saw her plunge into the smoke. However, she would not leave her horse to die like that, or any of them, indeed. Her courage was keen and he was proud of her. Then he recalled the sight of her in the sodden kirtle and his mind turned in a new direction. He tossed off the rest of his ale and was about to bid his men goodnight when he overheard his wife's name being spoken across the room.

'It was thanks to the Lady Elgiva that we saved the horses at all,' Ironfist was saying. 'But for her the outcome could have been very different.'

'Did you see her go into that stable?' Ida shook his head in wonder. 'Didn't even hesitate. Courage of a lion, that one.'

'Aye, she has.'

'When she thought Wulfrum wasn't coming out that last time, she was all set to go back after him too. I only just managed to hold her. Struggled like a fury.'

'Oh?' Ironfist's ale horn paused in mid-air.

Wulfrum was listening intently now, though the pair seemed quite oblivious to the fact they were overheard.

'Almost beside herself, she was. Kept saying, "Wulfrum's in there", and begging me to let her go. She's crazy about him, obviously.'

'Only the gods know why,' replied the giant. 'I've never seen anything in the bastard.'

The two of them guffawed. Wulfrum reddened, feeling strangely pleased. Had Elgiva really been so anxious for his safety? She had once said he was more use to her alive, but her actions tonight suggested that she cared rather more than he could have hoped. He smiled to himself and made his way to the stairs.

When he entered the chamber, it was to see his wife drying her hair with a large linen cloth. Her sopping kirtle lay discarded nearby and she had wrapped a pelt around herself against the chill from the rain. For a moment he watched her, then shut and barred the door before crossing to join her. Elgiva watched him strip off his wet clothes and rub himself dry.

'I have you to thank for being in time to save the horses,' he said then. 'If you had not raised the alarm when you did, they would have been lost.'

Elgiva shuddered. 'Don't, Wulfrum. It doesn't bear thinking about.'

He reached out and caressed her face with his hand, then gently removed the towel from her and took over the business of drying her hair. Elgiva remained very still. In truth, the gentle movement of his hands was soothing and gradually she let herself relax.

'How did you know?'

'I was watching the storm approach and smelled smoke.' Then she froze, remembering. 'There was something else too.' She told him about the figure she had seen just before the fire broke out. Wulfrum's hands stopped what they were doing.

'Did you see his face?'

Elgiva hesitated. The evidence was circumstantial and she was reluctant to name Drem and put him in danger.

'No, and it is possible the two things are not connected anyway.'

'I think it was no coincidence.' For a moment his expression was grim. 'But I will find the man who was responsible, I swear it.'

She laid a hand on his arm. 'Do you think it is one of our own people?'

'I don't know—yet.'

For a moment there was no sound save for the rain, which had slackened from a torrent to a steady downpour.

'Do you think they will strike again?'

'Undoubtedly. It is why they must be found.' Then he smiled. 'However, that is for tomorrow. Tonight I would show my appreciation.'

He drew her to her feet and took her in his arms. The kiss was long and passionate and Elgiva shivered. Wulfrum looked down at her in concern.

'You are cold, my love. Come.'

He took her to bed and lay beside her, holding her close, sharing his warmth. Elgiva lay still in his arms, the heart thumping in her breast, wondering if she had heard him correctly. *My love.* He had never used the word before. Did he mean it? His hand brushed her skin gently and she turned towards him, her mouth meeting his in a long passionate kiss, her hands stroking him, rousing him, bringing him to an equal pitch of desire. This time she took the lead and Wulfrum knew all the sweetness of her willing compliance as they came together in fierce and urgent joy, meeting in a mutual climax of shuddering delight.

Later, lying in his arms, Elgiva pondered his words anew. He trusted her, she knew that. Was he beginning to love her too? She bit her lip, glad of the darkness that hid her face. Would he love a woman whose silence aided his enemy? Had it been part of Aylwin's plan to burn the stables tonight? Would there be an attempt on the barn next or the hall? Matters had taken a turn she would never have believed. Wulfrum would not let this go unanswered. She closed her eyes. What to do for the best? She was still considering the matter when the spreading warmth and the sound of the rain lulled her to sleep.

CHAPTER FOURTEEN

BY SUNRISE the following morning the storm was long gone. The only sign of its passing was damp earth and a few puddles, for the sun shone again in a clear sky. However, the stable was a blackened ruin with half the roof burned away and the remaining timbers sagging under the weight of the thatch. The charred and sodden straw stank and everywhere dark ash stained the ground. Elgiva shuddered, hearing in her imagination the screams of the frightened horses once again.

'We'll have to rebuild it, all right,' said Ironfist, surveying the wreck with a critical eye. 'We couldn't put a hog in there, never mind a horse.'

Beside him Wulfrum concurred. 'It's fortunate the weather is warm. The horses will take no harm from being out at night. In the meantime, we'll organise a team of men to start clearing away the mess.'

'I'll see to it.'

Ironfist was about to depart when Ida appeared from inside the shell of the stable. His face was grim.

'My lord, I think you'd better take a look at this.' He paused, throwing a speaking glance at Wulfrum. 'It might be better if the lady remained here. It is not a sight for her eyes.'

Puzzled, Elgiva watched as the two of them drew closer to the ruin, to a place where part of the wall had crumbled, allowing ingress. She heard the sound of timbers being kicked aside and then the men's voices, too low to be overheard. After that was silence. When finally they emerged, her husband's expression was chilling. With a dreadful sense of foreboding, she summoned up the courage to ask.

'What is it, Wulfrum?'

'It's the body of one of the stable-boys. He must have been in the loft and he didn't get out. Unfortunately, no one knew he was there.'

Elgiva's eyes filled with tears and she could only stare at him in dumb horror. All around her she heard a buzz of angry voices as the news reached the others.

'The person responsible will pay dearly for this,' he went on. 'Had the boy any family?'

'Just his mother, I think,' replied Ironfist. 'I have seen her hereabouts on occasion.'

Before anyone else could volunteer information Ceolnoth approached, bringing one of the Saxon serfs with him. The latter looked fearfully about, but could not escape the firm hold on his arm.

'Now what have we here?'

Wulfrum looked round, following Ironfist's gaze.

'My lord, this man may be able to shed some light on what happened last night,' said Ceolnoth.

'Oh?'

'Yes, lord. It seems one of the other hands did not turn up for his work this morning.'

Wulfrum frowned. 'What has this man to do with it?'

The serf paled and began to tremble. 'Nothing, my lord, I swear it. 'Twas I that discovered Drem was missing this morning, that is all.'

Elgiva froze in stunned disbelief. Then her mind threw back the memory of a man at the whipping post and she knew with sick certainty that it had been he whom she had seen.

'Drem?' demanded Wulfrum.

'One of the field hands, my lord,' said Ceolnoth.

'I know the man.' Wulfrum's gaze never left the serf's face. 'Go on.'

'That is all I know, lord. Drem was there last night and gone this morning.'

'Have you made a search for him?'

'Yes, lord. He is nowhere to be found.'

'What more?'

'Nothing more, lord.'

'Well, I think we can guess who fired the stables last night,' said Ironfist.

Ceolnoth nodded. 'Belike the rat has slipped away into the forest to join the rebels.'

'Is that so?' demanded Wulfrum.

The serf began to shake. 'It may be so, my lord, but he did not confide in me.'

'Then who were his friends?'

The man remained silent, crushed by the sombre looks cast upon him, a picture of abject terror.

'I'll get it out of him,' said Ironfist.

Elgiva laid a hand on his arm. 'Wait, Olaf.' She turned to the serf. 'How are you called?'

'Oswy, my lady.'

'Then, Oswy, I beg you to say what you know. Those who are innocent have nothing to fear. We must find out who did this. A boy is dead.'

He blinked rapidly. Clearly this was news to him too.

'A boy, my lady?'

'Yes, one of the stable lads. He must have been trapped by the flames for he did not get out.'

Oswy was shocked and his face went a shade paler. 'Elfric and Leofwine knew Drem best, my lady, for he sometimes helped out at the forge. Even so, I think he would not have told them what he planned. They would never have agreed.'

Elgiva turned to Wulfrum. 'What he says is true, my lord. I know these men and they have ever served Ravenswood loyally.'

Even as she spoke, she knew he would recall the incident when they had tried to help Hunfirth and Brekka. Would he hold that against them now?

Wulfrum heard her out impassively. 'Nevertheless, I would speak with them.' He turned to Ceolnoth. 'Bring them here.'

The two men arrived a few minutes later, looking round uneasily at the assembled group of stony-faced warriors. However, they answered readily enough to the questions put to them. Wulfrum heard them without interruption. Beside him Elgiva watched his face, trying to glean any clue from his expression as to what he might do next but, as was usual in these affairs, he gave nothing away. Once, her gaze flicked to the smith and his son and thence to Oswy. They stood in silence, never moving a muscle, but the tension was almost palpable. Behind them stood half a dozen of Wulfrum's men, all armed to the teeth. If he gave the word, the three would be dead before they hit the ground. He deliberated a moment longer.

'Very well,' he said at last. 'You may go.'

The exhalation of breath was audible, but they needed no second bidding.

'You believed them?' said Ironfist, watching the retreating figures.

'Yes. If they knew anything at all, they would be with Drem in the forest,' replied Wulfrum, 'which is where we shall find him, I have no doubt.'

'How are we to do that, in the name of all the gods?'

The earl's smile was grim. 'Have the horses saddled, Olaf, and fetch the hounds. If Drem left this morning after the deluge ceased, there is a good chance of picking up his trail. Ceolnoth, find something that has the man's scent on it. Something from his sleeping place, maybe. 'Tis time to go a-hunting.'

Elgiva saw understanding dawn in the faces of the listening men, and they hastened to do his bidding. Wulfrum turned and strode back to the hall, heading for the stairs. Elgiva had almost to run to keep pace. Presently they reached their chamber and she watched anxiously as he donned chain mail and buckled on his sword belt, settling Dragon Tooth firmly in the scabbard. He checked the dagger in his belt and slid a smaller, slimmer blade into his sleeve before finally taking up the linden-wood shield embossed with iron.

'Wulfrum, take care, I beg you. These are desperate men and you know not how many there are.'

'True, but I know how many there will be by the time I return tonight.'

Elgiva shivered. Then she felt his hands on her shoulders drawing her closer.

'Have no fear, my lady. I will return. But I must smoke out this nest of rats or live in fear of them ever more.'

She nodded unhappily. There would be more killing before the day was done, but she knew he had no other choice. The raiders might have got away with the theft of a sheep or two, but the moment the stable was fired their fate was sealed. Wulfrum would find them, she was certain of it, and he would show no mercy this time.

'Wulfrum, I fear that Aylwin may be with them.'

He frowned, his expression suddenly intent. 'Aylwin?'

'Yes. After he fled Ravenswood, he went into the forest. You trailed him that far yourself. He could be with the rebels there.'

'Pray he is not.'

'You intend to slay him.'

'Can I do anything else?' He took her by the shoulders and looked down into her face. 'I know you have had ties of friendship with this man in the past, but you cannot have divided loyalties, Elgiva.'

'I know it.'

Her heart felt leaden in her breast but she knew he was right. An innocent child had died in the fire. Had Drem been taking his orders from Aylwin? It did not bear thinking about. Reluctantly, she followed her husband out to the waiting horses.

Olaf and Ida had returned with twenty mounted men. Beside them were four great hounds, leashed. Wulfrum swung into Firedrake's saddle and looked down at his wife. For a moment their eyes met.

'Until later, my lady.'

Then he turned the horse's head and rode away at the head of his force.

Elgiva watched until the column was out of sight and then recollected her own duties. Before anything else, she must speak with the mother of the murdered stable lad to offer what poor comfort she might. Accordingly she made her way to the village. She arrived to find that Father Willibald had anticipated her and he looked up thankfully as Elgiva entered the mean dwelling. As she expected, the wretched woman was distraught, for her son was the only surviving member of her family, her husband having died of fever the previous year. Now she wept inconsolably. Elgiva could well understand that terrible outpouring of grief and knew that no words of hers could possibly suffice. Instead she put her arms round the sobbing figure and held her close. It was a long time before the tears abated sufficiently for coherent speech.

'Why? Why, my lady?'

'To strike back at the Danes.'

'They have not hurt the Danes. They have murdered my boy.'

'He will be avenged,' replied Elgiva. 'Those responsible will pay a terrible price.'

'That will not bring him back.'

'No, but it will stop them from ever doing it again.'

Elgiva glanced at Father Willibald and saw the sadness in his kindly face. He too had suffered since the taking of Ravenswood, his church burned and his life threatened. Would there ever be an end to the violence, to the killing? Would this land ever know peace again?

Father Willibald cleared his throat. 'My lady, the boy should be given a proper Christian burial.'

'He shall be. I will speak to Lord Wulfrum.'

He regarded her in some surprise not unmixed with hope. 'Then perchance we shall say a mass for the child's soul.'

It was a small comfort, thought Elgiva when she left them some time later. Truly death was absolute. Her own powerlessness appalled her. If only she had given the alarm sooner, had realised the child was in the stable. It was her fervent prayer that he had been overcome with smoke very quickly and not suffered pain before he died, but in her heart she doubted it. Anger vied with sorrow as she relived the night of the fire. One stupid act by a vengeful man and an innocent child had lost his life. This day others would die too. She knew that Wulfrum had no choice but to follow his present course of action. The renegade Saxons were her own people, but her loyalty now was with her husband and she prayed that he would prevail and return safe to her.

All the rest of that day Elgiva looked for his return, though she knew it likely would not be till eventide. All day she tried to occupy herself with familiar tasks but could concentrate on none of them, her hands falling idle in her lap and her mind elsewhere. Beside her Osgifu worked on her mending, saying little, though her eyes went often to Elgiva's face.

In her mind's eye Elgiva saw the forest paths and the great trees whose green domain held so many secret places. She saw the mounted men and the dogs. Would they pick up the trail? Would the hunters come upon the raiders' hideout? She closed her eyes, hearing in her imagination the clash of swords and the shouts of men, the blood and the screams. Her stomach heaved and she rushed from the bower just in time to vomit in the grass. With a shaking hand she pulled her kerchief from her sleeve and held it to her lips, waiting for the nausea to die down. The other rested lightly on her belly as she struggled to come to terms with the knowledge she could no longer ignore.

'How often has that happened?' asked Osgifu.

'Two or three times, perhaps.'

'Have you missed your monthly bleeding?'

Elgiva nodded.

'How many times?'

'Twice.'

Osgifu's hand covered her own against her belly. Its warmth was reassuring.

'Does he know?'

'Not yet.'

'When will you tell him?'

'I don't know. Soon. I needed to be sure.' Elgiva drew in a deep breath. She would indeed have to tell him soon. The matter could not be kept quiet for long in any case. 'I just haven't found the right moment yet, that's all.'

'I'd like to be a fly on the wall when you do.' Osgifu smiled. 'It would worth something, I think, to see the Viking's expression then.'

'Oh, Gifu, how do you think he will take it? Will he be pleased or angered?'

'What man is angered to learn his wife carries their first child?'

'Wulfrum is not like other men. I hardly ever know what he is thinking.'

'He is not so different from other men,' replied Osgifu, 'at least not in essentials anyway. And he is not so hard to read, either, not when he looks at you.'

She made Elgiva sit down then and fetched a cup of cool water.

'Sip this. It will make you feel better.'

Elgiva took the water, turning over their conversation in her mind. If only Osgifu was right. Then she thought about the grim hunt being enacted in the forest. If only it might be over soon. If only Wulfrum might come back safely.

It was sunset when the hunters returned, the cavalcade emerging from the trees in a slow, steady line. The men did not talk, but their sombre expressions spoke more than words. Elgiva watched from her chamber window as they rode in, her heart leaping as she saw Wulfrum at their head with Ironfist beside him. With a final glance at the preparations she had made, she hastened down to the hall, calling instructions to the servants to bring ale and food before going to the door.

From that vantage point she watched the riders approach, their tired horses dark with sweat and mud. Elgiva's eyes went to the men, noting well the sinister darkening stains on their armour and weapons. All looked weary. One or two nursed obvious injuries and one horse was led with its dead rider slung across the saddle. Then her gaze came to rest on Ironfist and she swallowed hard as she realised for the first time what it was he carried on the point of his spear. Drem would fire no more buildings.

'Put the traitor's head on a spike by the gate,' said Wulfrum. 'Let all see it and know that justice has been done.' He swung down from Firedrake's saddle and crossed the intervening space to the door of the hall.

'Osgifu, some of the men are hurt. Tend to them.'

Wulfrum turned to his wife. For a long moment neither spoke. Elgiva looked anxiously at the blood staining his chain-mail shirt. Seeing the direction of her gaze, he smiled.

'The blood isn't mine.' He paused, surveying her in his turn. 'You look pale, Elgiva. Are you well?'

'Quite well, my lord.'

He saw the tears start in her eyes. 'Never tell me you feared for my safe return, wife.'

'Oh, Wulfrum, I was afraid. All day I have been imagining terrible things.'

'No cause, my love.' He bent and kissed the top of her head. 'It would take more than a few thieves to take on a Viking war band and win.'

'You found all the raiders, then?'

'Yes. We found them.'

'Did you... Are they...'

'Yes. All are dead and the carrion birds feed on their remains.'

Elgiva shut her eyes, fighting faintness, but she had to know. 'And Aylwin?'

'He was not among them. There was nothing to connect him to the band we found.' He paused, regarding her with shrewd eyes. 'After we let the hounds learn the scent, we cast a wide circle round the hall until they found it. Drem's trail led us straight to them. An arrow could not have flown more true to its mark.'

The relief on learning that Aylwin had not been there was huge, but she strove to control it. 'How many were there?'

'About twenty, all told. We took them by surprise. Even so, they fought well; I lost one man and four are injured. They will require your help, I think.'

'Of course.'

'Meanwhile I would wash off the sweat and stink of battle.'

'There is a kettle of hot water prepared for you. Or, if you would prefer it, the meal is ready.'

'I will wash first and eat after.'

He put an arm through hers and they went in together. At the foot of the stairs Elgiva left him and went to help Osgifu, who was laying out her things in readiness to treat the injured. Fortunately the wounds were simple enough—sword slashes and bruises for the most part, though one or two of the wounds were deep and needed sewing. They dealt first with the most serious cases, the others waiting their turn with good humour, refreshing themselves with a horn or two of ale in the meantime. Others had sluiced themselves at the trough or the well, divesting themselves of their weapons before washing off the grime of battle. When the last of the wounds had been dressed and more ale drunk, it was time for the food.

Wulfrum rejoined them, changed now into a light tunic and leggings, all signs of battle gone. He took Elgiva's hand and led her to the table. The atmosphere was lively enough, for the raiders had been overcome and would not trouble Ravenswood again, and almost all of Wulfrum's men had returned without serious hurt. It was cause enough for celebration. She thought it did not need much cause for the Danes to celebrate.

'What is it, Elgiva?'

She turned to see Wulfrum's gaze on her. 'I am thinking about that stable-boy.'

'He shall be buried properly with the priest to perform the ceremony, if you wish.'

'I do wish it, Wulfrum.' She hesitated a moment. 'His mother... I visited her today.'

'She shall receive the wergild. Since Drem cannot pay it and has no kin, I shall do so. Nothing can bring the boy back, but the money may help his surviving family.'

'Thank you.'

'It was a bad business, Elgiva, but the traitor has paid; when the fate of the raiders is known, it will deter others from thinking Ravenswood a soft target.'

'I think no one could ever make such a mistake again.'

Wulfrum was silent a moment, then bent on her the familiar easy smile that made her heart leap. 'And now we shall feast, and celebrate.'

'Because your enemies are slain?'

'No, because I can sit here and look at you.'

Elgiva blushed as a glow of happiness spread over her. Perhaps he would be pleased to hear the news she had to impart after all. However, this was not the time or the place. She glanced round surreptitiously and decided it must be later, when they retired to the privacy of their chamber.

For all he shared the sentiments of his men that evening, Wulfrum was not disposed to linger late and he and Elgiva left them carousing to seek their own room. Wulfrum undressed and climbed into bed. She heard him yawn and saw him settle back comfortably, watching her undress. She cast a swift look down her body, but the slight round-

ness of her belly showed no sign yet of the life within. Her
breasts were bigger, but her waist was as slim as it had ever
been. Slowly she unfastened her hair and began to comb
it, teasing out the small tangles. It took her some time, but
eventually she was finished. However, when she turned
towards the bed it was to see that Wulfrum was watching
no longer. He lay on his back, eyes closed, his breathing
regular and deep.

'Wulfrum?' There was no sign that he heard her. 'My
lord?'

For a moment she regarded him with strong indignation before her sense of humour got the better of her. Trust
him to fall asleep now. Evidently her news would have to
keep till morning. She crossed the room and blew out the
lamp before climbing into bed beside him.

She had slept well, snuggled close to the familiar warmth
of the man beside her. The sun was fingering its way
through the shutters when she woke, aware suddenly that
a gentle hand was stroking her back. Elgiva smiled and
stretched, arching her body towards the hand, for its touch
was sensual and exciting. Wulfrum drew her backwards
and pressed her down into the bed as he leaned across her,
holding her there with an arm either side of her shoulders.
He kissed her then, long and passionately. Elgiva felt the
familiar glow inside her, then her arms were about his neck
and she was kissing him back, moulding her body to his,
feeling his arms tighten around her. With the familiar
feeling of astonishment and delight, Wulfrum looked into
her face and saw her smile. Then she was kissing him
anew. He felt her mouth open to his tongue, felt her yield,
felt her body press closer. Elgiva shivered as she felt his

lips move on to her neck and throat, his hands brushing the peaks of her breasts, raising sensations that both thrilled and appalled. Yesterday he had shed Saxon blood, but he was no longer the enemy in her eye, for she loved him. To lose him would be like losing part of herself. Warming to his touch, she gave herself now unreservedly.

Wulfrum felt her shudder, sensed the desire rising through her blood. He entered her then, gently, but Elgiva wanted him now every bit as much as he wanted her. He felt her legs close around him, her hands on his shoulders, pulling him deeper inside her. Still Wulfrum held back, fanning the flame to a blaze that would eventually consume them both, reaching a peak of ecstasy so intense he thought he might die. Looking into the depths of the amber eyes beneath him, he knew it had been the same for her.

The intensity of the feeling took him by surprise. Nothing that had gone before compared to this. In his experience hitherto, women had been a means to an end. They satisfied a need and afterwards were quickly forgotten, but this Saxon wench had woven a spell that had him in its grip. He found himself thinking about her all the time, seeing her face, wanting her. He knew then that he would hold her till death.

Watching him closely, Elgiva saw his expression change as he looked at her and felt in her heart the stirrings of disquiet. However, he reached out a hand and touched her cheek, brushing away stray wisps of her hair, his fingers tracing a line along her nose, across her lips and chin and thence down her throat to her breasts. Then he kissed her lightly. She could not fathom his mood, but it showed yet another side of him she had not seen before.

It was new and disturbing and hinted at so much more to learn. Suddenly she wanted to know, all of it, for there could be no more pretence. She loved him, had loved him since that day in the forest glade when he had risked his life to save hers. If Ida had not prevented it on the night of the fire, she would have gone back into the flames, for the thought of a future without Wulfrum was inconceivable. He was as necessary to her as sunlight and breathing.

Seeing her preoccupation, he smiled down at her. 'I never know what you are thinking.'

'I was thinking about you.'

'Good. What about me?'

'I shall not tell you, for it would only make you conceited.'

He laughed. 'I think it would not be easy for a man to be conceited too long in your company. You have a way of cutting us down to size. One look at those amber eyes and we crumble.'

'You credit me with powers I do not possess, my lord.'

'Not so. I must speak as I find.'

'And what else do you find?'

'A Saxon wench beautiful enough to make a man forget all others.'

Her expression was suddenly serious. 'Have you forgotten them, Wulfrum?'

'You are the only woman in my life now and always will be.' He leaned over and kissed her very gently. 'You are my love, Elgiva.'

For a moment she stared at him in stunned surprise and then felt only intense happiness. His arms closed round her again and she laid her head against his shoulder, revelling in his nearness and warmth. They lay thus in silence for some time until Wulfrum smiled and glanced down at her.

'What?'

'I was thinking that I want our son to be like his father,' she replied.

For a moment he did not stir, but then the import of the words struck him.

'Elgiva?' He shifted his weight until he could see her face. 'You don't mean…'

'Yes, I do.'

'Oh, my love. When?'

'In the spring.'

'That's wonderful!' Then another thought occurred to him and his face registered concern. 'But you should have told me sooner. I might have hurt you.'

'You haven't hurt me, Wulfrum.'

'Are you sure?'

'Quite sure.'

He threw back the coverlet and looked at her, running a gentle hand down her body until he came to her belly. As yet he could detect no sign of the life within, but a fierce joy burned in his heart to think she carried his child, their child.

'It will be a while yet before you see any sign.'

'No matter. It is enough to know.'

He kissed her then, but too decorously for Elgiva's liking. Taking his face in her hands, she returned the kiss with passion.

'Have a care, wench,' he warned. 'You play with fire.'

'No, my lord, 'tis you who play with fire.'

'Were it not for your tender condition, I might have put that to the test.'

'Let's put it to the test anyway.'

He was about to reply in kind, but found he couldn't, for her tongue was subtly probing his ear, sending a delightful shiver through his entire body and temporarily robbing him of the power of speech. Then her lips moved to his chest, then lower and lower still. Wulfrum drew in a sharp breath.

'Elgiva?'

She made no reply, but glanced up, once, just long enough for him to glimpse a new and unfathomable expression in those amber eyes. Then she resumed. Wulfrum gasped as he began to experience other infinitely more exciting sensations.

'Elgiva?'

'Mmm?'

'Elgiva, I'm not sure we should…'

The sentence ended in a groan as the first shock wave of pleasure hit him.

CHAPTER FIFTEEN

THE HARVEST that year was a good one and every man and woman who could lift a scythe or thresh grain was pressed into service. The granaries and barns filled rapidly. Wulfrum spent his days out in the fields or in the storehouses and saw it all with satisfaction. According to Gurth's careful accounting, there would be more than enough food for the winter. Besides, soon the apples and root crops would be laid down. Cheeses ripened in the storerooms. Game was abundant. With care, no one need go hungry. In the late autumn the cattle would be killed and the meat salted for, despite a good hay crop, the fodder would only be sufficient to see the breeding stock through the cold weather to come.

In the forest the first leaves began to turn and the time drew near for Wulfrum to leave Ravenswood for York. He was loath to go but knew he had no choice. Lord Halfdan required his presence and would take it much amiss if he were denied. Accordingly he chose a dozen men to accompany him on the ride, leaving a large contingent behind to look after matters in his absence.

'It is only for a week,' he told Elgiva. 'If there are any

problems, you can consult Ida. However, I do not think there is cause for concern.'

She forced a wan smile. No cause for concern? With Aylwin and the dispossessed Saxons seeking his life? They would never have a better chance to act than now. Elgiva was racked by guilt, for the knowledge of her own complicity weighed heavily on her conscience. With it her fear grew apace. Time and again she had tried to summon the courage to tell Wulfrum, but the thought of his reaction stayed her. Already she could see the hurt in his eyes. How could she bear it? How could she bear to see his love turn to suspicion and hatred? Yet how could she remain silent while he was threatened by a danger that was, in part, of her making? She had to speak now, to warn him before he left. Yet how to find the words? How to tell him what she had done?

Unaware of her inner turmoil, Wulfrum finished dressing for the journey and then came to stand before her, drawing her to him.

'Take care of yourself, Elgiva, and look after my son.'

'Depend upon it.'

'I do.' He paused. 'Do you wish me to bring you anything from York?'

'Only yourself.'

They kissed, Elgiva holding him close. Then he buckled on his sword and slid his knife into his belt. The second, slimmer blade was slid into his sleeve.

'It never hurts to be prepared,' he said humorously, seeing the direction of her gaze.

Elgiva took a deep breath, her heart hammering. 'Wulfrum, I must tell you…'

He smiled. 'Tell me what?' Then he saw her unwonted

pallor and the anguish in her eyes and his smile faded. 'My love, what is it?'

'Be vigilant on this journey. I think Aylwin is planning your death.'

For a moment or two there fell a silence so intense that Elgiva could hear the blood pounding in her ears. Throughout, Wulfrum's gaze never left her face.

'How can you know this?'

'Because he…he as good as told me.'

His eyes narrowed. 'How could he have told you?'

'After he escaped from Ravenswood he took refuge in the forest but…' she licked dry lips '…he returned.'

'Returned? When?'

'After his escape. He came here twice, the last time when Halfdan's messengers were here.' She paused. 'He told me that he planned to unite the rebels and take back what was his.'

'Did he so?' Wulfrum was very still, his expression stony as the implications sank in. 'And all these months you have aided and abetted him behind my back.'

'No. I urged him to flee and prevent more bloodshed. I had to try. I had no choice.'

His brow darkened further. 'No choice?'

'I owed him that much, Wulfrum.'

'What did you owe me, your husband?'

'I wanted him to abandon all hope of revenge. I never meant to hurt you.'

'No? Yet knowing he wanted revenge, you still waited all this time to tell me.'

The tears started in her eyes. 'Forgive me. I did not tell you earlier because I could not.'

'Could not or would not?'

'Both, since you will have it.' She swallowed hard. 'There is more.'

Wulfrum remained silent, waiting.

'I warned him of the plan to seek out and destroy the rebel group. That was why the men you caught were not his.' Elgiva closed her eyes a moment, waiting for the explosion of rage. It never came, but the calm was infinitely more chilling.

'Why have you chosen to tell me these things now, Elgiva?'

'Because I don't want any more secrets between us.'

'And I am supposed to trust you from now on?' The coldness in his voice was worse than anything she had anticipated.

'I can only beg your forgiveness and ask you to try to understand.'

'I understand, all right. You love him.'

Elgiva's head jerked up. 'No. I have never loved him. I love you.'

He laughed then, a harsh sound as cold as the expression in his eyes. 'You speak of love! I trusted you and you betrayed me.' Taking a step closer, he seized her shoulders in an iron grip. 'How else have you betrayed me with him, Elgiva? What else have you not said?'

She stared at him in shocked disbelief. 'Nothing. You cannot think so.'

'Why not? How was it—a passionate woodland tryst with the fugitive lover? It would be a fitting revenge, would it not?'

Elgiva, at first appalled, felt her own anger rising at the injustice of this.

'That's not true.'

'Isn't it?'

'No, and you know it.'

Wulfrum's eyes glinted. 'I know only that I was a fool blinded by your beauty. A fool who believed you when you spoke to him of love.'

'The words were true, Wulfrum, I swear it.'

'If they were true, you could not have protected him. You could not have betrayed me.' He paused, his face white with anger. 'By rights I should kill you now, you faithless whore!'

'Do it, then!' Before he was aware of her intent, Elgiva had seized the dagger from his belt and held the point to her breast. 'If you really believe I have cuckolded you with Aylwin, then it is your right. All you have to do is lean upon the point.'

Her gaze met his, unflinching. In it she read anger and pain, a hurt far deeper than she could ever have guessed. His hand closed round hers and the blade touched her throat. He would kill her, then. Suddenly she didn't care. She had lost his love and the look in his eyes was more than she could bear. Unheeded, the tears flowed down her face as the silence stretched between them. Then, without warning, his grip changed, sliding to her wrist before tightening with brutal force. Elgiva gasped. The dagger fell to the floor. He flung away from her and retrieved it.

Elgiva lifted a hand towards him. 'Forgive me.'

Wulfrum made no answer. Casting her a last contemptuous look, he grabbed his cloak and strode to the door. He threw it open with a crash and marched out. In sick horror she heard his receding footsteps and then only silence. Gradually, from outside, the sound of horses' hooves impinged on her consciousness and she ran to the window. Through her tears she watched in hopeless longing as Wulfrum mounted and moved to the head of the column. Elgiva willed him to look her way as her hands clenched over the wooden sill. Almost as if he sensed the intensity of her gaze, he glanced up once and their eyes met. Her heart skipped a beat. Let him smile, she thought, let him give some sign that he forgave her. His expression was forbidding as he held her gaze for a moment, and then he looked away, touching his heels to his horse's sides. Elgiva felt her throat tighten. She watched until he was out of sight and then she wept.

Wulfrum rode fast and his men, seeing that flinty expression, left him alone with his thoughts. In truth he had only one: Elgiva. Their conversation had shaken him to the core and the knowledge of her deception turned like a knife in his guts. For a moment back there he had wanted to kill her. He had no idea what had stayed his hand or how he had governed his ire. It burned still and for some considerable time after until eventually fresh air and exercise tempered it a little. Even so, the memory of the scene was bitter. Her look as he left haunted him. His last words to her had been spoken in anger, anger born of pain the like of which he had known only twice before. He wanted to believe it was all baseless, but he had the evidence of her words. Why had she kept silent so long, only to tell him now? Who could understand the workings of a woman's mind? What traps did subtle beauty lay for the unwary? How could he have been so naïve as to fall for melting looks and tender words of love? And yet she had seemed so sincere. Had she meant *any* of the things she had said? Once he had thought so, but now…

For a long while he rode thus, his brain a ferment of tormented thought. Then, as his rage cooled and he grew calmer, his mind began to clear. In truth, he had been much to blame for allowing himself to grow too fond, to let beauty blind him. He had known from past experience that loving made a man vulnerable and in so doing he had broken a cardinal rule. His marriage to Elgiva had been made for political reasons by and large, something he had forgotten. Only a fool would think a woman could take an enemy to her bed and love him.

In the days that followed Wulfrum's departure, Elgiva kept herself busy about her household tasks, but she found herself thinking about him all the time, wondering what he was doing just at that moment. She had no doubt that he would receive a warm welcome from Halfdan and his mind would be filled with men's business, leaving no time to think of anything else. While their days would be filled with council matters, the nights would be left to carousing. There would be women too, young and attractive and only too pleased to be the object of attention to a handsome earl. And he was handsome, dangerously so. Elgiva bit her lip. So many times she had relived that last quarrel and seen again the hurt in his eyes. He had trusted her and she had betrayed that trust. It mattered not that her motives had been of the best. It was betrayal. Now he had gone with his heart full of anger. Would he seek his pleasure elsewhere? Out of sight, out of mind, the proverb said. For her part it had proven manifestly untrue. Now each day passed much the same as the one before it with nothing to break the monotony. Sometimes she would hear a footfall behind her and turn round, half-expecting to see him there, but it would be Ida or one of the other men. Most acutely she was aware of how big their bed-chamber seemed without him. She could not but recall the scenes that had taken place there. Now all that remained was echoing emptiness.

'You miss him, don't you?' said Osgifu. They were sitting outside the women's bower, spinning. Elgiva's attention never left the yarn, but a telltale blush crept into her face.

'Yes.'

'Well, 'tis only a week he'll be gone and the time will pass swiftly enough. Then you might regret that it was not longer.'

Elgiva burst into tears. In a moment Osgifu was beside her.

'What is it, child? What's wrong?'

Between sobs she managed to glean an account of the events that had preceded Wulfrum's departure.

'I wanted things to be right between us, for there to be no more lies. Now I've made it a hundred times worse. I have never seen him so angry. He looked at me as though he hated me.'

'His pride has been hurt and he's jealous. It's a danger-ous combination, but he'll get over it.'

'But he had no cause to be jealous. I love him, not Aylwin. I thought he knew that.' Elgiva sobbed harder. 'Now he has gone away. What if he never comes back?'

'He'll come back. He's too bloody minded not to.'

Sick with fear and doubt, Elgiva endured the long days of Wulfrum's absence with a heavy heart. She performed all that was required of her with regard to the household affairs, but could take no pleasure in any of it. When her duties were done she sought solace out of doors, for the chamber she had shared with Wulfrum was too full of bitter memories to allow of its being a sanctuary now. The quiet burying ground offered most tranquillity and the prospect of being undisturbed. Having told Osgifu of her intent, it was thither she bent her steps.

However, she found that she was not alone. A man was already standing there in the shade beneath one of the trees on the far side. With a start, she recognised Brekka. For a moment she regarded him with resentment. What did he want? Why couldn't he leave her alone? Did he not know the peril he put them both in if he were seen? She looked around, but there was no sign of anyone else. Taking a deep breath, she calmed herself, ashamed of such uncharitable thoughts. Then she made her way towards him.

'My lady.' He bowed. 'I have been waiting here in the hope of meeting you.'

'What is it, Brekka?'

'I bring word from Lord Aylwin.'

'From Aylwin?'

'Aye, my lady. He bade me say that he has reconsidered your advice. He said you would understand what that meant.'

Elgiva's heartbeat grew a little faster. Aylwin was going to leave after all. Wulfrum was safe. Her spirits lifted as they had not for days. Before she could question further, Brekka continued.

'He asks that he be permitted to see you once more.' He paused. 'If you refuse, he will understand.'

Elgiva looked over her shoulder. There were still no Danes in evidence. Of late, the watch on her person had been relaxed, proof of Wulfrum's growing regard and trust. Guilt stabbed. Then she thought of Aylwin, of his long and lonely exile in the forest, hunted by his enemies, never knowing if each day would be his last. He had been her betrothed. He had fought for Ravenswood, for her, and been wounded in their cause. Surely it was not too much to ask that he should be allowed to say farewell.

'Where is he, Brekka?'

'At the clearing where stand the old woodsmen's huts.'

She nodded. It wasn't far. She could be there and back before she was missed.

'Very well. I will come.'

As she had anticipated, it was but a short distance they had to walk and twenty minutes later they reached the clearing. As they did so, Elgiva could see the men and horses gathered there, perhaps twenty in all. Evidently they were on the point of departure. Elgiva stopped, looking around, relieved to think that sense had prevailed.

'He is within, my lady,' said Brekka, nodding towards the foremost of the huts.

Even as he spoke three men emerged and she saw the familiar figure of Aylwin. The others she did not know. They had been deep in conversation, but, seeing her and Brekka, they stopped. For a moment there was silence, then Aylwin hurried forwards to greet her. He took her hand and pressed it to his lips.

'I knew you would come.'

Elgiva glanced at the mounted men. 'I think my arrival is opportune.'

'Indeed, there is little time. We must be gone.'

'Where do you go, my lord?'

'To Wessex, to throw in our lot with Alfred and the free Saxons.'

Elgiva felt a surge of relief. He would be safe and now so would Wulfrum. 'I am glad. After our last conversation, I did not think you would leave.'

'Indeed, there is nothing now to stay for.' He smiled. 'Your arrival makes everything complete.'

'I don't understand.'

'You are coming with me, Elgiva.'

Apprehension prickled as she glanced around her. All the men on the far side of the clearing had mounted and were waiting. The two who had been with Aylwin before were now just a few yards off, flanking her. Brekka stood a pace behind.

'I apologise for the ruse used to get you here,' Aylwin went on, 'but it seemed the safest way, all things considered. Besides, according to my intelligence, Earl Wulfrum is in York and not due back for days. By the time you are missed this evening, we shall be long gone.'

'I cannot go with you, you know that.'

'Did you think I would leave you behind, Elgiva?'

'You must. Wulfrum will follow. He'll kill every last one of you.'

'No. The noble earl will not follow.'

Apprehension turned to real alarm now. 'What do you mean?'

'Our Saxon allies have undertaken to prevent it. An ambush has been laid for him on his return from York.'

'What?' She was aghast. 'You can't mean it.'

'I was never more serious in my life,' he returned. 'And with your husband dead, I take back what is mine.'

Elgiva shook her head, feeling sick with dread. 'I cannot let you do this, Aylwin.'

'You cannot prevent it,' he replied. He nodded to his companions. 'Take the lady to her horse.'

'No!' Elgiva confronted him in anger. 'I will not go with you.'

'You're coming with me, Elgiva, whether you will or not.'

Aylwin nodded to his companions. In a moment she was held and her wrists bound securely in front of her. Then, despite all protest, she was carried to the horses and lifted into the saddle. Someone took hold of her reins and the whole cavalcade set off.

Frightened and shocked, Elgiva concentrated first and foremost of staying in the saddle, for the pace was swift. With every stride all she could think of was Wulfrum riding into an ambush. And if by some miracle he survived it and returned to Ravenswood to find her gone, he would think her complicit, that she had gone with the Saxon rebels of her own free will. It would be for him the ultimate proof of her guilt. Heartsick, Elgiva saw in her mind her husband's face and the hurt in his eyes, the silent accusation and the killing rage. He would never forgive her.

CHAPTER SIXTEEN

THE council had been a notable success so far as Wulfrum was concerned; it had finished ahead of time and Halfdan had acceded to his request for reinforcements to crush the Saxon rebels in Ravenswood, offering twenty-five men. It wasn't as many as Wulfrum had initially hoped, but Halfdan had his own problems with local uprisings and could spare no more. Even so Wulfrum knew it would give him the advantage. With skilful deployment he could achieve his goal. The only negative was that Sweyn was among their number, but Wulfrum would not let personal matters cloud his judgement here. For all his faults Sweyn was a good man in a fight, being both experienced and ruthless. Once the rebels had been crushed, then there would be time to consider past grievances, but not until.

Having turned their backs on York, they made good progress with Wulfrum calling a halt at noon to rest the horses and let the men refresh themselves. Then they rode on. The mood was buoyant; as they reached the edge of the forest, they knew they were within ten miles of Ravenswood. Wulfrum breathed in the subtle evocative scent of the woodland and smiled, for he associated it with home and with Elgiva.

Elgiva! Despite all his efforts not to, he had missed her more than he had ever dreamed possible. Yet their last words had been filled with anger. How much he had regretted it since. While his days had been busy enough, the nights had afforded leisure to think; it had occurred to him then that she could have kept silent and he would never have known of those meetings with Aylwin. She could have kept silent and let him ride unsuspecting into possible danger. That way she would have been free of him, free to join her Saxon lover—if, indeed, he was her lover. She had told him long ago that she respected Aylwin, but had denied ever loving him. A marriage of convenience, she said. It had sounded like the truth, but was it? If not, why had she chosen to speak at last, to risk his wrath and worse? He had been so close to killing her. The truth hurt, as she had known it must but, as she said, what was the alternative—to build a future on secrets and lies? He knew it was not a future he wanted. She had begged for his forgiveness and he had spurned her, too angry to realise that she was asking for a completely different relationship with him. A prize of war, forced to marry the victor, she had had no say in the events that would shape the future. Her world had been turned upside down. Torn between two loyalties and put, by him, into an impossible position, Elgiva had only done what she thought she must. Should he blame her after?

Wulfrum sighed, calling himself all kinds of fool. He had regarded his marriage with complacency and then, at the first real test, he had allowed rage and jealousy to impair his judgement. While he was familiar with the former, he had never known jealousy before. No woman had ever mattered enough—until now. He had told Elgiva he loved her, but he had not taken her part or even given her the benefit of the doubt. Could she ever forgive him? Could they make a life together after this? He prayed it might be so for the idea of any future without her was meaningless. When he had taken her to wife he had little thought he would come to love her to the point where only she could do him hurt.

Wulfrum was given little more leisure to indulge these thoughts for the road narrowed among the trees, forcing the party to slow the pace. The forest around them grew denser and the landscape more rugged. Presently the way passed between two steep banks, compelling the horsemen to ride in single file. Firedrake slowed and snorted. Wulfrum frowned, snapping out of his reverie instantly, reining in while he scanned the path ahead and the trees around.

'What is it?' Ironfist drew rein behind him.

'I don't know. Listen.'

At his signal the men ceased all conversation. Apart from the occasional stamp of a hoof and the creak of saddle leather, there was silence.

'I don't hear anything,' said Ironfist at length.

'Exactly.'

The giant's eyes narrowed as he looked at the defile ahead. 'A good place for an ambush.'

'Aye, but our way lies through it all the same. Have the men keep their wits about them.'

Wulfrum heard the word passed back, heard swords loosened in scabbards. Then he urged his mount forwards. The stallion's ears flicked back and forth and he snorted anew, placing his hooves with neat precision on the path, his steps more reluctant. It confirmed Wulfrum's suspicions, but still he could detect no sign of life. The skin prickled on the back of his neck. He guessed if there was an attack, it would be when his men were deep in the defile. Closing his legs around the horse's sides, he urged him on. From out of nowhere an arrow hissed past and a man behind him cried out. More arrows followed, thudding into shields amid warning shouts from his escort. He saw a man fall, pierced through the throat. Then came whoops and yells and suddenly the trees were alive with armed men hurtling down the steep banks towards their quarry. He had an impression of woodsmen's garb and rough bearded faces, but the attackers were not without courage or skill and laid on right willingly.

Wulfrum drew Dragon Tooth from the scabbard. Moments later the sword became a deadly arc of light, cutting down the first two attackers before they knew what had hit them. Then the third was upon him. Wulfrum parried the blow aimed at his head, but the blade slid off his own and left a bloody gash along his arm. Gritting his teeth, he fought grimly on, knowing there could be no quarter. He dispatched his opponent with a wicked slash to the throat. The man dropped where he stood, his life blood gushing from the wound. As he fell, another took his place. The outlaws were violent men, who preyed on travellers and would sell their lives dear. Wulfrum knew it was unusual for them to attack such a large group, but desperate fugitives would do whatever they had to. His men gave a good account of themselves, but, hampered by the cramped conditions and milling horses and the bodies of the slain, their situation was precarious indeed.

From the corner of his eye he saw Ironfist swing his war axe and take off a man's head before slicing for another. He heard the foe scream and fall as the blade severed an arm. Wulfrum fought on, a cold anger burning in his gut and a fierce determination not to meet his end here on this forest trail. He accounted for three more of the attackers before their leader, seeing the tide of battle turn against them, shouted the command to retreat. The outlaws fought their way free and began to back off before turning and scrambling up the banking towards the safety of the trees. There was no order about their going, just a desire to escape. Soon the last of them vanished among the trees.

'Shall we give chase?' demanded Ironfist.

'No. Let them go.'

Wulfrum leaned on his sword, breathing hard. He turned and looked around at the scene of carnage. Apart from several casualties among Halfdan's men, of the dozen who had originally set out with Wulfrum, only five were standing alongside himself and Ironfist. Three more were injured, the rest were slain. His anger grew.

Then Ironfist noticed the blood dripping over Wulfrum's wrist and hand. 'You are hurt.'

'A gash, no more.'

'Best let me bind it.'

Wulfrum stood while the big Viking took a cloth from his saddlebag and bound it expertly round the wound. Having done so, he looked around, surveying the bodies of the attackers.

'Saxons,' he said, 'but why would they risk attacking such a large group?'

Wulfrum shook his head. 'I don't know.' Then he remembered Elgiva's words: *Be vigilant on this journey.*

Had she known more about this than she confessed to? Was she implicated? As he beheld the bodies of the slain, all his former doubts resurfaced and with them his anger.

'It seems the rebels grow bolder,' said Sweyn, looking around him with casual interest. 'You will have quite a task on your hands, Wulfrum.' He wiped the blood from his blade before sheathing it again. 'But at least we can look forward to a good fight.'

'No doubt.' Wulfrum turned to Ironfist. 'Have the men mount up. I want to get back to Ravenswood.'

As Ironfist moved away, Sweyn grinned and his expression grew mocking.

'Missing the lovely Elgiva, Wulfrum?' Then, seeing the other's expression, he feigned contrition. 'Not that I blame you, of course.'

'You take a deal too much interest in my wife. I should resent it if the time were right.'

'Let it be a quarrel between us then, if you live.'

'I'll live.' Wulfrum's voice was cold. Retrieving his horse's reins, he remounted, pausing a moment to survey his rival. 'Whether you will do the same is another matter.'

'Trust me…' Sweyn bared his teeth in a vulpine smile '…I'll have Elgiva yet.'

'Over my dead body.'

'Why, so I hope.'

Refusing to be drawn further, Wulfrum touched Firedrake with his spur and the big horse cantered away.

Elgiva breathed a sigh of relief when eventually the pace slowed for a while to let the horses breathe. Already they were many miles from Ravenswood and all hope of aid. Her heart sank to think that she would likely not be missed for some time. Even then, no one would have any idea where she was. Aylwin had laid his plans well, baiting the trap with expert care. All sympathy for him had evaporated now. In following his own desires he had completely ignored hers, thinking to take by force what she could not give. She shivered. If once he and his men reached Wessex, she would be beyond all help. Even Wulfrum could not pursue her there. Wulfrum! If only he might be spared the ambush laid for him. If only he might live. Nothing else mattered.

She was so preoccupied that she failed to notice Aylwin beside her until he spoke.

'Why so sad, Elgiva?'

She turned to look at him, hoping to find some trace of remorse in his expression, some small expression of pity that she might exploit.

'You know why,' she replied.

'Have I not rescued you from the Viking's clutches? Do I not deserve your thanks?'

'Wulfrum is my husband.'

'Not for much longer.'

'He is not so easy to kill.'

'It matters not.'

'What do you mean?'

'A marriage made under duress to a pirate raider is no marriage at all. When we reach Wessex I shall appeal to Alfred. He will be exceeding grateful for the reinforcements I bring and he is withal a most pious king. I anticipate no difficulty in having your marriage to the Viking set aside.'

'And say you do. What then?'

'Then you will wed me as is my legal right as your betrothed.'

'I will not marry you, Aylwin.'

'You will have no choice, my dear, when it is a matter of royal decree.'

Elgiva closed her eyes for a moment, striving against the knowledge that he was right. If the king ordered it, she would be forced to submit to his will. Aylwin could then marry her within the hour. In desperation she made a last appeal to his better self.

'What point, my lord? Would you have an unwilling wife?'

'I would rather have you willing, Elgiva, but if not I'll have you anyway.' His gaze hardened. 'Forget your Viking earl. You belong to me now.'

She drew in a deep breath, fighting down panic. He would not see her weep and plead. In any event it would be useless for all appeals would be denied. She would not give him that satisfaction. Aylwin saw her chin come up and nodded.

'That's better. Do you know, I've always admired your spirit and your good sense. You fight well, Elgiva, but you know when you cannot win.'

'It isn't over yet.' Even as she said it, she was not at all sure it was true. He was strong and resourceful and now he had her in his power.

'Shall we have a wager on that?'

'I would wager only that you will die on the point of Wulfrum's sword.'

'Then you will lose. I am your lord now.'

Wulfrum urged the stallion to a gallop, a mile-eating pace that closed the distance between him and Ravenswood. As he rode, a lot of things became clearer in his mind and he knew for a certainty that he was supposed to have died in that ambush along with his men. It had been no random incident. The attackers had been Saxons and only one man hereabouts had the necessary knowledge to order it—the knowledge *and* the motive. Aylwin. He had not bowed to the Viking yoke, nor had he forgiven the loss of his lands or his betrothed. He would take Elgiva if he could. His wife's face floated before him in memory and with it fresh suspicion. On her own admission Elgiva had been in contact with the rebel leader. It begged the question—had she aided him in this business? Had the two of them planned his death? The thought was chilling but he could no longer suppress it. It must be faced. She had deceived him before and might have again. However it might be, he would learn the truth soon enough.

He and his companions covered the last miles in a short time and at length saw Ravenswood in the distance. On seeing their approach, the look-outs gave word and serfs came running from all directions. Wulfrum rode through the gateway at the head of his escort and drew rein outside the hall. Ida and several of his men came out to greet the new arrivals. Of Elgiva there was no sign. The feeling of foreboding grew stronger with every passing moment. Dismounting, he flung the reins at a serf and strode into the hall.

'Elgiva!'

His voice echoed round the building, but brought forth no reply. Setting his jaw, he took the stairs three at a time, coming at length to their bedchamber. One glance revealed it to be empty. Wulfrum searched the other room, then went down again to the hall. In the women's bower he accosted Osgifu, but she professed no knowledge of

Elgiva's whereabouts. His anger rising fast, Wulfrum grabbed hold of her and shook her.

'Don't lie to me, old woman. Where is she?'

Osgifu went pale. 'My lord, I'm not sure.'

'What do you mean, you're not sure?'

'She said she was going to the burial ground earlier this afternoon. I have not seen her since.'

'The burial ground?' Mentally Wulfrum saw the place. It was but a stone's throw from the forest. He glared at Osgifu. 'What more?'

'My lord, I know nothing more, I swear it.'

'If you're lying to me, this day will be your last.' He let go his hold. 'Now fetch me one of your mistress's gowns and be quick about it.'

Much disturbed, Osgifu scuttled off. Wulfrum turned to Ida.

'Tell the kennel men to bring out the hounds and have someone saddle me a fresh horse.'

'At once, my lord.'

As Ida disappeared, Wulfrum drew in a deep breath, trying to collect his thoughts, to force his anger down. Ironfist's voice broke the silence.

'You think she's run away.'

'I don't know yet, but I will find out.'

'It's possible she was taken by force.'

Wulfrum's fists clenched. 'It's possible.'

'Perhaps you should give her the benefit of the doubt.' The giant met the basilisk glare unflinching. 'I do not think her treacherous.'

Had it been anyone else, there would have been bloodshed. Wulfrum closed his eyes a moment, striving for control.

'Tell the men to mount up.'

Ironfist walked away and for a moment Wulfrum followed his retreating figure. Then Osgifu returned with one of Elgiva's gowns, hastily snatched from the coffer. It was the gold one she had worn for their wedding. The memory cut like a blade. Without a word, he seized the dress and strode out to the courtyard in the other's wake. If they were to find his wife, the hounds needed a scent.

From the burying ground the trail was clear enough and they followed at a cracking pace, coming soon to the clearing and the now abandoned woodsmen's huts. At that point the scent grew confused and there was no clear trace of Elgiva anywhere in evidence. Then, after some casting about, Ida called out, 'A lot of horses were here, my lord. Fifteen or twenty, I'd say.'

For a moment Wulfrum was silent, his face deathly pale. Elgiva had chosen her moment well. By now she and her Saxon lord were well away. His fingers clenched round the fabric of the gown and he bit back the cry of rage and despair welling in his heart. Forcing his voice to a level tone, he turned to Ida.

'We follow.'

The trail wasn't hard to find and the fugitives had made no effort to conceal their passage. Moreover, they were travelling fast. Wulfrum pushed his horse hard, determined to narrow the gap. The party was riding west by south. That could only mean one thing. He gritted his teeth. If they once reached Wessex, Elgiva was as good as lost to him. Her face intruded on to his thoughts once more. How cleverly she had deceived him, using her beauty and her wit to lull him into believing she really cared, only to betray him so thoroughly in the end. Except it wasn't the end, he vowed. Not yet. Not till he caught the fugitives. He would slay Aylwin with his own hand and then... Heartsick, he suppressed a groan for grief had taken on all the sharpness of physical pain, one deeper than any sword thrust. Yet even now, with all the evidence in front of him, he could not bring himself to believe her capable of such treachery. Could Ironfist be right? Could she have been taken by force? How much he wanted to believe that, to believe her innocent for he knew now that the alternative meant her death.

The Saxon fugitives rode until the sun was low on the horizon before stopping to rest the horses a while. Aylwin dismounted, lifting Elgiva from the saddle. Bone weary and sick with dread, she made no resistance now, knowing she was lost. Wulfrum was in York, would be for another day at least. He would return to find her gone. Worse, he would think she had gone of her own volition. His pain and his anger would be great indeed, but not as great as the desolation in her heart.

Throughout the long ride she had sought the means to escape, but none presented itself. She was kept in the midst of the riders and her horse was led. Besides, with her wrists bound, it would have been impossible to try anything. Even now they had halted, Aylwin was still taking no chances. On his orders, Elgiva was led aside and tied fast to a tree. The bonds were not cruelly tight, but they were secure enough when tested to preclude all hope of escape. Aylwin surveyed the proceedings with a rueful eye.

'I'm sorry, Elgiva. I do this only for your own good.'

'No,' she replied. 'You do it for yours.'

'I wish it had not been necessary.'

After he left her to speak with his men, Elgiva struggled again against the rope, but it yielded not a whit. Hot tears scalded her eyelids and she slumped into despair. She knew now that she would never see Wulfrum again.

CHAPTER SEVENTEEN

SEEING a telltale cloud of dust some way ahead, Wulfrum experienced a sense of savage satisfaction. When the cloud dissipated, the feeling intensified. The Saxons had stopped. They weren't expecting pursuit yet. Wulfrum reined in and raised a hand to halt his men. Then he gave the order to dismount.

'We'll move up as close as we can. Then we go in fast and we go in for the kill. Take no prisoners save one.' He paused, drawing Dragon Tooth from the scabbard. 'My wife is to be brought to me—alive and unhurt.'

In obedience to the command, the Viking host moved forwards with stealthy stride until they were within fifty yards of their prey. Then they surged forwards in open attack upon the startled Saxons. Wulfrum launched himself forward, Dragon Tooth in his fist, hacking and slashing at the hapless foe. Several fell before they had time to draw a blade. All around him he could hear shouts and curses and cries of pain in the ensuing mêlée. Though surprised and outnumbered, the remaining Saxons fought with desperate courage, determined to sell their lives dear. Surrounded on all sides by the battling throng, Wulfrum

had but one immediate aim: to find Aylwin and carve the
Saxon cur into small slivers. Seeking his man, he cut down
three others on the way, his sword running with their
blood. A moment later exultation became impotent rage
to see his quarry locked in mortal combat some twenty
yards off and half-a-dozen other fighting pairs between.
Wulfrum's wrath became incandescent when he saw who
it was in that fatal conflict.

'Sweyn!'

If the man heard that furious yell, he gave no sign. Even
from his present position Wulfrum could see the fearsome
light of battle joy on the berserker's face, the savage delight
with which he pressed the attack, forcing his opponent
back step by step. Even in the midst of frustration and rage,
Wulfrum had to admire the sheer gall of this man who
dared steal his earl's rightful opponent thus. Gritting his
teeth, he carved his way forwards, determined not to lose
this enemy to Sweyn. However, even as he slew one man,
it seemed another rose up to take his place. Cursing, he
fought on.

Elgiva struggled in desperation against the rope that held
her, her terrified gaze following the conflict even as her
heart leapt. They were Wulfrum's men. He had come for
her. Frantic, she looked for him among the heaving throng,
but failed to spot him. She swallowed hard. Dear God, let
him win. Let him come through unhurt. Her anxious eyes
found Aylwin locked in deadly confrontation with a tall
fair-haired Viking warrior. Anxiety became fear as she
recognised his opponent: Sweyn! Appalled and fascinated
together, she watched as the swords clashed, sparks
leaping from their edges with each savage blow. Aylwin

fought well, but he was twice the other man's age and no match now for Sweyn in speed or stamina. Already his tunic was stained with the blood from half-a-dozen gashes. Beads of sweat stood on his forehead as he was pushed relentlessly back. Unable to see where he put his feet, he caught his heel on a rock and stumbled. He was off balance for no more than a second, but it was enough. Elgiva stifled a cry as Sweyn's blade thrust deep into his opponent's unprotected body. For a moment or two Aylwin hung impaled on its point before the blade was withdrawn and he buckled at the knees, sinking to the earth. The Viking paused a moment to look down at the fallen foe. Then he laughed, exultant. A moment later he was challenged anew by three furious Saxons who, having seen their leader fall, were bound on revenge. Sweyn fought like a madman, killing one and wounding another before the odds swung against him and the third sword thrust past his guard and through the ribs behind. Checked mid-stroke, he staggered and fell, dead before he hit the earth, the sword still in his hand and the ghost of a smile on his face. Elgiva shuddered and turned her head away.

Wulfrum saw Sweyn go down, but by the time he reached the place, the fighting had moved on and the berserker was dead. Darting fierce glances about him, he found Aylwin hard by. The man lived yet, but his lifeblood was flowing fast from the great wound in his side. For a moment Wulfrum was still, glaring down upon his fallen enemy, knowing he had been cheated of the revenge he had so ardently desired. With dimming eyes, the Saxon registered his presence and spoke through ragged, gasping breaths.

'So it ends, Viking.'

'Aye, it ends.' Wulfrum bent and he seized the front of the other's tunic. 'Where is my wife? What have you done with her?'

'She is unharmed.' The Saxon coughed and blood trickled from his mouth. Every word was an effort now. 'I forced her to come…thought to take her from you but…it is you she loves.' He paused, fighting for breath. 'You must…take care of her.'

There followed a slow exhalation of breath and nothing more. Meeting the Saxon's sightless gaze, Wulfrum bestowed on him a grim smile, his fist tightening round the hilt of the sword.

'I shall take care of her. I swear it to you.'

He straightened, his gaze scanning the scene for the one he sought. Above the din of fight he heard a woman scream and then he located her at last, not twenty yards away from him. Anger blazed anew, but he controlled it now, letting it fuel his strength as he cut a path towards her, relentless, determined, his opponents falling like corn beneath the scythe.

Ashen faced, Elgiva watched him come and, as he reached her, joy was drowned by flooding terror for he was suddenly a stranger to her—not Wulfrum any longer, but a warrior bent on vengeance and fearsome in battle rage, all dark with gore, his sword reeking and bloody, a sword whose naked point was levelled at her. For a moment he stood quite still, the icy gaze taking in every detail of the scene before it met and locked with hers. Then ice became fire. Like one transfixed, she watched him lift the sword, saw it descend. With a solid thunk the blade bit wood, severing the rope that bound her to the tree. Elgiva slumped, barely aware of the powerful arm that caught her just before she fell into a dead faint.

She had no idea how long she lay there. Perhaps no more than a few moments, though the sounds of fighting seemed muted and distant now. Someone was with her, cradling her in strong arms and a man was speaking her name.

'Elgiva, my love. My heart. Speak to me, for the love of Odin.'

Her eyelids fluttered open. What had he just called her?

'Wulfrum?'

'Oh, my love. Thank all the gods. I thought I'd lost you.'

'You came for me.' Unable to help herself, Elgiva began to cry, her body shaken by great racking sobs even as she clung to him.

'Shh. Hush now. It's all right. It's all right.' He rocked her in his arms until she quieted a little. As he did so, he noticed her bruised wrists and his gaze hardened. 'He has hurt you.'

She shook her head. 'Rope burns, nothing more.'

'No one shall ever hurt you again. I swear it.'

'Oh, Wulfrum, he told me you were dead.' Elgiva began to sob again. 'He said he was going to keep me…that he would take me by force to Wessex. I thought I'd never see you again…'

Wulfrum, feeling her body shake in terror and revulsion, dropped a soothing kiss on the top of her head. 'Surely you did not think I would let another man steal you away?'

As the sobs racked her, his jaw tightened as he bore witness to her anguish. Then, as if that were not bad enough, another thought occurred to him.

'Elgiva, the child. It is not harmed?'

'No. I think it is well.'

Even as he knew relief, it chilled Wulfrum to think of what he might have lost that day. In a moment of blinding clarity he understood then that love was stronger than hate. Love made a man vulnerable, but it empowered him too. It gave his life reason and purpose. Aylwin might have died this day, but his battle had been lost long ago. Anger evaporated on the heel of that realisation and he knew the Saxon had done only what any man worthy of the name would have done—he had fought for his land and his kin and for the woman he loved. The knowledge that his love had not been returned must have been bitter indeed and yet he had acknowledged it at the end. That too required a kind of courage. His heart full, Wulfrum bent his gaze on his wife's face.

'How I have missed you, lady.'

Looked up at him through her tears, Elgiva drew in a shuddering breath. 'Wulfrum, can you ever forgive me for—'

His finger on her lips silenced her. 'There is nothing to forgive. The fault is mine for allowing jealousy to blind me.'

'You had cause enough to be angry but I never meant to betray you. I swear it.'

'I know. As I know there could be no future for me without you. You are my life, Elgiva. My life and my love.'

Then he crushed her to him in a close embrace that needed no further explanation.

EPILOGUE

Spring—868 A.D.

WULFRUM stood by the casement, watching the first grey light of dawn stealing over the quiet earth. He let his gaze travel over the roofs of the outbuildings to the fields beyond, surveying it all with a sense of pride. The first time he had set eyes on Ravenswood he little thought it would be his or that it would become the place he called home. Yet in the last year he had come to know it intimately, every field and farm, every hedge and ditch. It was good land, rich and fertile, his land. And yet it was more than that—the land had a power of its own that spoke to the heart of a man. Sometimes he thought it had claimed him rather than the other way round. And always there was the great forest, at this season decked again in the fresh green of new growth, new life. He felt its peace steal into his soul as he breathed its scent on the cool air. With a faint smile he glanced at the sword lying on the chest nearby. Let others follow the winds of war or launch the sea dragons to go a-viking. They would do it without him.

A faint sound from the bed drew his attention from the

view outside and he smiled to see Elgiva stir. Beside her, in the crib, their son lay sleeping: Wulfgar. Born in the teeth of a March gale, he was a fine lusty babe with a thatch of dark hair and eyes as blue as harebells. Watching them both, Wulfrum felt his heart swell with love and pride, touched alike by their vulnerability and the beauty of the simple scene. Once fate had snatched away everything he held dear, but it had been restored in full measure.

Elgiva stirred and, feeling the empty space beside her, opened her eyes. 'Wulfrum?' Seeing him across the room, she smiled and reached out a hand.

'Come back to bed. It's early yet.'

Nothing loath, he left his station by the window and returned to her, sliding beneath the pelts and drawing her close, sharing her warmth. Feeling his arms about her, Elgiva smiled and closed her eyes and slept again. For a while he lay there, listening to her soft breathing, and then he too began to drowse and sank at last into peaceful slumber. Outside, the first rays of sunlight touched the canopy of the sheltering forest.

* * * * *

The Nurse's Baby Miracle

JANICE LYNN

Janice Lynn has a Master of Science degree in nursing from Vanderbilt University and works full-time as a family nurse practitioner in a small rural town in the southern United States. Juggling the aspects of day-to-day life and her life-long dream of writing happily-ever-afters, Janice lives with her husband, David; their four children, Jessie, Jacob, Abby and James; their three dogs, Lily, Trouble and Jackson; and a lot of unnamed dust bunnies that have moved in since she started her writing career.

As a teenager, Janice fell in love with romance while sneaking her mother's Mills & Boon® novels. She dreamed of fictional worlds where good always triumphs over evil and where the girl gets her man. Since then, she's dreamed of creating stories that touch readers' hearts and takes them into fantasy worlds of their own.

Prior to publication, Janice won numerous writing contests and finalled in the prestigious Golden Heart in 2003. Then Janice won the 2006 Golden Quill for Best First book and her first Mills & Boon® Medical™ romance, *The Doctor's Pregnancy Bombshell*, won the 2007 National Readers' Choice Award and was a finalist for the Award of Excellence and Touch of Magic writing contests. Janice has published four additional novels with Harlequin Mills & Boon.

Janice belongs to Writers At Play, the Romance Writers of America and various RWA chapters where she's served in numerous capacities.

Janice loves to hear from readers. Please e-mail her at Janice@janicelynn.net, write to her care of Mills & Boon or visit her at www. janicelynn.net.

To Janie Green,
who inspires me in so many ways.
I love you, Grandma!

CHAPTER ONE

HE'S the one.

Natalie Carmichael's heart pounded the words through her mind while she listened to the orientation speech at the East Atlanta Shopping Complex parking lot. The previous evening she'd arrived at this year's breast cancer walk's campsite expecting to find things similar to other walks she'd participated in.

But she hadn't counted on Dr. Caleb Burton, a hot, sexy, ohmigosh-do-doctors-really-look-this-good-off-television? volunteer at this year's three-day, sixty-mile fundraiser.

Her gaze collided with hot blue eyes fringed with thick, sooty lashes. Heat crawled up her neck, prickling the tiny hairs at her nape, coating her skin with a sweaty sheen. She couldn't blame the weather. The sun had barely risen above the mall, casting orange and pink streaks across the early-morning sky.

He's the one.

What was wrong with her? She couldn't go up to a virtual stranger and tell him that she wanted a baby, wanted to be a mother more than anything in the world, and would he please consider helping her with that? That she'd taken one look at him last night at dinner and known that, despite her aversion to one-night stands, what she really wanted was *his* baby.

No, she couldn't ask Caleb Burton to donate his sperm after having met him only the day before. He'd think she was crazy.

She *was* crazy.

Crazy in lust. The man was hotter than the steaming Atlanta asphalt. That had to be why she was thinking the way she was. Thanks to the fertility drugs, her hormones were in baby-making overdrive, and being attracted to Caleb was only natural. He was a gorgeous, testosterone-laden hunk who made her insides quivery, made her envision cuddling a dark-haired darling who looked like him.

Okay, so he made her envision a lot of other things, too. Like when his fingers had brushed hers and she'd imagined how they'd feel in other more sensitive spots. When he'd walked her to her sleeping bag in a partitioned-off section of the medical tent, she'd gotten the impression if they'd been truly alone he'd have kissed her. She'd envisioned that kiss.

He'd wanted to. She'd wanted him to. But their attraction only complicated her well-laid-out plans. Very soon she'd be pregnant, and focusing her energy into a healthy pregnancy. Admittedly via a sperm bank wasn't how she'd imagined starting her family, but she'd learned to improvise long ago.

Her gaze lifted. Caleb was watching her—again—and her face caught fire. Lower spots on her body caught fire, too. Burning so hot she melted to the very core. Lord, the man was so sexy. She was tempted to put off her plans for a few months to enjoy the promises his eyes made.

What if she didn't have a few months?

She'd already failed two artificial inseminations. Time could be running out. Which was why she was emptying her savings account for IVF. It was expensive, but what was one more medical bill when compared to those of the past year? When compared to a mangled uterus that wouldn't carry a baby if she waited too long to get pregnant, thanks to growing scar tissue? She wouldn't risk never having a baby. Not even for an attraction as strong as what she felt for Caleb.

He sent her a quick grin—a friendly one, not attempting to hide his interest. He moved close, bent near her ear. "What are you thinking about so seriously?"

That she wanted a baby with twinkling blue eyes, dimples to die for, and an obvious zest for life.

She needed to get her mind on task. Pursuing whatever this was between them was not worth the price of never having a child.

"Just hoping all the walkers make it safely today." She gestured to the crowd of more than four thousand, anxiously waiting to start their adventure while the emcee continued her motivating speech, regaling them with statistics on breast cancer and the strides being made in prevention, detection and treatment.

"There are stop points all along the way for the walkers to rehydrate and grab a snack," she assured them. "Plus, one of the rescue vans will pick up any who have problems."

Natalie fanned her face to stir some air. Standing behind a 747 at take-off wouldn't stir enough air to cool the heat looking at Caleb caused.

"You weren't in Atlanta last year. Which walk did you volunteer with?"

"St. Louis." Caleb grinned at her obvious appraisal, causing more heat to suffuse her face.

"What brought you to Atlanta?" she asked, hoping her question sounded friendly, professional, not too interested.

"One of the doctors lined up to volunteer had something come up last minute. A mutual friend gave John Scarbrough my name, and when he called saying he desperately needed someone to fill in I couldn't say no." He looked straight into Natalie's eyes. "I'm not heading home until Monday afternoon. We could grab a bite to eat Sunday evening, after the hoopla dies down."

His expression promised much more than food.

Why now? She couldn't help but wonder. A whole lifetime of less-than-interesting men, jerks and losers, then *boom,* the most fascinating man showed up.

He's the one.

God, would that voice inside her heart please just shut up? He was not "the one". The only "one" for her at the moment was an anonymous donor she'd pre-selected months ago.

She coughed to clear her throat.

"I'm glad you were able to do the walk." She ignored his invitation for the simple reason she couldn't bring herself to say no, and she certainly couldn't say yes. "It's a great cause, and volunteers are needed to make the walk successful."

"Yes," he agreed after a moment's hesitation. She thought he was going to call her on her non-answer. Just when she reached the point of wanting to squirm beneath his intense stare, he glanced toward the opening day stage in the middle of the mall's parking lot. Music blared from the speakers and the walkers stretched to the beat, preparing their muscles for the taxing day.

"Do you have a family member with breast cancer?" he asked, leaning in close. So close she fought against inhaling as much of him as her lungs would hold. God, he smelled heavenly.

"While I was in nursing school I had the pleasure of meeting a special lady with breast cancer. She was my first real patient assignment and we clicked." Although she wasn't generally one for talking about her personal life, Natalie responded openly. Probably because of the way his expectant expression said he genuinely wanted to know. "I've kept in touch and consider Lydia a dear friend. She got me involved with a local support group for breast cancer victims."

He nodded. "How many years out is she?"

"Five. She's walking this weekend." She glanced up at the rising sun. "I worry about her in this heat."

"One-hundred-degree weather isn't the time to take twenty-mile treks around Hotlanta three days in a row, that's for sure," he mused.

Natalie bit back a smile at his use of the slang nickname for her hometown. "It got up to the high eighties last year, but the weather's been so crazy this fall."

The forecast for the entire weekend was sunshine, sunshine, and more sunshine. Normally a good thing, but with the current drought, and temperatures still soaring into three figures, too easily a charity event could turn dangerous.

"Are you assigned to the main medical tent at the

campsite or rotating at the stop points?" he asked, his eyes holding a mischievous gleam she didn't quite understand.

A loud cheer went up. It seemed they were minutes away from the walk's official start.

"I'm traveling between stop points. Team B."

"Me, too." His grin widened. Clearly he'd already known the answer to his question. Not seeing him all day would have been a lot easier on her libido.

"What about you? Do you have a family member with cancer?" Now, why had she asked that? It wasn't as if it mattered if he was genetically clean. She was not going to ask him to donate sperm. She wasn't.

Nor was she going to have a quickie relationship with him.

Struggling not to appear as if her very future hung on his answer, she let her gaze meet Caleb's. A deep glimpse of sadness in his eyes made her think she'd pried where she shouldn't have. The urge to reach out and touch him, comfort him, hit her.

After a moment he shook his head.

Praise the Lord. No, not praise the Lord. Caleb's health history bore no relevance to her pregnancy plans.

He started to say more, but the emcee let out a yell and the crowd went wild.

"Look." Glad for the distraction, Natalie pointed toward the stage. "The first walkers are preparing to cross the start line."

They watched a cancer survivor lead a group of women into the crowd and through the partitioned-off walk start. Onlookers cheered, giving high-fives and applause as the ladies forged the way for the approximately four thousand walkers.

Natalie and Caleb stayed with others from the medical crew until most of the walkers were on their way. Natalie had worked with Martha and John Scarbrough each year she'd volunteered. In their late fifties, the couple had been coordinating the medical volunteers for almost a decade.

"How are you feeling this morning?" Martha asked, walking up to where they waited.

Caleb's concerned gaze cut toward Natalie.

Self-consciously she dismissed the question, and straightened the pink ball cap she wore. "Couldn't be better."

"I wasn't sure if you'd opt to do this year's walk or not," Martha continued, oblivious to Natalie's discomfort. "I was glad to see your name on John's list."

"Work's busy, but I wouldn't dream of missing out on the walk."

Martha gave her a funny look, caught site of Caleb's curious expression, then nodded. "Yeah, work. Speaking of which, how's Dot?"

Dr. Dot Watson was a gynecologist who'd volunteered with the walk the past two years and worked at the same hospital as Natalie. Although she didn't know her well, she liked the pleasant doctor. "Working too hard, but I believe she's taken some time off this weekend."

"Excellent. She deserves a break."

Caleb cleared his throat, and Natalie realized how rude she'd been. "Martha, have you met Dr. Burton? He's a physician from St. Louis who is volunteering with the walk this year."

"St Louis?" the petite woman looked thoughtful, then shrugged, brandishing a brilliant smile at Caleb. "We met briefly last night. My husband John heads the medical team. You were added on last minute, weren't you? We're sure glad to have you. John was worried we were going to be short-handed after Dr. Rose canceled. No matter how many volunteers we get, we always need at least a dozen more."

They chatted a few minutes before loading into a motif-decorated van that would later be used to pick up walkers needing assistance.

Caleb and Natalie were dropped off at the first pitstop, a mere two miles from the mall parking lot. A medical tent was marked with a red cross at the top. Another tent was supplied, with a variety of snacks and water. Currently, only the volunteers manning the tents were there.

"Some of the first walkers will arrive soon." Martha gave them a heads-up.

"Have you ever done the actual walk?" Caleb asked Natalie, watching her recheck their supplies.

"Three years ago I walked with Lydia, the patient who got me involved with breast cancer," she reminded him. "I'll introduce you if she stops by. She was in the first group who crossed the start line this morning."

"I'd like to meet her." He glanced around the pitstop. Volunteers made last-minute checks so that they were fully prepared for the onslaught of walkers. A local newsstation's camera crew awaited their arrival. A helicopter flew overhead, no doubt filming the walkers' progress. "There's a lot of media attention, isn't there?"

"Not nearly enough. This walk is all about getting attention. About making people aware that one out of eight women will have breast cancer. Those are scary statistics. Early detection is key to saving lives, yet so many women don't bother having their mammograms. Imagine how many lives would be saved if we could just convince women to take their annual screens."

Caleb leaned against the table in the medical tent and suppressed an appreciative whistle at the beautiful blonde who had instantly captured his attention yesterday evening. Natalie spoke with such passion, such conviction. Her verve had been the first thing he'd noticed.

Well, maybe not first thing.

He'd be lying if he didn't admit to being lured in by the shapely legs beneath the khaki shorts she'd worn. He'd always been a legs man. But it took more than a great pair of legs to keep his attention, and Natalie *had* more. Lots more.

He'd gravitated toward her the entire night. He'd even gone so far as to position himself where she'd had to sit next to him during the meal the medical volunteers had shared last night while discussing their role in the walk.

Natalie excited him. From the way her eyes flashed when she got on her soap box to the way desire flickered in the dark blue depths—as it had last night, when he'd wanted to pull her into his arms and do a whole lot more than he should want to do with a woman he'd just met.

Plus, the woman could hold a conversation. Last night they'd talked about everything, from the ethics of genetic cloning to baseball, and Natalie's diehard loyalty to her local team the Atlanta Braves. No matter what they'd discussed, her zest for life had shone through.

Natalie was the kind of woman who put her whole heart into everything she did.

He was the kind of man who recognized the rarity of the woman now rearranging the containers of moleskin, bandages, acetaminophen and ibuprofen tablet packets, and other items the walkers might need.

And she knew Dot.

"Which hospital do you work for?" he asked, having to be sure. Although the odds of there being another Dot, who was an Atlanta gynecologist and on vacation this weekend seemed highly unlikely.

"Atlanta General. Why?"

"You work in Labor and Delivery?" He knew she did. She'd mentioned it the night before. Something else they'd had in common.

"Yes. It's my first love. There weren't any openings in the department when I first graduated, but I transferred the moment one became available."

He bit back an ironic smile. Bingo. Natalie worked with Jamie's sister.

Prior to his wife's death, he and Dot had been close. He'd pulled away after Jamie had died. Truth was, he'd had to leave Baltimore—had to have a change of scenery. To survive he'd had to put distance between himself and reminders of his wife. A residency in Nashville had been offered, and he'd snapped it up. But Nashville hadn't ever felt like home.

Could Atlanta? It was Jamie's hometown after all.

What about Emily? Nashville might not feel like home to him, but his daughter wouldn't remember living anywhere else. Would gaining her aunt Dot and her grand-parents be worth the upheaval she would have to go through?

Although Jamie's family visited on birthdays and Christmas, it hadn't been until the past few months that he'd started taking Dot's requests to move to Atlanta seriously. He did everything he could to give Emily a good life. But by staying away from Jamie's family except for their bi-annual visits, wasn't he depriving Emily? He hadn't meant to cut his daughter off from her mother's family, but in trying to survive the pain in his heart wasn't that exactly what he'd done?

He had, and if he moved to Atlanta he could correct some of the wrongs he'd done.

"This is the quietest you've been since arriving," Natalie accused him, gently pushing him away from the table so she could straighten the bins he'd bumped.

"Just thinking."

"Dare I ask what about?" She didn't look at him, just realigned the containers. The walkers wouldn't care if the bins were perfectly aligned, but apparently she needed something to keep her busy.

"Life."

His answer stopped her, had her brows veeing together. An odd, *déjà vu*-type look came over her face.

"That wasn't what I expected you to say." She crossed her arms over her light gray tank, emblazoned with a tiny pink breast cancer emblem over her heart. "Explain."

When she'd asked him if he had family with cancer he'd meant to tell her about Jamie, about how he'd lost his wife to the disease they were volunteering for this weekend. But the words had stuck in his throat. He'd tried to shake them free, but she'd taken his action as a no and before he could correct her the walk had started.

He really should tell her now. But the truth was he didn't want to talk about Jamie. Or why he hadn't corrected Natalie's incorrect assumption that he lived in St Louis. He didn't even want to talk about Emily, although usually he would brag about his daughter's talents to anyone willing to listen.

For this weekend he'd been granted a rare opportunity to simply be a man who'd met a beautiful and exciting woman. He desperately clung to that notion.

Just this once he didn't want the looks of pity, the looks of disgust that he came as a package deal. Just because he was a widower and a father it didn't mean he wasn't still a man.

Natalie made him feel manly and glad of it.

He gave a flirty grin. "What were you expecting me to say?"

Natalie's cheeks pinkened, broadcasting her thoughts.

"That I was thinking about you?" he pressed. "About last night?"

Long into the night he'd lain awake thinking about her—had awakened thinking about her. Could think of little else. It had been a long time since a woman had excited him.

Since Jamie.

Not that he'd been celibate for the past five years, but women had been far and few between. Emily was his life, his priority, to the exclusion of pretty much all else with the exception of medicine.

"Last night?" Pink blossomed to red on Natalie's face.

He enjoyed her reaction, enjoyed the chemistry zinging between his body and hers.

Would she flush as prettily elsewhere when aroused? If he ran his fingers over her cheeks, the bow of her neck, the fullness of her breasts…? His gaze dropped to the delicate curves her tank hugged.

"I almost kissed you last night." Just like he wanted to

kiss her now. But she wouldn't welcome his affections in the broad daylight, in the middle of their workstation. Still, those rosy cheeks hinted her mind was racing with possibilities.

He, of all people, knew how short life could be, and he didn't plan to waste a precious moment of this unique situation. He was going to know this pretty blonde much better before the weekend was over.

Unable to resist, he stepped forward, touched a strand of golden hair peeking out from beneath her pink cap.

Natalie backed up, nervously wet her lips.

"I wanted to kiss you," he admitted, staring at the moist shine to her lips. "I've wanted to kiss you from the moment I saw you."

CHAPTER TWO

GENTLY cleansing a walker's foot, Natalie patted the area dry then applied a layer of moleskin to the angry heel. Eyeing her work, she wiped sweat from her brow with the back of her forearm.

The lady had bought new tennis shoes, thinking they'd help on the walk. Instead, the stiff leather had rubbed against her heel, irritating the skin. Before the day was over she'd have a nasty blister if she weren't careful. Hopefully the moleskin would protect her tender skin.

"I know it sounds gross, and may feel funny, but I'd recommend putting petroleum jelly between your toes," Natalie advised.

"Petroleum jelly?" The woman's brows rose and she paused with her thick white cotton sock half on.

"It cuts down on the skin-to-skin friction between toes, plus provides a protective layer to the skin." She gave a compassionate smile. "You're less likely to have blisters."

The woman shrugged, pulling her sock free from her foot. "At this point I'm willing to try anything."

She handed the lady a sample packet of petroleum jelly.

Another walker came to the tent, pulled off her shoes, and rubbed the back of her heel.

Natalie smiled in empathy, cleaned her hands, and moved to the newcomer. "Need some help?"

A steady stream of walkers had visited the medical tent, most in search of protective skin barriers or anti-inflammatory tablets. Fortunately the first walkers had arrived seconds after Caleb had caught her off guard by saying he wanted to kiss her, saving her from having to respond.

What would she have said? He'd admitted he'd lain in his sleeping bag thinking of her. Admitted that he wanted to kiss her.

Her few sexual experiences hadn't been bad, but, actually, she'd often wondered if she even *liked* kissing all that much.

Somehow with Caleb she suspected she would be trying to catch the breath just looking at him stole away from her.

Truth was, she'd never felt such an instantaneous attraction, and didn't know how to deal with it.

Apparently Caleb knew exactly, and he wasn't planning to play games about what he wanted.

Which turned her on all the more.

A man who knew what he wanted and wasn't afraid to go after it. A man who looked at her in a way that made her feel sexy. A man who had lain awake long into the night imagining.

What he wanted was her.

She wasn't supposed to be turned on in going on a hundred degree weather, during a volunteer stint for a great cause, only days before she'd be undergoing egg-harvesting for IVF.

She glanced his way, watching as he gently examined an elderly lady's knee.

The fact he cared about people came shining through with each and every contact he had with the walkers. He was a hit. She suspected women would be stopping by the medical tent in the hope Caleb would be there, just so they could get some of his tender, loving care. More than a few of the younger walkers had flirted with him, and she'd swear one had given him her phone number.

The unfamiliar quiver that had run through her belly had not been jealousy. It hadn't. She couldn't possibly feel jealous over a man she barely knew and certainly had no right to.

"Natalie?" he said, turning toward her and flashing that special smile he seemed to reserve for just her. "Would you mind icing down Mrs. Jones' knee?"

Ice sounded divine.

"No problem." She opened the cooler containing their icepacks and turned, surprised to find him standing behind her.

He caught her elbow, steadying her. It amazed her that the ice didn't hit an immediate rapid boil at the heat zapping through her body. His megawatt touch fried her nerve-endings.

He smiled. "Thanks."

"You're welcome," she gulped, pushing past him to put the ice pack on Mrs. Jones' knee while there was still ice to be had.

With the way her libido was burning, she should probably pour the cooler's entire contents over her head.

An hour later Martha came by with a couple of volunteers.

"That was the last of the walkers," she informed them, giving them a quick round of applause. "Y'all did a wonderful job. John's at the third pitstop. We're going to relocate you two to the lunch stop, and let you eat while the crew sets up your tent at the last stop. Y'all can help at the lunch medical tent if you finish before the van arrives to take you onward."

Along with other volunteers, Caleb and Natalie helped pack the medical supplies. The volunteers would take the truck to the next stop and set it up.

When Natalie climbed into the van, several people she'd met the previous year greeted her, asking how she was doing and making general small talk. Although she refused to look his way, she was acutely aware of Caleb sliding in next to her, sitting close despite the still empty seat in front of them.

The ladies she'd been talking to smiled, giving Caleb a more curious appraisal, but neither missed a beat in their conversation. Soon they turned to Caleb, questioning him.

Within moments Caleb had them eating out of his hands—including Martha, who'd settled into the empty seat.

Natalie didn't want to pay him any attention, but her lips twitched at Caleb's animation as he regaled tales of previous volunteering experiences. The man was a natural-born charmer.

Taking advantage of the moment, she studied him to try and figure out what it was that made her so acutely aware of him. He was gorgeous. No debating that. But she'd been around gorgeous men before and had not wanted to strip off their clothes.

Caleb's hand slipped over to hers, his thumb brushing the top of her hand in a caressing motion.

There was nothing innocent about the touch.

Sparks shot back and forth between them. Any moment she expected the ladies to peek over the back of the seat to see what had caused the fireworks display. But other than the tiny explosions going off inside her body nothing tangible was happening.

Nothing anyone could see, at any rate.

She jerked her hand away and gave a look she hoped said "back off."

He grinned, not appearing at all like he'd gotten the message. Had her body betrayed her and sent the wrong signal?

The lunch stop was eleven miles into the walk, and located at a scenic state park. Food tents and a medical tent much larger than the station they'd manned at the previous point were already in full swing. Volunteers buzzed around making sure boxes were open and that there would be plenty of food and water for the walkers. A few of the more fast-paced had already arrived, and were eating their sandwiches, fruit and cookies in the grassy shade beneath tall oak trees.

As she and Caleb went through the lunch line he held out a Red Delicious toward her. "Apple?"

Visions of sin and temptation filled her mind. Wasn't *she* supposed to be the one tempting him with forbidden fruit? Her uterus contracted, as if to remind her where her priorities lay. No, she wasn't supposed to be tempting him or being tempted. She was supposed to be focusing on her future. A dalliance with a sexy doctor was not in the plan.

She took the apple with a softly murmured thank you.

Holding her paper sack lunch, she looked for a shady

spot. Settling beneath an oak tree with sprawling roots, she opened her bag and surveyed the contents. Sandwich. Chips. Cookie. Bottled water.

Apple.

She'd no more than peeled the wrapper off the sandwich when Caleb plopped down on the grass beside her.

"Nice spot. Hope you don't mind if I join you?"

Why now? No man would take her seriously during a time when she was paying thousands to become pregnant.

Would they? Would he?

"You never answered my question."

She didn't look at him, just spread a tiny dollop of mustard over her sandwich. "Which question would that be?"

He unwrapped his sandwich and took a hearty bite. "Whether or not you thought about me last night."

She glanced toward him. Sunbeams broke through the shade of the tree and reflected off the silky sheen of his dark hair. A light breeze blew, breaking up the insufferable heat, causing his hair to sway to its tune.

"I don't recall you asking me that." Her gaze lowered to his mouth, lingered on the pink fullness, on how his lips curved upward so easily—like smiling was the most natural thing in the world for him, like he smiled a lot.

That mouth wanted to taste her.

She swallowed, almost choking on the bite of sandwich she hadn't even realized she'd bitten off.

"Not in so many words," he admitted, meeting her gaze head-on, "but I hoped you'd say I wasn't living in a fantasy for one, because I like you."

"I'm not interested." She took another bite of her

sandwich to keep from saying more. What was it about him that made her feel so good inside? So aware? So alive?

His smile faded and his expression became thoughtful. "Are you seeing someone? If I misread the chemistry between us and have made you uncomfortable, I apologize."

Tell him yes. Tell him you're involved.

"My life is complicated right now." That wasn't what she'd meant to say. Letting him think there was someone else would be so much simpler than the truth.

He looked surprisingly insulted. "I'm a grown man, not a boy. Complicated doesn't scare me."

She'd definitely noticed his manhood. No mistaking him for a boy. No, siree.

"You don't understand." Which sounded lame even to her own ears.

"Then explain. You'll find I'm a good listener."

She'd noticed that about him, too. Last night he'd listened when she'd talked, really listened, like he found her thoughts fascinating. She couldn't recall a date ever being so attentive.

Last night had not been a date.

She had to put some distance between them. Now.

"Look—" she took a steadying breath "—I'm sorry if I gave you the wrong impression, but I'm not interested in a relationship or a casual fling this weekend. Because that's all it could ever be. Nor do I have any interest in sharing the details of my life with a complete stranger." Before she could change her mind and spill the sordid story of the past year, she gathered her lunch in a quick grab, not caring that she toppled her water. She needed to catch her breath, and she couldn't do that when Caleb was anywhere near.

When she sat down far away, on the other side of the shady area from where Caleb sat, she realized she'd left her apple.

Somehow leaving the fruit behind seemed fitting.

Grateful for the shade the medical tent provided from the scorching heat, Caleb placed a plaster upon a lady's large toe and smoothed it. He knew his mind should be on what he was doing, but instead it kept wandering to where Natalie cleaned a foul-appearing blister on a walker's heel.

His stomach tightened from just watching her fingers gently glide over the lady's foot. She smiled and chatted with the walker. About what he couldn't say, as his mind was too distracted. Too mesmerized by the healing strokes of her touch.

He wanted her hands on *him*.

He wanted her.

More than he could recall wanting anyone, period.

But she'd said she wasn't interested and he had to respect that. Not that he had to like the fact she'd given him the major brush-off at lunch, but he wasn't the type of man to pursue a woman who point-blank said she wasn't interested.

At least he didn't think he was. His forehead crinkled. He honestly couldn't recall being presented with that scenario before. It had always been *him* with other priorities, *him* with the complicated life.

His life *was* complicated.

He was the single father of a five-year-old daughter. He

was in the process of deciding whether or not to relocate to Atlanta to be closer to his dead wife's family.

From the time he'd met Jamie he'd been smitten.

Then he'd lost her.

She'd only been six weeks pregnant when they'd discovered her breast cancer. He'd tried to convince her to start chemo immediately, but she'd refused. After Emily's delivery, treatment had been too little too late. The cancer had spread to her hip, her pancreas and her liver. He'd focused his energy on ensuring each of her days overflowed with love, lived to the fullest of her capabilities.

Jamie hadn't lived to see her daughter's first birthday.

"Ahem." The walker cleared her throat, bringing Caleb back to reality. What was he doing, daydreaming while treating a patient?

"Sorry." He gave the rosy-cheeked woman with snow-white hair a final check, then patted her hand. "If your feet swell any worse, grab a ride on the van and get rechecked."

"Thanks." She didn't stand, though, just looked toward Natalie. "She's lovely, isn't she?"

"Lovely?"

Could Natalie hear them? She'd made it clear as day she wasn't interested. At least verbally. But what about what her eyes said when they met his? What was so complicated in her life that she said one thing with her mouth and another with her eyes? Regardless, he didn't want to make her uncomfortable.

"Yes, she is." He didn't elaborate.

"My neighbor says she's an angel dropped straight from heaven."

Caleb blinked at the petite, grandmotherly woman

sitting at his station with renewed interest. "Your neighbor knows Natalie?"

"Oh, yes." She gave him a *duh* look. "Lydia was one of her first patients. After she was released to go home, Natalie visited her, bought groceries, even did odd jobs around her house during Lydia's chemotherapy."

Lydia. The patient Natalie had mentioned. But he still didn't know what to say. He wanted to know everything he could about the amazing woman he was volunteering with, but he'd prefer Natalie to tell him. Somehow he'd have to convince her that he could deal with complicated.

"It was a shame about what happened to her last fall," the woman mused.

What had happened to Natalie last fall?

Caleb winced. He had no right to ask. He wouldn't pry.

"What with that drunk driver hitting her and all. She was pretty banged around." The woman shook her head in remembered disgust, giving Caleb a moment to digest her words.

Natalie had been hit by a drunk driver.

His gaze traced over her where she was now finished with her patient. There were no telltale scars visible, although her shorts and T-shirt could be hiding a multitude of sins. The thought that someone's carelessness had hurt her, caused her pain of any kind or measure, angered him, made him want to lash out at the reckless fool. Thank God she seemed okay.

Was the car wreck her life complication?

"Lydia and I made cookies for her every week while she was recovering," the woman continued, seemingly oblivious to Caleb's reaction. "That girl loves oatmeal chocolate chip cookies like you wouldn't believe."

"Really?"

"I swear she'd sell her soul for my secret recipe." She beamed proudly.

Having caught on to the fact she was the topic of conversation, Natalie joined them. She hugged the woman's neck. "Mary Baker, are you telling my secrets? You know word is not to get out about my obsession for your cookies."

The woman chuckled, pleased with Natalie's praise. "What woman doesn't love a warm, melt-in-your-mouth chocolate chip cookie baked to absolute perfection?"

"True." Natalie gently squeezed a wrinkled hand. "How are you holding up? I was surprised when Lydia said you were going to walk this year."

"Figured I wasn't getting any younger, and if she could do it so could I." The woman's shoulders straightened.

"Lydia walks every day. She prepares herself for this event year-round." Natalie's eyes grew concerned when her gaze landed on the woman's swollen ankles. "Are you sure you're up to this? What did your doctor say? This can't be good for your bunions."

"My doctor signed the release form." The woman looked offended. "If I have problems, this handsome young doctor will fix me right up." Mrs. Baker patted Caleb's knee.

"Besides," his patient continued, "I've trained, too. I've been walking with Lydia and Barney every morning."

Natalie's lips compressed into a worried smile, then she gave a resigned nod. "How *is* Barney? Still as ornery as ever?"

"Of course. The devil runs circles around me. He should be the one doing this walk, but he couldn't be bothered.

Says he'll surprise Lydia and me with goodies at the finish line."

Natalie laughed. "I'm surprised Lydia didn't sign him up, too."

"Said she didn't want an old fogey slowing things down."

Not paying any heed to Caleb's presence, they chatted until another patient came to the tent. "You two keep talking. I'll take care of—" he checked the newcomer's name badge, which swung around her neck "—Gladys."

The pretty, fortyish woman gave him a grateful smile. "I think I've pulled something in the back of my leg. Every time I take a step, sharp pain shoots up my back."

"Your back?"

She nodded, grimacing as she lowered herself into a folding chair. "A lightning-sharp pain that burns. It literally takes my breath away."

"You didn't fall or anything?"

Gladys shook her head. "I've just been walking. Although I did step off a curb wrong at one point, and jarred my back a bit."

"Sorry to ask you to do this, but I need you to stand up again so I can check your back."

Slowly, and with her hand low in the center of her back, the woman stood. "Agh," she moaned, using her free hand to push herself up.

"Sorry, but I need access to the spine to fully check you."

Wincing, she nodded in understanding. "No problem— just so long as you figure out what's going on."

Caleb examined the lady's spine, then checked her hip and thigh. When he ran his palm over her hamstring, she cried out.

"I take it that's where you hurt the most?" he said, as he continued to examine her leg, concerned that she also hurt in her low back.

"Yes, it's sharp—almost spasmodic."

"The hamstring muscle is pulled tight as a bow. I think you've strained your muscle."

"Can you give me a pill to fix it so I can finish the walk?" The woman looked hopeful, massaging her low back with her fingertips.

"There's not a quick fix. You won't be able to finish the walk." He patted the woman's hand. "I'm sorry."

Her eyes teary, the woman nodded.

"I'll arrange for one of the vans to carry you to the campsite whenever you want. There's an orthopedic doctor volunteering at the main medical tent. Let him have a look at your back and leg after you arrive. Is your transportation there?"

The woman shook her head. "I live in Madison and drove into town this morning. My car's at the shopping center. I really wanted to do this weekend." She inhaled deeply. "I feel like such a failure."

Caleb looked thoughtful. "If the orthopedic doctor agrees that it's okay, I'm sure there's somewhere you can volunteer at the campsite, if you'd like to continue with this weekend. Somewhere you can sit, and stretch when you need to."

The woman's face brightened. "Oh, that would be wonderful. I really didn't want to go home a failure."

"Injuring yourself during a walk of this distance isn't a sign of failure. That you participated at all is a sign of your success," he praised her, before using his walkie-talkie to see what could be arranged for Gladys.

* * *

Natalie tried to ignore what Caleb was doing, what he was saying. Unfortunately she couldn't. His compassion with his current patient touched her. His insight that Gladys didn't want to go home told her he looked beyond the obvious and really cared about the people he took care of.

She didn't want to like him so much. She didn't. Just looking at him was temptation enough. The fact he had heart made him all the more appealing.

Like he needed more appeal.

She had to stay away. Far, far away. Tomorrow she'd make sure to get a different assignment. There was no avoiding Caleb at night in the medical tent, but if she didn't have to see him all day—see what a great doctor he was, what a great person he was—well, that would make sticking to her plans a lot easier.

Lord knew she needed all the help she could get, because immaculate conception was looking less and less appealing.

CHAPTER THREE

IF NATALIE hadn't been so starved she'd have gone any-where other than the food tent. Of course if she'd headed in a different direction people would have wondered.

She wasn't surprised when Caleb slid into the folding chair next to hers at an otherwise empty table.

"Hungry?" he asked, grinning at her heaped plate of spaghetti, garlic toast and salad.

"Aren't you?" she challenged, with a pointed glance at his own full plate.

"Starved," he agreed, forking a bite of salad. "I feel like I haven't eaten in years."

"Imagine how the walkers feel."

"Twenty miles in this blazing heat?" He shook his head. "I hope they all remember to come straight to the food tent rather than head to the showers."

"It's so tempting to want to wash off first," Natalie agreed, "but hydrating and eating are more important."

He nodded, met her gaze. "Earlier today you overheard Mrs. Baker and I talking…"

Was he asking her a question?

"She mentioned you'd been involved in a motor vehicle accident last year. What happened?"

Natalie grimaced. She'd wondered what he and Mary had been talking about. "It's really not that big of a deal."

"She said you were hit by a drunk driver."

"Yes." She gave a bright smile. "But, as you can see, I'm fine, and I'd rather not talk about the past."

He stared at her thoughtfully, then asked, "What *would* you like to talk about, Natalie?"

She said the first thing that popped into her head. "Tell me about St. Louis. Have you been up in the arch?"

Natalie ate, fought her attraction for Caleb, and made small talk with him and the walkers who quickly joined their table. Two were sisters from Chattanooga, named Ivy and Gail, and the other a young girl named Beth.

"Are you feeling okay?"

Even before Caleb said anything to the woman who appeared to be in her late fifties or early sixties, Natalie noticed Ivy placing her hand over her chest every so often. She'd planned to discreetly ask the woman about her symptoms and suggest she stop by the medical tent for evaluation.

"Just a bit of heartburn." The woman cleared her throat. "I forgot to bring my antacid with me, and I imagine I'll be paying for it all weekend." Her gaze touched on her half-eaten spaghetti. "Especially if I keep eating like this."

"You should stop by the medical tent." Caleb's suggestion echoed Natalie's thoughts. "We have samples of antacids available." His eyes assessed her more closely.

He was worried about Ivy, concerned her pain might be more than just indigestion. Yet, despite Natalie being able to read him, she knew the other ladies at the table couldn't. They saw a handsome doctor showing concern, and at any moment she expected the *ahhhs* to break out. Caleb probably got that reaction a lot.

"Natalie and I are headed that way when we're finished here. You're welcome to tag along with us." He gave one of his killer grins. "We'll be glad to check you over and get some of those samples. That way you can bypass the usual lines and be checked more quickly." He winked conspiratorially, and the first *ah* sounded from Gail's parted lips.

"Perks of sitting at the right table," he added.

Beth practically sighed her *ah*. Natalie expected the girl to bat cow-eyes in adoration any second.

Completely melted by Caleb's charm, Gail nudged her sister. "You should go, Ivy. You've been complaining all evening about your chest bothering you."

All evening?

"Do you often have chest pain with your heartburn?" she asked, hoping Ivy's pain wasn't cardiac in nature.

"Not usually. But I forgot my medicine this morning. If I take my medicine—" she said the brand-name "—I don't have any problems with my stomach."

"Do you get short of breath when it flares?" Caleb asked, in between bites of spaghetti.

"Not usually. But I am today. I figure that's from the walking."

Caleb set his fork down on his plate. "Did you manage the full twenty miles?"

The sisters exchanged glances.

"No," Ivy admitted reluctantly. "I had to flag down a van at a couple of different points throughout the day. I probably only got in half the miles."

She sounded so despondent over not making the full

walk Natalie's heart squeezed in empathy. "Even so, ten miles isn't anything to scoff at."

"S'pose not," she agreed, toying with her spaghetti. "If I even made it that far. I probably didn't."

Losing her appetite to her concern over the woman sitting across from her, Natalie gathered her half-full disposable plate and utensils. "I'm heading to the medical tent to see if they're ready for extra help. Ivy, would you like to go with me?"

Caleb's hand covered her wrist. "Wait. I'll go with you. Ivy, too."

Natalie's gaze dropped to Caleb's empty plate. Had he been waiting on her to finish? Although he didn't let go of her wrist, he gave Ivy a compelling look.

The woman nodded and pushed away her barely touched plate, her hand immediately returning to press against her chest. "That'll be fine. I'm finished."

Ivy's sister followed behind them as well, concern etched on her face.

When they got to the medical tent, the lines were in full force. Several volunteers with various medical backgrounds triaged the patients as quickly as they could.

"Oh, I feel guilty coming on back when all these ladies have been waiting."

"As I said, the perks of picking the right table to join," Caleb teased, keeping the mood light, although Natalie could tell he was worried.

"Are we ever glad to see you two?" one of the volunteers called out. "It's a mad house in here."

"Where do you need us?" Natalie asked.

"There's an empty station over in the back if you and Caleb want to get started. We'll triage patients your way."

528   THE NURSE'S BABY MIRACLE

"First we're going to check Ivy." He gave the woman a reassuring smile. "Here." He handed Gail a clipboard with a standard contact and medical information form. "We'll let your sister fill out this paper while I examine you. Any allergies?"

Caleb washed his hands while quizzing Ivy on her medical history. He picked up a stethoscope and cleaned the diaphragm and ear tips with alcohol. Natalie did the same, then got a 325mg aspirin from the limited supply of medication kept onsite at the medical tent. After Ivy had swallowed the tablet, Natalie picked up a blood pressure cuff to check her vitals.

"Ivy, do you have any personal or family history of heart disease?"

"Who doesn't?" The woman shrugged at Caleb, then returned her attention to where Natalie had wrapped the cuff around her left arm and secured the Velcro fastener. "My cholesterol runs around two-hundred-and-fifty. Although it may be down since my doctor started some medicine at my last check-up, and I've been walking each morning to train for this weekend."

"Your blood pressure and sugar run normal?" Caleb asked, placing the stethoscope against Ivy's chest and listening to her heart and lung sounds.

"Oh, yes." The woman took deep, exaggerated breaths for Caleb's benefit, grimacing as she did so. "I haven't had problems with my blood pressure or sugar in years."

"Years? Meaning you used to have a problem with them?"

"Yes, but I started taking some pills, and I've been normal since."

Caleb and Natalie exchanged a look. Too many patients

believed that, once it was controlled, they no longer had the actual disease. Natalie hoped the readings would be as favorable as the woman claimed.

Tightening the valve, she pumped up the cuff and slowly released the air. Immediately she heard a beat, meaning the systolic pressure was higher than expected. She'd pumped it up to a hundred and eighty. Completely releasing the valve, she took the cuff off the woman.

"I'll try again in just a minute," she assured her. "When Caleb's finished listening to your chest."

The woman nodded, as if she'd been through the scenario before. Natalie suspected she had. Probably several times.

Waiting while Caleb listened, Natalie placed her fingertip against Ivy's wrist. Radial pulse: one-hundred-and-twenty beats per minute. Leaving her finger against Ivy's wrist, so the woman wouldn't become conscious of her breathing, thus changing it, Natalie counted each inhalation. Respirations: twenty-two breaths per minute.

Caleb finished listening to Ivy's heart and indicated for Natalie to retry the blood pressure. She pumped the cuff to over two-hundred this time, and first heard the systolic beat at two-twenty. The diastolic beat faded out at one hundred and fifteen. Natalie winced.

Rapid breathing, rapid pulse, high blood pressure and chest pain. She suspected more was going on with Ivy than just forgetting to take a heartburn pill.

"Did you remember your other meds this morning?" she asked, handing Caleb the paper she'd jotted the numbers on.

Ivy shook her head in derision. "No, I left all my medicines at home. I feel like such an idiot. I'd set them out so

I wouldn't forget, but I forgot. I figured one weekend wouldn't hurt anything."

Diabetes, blood pressure, stomach—and who only knew what other health problems Ivy was being treated for? One weekend could hurt lots.

"Do you have a list of the medicines you take?"

"Not on me, but I can tell you the names." Ivy began rattling off the names of medicines, helped by her sister's interjections when she forgot one.

"That sounds like everything," she said, after naming nine medicines. *Nine.* No wonder the woman hadn't felt well after forgetting them.

Natalie went to a supply station and grabbed a glucometer, an alcohol swab and a lancet.

"You read my mind," Caleb praised her from where he squatted, checking Ivy's pedal pulses. They'd both been doing that throughout the day, second-guessing each other's next move.

"Two hundred and eighty."

"That's not too bad," Ivy said, making Natalie question just how "controlled" Ivy's sugar normally was.

Caleb's eyes darkened. His thoughts were likely the same. "It's much higher than it should be. Around a hundred is normal. I'm going to call for an ambulance to take you to the hospital."

"An ambulance? Over my sugar?" Ivy's face pinched. "My sugar's been higher than that in the past. I didn't have to have an ambulance then. I really think you're overreacting."

"Perhaps," Caleb conceded. "But you need medical care that we aren't able to give you here. Tests and medicines to get your sugar and blood pressure under control."

He turned to Natalie. "Let's get an EKG. While you're doing that, I'm going to get a nitro, if we have any available. If not the aspirin will have to do." Caleb turned to Ivy's sister. "Can you come with me, in case the ER has any questions when I call?"

With one last worried look at Ivy, the woman followed Caleb away from the screened-off area of the tent.

Natalie spotted the portable EKG machine and quickly began hooking the leads to Ivy.

"This won't hurt a bit," she assured her. She draped a white cotton towel over Ivy's breasts to give her some sense of privacy. It was the best she could manage with their limited supplies, and her lack of knowledge of where she might find a gown. "Have you ever had an EKG before?"

"Once. Several years ago." The woman's eyes had turned pleading, and she placed her hand on Natalie's. "Am I dying? Is that why Dr. Burton is sending me to the ER? Did he hear something when he listened to my chest?"

"Of course you're not dying." If Ivy panicked her symptoms would worsen, could become fatal. Natalie would do everything within her power to reassure her, keep her calm. "I'm not sure what Dr. Burton heard, but your blood pressure and sugar are up. You're also having chest pain. He wants you to get the best care possible and he isn't going to take any chances. You need to be in the hospital where they can monitor your symptoms, make sure everything's truly okay."

She hit the button on the EKG machine and watched the strip print. Right Bundle Branch blockage. Elongated ST segment. Inverted T-wave. Not good.

Her own heart kicked up a flutter, racing in her chest.

She was glad Caleb had called for an ambulance. She needed him back here with the nitroglycerin. *Stat.*

Ivy was having a myocardial infarction.

On cue, Caleb rounded the screen. Among other items, he carried a clear disposable cup with a tiny white pill at the bottom.

He dropped all the items except the cup onto the medical tray stand.

"Place this under your tongue." He handed the plastic cup to Ivy, who frantically attempted to cover her bare chest with her arms and the cotton covering.

Caleb set the other supplies—a vial of regular insulin and an insulin syringe—down on the tray stand. Natalie handed him the EKG strip.

He frowned, but quickly masked his reaction before Ivy spotted it. Raising her anxiety would only make things worse.

"The ambulance is on its way," he said with calm assurance, taking Ivy's hands and giving them a quick squeeze. "Your sister is getting your bags from the transport truck. We've arranged a ride to the mall, so she can pick up your vehicle and meet you at the hospital."

"I really don't think all this is necessary. Give me an antacid and I'll be fine." But even as she said the words she winced and pressed her hand against her sternum.

Natalie gave Caleb a questioning look. He nodded, reaching for the insulin. He drew up ten units. In a matter of seconds he explained to Ivy what he was doing, and why, and injected her with the medicine that would bring her blood sugar down.

"Ivy," Natalie said in what she hoped was a reassuring voice, "I'm going to start an IV line for you."

Pale, Ivy widened her eyes. "An IV? Whatever for?"

Detaching the EKG lead attachments, Natalie rearranged the towel to keep Ivy's chest from being exposed. She turned to gather the supplies she'd need to get the IV started, but Caleb had left and was already coming back with the items in hand. Even coworkers she'd worked with for years weren't so in tune with her thoughts or her next move. She studied his calmness, the confidence he exuded, and how Ivy's expression brightened just at his nearness. She didn't blame Ivy one bit.

"How's your pain, Ivy?" he asked, bending next to her and looking at her veins, rubbing his finger over the one on the back of her hand. The vein plumped from the attention. Natalie expected him to step back and let her insert the catheter, but instead he prepped the area and slid the needle into the vein with expertise. Within seconds he had a Hep-lock in place.

"Nice work," she praised when he'd finished.

He turned, grinned. "Did you expect otherwise?"

She was saved from answering by a siren's wail in the distance.

"Sounds like your ride is almost here." Caleb patted Ivy's IV-free hand.

"I'm so embarrassed. Even if I needed a trip to the hospital Gail could have taken me once we got our car. I hate to be such a bother."

"No bother," Caleb and Natalie assured her in the same breath.

Speaking in harmony with him only brought home to Natalie the uneasy connection she'd felt all day. How could she possibly feel like she'd known him for so long when they'd just met?

Quickly, they gave a report to the paramedic and helped get Ivy loaded onto the stretcher and into the ambulance. Within minutes she was on her way to the closest hospital.

A crowd of onlookers had gathered to see what the commotion was all about, and it took a few minutes for everyone to go back about their business.

"Do you think she'll be okay?" Natalie asked as the siren faded into the distance. "I wish we'd dragged her to the medical tent the moment she mentioned she was having chest pain."

Caleb took a deep breath. "Things are always clearer in hindsight, but we got her to seek care when she'd obviously had no intention to do so up to that point. We quickly figured out what was going on and took appropriate action to get her to a hospital where a cardiologist can take over."

When he put it like that… "Still, every minute counts, and we both knew something wasn't right at dinner."

"Quit beating yourself up. She's going to be fine."

"Hopefully."

"She will." He placed his arm at her waist and guided her back toward the tent. "We'll call and check on her later. In the meantime, there are a lot of blistered feet, sore muscles and aching joints waiting for us."

"Oh, boy." She smiled in spite of herself. "I can't wait."

"Me, either." He grinned. "Don't you just love our jobs?"

She did, of course. She could tell he did, too.

"Do you normally work emergency medicine?"

He shook his head, flashed her a conspiratorial grin, then winked. "Gynecology. But I did a stint in a rural hospital's emergency room and treated a little bit of everything there."

He was a gynecologist?

For the next four hours they worked side by side, seeing patient after patient for various ailments. Mostly blistered feet, sore muscles and aching joints, but with a few other issues thrown in to keep things interesting.

At past eleven, when the last patient had been seen, Caleb dropped into the folding chair at their station. "That was really the last one?"

Natalie nodded, thinking he looked tired. She probably did, too. It had been a long day. A long evening. Tomorrow would be just as long. She still hadn't made it to the showers.

Eighteen-wheel semi-trucks had been set up, which contained portable showers. Each truck housed sixteen showers. Tiny stalls that were separated by thin sheets of metal that provided minimal privacy. But at the moment she'd settle for whatever she could get, just to wash off the day's grime.

"You headed to the shower trucks?" Caleb read her mind yet again.

"Yes. I need to shower before getting some sleep."

He nodded. "You and me both."

Together they headed into the large open sleeping area, where the numerous medical volunteers had stashed their sleeping gear and duffle bags. They all slept in one big open area that was partitioned off from the rest of the tent by thick canvas flaps.

Natalie was too tired to argue when Caleb fell into step next to her, his towel, toiletries and clean clothes in hand.

"It's late and it's dark," he informed her unnecessarily. "I'll walk you over."

"I have a flashlight." She held it up to prove her point.

THE NURSE'S BABY MIRACLE

She hadn't clicked it on, as the moonlight and the light spilling from the main tents provided enough for her to see she was going in the right direction.

"Still, you shouldn't be out by yourself this late at night."

Natalie stopped, gave him an odd look. "I'm not afraid of the dark."

"No, but you need to remember to use good sense. Going out this late at night by yourself isn't smart."

"We're in the middle of a campsite with four thousand women and a few hundred men, if that. You act like we're in the middle of a crime-ravaged city."

"Just humor me."

She wanted to roll her eyes. She felt completely safe inside the camp, and there were security volunteers who patrolled the grounds just in case. But it had been so long since someone had been concerned about her safety—not since her mother—that instead of arguing she resumed a brisk pace toward the showers. He stayed beside her but didn't attempt conversation again, just stayed with her until she was at the shower trucks. Apparently reassured that there were still others at the sink stations set up in front of the showers, he then headed toward the much smaller men's area, several hundred yards away.

Despite the tiny cubicle and the poor water pressure, Natalie felt amazingly refreshed after her quick shower. She'd rushed through shampooing her hair, conditioning and rinsing it, and then had run a razor over her legs and underarms.

Toweling dry, she dressed in a baggy T-shirt and comfy black stretch pants. She combed her hair, gathered her things, and headed outdoors to the sink station to brush her teeth, apply moisturizer, and head back to the medical tent. Hopefully she'd finish before Caleb came back.

Before he came back? Wasn't she assuming a lot? That he'd come back? Crazy when she'd never expected much from the men in her life in the past. Nor had she gotten much.

Caleb was *not* a man in her life.

Not in that sense.

But it didn't surprise her in the slightest to see a freshly showered Caleb sitting on one of the benches scattered around the grassy area in front of the shower trucks, his towel draped around his neck. Although the lighting was dim at best, she knew his eyes were trained on her. He watched her carefully make her way down the metal steps. If she slipped he'd be there in a flash to attempt to rescue her.

That knowledge did funny things to her insides.

The wall she kept trying to erect between them crumbled to an irreparable heap.

Ignoring the curious looks the two other women at the sink station kept giving him, Caleb watched Natalie brush her teeth, floss, and smooth cream over her face.

She was stalling, purposely dragging out each action.

Life was complicated. Her words haunted him.

When he looked at her, life didn't feel complicated.

They were attracted to each other, but she was afraid to acknowledge that attraction, seemed determined to shove it aside. He should respect that and do the same. But it had been so damn long since he'd felt…anything. He couldn't ignore the sparks even if he wanted to.

Natalie's fingertips brushed over the delicate skin at the corners of her eyes, over her forehead, around her mouth.

He imagined his fingers doing the same, his lips kissing each and every spot. He imagined much more.

By the time she turned to him, and slowly walked to where he waited, he was thankful for the dim light.

"You should have gone back to the tent," she scolded softly, but her eyes said she was glad he'd stayed.

His stomach somersaulted into his chest.

"You knew I wouldn't," he said, gathering his grooming kit and bag of dirty clothes. "That I'd wait for you."

She nodded, accepting his answer, and turned toward the direction of the medical tents. When they were away from the showers, away from everyone, they could be the only two people in the world.

He shifted his belongings to one hand and grabbed her wrist with the other. "Talk to me, Natalie."

She trembled beneath his touch. "What do you want me to say?"

"That you want me to kiss you."

She glanced around them in the darkness. "Here? Right now?"

"Yes."

"Someone could come along any minute." She hesitated, which gave him hope, but she shook her head. "Besides, I told you I'm not interested in a fling this weekend."

"Neither am I." It was what he'd thought he wanted when he'd made that foolish decision not to tell her about his family, but, after only knowing her for a little more than a day, he now wanted much more than a casual weekend.

"Whatever it is you're wanting from me," she corrected, "I'm not interested."

"Not interested? Or not willing to admit you're attracted to me?"

She shrugged, and he got a whiff of her shampoo. Fresh, fruity, mingled with Natalie's unique scent, which he found more seductive than the most exclusive perfume.

"Why are you doing this, Caleb?" Her voice quavered. "There are dozens of women who'd be more than happy to have your attention this weekend. Probably hundreds."

She sounded so distressed and in misery that he lifted her wrist to his mouth and kissed the tender pulse beating there. "I've never met anyone like you, and I can't get you out of my head."

"That's ridiculous. I'm just plain, ordinary me."

"There's nothing plain or ordinary about you," he whispered against her wrist, before gently lapping his tongue over the pulse.

"I don't do this," she warned him, but he felt her sway toward him. "I don't meet men and let them kiss me."

"You sound as if you think I do this all the time."

"Don't you?"

He nuzzled her wrist one last time, a slow caress, then let go of her arm to cup her chin. "No."

"But…" Her mouth was only centimeters from his.

"I'm not a playboy, Natalie. I'm attracted to you, and would like to spend the weekend getting to know you."

"And after the weekend is over?"

"Like any other new couple, we take it day by day and see what happens."

"Couple?"

"I'm not saying I want any more than to spend time with you here, but I'd like the opportunity to find out how we feel about each other on Sunday night. To find out if we want to see each other beyond this weekend." He skimmed his thumb over delicate skin. "Give us that chance."

She hesitated, and he could almost hear the wheels turning in her sharp mind.

"I told you my life is complicated. I wasn't kidding."

"And I told you I can handle complicated." He dropped his toiletry gear onto the ground and cupped her face with both hands. "My life's complicated, too. We've been given an opportunity to get to know each other away from life's everyday complications. For this weekend we're in our own little world."

"Along with four thousand others," she mumbled under her breath—probably in an effort to distract him, or to lighten what he was saying. He wouldn't stand for it. Not when his every gut instinct told him not to let her go.

"Look around, Natalie. It's just you and me beneath the moon and stars. No one can see us."

"What is it you *want* from me?" she cried in a hoarse whisper.

"To kiss you."

She took so long in responding that if he hadn't been able to feel the tension beneath his palms he might have thought she'd fallen asleep on her feet. He could feel the stress emanating from her tiny frame.

"Then be done with it." Her face crinkled in a grimace as she waited for his kiss.

Caleb peered into her upturned face. Moonlight gave her flawless skin an ethereal glow. She looked fragile, like the wrong move could shatter her into a thousand pieces. Her eyes were closed, her lips slightly parted, her breathing ragged, as if she were afraid to drag in her next breath. As much as he wanted to claim her lips, he suppressed the urge and gave a low laugh.

"Is my kiss *that* unpleasant a thought?"

Her eyes sprang open, glinting in the moonlight. "You've changed your mind?"

A mixture of relief, hurt, and something more poured out with her words. Her knees buckled. Her hands went to his shoulders, her fingers digging into his flesh for support.

"No, I want to kiss you more than I want to draw my next breath, but I need to be sure you want me to kiss you—because it sounded like you were just trying to get rid of me."

"Shut up and kiss me, Caleb."

His body strumming with anticipation, he grinned. Gazes locked, he closed the small gap between him and the soft fullness of her mouth.

Oh, hell, but she tasted as sweet as he'd imagined.

One kiss was never going to be enough.

CHAPTER FOUR

SUNDAY morning came quicker than Natalie would have preferred. Actually, the weekend had passed in a dazed blur. A happy dazed blur thanks to Caleb.

She glanced across the medical tent at his profile as he talked with a walker. While they'd had a brief lull, she'd gone to grab a couple of bottled waters.

It was early, barely ten, but the majority of the walkers had headed out not long after the sun came up, and had already passed through the first checkpoint. Only a few stragglers remained. Soon they'd be packing up and moving onward. Probably to the lunch site.

When he caught sight of her standing on the outskirts of the sideless medical tent they used at the smaller stations, Caleb flashed the smile he reserved just for her. "Hey, you."

"Hey, yourself." Tossing him one of the bottles, she smiled at the walker, a brunette in her late thirties. Her T-shirt had an iron-on photo of a woman who bore a striking resemblance to her. Beneath were dates, probably signifying birth and death, and a handwritten message: "Don't let breast cancer claim another mother."

Natalie's smile faded at thoughts of *her* mother. At how much she missed the woman who'd raised her alone. But her mother wouldn't want her to be melancholy on such a glorious day. Natalie tucked her sadness back into its special place in her heart and let the joy of the weekend fill her.

Although she and Caleb had worked hard this weekend, pulling sixteen-hour days on Friday *and* yesterday, she'd had to remind herself not to be giddy on several occasions.

Giddy. Her. Ridiculous. But once she'd decided to give in to what Caleb made her feel, if only for the weekend, she'd been able to enjoy what was happening between them.

They'd not done more than kiss—wouldn't do more than kiss. Because they'd say goodbye this evening, at the end of the celebration, and she'd proceed with her IVF. Caleb lived in St Louis. It wasn't as if she'd ever see him again. But his kisses were magical, warm, delicious, laced with heaven and hell. He was one delectable man.

Last night they'd walked to a picnic table and sat talking into the wee hours. When they'd kissed she'd wanted much more—had wanted him to push her back on the cold concrete and ravage her.

She swallowed, refocusing her attention on the walker Caleb was examining. No, he wasn't examining the lady. He was checking out Natalie.

Getting caught, he winked at her, then at his patient. "Sorry, my girlfriend distracts me from time to time."

His *girlfriend?*

If he hadn't already charmed the walker, his comment now hooked her. She eyed him warmly. "How sweet. How long have you two been together?"

Natalie started to deny the girlfriend comment, but before she could speak a single contradictory word Caleb was making assurances he had no right to make.

"Not nearly as long as we're going to be," he claimed.

She wasn't his girlfriend. Beyond what had been said between them on Friday night, on their walk back from the showers, they hadn't attempted to define their relationship. She *wasn't* his girlfriend.

One didn't qualify as a girlfriend when a relationship was fated to only last three days.

Natalie gave a weak smile, set her water bottle down, and was thankful when another walker ambled into the station.

"Mary!" she exclaimed in recognition of the rosy-cheeked woman who looked ready to drop. She crossed the divide and laced her arm beneath the older woman's to help guide her in. "What hurts?"

"Everything," the woman groaned miserably. "I had to flag down a van to bring me here. I couldn't take another step my feet hurt so badly."

Natalie's gaze dropped to her friend's ankles, which bulged over her socks. Her skin was stretched tight from the amount of swelling, and it was difficult to tell if the moisture was from sweat or from weeping edema.

She assisted the sweet lady into a folding chair and bent to pull off her tennis shoes and socks.

"Honey, if you take those off there ain't no way we're going to get them back on," Mary warned her. "I barely stuffed my feet into them this morning, and they've doubled in size since then."

"If your swelling was that bad, why did you walk?" Natalie asked, although she knew the answer. Mary didn't want Lydia thinking she couldn't keep up.

"You know I didn't walk but a mile in total yesterday, right?"

The night before she and Caleb had dined with Lydia, Mary, and a group of ladies, many of them breast cancer survivors. Lydia had been very taken with Caleb. With his gorgeous looks and natural charm what female wouldn't be?

"That doesn't mean you had to go out and try again today. Actually, it means you should have stayed behind at the campsite and kept your feet propped up so the swelling would go down." Natalie got a cloth and began washing Mary's feet and ankles so she could assess the swelling more accurately. "You could have ridden the bus over to the last stopping point and gotten out to cross the finish line with the other walkers. No one would have thought less of you for doing so."

She gave a grunt. "*I* would have. I ain't no quitter. Lydia would never let me live it down if she found out I didn't walk today."

"Lydia adores you and would never want you to put yourself in harm's way." Natalie gestured to her ankles. "She'll have a fit when she finds out what you've done to yourself."

"Guess she better not find out, then," Mary said, so matter-of-factly that Natalie paused to frown up at her serious expression.

Natalie gave another pointed look at the ankles that were double their normal size. "Somehow I don't think you're going to be able to hide these."

Mary waved her hand nonchalantly. "Oh, pudding cakes. They'll be down long before Lydia crosses that finish line this evening."

Natalie wasn't so sure about that. Even apart from Mary's ankles, her fingers appeared pudgy around the too-tight single golden band she wore on the third finger of her left hand.

"What do we have here?" Caleb asked, immediately catching sight of Mary's ankles and whistling. "I'd ask what the problem is, but..."

He stooped and ran his palm over her ankles. "Three-plus pitting edema. Mrs. Baker, have you been short of breath or coughing?"

"I got winded while I was walking," she admitted reluctantly. "Guess I should have trained more with Lydia."

"Or not." Caleb pulled a stethoscope from around his neck and listened to her heart and lungs. When finished, he crossed his ankles and stared thoughtfully at the woman sitting in the chair. "Have you ever been diagnosed with congestive heart failure?"

Mary nodded. "Several years ago. But I don't normally have problems. Just have to avoid salt and the like."

"But you normally take diuretics, and my guess is that you've been skipping those the past few mornings."

Mary eyed him as if he were crazy. "They don't have enough port-a-potties between here and the finish line for me to take that pill during this walk."

Natalie was impressed at how Caleb had honed right in to the root of the problem. Quicker than she had, she admitted, although she should have thought of it. She wondered how many other women were skipping their meds due to unwanted side effects such as increased urination? Didn't they realize how dangerous that was?

Caleb's dark brow lifted. "So instead of taking bathroom breaks you're taking emergency stops at the medical tent?"

"This isn't an emergency. Just a fashion no-no." Mary made light of her condition.

"I'm going to diurese you and send you home."

"Oh, no, you're not." Mary wagged her finger at him. "I'm going to cross that finish line if you have to carry me piggyback."

Caleb's gaze narrowed. "This is nothing to make light of, you know. You could have drowned in your own body fluids because you didn't take your medicine. I should have realized on Friday when you stopped by the tent. I want you to promise you'll never do this again."

Mary snorted. "No worries there. This is my one and only shot at this particular walk. Next year I'm just going to sponsor Lydia and bake cookies to feed her along the way."

Caleb nodded, then turned to Natalie. "Will you see if you can rustle up some furosemide? I'd prefer IV or IM, but I'm guessing we'll have to settle for a tablet."

Natalie guessed they would, too, as the majority of IVs they'd given had been to rehydrate rather than pull off fluid.

"Once we get you infused and we're happy with your status, we're going to put you on the bus."

Mary looked ready to protest.

"There's a toilet on board, and the driver will take you to the finish line. What you do once there is your business," Caleb said, although he didn't look pleased. "My recommendation is for you to keep your feet propped up until your husband picks you and Lydia up this afternoon, Mrs. Baker. They're playing *Pirates of the Caribbean* on board the bus. Enjoy."

Natalie couldn't hear Mary's response, just the gruff

sound of her talking with Caleb. She found some diuretic tablets and brought them to where Caleb still talked with Mary.

"What dosage would you like me to give?"

"Let's give forty now, reassess, and give another forty if needed." His gaze dropped to the tight ankles and he shook his head. "We'll likely need it."

In the busy lunch line, Natalie picked up an apple, turned to Caleb and flashed an innocent smile. "Apple?"

His eyes danced. "Please."

"Such manners." She handed him the fruit and started to grab one of her own, but his hand stayed her.

"We'll share."

Share? "That sounds interesting."

His grin took on a lethal appeal. "It will be."

If Natalie didn't know better she'd swear she giggled. But she knew better. She hadn't giggled since before her mother had died and left her all alone in the world.

Even before her mother's death Natalie had craved a family of her own, but the utter aloneness that had hit her had increased that longing tenfold. Still, she'd been content to wait to meet a man who loved her, and who she loved in return. She'd thought she had plenty of time.

She'd been wrong.

When she'd learned of the ticking time bomb of her fertility, she'd weighed her options and come up with the perfect plan. Artificial insemination. Which had failed. Twice.

Please let the IVF be more successful.

"Hey, where'd my smile go?" Caleb asked, joining her beneath a giant oak in the park where they lunched.

Natalie shook off her thoughts. "Just a moment of reality creeping in. Sorry."

Caleb placed his palm over hers and gave a reassuring squeeze. "No reality is allowed this weekend, remember?"

She stared at their hands, wondering how his touch could make her feel better and so bothered at the same time.

"I remember." She slid her hand out from under his and unwrapped her sandwich. She took a bite and considered how strange life was. Why meet Caleb now? At a point in time when she'd opted to take a different path?

They ate in silence for a few minutes, then she pointed at the apple. "Are you going to share that with me like you promised, or am I going to have to take it from you?"

His mouth turned up at the corners. "As much as I'd enjoy letting you take my apple…" his expression screamed with naughtiness "…I'll play nice and share." He took his napkin and wiped off the apple. "I'll even let you have the first bite."

"Such a gentleman."

"You better believe it."

Natalie took the fruit and bit down. Sweet juice ran into her mouth, trickling from the corner.

"Mmmm." She licked the juice from her lips. "It's good. Want a bite?"

He swallowed, his Adam's apple bobbing. "Hell, yeah."

But as he took the fruit from her extended hand she got the impression he wasn't talking about the apple.

His gaze connected with hers as he took a bite from the exact area she had. There was something sensual about knowing he'd intentionally placed his mouth where hers had been, that shared bite somehow creating an intimacy hard-found in the midst of thousands of walkers.

He chewed the bite slowly, and Natalie decided right then and there that an apple a day might keep the doctor away but this particular nurse was totally hooked.

"Go out with me tonight, Natalie?" he requested, his eyes compelling her to say yes. "I'd like to spend every minute with you between now and when I have to leave tomorrow."

She glanced away, watching as a group of walkers passed, "In memory of" blazed across the front of their T-shirts in bright green. Women's names were handwritten at all angles over the material. Women who'd died from breast cancer. Women who had left someone behind to care that they were gone. If *she* left this world right now who would miss her? Sure, she had friends, but how long would pass before they forgot all about her?

"Say yes," he said from close to her ear, his breath caressing her skin. "Say you'll spend tonight with me."

Spend tonight with him? What had happened to going out with him? "I can't."

"Can't or won't?"

"Doesn't matter. The end result is the same." She wadded up her trash, squeezing the papers tightly in her grasp. "This weekend has been wonderful, but we both know it's an aberration from our real lives."

"Things don't have to end with the walk, Natalie. I'd like to see you again." His gaze held hers. "I'm not just talking about tonight, but beyond that."

"You live out of state," she pointed out, feeling her resistance waning.

"We could make a relationship work. Let's see where this goes between us."

"That's what the past few days have been about." She tossed his argument from Friday night back at him.

"Exactly, and they've been wonderful. You said so yourself." When he looked at her with such longing, such earnestness, his smug comment came out as imploring rather than arrogant. "I want more. Lots more."

His words were sweet music, but she knew better than to be sidetracked by a tempting melody.

"Hand-holding and a few kisses beneath the moonlight not enough payout for the time you've invested in me?" She wasn't sure where the nasty accusation had come from, but in her heart the words rang with truth.

He winced as if she'd slapped him, his eyes turning a steely blue. "That comment doesn't deserve a response, but I'm going to give you one."

Natalie gulped, almost afraid of what he was going to say. The veins in his neck bulged, and he gritted his teeth as if restraining his words took a great deal of willpower.

"I want you," he ground out. "In a bad way I want you. I won't deny that if you had been willing this weekend would've ended with me making love to you. Hell, if you'd been willing I'd have taken you in the woods, or anywhere we could have found a private spot. But if that had happened it wouldn't have been about a payout for time invested. I'm offering a relationship, not a one-night stand."

He tossed the apple to her and she stared at the single bite of white flesh showing through the missing red skin. How had they progressed to this harsh tension?

"I'm not sure what's happened in the past that's given you such a jaded perspective of men, but that's not how I operate. We've only known each other for a few days, but I expected you to know that about me." He stood, stared down at the apple with the same intensity she had. "I'm going to the medical tent."

He turned his back to her and took two steps before she stopped him.

"Caleb?"

He paused, turned, locked his gaze with hers, and waited for her to say whatever she'd stopped him for.

I'm sorry, she whispered in her heart. Aloud she didn't speak, though. She didn't tell him all the things she was sorry for.

Like that she felt she had to choose between him and having a family.

He didn't understand that even if she chose him ultimately he'd leave her, like everyone else in her life had, and then she'd be alone yet again.

When she still didn't speak, he shook his head in disappointment and walked away.

CHAPTER FIVE

INSTEAD of going to the medical tent, as he'd told Natalie, Caleb headed away from where the majority of walkers and volunteers were clustered around the food tents. A wide creek ran through the park, but it was enough of a trek that few of the exhausted walkers made the effort.

How could Natalie be so stubborn? Surely she didn't believe whatever was going on in her life was so "complicated" that they couldn't deal with it together?

Was it to do with her accident? He'd let her subject-change slide because he'd figured she'd open up to him before the weekend was over. Now he wasn't so sure, and wondered if he'd made a grave miscalculation.

Just as he'd made a grave miscalculation in not telling her he was the single father of a beautiful, precocious five-year-old, and he'd once been married to her co-worker's sister.

He hadn't been too forthcoming himself. A mistake he intended to correct before the weekend ended.

These past couple of days with her had been amazing, like a fresh breath of air to a dying man.

In many ways he *had* been dying.

Except for with Emily he'd packed away his heart when Jamie had died, and had forgotten it existed. Until now.

Whether he'd wanted to fall for Natalie or not he had, and her reluctance to give them a chance ticked him off. How could she so easily toss aside what they shared when an attraction so strong was so rare?

"I thought that was you."

The friendly voice startled him out of his reverie. "Lydia."

"You were expecting someone younger, with big blue eyes, perhaps?" the older woman teased.

No, he hadn't expected Natalie to follow him.

"I should be so lucky."

Lydia's expression softened. "My Natalie giving you a run for your money?"

"Run would be the right word," he muttered under his breath.

"She's worth fighting for, you know."

"I know." He did know, and he would fight. Once he figured out what he was fighting against. "She doesn't want me in her life beyond this weekend."

"If you believe that you're not nearly as intelligent as I gave you credit for last night." Lydia motioned for him to sit down on a large flat stone overlooking the creek bank.

He settled next to her and picked up a flat rock, skipped the stone across the creek. "She told me so."

"Then you should start listening with more than your ears," Lydia said bluntly. "Nice toss. I never could do that."

He searched the rocky bank until he found another good stone, placed it in Lydia's hand just so, then guided her in a fling. The rock skipped twice.

"This old girl's never too old to learn a new trick," she said in glee, and turned delighted eyes on him. "Now, let me teach *you* something."

His brows veed. "What?"

"Natalie is a wounded soul. Precious, but wounded," she pointed out. "She was involved with someone who hurt her dearly."

He wasn't sure he wanted to hear this. "Natalie wouldn't like us talking about her."

"No," Lydia agreed. "She wouldn't. But before you make any hasty decisions regarding my girl you should know how special you are."

Special? His lips twisted.

"She's not dated since Bob. Says she doesn't have time, but it's because she's afraid of being hurt again."

He shouldn't ask, but he did. "What happened to Bob?"

"He dumped her while she was recovering from the wreck."

He called the man a choice word.

"And then some," Lydia agreed.

"She was in love with him?"

"She thought she loved him, but I was never convinced. Bob came along at a point in Natalie's life where she was vulnerable and needed someone to care for. Her mother had died not long before they met, and her heart latched on to Bob and his family." Lydia shook her head. "Really he's a nice enough guy, I suppose, but they weren't right for each other. In the long run he did her a favor when he set her free."

The furrows on Caleb's brow deepened. "I don't understand."

"Natalie—"

"Caleb?"

Both Caleb and Lydia twisted toward the sound. Natalie stood behind him, her eyes huge pools of azure, her face pale. She glanced back and forth between them.

His gut wrenched that she'd caught him talking about her—again. But she'd come after him. That had to mean something.

"I, uh, came to tell you…" She paused, giving a quick glance Lydia's way before returning his stare. "Yes."

Caleb's heart leapt and lodged in his throat. He wanted to reach out and take Natalie in his arms, to hold her until every hurt she'd ever felt faded into distant memories. Until she forgot all about this Bob guy and all her thoughts centered around him—Caleb.

Lydia patted his hand, thanked him for showing her how to skip a rock, gave Natalie a quick hug, and headed in the direction of lunch.

Natalie sat down next to him, wrapped her arms around her knees, and stared out over the bubbly creek. He wasn't sure she saw the beauty of their surroundings. Her cheeks were red, and the pulse at her throat hammered as if she'd run the ten kilometers in record time.

He reached over, took her hand in his. So tiny, yet so capable. Her hands held the strength to cure an ailing body. Perhaps the strength to cure an ailing heart. "You changed your mind? You'll have dinner with me?"

She nodded.

Thank God. He'd tell her everything—about Jamie, about Emily, about how he wanted Natalie as a part of his life. Was she willing to give them a chance? To give them time to explore the feelings between them? To see if what they shared was for forever?

"And after?" Surely her agreeing to dinner meant she'd give them time, agree to see him again?

She looked at him with her bright blue eyes and sucker-punched him. "I'll spend the night with you."

His ears roared. "You'll what?"

He'd meant tomorrow, the next day, the following week, month—however long this feeling existed between them.

"I want to spend the night with you." She ran her palms over her legs, visibly uneasy, but her gaze held his. "It's what we both want—what this weekend has been about."

Caleb didn't know whether to kiss her or strangle her.

He wanted to argue, to point out that this weekend was about much more than taking her to his hotel room. But if she couldn't see that for herself, his saying the words wasn't going to change anything. He'd show her.

By the time they parted tomorrow she'd be as anxious to see him again as he knew he'd be to see her.

Because he wanted Natalie in his life.

The superior gleam in Caleb's eyes worried Natalie, but only a little. She'd known what she was letting herself in for. A night of sex and then they'd go their separate ways.

She was likely to suffer heartache, but, unlike with Bob, she knew that going in. Why be deprived of Caleb's company when she desperately wanted more time with him?

One night with a sexy man wasn't going to prevent her from going through with her plans for IVF.

Watching him walk away from her had hurt. Hurt way too much. She'd been struck by two strong compulsions. To run far away from him while she still could. Or to go after him. Her ultimate goals hadn't changed. Only now she'd have more memories with Caleb. Perhaps those memories would see her through whatever her future held?

"Say something." She couldn't stand him just grinning at her that way. "Please."

He laced his fingers with hers, kissed her knuckles. "I'm going to show you the best night of your life, Natalie."

That was what she was counting on.

Cheers went up as walker after walker crossed the finish line. Volunteers handed out T-shirts, and stations were set up with bottled water and snacks. Despite the crowd, Natalie bumped into Barney moments after the van had dropped the medical crew off at the finish celebrations. Together they waited on his wife and Lydia to cross the line.

Caleb had disappeared to help at the medical tent. Natalie supposed she should go see if they needed more help, but the excitement of cheering the bedraggled walkers thrilled her too much to step away.

Or perhaps the flutters in her stomach had nothing to do with the walk and everything to do with the way Caleb kept looking at her. Like he planned to gobble her up.

She shivered at the intensity of what his eyes promised.

Had she made a mistake?

No, she wouldn't second-guess herself. She'd decided to go for tonight, to enjoy Caleb's attention if only for one night, to let him heal that part of her deep inside that Bob had made feel unlovable. That had perhaps always felt unlovable when it came to the opposite sex.

"Who was that young man you were with when I spotted you?" Barney asked, waving a pink flag as more walkers crossed the line.

"Dr. Caleb Burton. I was his nurse this weekend."

"Oh?" Barney's bushy brows lifted in interest. "Y'all played doctor together?"

Natalie couldn't help but smile at the eighty-year-old's suggestive eyebrow wiggle. "We worked well together," she corrected. Quite well together.

"All work and no play—" Barney began, but Natalie spotted a familiar face.

"Look, there's Lydia! Lydia! Woo-hoo," she cheered, as the breast cancer survivor experienced yet another triumph over the disease that had once invaded her body.

Barney let out a holler of encouragement to his neighbor, and together they made their way to hug Lydia after she'd gotten her T-shirt.

"I am so proud of you," Natalie said, wrapping her arms around her friend. "So very proud."

"Me, too," Barney praised, giving Lydia a hug of his own. He glanced around. "Where's my wife? Unable to keep up?"

Lydia winked conspiratorially. "Actually, she got herself a better offer."

Poor Mary. She'd wanted to cross the finish line so badly. Her edema just hadn't permitted it. As Caleb had ordered, she'd ridden the bus to the finish line earlier that afternoon.

"Huh? What kind of offer?" Barney asked, at the same time as a bevy of loud hoots and hollers went up from the crowd. Good-natured cheering and laughter sounded all around.

Natalie, Barney and Lydia craned their necks to see what all the commotion was about.

"Oh, my." Natalie's eyes widened as she spotted Mary.

The older woman was going to cross the finish line after all.

In Caleb's arms.

After the closing ceremony, Natalie and Caleb said their goodbyes to Lydia, Barney and Mary. As they waved one last time before heading toward the medical tent, Mary beamed at Caleb with a light in her eyes that said she'd never forget what he'd done.

"I can't believe you found Mary so you could carry her across the finish line." Natalie stretched up and kissed his cheek. "That was a really nice thing to do."

His eyes twinkling, he grinned. "You should have seen me trying to convince her to ride piggyback. She'd have none of it."

Natalie laughed. Caleb had swooped Mary into his arms, carried her a good way down the lane, and cut into the walkers' path lined with well-wishers. To the amusement of the onlookers he'd carried the petite woman the rest of the way much as a groom would carry his bride over the threshold.

"You made her day. Instead of hanging her head in shame that she didn't cross the finish line she'll be bragging about this for weeks. Longer."

"Good." He took Natalie's hand in his and they walked toward the medical tent. "As long as she keeps talking, you won't be able to forget me."

Did he think she'd need reminders? He'd be impossible to forget. She suspected after tonight she'd be hard pressed to take a breath without thinking of him.

Butterflies fluttered in her stomach. *Tonight.*

"Did you see Barney's face?" She changed the subject, unable to dwell on what the night might hold. "He was stunned, and a bit jealous, I believe."

"A bit?" Caleb let her get away without commenting on what he'd said. "He pulled me aside and point-blank told me to keep my hands off his wife."

Despite the quivery emotions still gripping her insides, she laughed. "I wondered what he was saying to you."

"Mary seemed to enjoy the attention. Did you see how Barney was fussing over her? He'll see to it she keeps her feet propped and follows up with her primary care provider."

"Thankfully her ankles looked much better this evening."

"Yeah, hopefully she's learned her lesson about skipping medicines. Next time she might not be so lucky."

They gathered their personal belongings, said their goodbyes to the medical crew, the volunteers, and to John and Martha. Dusk had begun to fall. Pink, purple and a deep blue streaked the darkening sky.

"Anywhere in particular you'd like to eat?" Caleb asked as they hiked toward where Natalie had parked her car.

Natalie glanced down at her dirty clothes. "Anywhere is fine. We don't look up to anything fancy."

"If you want fancy, I'll take you any place you want to go," he quickly assured her.

She shook her head. "No, I'm tired and grimy. Let's shower, then decide." Her lips curved in anticipation. "In a real shower, rather than a cubicle not much bigger than my high-school locker. We take such simple pleasures for granted until we have to do without them for three days."

He laughed. "I have a reservation." He named an

upscale hotel. "We can shower there and then decide on where we eat. My car's there, so I'll have to hitch a ride with you."

Her belly somersaulted. "Sounds perfect."

On the drive to his hotel, Natalie thought about what the night would hold. She wanted Caleb—cared for him much more than she should, considering the short time they'd known each other. Amazingly, he wanted her, too, and cared enough that he wanted a relationship. At least that was what he'd said.

The reality was that they'd go their separate ways in the morning and likely never see each other again. She knew that. Yet, despite the fact she hadn't been with many men, she wanted tonight with Caleb.

Perhaps she should have held out to the last, let Caleb seduce her, but she was a grown woman and she was going into this with her eyes wide open. One night with a man who made her feel amazingly alive, then she'd move on to her future.

"If you've changed your mind and want me to take you to a restaurant I will," Caleb offered when she pulled the car into the hotel drive.

She parked the car in front of the entrance and blinked at him. "I've not changed my mind. Why would you think I had?"

"You've not said a word since we got in the car."

"Sorry—guess I'm just tired. I was just thinking about the walk." Her mind had been running a mile a minute. But not about the walk. All her thoughts had centered on Caleb.

"Natalie…" He hesitated, took her hand in his and stared at their twined fingers. "I'm not averse to taking things slow."

Her mouth opened, but he rushed on.

"Don't get me wrong. I want you desperately. Since the night we met I've ached for you."

He lifted her hand to his lips and kissed her fingers one after the other. His lips lingered over the tip of her pinky as he stared directly into her eyes.

"But I want you with me all the way when we make love for the first time, and I'm willing to wait. I didn't mean to pressure you earlier. If you have the slightest doubt about the rightness of sharing my bed tonight, well—" He looked torn. "Well," he repeated, "we could always keep our clothes on."

His thoughtfulness melted away any lingering self-doubt. In an effort to hide just how much his words touched her deep inside, she chuckled. "Have sex while we're dressed?"

He frowned. "No. As in you and I share a bed while fully dressed and not have sex."

"Where's the fun in that?" She continued to try to make light. Otherwise she might just throw herself into his arms right this minute.

"I get to hold you," he answered bluntly. "To wake up with you in my arms."

It took her a moment to decipher that he was serious. He *was* willing to just hold her.

Oh, Caleb. She leaned across the car seat, threw her arms around his stunned body and hugged him, grateful such an amazing man had come into her life to give her precious memories.

"I'm the one who came after you today," she reminded him, loving his musky scent. "I'm the one who said yes." Yes, yes, yes—oh, yes. "I haven't changed my mind. Nothing could be further from the truth."

He didn't look convinced. "You're sure?"

"Positive." She'd never been more sure of anything. "Let's go inside."

Being with Caleb felt like the most natural, perfect thing in the world.

CHAPTER SIX

SWEET dreams filled Natalie's mind.

Dreams of her and Caleb sitting on a sofa, with his hands rubbing over her swollen belly.

Dreams of her and Caleb picking out baby clothes, decorating a nursery together, laughing, kissing, touching.

Dreams of rocking Caleb's baby during the long hours of the night.

Dreams of a dark haired, blue-eyed darling who looked like her father.

Caleb.

Trying to focus through the cloudy world of her dream, Natalie attempted to see more clearly.

They were in a park not so dissimilar from the one where they'd had lunch the day before. Holding hands, she and Caleb sat on the bank of a creek while a little girl splashed in the ankle-deep water. Her dark curls bouncing, she giggled in glee as she sent a spray of water toward them.

"Mommy," she called. "Come play with me."

Natalie attempted to stand, but Caleb's hold on her hand tightened, staying her. "No. Stay with me."

Looking back and forth between them, she struggled, feeling torn.

The little girl reached for her. "Mommy."

Natalie's eyes opened. Her heart pounded against her ribs, her dream so vivid in her mind that she longed to search for the child. *Mommy.* The endearment echoed through her heart.

Clearly the little girl in her dream was her and Caleb's child.

Caleb.

Oh, sweet, sweet heavens, he'd been a tender lover. Tender, passionate, demanding, giving—everything a man should be in bed. Even now, the morning after, he held her as if even in sleep he wanted her close.

She rolled over to look at the man who'd done amazing things to her body during the night, who'd freed her inhibitions and made her feel both precious and like a sexy siren. Unable to stop herself, she ran her fingertip over his face.

His even breathing signified he was sound asleep, and she studied his relaxed features, put them in her memory.

She wanted to look into those features over and over, to spend all her mornings waking up to him, to look into her child's face and see Caleb.

Her dream only brought the realities into clearer focus.

She didn't want an anonymous donor as the father of her baby. She wanted Caleb, so that she'd always have a part of him to love.

"If I asked, would you?" she wondered out loud, her whisper barely audible.

One thickly lashed lid opened at the same time as a lazy smile curved his lips. "If you asked me what?"

Her heart made the mistake of thinking it was vying for pole position, and took off at a hefty speed.

"Never mind."

He stretched, then wrapped his arm around her waist, tugging her toward him. "After last night, surely you can ask me anything?"

No, she couldn't. She couldn't ask him to give her a baby.

"I want to get pregnant."

Oh, my God. Had she really just said that out loud, to the man she'd spent the night making love to?

The way his eyes popped, fully awake, the way the skin paled and stretched tightly over his cheekbones said she had indeed revealed her innermost wishes.

He shook his head as if trying to jar some sense into it. "What did you say?"

Her face was likely as red as his was pasty white.

Embarrassment flooded through her, but she'd already said the words aloud. There was no going back.

"I want to get pregnant. Will you give me a baby?"

Caleb pushed himself up in the bed, staring at her as if one of them had lost their mind, and his money was resting on it being her.

"We've only known each other for four days." His words came out slow, measured, attesting that he'd given enormous thought to each one yet wasn't sure how to proceed. He looked dumbstruck—like he wanted to grab his clothes and run.

Seeing how he so clearly abhorred the idea of her being pregnant with his child, she hung up protective walls built long ago in her defense.

"Yet here we are." She gestured to where the sheet barely covered their naked bodies.

A tic jumped in his temple and she thought he might be sick. "You were trying to get pregnant last night?"

"No, I wasn't. And you can wipe that horrified look off your face. We both know we used condoms."

They had. Which was okay. She'd never intentionally get pregnant by a man who didn't want to give her a baby. Which was why she'd opted to go the fertility treatment route rather than pick up some random guy.

There was the health thing, too. She didn't want to risk her health or her baby's.

"I'm not sure what to say, Natalie." He raked his hands through his sleep-ruffled hair.

How was it possible for him to look even sexier in the early-morning light with his features sleep-roughened?

Natalie's anger lost momentum. She realized she'd truly blindsided him. To his credit he hadn't run, despite that initial appearance of the need for flight.

The reality was they had just met. She'd been a fool to think he might agree to give her the baby she longed for. From the moment they'd met she'd been envisioning having his baby. Last night, his tender lovemaking had only strengthened her desire for her baby to be *his* child. She'd asked, and now she knew.

"I'm sorry." She sighed. "It was a crazy idea to begin with."

She *was* sorry, because the precious feeling she'd had upon waking in his arms was gone. In its place was an ugly reminder that the entire weekend with Caleb had been an illusion. She needed to get back on task.

"You're upset." Still looking shell shocked, he placed his hand under her chin, lifting her face toward him. "I didn't mean to hurt you."

"Just forget it." She jerked her chin free. "I'm going to take a shower." She pulled the sheet protectively around her bare breasts—which was ridiculous since he'd seen, held and tasted every inch of her. But she felt exposed, conscious of her nakedness, and needed something to shield the pain riveting through her.

She'd known better than to ask. Women didn't ask strangers to make them pregnant.

She'd known Caleb less than a week.

But, as much as he *was* a stranger, he wasn't one. How could he be when she felt as if he'd always been a part of her life? Like she could look at him and know what he was thinking. Like right now.

He thought she was crazy.

She was.

Crazy about a man she needed to let go so she could get on with her life.

Of all the things Caleb might have guessed would come out of Natalie's mouth first thing this morning, asking for a baby wasn't one of them.

"Natalie."

He grabbed her wrist, hating that she hid behind the sheet. After what they'd shared there shouldn't be anything between them, and he suspected the sheet provided more of a barrier between them than just hiding her nakedness.

"Like I said, you caught me off guard. I didn't mean to hurt you." Nothing he said seemed to be coming out right, but he stumbled onward. "Hurting you is the last thing I want."

Her lower lip quivered and she didn't meet his eyes.

"What I want is you in my life. But don't you think it's a bit soon to start talking babies?"

"I plan to raise my baby by myself. I didn't mean that I expect you to be a permanent part of my life. Just that I want your baby." Her face squished up and she shook her head. "This isn't coming out right."

Her eyes watered, her hands shook, and she refused to look at him. She'd been serious.

Natalie had asked him to make her pregnant.

Oh, hell.

"I made a mistake, Caleb. Just forget I ever said anything." Keeping a tight grip on the sheet, she tugged against his hold. "I need to go to the bathroom."

"Natalie." He had to say something—anything to take that rejected look off her face.

But she shook her head, gave a brave smile, and said, "I'm fine. It was just something silly that popped into my head. No big deal."

No big deal? She had no idea.

He loved Emily with all his heart, but having watched Jamie go through such hell during her pregnancy, knowing having his baby had contributed to her death, fathering another child was the last thing he wanted to do.

He needed to tell her about Emily. He *wanted* to tell her. But telling her about Emily meant telling her about Emily's mom. He'd meant to tell her last night, but from the moment she'd wrapped her arms around him his mind had focused on Natalie and no one else.

After they'd made love he'd remembered that he still hadn't told her. He wasn't the fun, sexy guy she'd spent the weekend with, but a single dad and lonely widower. Talking about Jamie while lying naked in bed after a night spent making love to Natalie had felt wrong, so he'd kept silent, planning to tell her everything this morning.

"Being a single parent is tough," he said, trying to segue into an explanation.

Natalie's gaze narrowed. "I've given having a baby on my own a lot of thought."

"Why? What's the rush? Wouldn't it make more sense to wait until you meet the right person and decide together to start a family? Going it alone isn't easy."

He couldn't imagine his life without Emily, but he didn't tell her he knew all too well the difficulties of being a single parent. He was a single father who'd rocked a crying baby to sleep, changed diapers, cleaned up spilt milk, stressed over preschool, read bedtime stories and gone to PTA meetings. He was a lonely, single father because he'd watched his wife die and been helpless to stop the disease claiming her.

"You don't understand."

"Kids aren't easy, Natalie. They're a lot of work. Being responsible for another person, having to be on call twenty-four hours a day endlessly—it isn't a game. Not having someone to share that workload with can be downright depressing."

"You sound like you don't like kids," she accused, her chin lifted in an angry tilt.

"There's nothing wrong with kids." He clenched her hands, wanting to pull her to him and kiss her until she was breathless, until the panic left her eyes and he didn't think she planned to rush out the door the moment he turned his back. "Purposely being a single parent—doing that to an innocent kid—that's wrong."

He watched every day the effects of being motherless

on Emily. That was why he'd come to Atlanta. To spend time with Jamie's parents. To talk with them about his and Emily moving here so she could be closer to her family and hopefully fill the loss in her young life.

"How could you intentionally deprive a child of having a real family?" he asked. "To put a child at such a disadvantage before he or she is even born?"

"There are a lot of single parent families, Caleb. And they're as real as it gets." She bristled. "You act like it's a horrible crime to be a single parent. My mom was a single parent and she did an excellent job of raising me. It was just her and me and we did fine—do you hear? Why don't you get to the real issue? It's not that you care if I'm a single parent or not, just so long as you aren't involved in the process. Well, no worries there, because I don't need you to have a baby."

Giving him one last look of disgust, she disappeared into the bathroom. The crisp white sheet wrapped around her body trailed in her wake.

She'd asked him to get her pregnant.

Nausea washed over him, leaving his palms sweaty. Thank God he'd used condoms.

Otherwise he could have already made her pregnant.

Natalie procrastinated in the bathroom for as long as she could. She'd left her bag on the floor beneath the sink, and dressed in her last pair of clean shorts and a T-shirt. She packed all her things back into the bag and stood leaning against the sink, staring into the mirror.

The steam had evaporated long ago, and now nothing hindered her view of the lost-looking woman staring back. She should be over the moon. She'd spent the night in bed with a generous man who'd focused solely on her pleasure. He'd even held her while they slept. She should be happy.

Instead tears clouded her eyes yet again.

Caleb had knocked on the door twice, checking on her.

"Natalie?" He knocked on the door a third time. "You about done?"

The poor man's bladder was probably protesting her prolonged hiatus.

Steeling herself, she reached for the handle. The bathroom door opened before she could turn it. Her mouth dropped and she glared at the man filling the doorway.

Since she was as clean-faced as she'd been all weekend, and hadn't done more with her hair than pull it back with an elastic band, he was probably wondering what she'd been doing for so long. But one look at her red-rimmed eyes and he'd know. She'd kept her sobs muffled beneath the sound of the shower, kept her sorrow and horror at having asked him for a baby under enough control not to be heard, reined in her anger at his ignorant comment about single parent households not being "real" families.

She brushed past his boxers-clad body so quickly that he couldn't see more than a brief glimpse of her face. That and the fact the bathroom beckoned him saved her from his being able to look more closely at her broken heart.

She'd expected him to jump in the shower before coming out, but after washing his hands he re-entered the bedroom.

"What are your plans for today?"

She glanced up at him. She was going home, doing laundry, catching up on all the things that accumulated when one had been away from home several days. "Why?"

"I want to spend the day with you."

"Maybe it's better if we go our separate ways this morning."

He stood in his boxers, bare chest, bare legs, bare feet, ruffled hair, looking sexier than he had a right. "It's not better for me."

She gripped her bag closer to her, using it as a buffer between them.

"You regret spending the night with me?" His eyes narrowed in on her bag. He was glaringly suspicious that she was going to run away any moment. He looked angry. Sounded angry.

"No." She didn't regret what they'd shared. She'd never felt so cherished, so loved, but how was she supposed to go through life without ever experiencing that again? She suspected not having Caleb in her life would hurt for a long, long time, but it was a price she'd willingly pay for motherhood.

"This weekend has been…" *the most amazing weekend of her life* "…nice, but let's just end things while we can both think of each other as a fond memory."

"I'll think of you as much more than a fond memory," he admitted, crossing to her and taking her hands in his.

She didn't like that she could feel his body heat, that his broad bare chest was so close she could lean her cheek against it, could lean on him. She couldn't, of course. She'd learned long ago not to lean on anyone, to depend only on herself.

She and her mom had been real. They'd been a family. Been being the key word. Natalie had nothing these days. Nothing but memories and the hope of someday having her own family.

Caleb wanted her right now, but he'd turn out to be another Bob, and when push came to shove he'd leave her too. It was what the men in her life did. Wouldn't it be much better to end things before she really did depend on him? Before her heart became so entwined with him that it would shatter when he left?

"Let's keep it that way. Let's walk away from this and keep it as something…" she paused, searching for the right word "…something precious."

"Do I mean nothing to you? Natalie, you just asked me to give you a baby." He couldn't quite hide his grimace. "Now you're saying I'm nothing more than a weekend fling you never want to see again?"

She winced. She couldn't see him again and stick to her plan.

"I want a baby. I'd been dreaming, and I was still foggy from sleep. The words came out of their own accord. I didn't know how to take them back."

"Does this have to do with your scars?"

At first she didn't know what he was talking about, but then it hit her. Not once had she given any thought to the marks on her body. After surgery, the surface scars hadn't been that noticeable. It was the scars beneath the skin that worried her. But what would be the point in telling him that?

"No."

He raked his fingers through his hair, then quickly took her hands again, obviously worrying she'd flee if he wasn't hanging onto her.

Her heart surged. He really wanted their relationship to continue. But what would be the point? He obviously didn't want kids; she desperately did.

To carry on with Caleb would mean putting off her IVF. And she had too much invested in proceeding—financially and emotionally.

"I...I'm..." He dropped her hands, rubbed his fingers across his jaw. "I don't know what to say."

"There's not anything to say, Caleb. Just goodbye."

CHAPTER SEVEN

ON THE day of Natalie's scheduled egg-harvesting, she woke up sick. Not a little sick, but dog sick. So sick she could barely crawl to the bathroom, could barely lift her head. Her heart broke at having to put off the harvesting, but she literally couldn't drive herself to the clinic, couldn't proceed with anything other than turning her body inside out with her wretchedness.

The next day wasn't much better, and she did the unthinkable and called in sick to work.

On the third day of spending more time on the bathroom floor than on her feet, Natalie whined to Dot for commiseration. She and Dot had always been cordial to each other, but since the walk Dot had seemed to go out of her way to talk to her, to be kind to her. Natalie had always liked the doctor, and welcomed the blossoming of their friendship.

"I think I have the flu," she moaned.

"The flu?" Dot asked. "It's a little early in the season for flu, but it's possible. Probably just a nasty virus, though. You've looked tired ever since you got back from the breast cancer walk. Are you sure nothing happened there that you need to tell me about?"

She *was* tired. From a lack of sleep that had little to do with her illness. But, although she treasured her new friendship with Dot, she didn't want to tell her about Caleb.

"Do you need me to stop by and check you over?" Dot offered. "I finally got my Disney pictures developed, and I'd love to show you my niece."

Natalie was miserably alone, and would have loved to have company. If only she *felt* like company. Plus, any company would likely catch this horrid bug.

"Not yet," she said reluctantly. "But if I'm not better soon I may take you up on checking me out."

"Maybe you're pregnant," Dot teased.

"I wish," Natalie sighed. She'd told Dot about her dream to get pregnant, about the lengths she was going to to make that dream come true. "Surely I'll be better by tomorrow?"

"I hope so." Dot sounded thoughtful, and like she really did hope Natalie returned to work soon. "You're missed. I delivered a breech today. You know I prefer working with you when delivering, and particularly when dealing with a hard delivery."

Natalie's stomach gurgled as Dot's teasing ran through her mind. Pregnant? Impossible. "Good to know I'm appreciated."

"Hey, guess what? My brother-in-law is going to be joining us at the clinic."

"The hotshot obstetrician who delivers all the country music stars' babies in Nashville?" she asked, distracted. She couldn't really be pregnant. This was just the flu or a virus. Caleb had used condoms.

"That's the one. I can't wait to have him and Emily close."

Emily was Dot's niece. Recently the little girl had spent

a long weekend with her aunt, and Dot had taken her to Disneyland. The trip had been the same weekend as the breast cancer walk.

Oh, Caleb.

She missed him so much.

So much that her mind was working overtime, teasing her that being pregnant was a possibility. She couldn't be.

"Actually," Dot mused, "it surprises me you didn't meet Cal at the breast cancer walk."

"Your brother-in-law was at the walk?" Oh, God, what if she *was* pregnant? What if somehow she'd gotten pregnant that weekend with Caleb? Natalie placed her palm over her stomach, fighting another bout of nausea.

"Cal signed up for the walk last minute. He dropped Emily off and headed directly there, apparently."

The queasiness that had been churning in Natalie's stomach launched itself up her throat and she couldn't fight it anymore.

"Sorry, Dot, got to go."

She dropped the phone and ran to the bathroom.

Leaning against her bathroom sink, Natalie stared at the blue line on the home pregnancy kit. A blue line: Her stomach twisted into a nervous knot. A blue line.

That was why she'd been so sick. Why the virus had lingered and lingered. Because she hadn't had a virus.

Dot had been right.

Natalie was pregnant.

Pregnant.

Strong emotions stormed through her. She wanted a baby desperately, but being pregnant by a man she knew didn't want her pregnant with his child felt wrong.

Recalling all the things he'd said about parenthood, she winced. He really didn't want a child—had sounded like he'd resent having his freedom taken away.

She flattened her palm over her belly. A baby. She was having Caleb's baby.

In her wildest dreams she wouldn't have believed it possible. She knew condoms occasionally failed, but she hadn't thought it would happen to her.

Her fingers tightly latched onto the plastic stick. Blue. Blue. *Blue.*

Happiness erupted within her, drowning out her guilt at getting pregnant by Caleb. Happiness that pushed outward and consumed her entire being.

Blue.

She was pregnant.

Her hand slid over her belly. She was going to have a baby—a family. Naturally. Without IVF. Although the fertility drugs she'd been taking so she'd release multiple eggs for harvesting had no doubt played a role in her getting pregnant.

She was having a baby with a man who'd given her so much in the one weekend they'd known each other.

She slid onto the cream-colored tile floor. Bursting into excited laughter, she ignored the pang of doubt that said she cared more than she was letting on that Caleb wouldn't be a part of their baby's life. A part of *her* life.

But he was back in St. Louis, where he belonged, and she'd never see him again—just as she'd said she wanted on the morning they'd said goodbye.

At the moment she no longer ached with heartbreak. He'd given her the most precious gift. His baby.

She was going to have Caleb's baby.

She had no way of getting in touch with him. She'd destroyed the business card he'd given her. First shredding it into the smallest pieces she could tear, then flushing the remains down the toilet.

Getting rid of temptation had been her only way of ignoring the magnetic pull of the card. The only way of ignoring the magnetic pull of the man who'd tempted her to forget her plans.

Instead he'd given her what she'd wished for most. A family.

She hated that she couldn't tell him, that he'd never know they'd created a beautiful life. But with the way he'd freaked out when she'd asked him to make her pregnant it was probably just as well.

He didn't want children, didn't want the responsibility. He wouldn't want to know.

Still, her conscience weighed heavy. How could she *not* tell him? Not give him the opportunity to know the wonderful life they'd created?

Truth was, she had to tell him. Despite his ravings about parenthood, she couldn't keep his child a secret from him.

After making sure she was going to carry on the pregnancy without problems, she'd find him. Closer to her time for delivery she'd give him the choice of whether or not he played a role in their baby's life. The rest was up to him.

Either way, joy sang in her heart.

She was pregnant.

"Thank you, Caleb," she whispered into the empty bathroom. "Thank you for granting me my wish."

Pausing in the hospital hallway, Caleb questioned his sanity.

Among other reasons, he'd moved to a different state

to be near a woman who'd told him she didn't ever want to see him again. He'd tried to forget her, to tell himself he was better off without Natalie because she wanted a baby. But he couldn't put her out of his head. Not with her so entrenched in his heart.

He constantly thought of her. Of the way her eyes twinkled when she smiled, of the sparkle in her laughter, of the way she tasted, of the way her body had felt beneath his.

Closing his eyes, he breathed in deep, trying to somehow recapture the time he'd spent with her.

He was going to see her. Today. In just a few minutes. What would she say? Would she pretend not to remember him? It had been almost three months. He'd wanted to come immediately, but he hadn't been able to walk away from his patients until other arrangements could be made. Hadn't been able to just rip Emily from her life without making plans for their future.

What if Natalie didn't care? What if he'd truly just been a fling for her? No, that couldn't be true. Her eyes had told him the exact opposite of what her lips had said. Natalie had been as affected by the chemistry between them as he'd been.

So why was he so nervous at the prospect of seeing her again?

"There you are," Dot said, greeting him with a bright smile and an excited gleam in her eyes. She brushed a piece of lint from his white lab coat sleeve. "I've been waiting for you. Come on, I want to introduce you to the gang."

His heart thudded in his chest at the prospect of seeing the woman who'd ripped his world apart in the space of one weekend.

She might not be working today.

She might…

He spotted her the moment they walked onto the obstetrics unit.

Natalie.

His Natalie.

Wearing brightly colored scrubs with happy faces all over the top, she was smiling at another nurse, a faraway look on her face. She was beautiful in the timeless way that he knew would carry her through a lifetime. Her skin was a smooth cream, her eyes a crystal blue, her hair a pretty blond bob, her lips a rosy shade that begged for a kiss.

She'd had her gorgeous hair cut, but otherwise she looked just as he remembered.

She hadn't even seen him, and already he wanted to kiss her.

Admit it, ole boy, you've never stopped wanting to kiss her. From the moment you saw her across that medical tent, you've wanted this woman in the worst kind of way.

"Natalie, I want you to meet my brother-in-law," Dot said, causing Natalie's gaze to lift.

His heart stilled in his chest as he waited for her reaction, waited for some acknowledgement that they'd met, known each other.

Her eyes widened in surprise and a huge smile curved her lips.

His heart sighed in relief. Everything was going to work out. Natalie was excited to see him.

But just as quickly the smile slid from her face, and her eyes lit with—was that horror? Anger?

"*You're* Dot's brother-in-law?" Her gaze met his and she pierced him with a look of betrayal shining in her eyes.

Quickly she masked her emotions. Probably for Dot's sake, she plastered a fake smile on her face.

"This is Dr. Caleb Burton, better known as Cal to his friends," Dot continued, beaming with pride as she glanced back and forth between them. She was ecstatic that he and Emily were in Atlanta. So were Emily's grandparents. "He's joining my practice. He mentioned you met briefly at the breast cancer walk."

Her mouth dropping open, Natalie's eyes narrowed accusingly. "You're moving to Atlanta?"

If he'd thought her *eyes* accusing, that paled next to the tone of her voice. She hated him.

Dot's smile slipped and she gave Natalie an odd look. "It would be difficult for him to commute back and forth from Nashville. Of course he's moving here—and we're thrilled to have him."

Natalie didn't look thrilled. She turned alarmed eyes toward Dot. "I thought he was from St. Louis."

Natalie looked panicked, sounded panicked. Well, he'd wanted an answer to his question and now he knew. She hadn't forgotten their weekend together. Far from it.

But why was she afraid of him?

They'd spent a wonderful time together at the walk. An amazing time together at his hotel. Even when they'd said their awkward goodbye nothing had occurred to justify *fear*. Yes, he'd made a fool of himself by doing everything he could to get her to agree to see him again, to get her number so he could call.

But he'd wanted Natalie to want him to contact her, to admit to that want. She never had, and with the way she was reacting now she really hadn't wanted to see him again. He was floored.

"Why would you think that?" Dot asked, glancing back and forth between them. "I never told you Cal was from St. Louis."

Caleb cut in, knowing he needed to explain. "My parents live in St. Louis, so I usually participate in the breast cancer walk there, but I haven't lived there since high school." He glanced toward his innocent-appearing sister-in-law. Had she figured out he had feelings for Natalie? No wonder, with the many times he'd "casually" asked about Natalie.

"St. Louis. Nashville." Dot shrugged. "Either way—" she beamed again, pretending oblivion to the undercurrents "—we're glad you're in Atlanta now. You belong here."

"I'll say." Tired of being ignored, the perky blond next to Natalie stuck out her hand. "Trish Wildes, registered nurse and, for the record, single."

She flashed the kind of welcoming smile Caleb would have liked to see permanently etched onto Natalie's face. A come-hither one.

Natalie gave her colleague a horrified look, re-met Caleb's gaze, glared, then quickly glanced away. "Nice to…uh…see you again. I've got to check on a patient."

Without another word she spun, leaving Caleb to watch her go, wanting to rush after her, but knowing now wasn't the time or the place.

He'd give her time to adjust to the idea of who he really was. Time to adjust to the idea he was going to be a part of her life. Although she'd apparently not wanted their colleagues to know they'd spent the weekend together after they'd met. That they'd shared something special.

At least what they'd shared had been special to *him*.

Judging by the look on her face, he wasn't so sure

Natalie would call memories of their weekend special. More like something that had left a bad taste in her mouth and that she'd really like to forget.

Caleb was Dot's brother-in-law—*Cal.*

Over and over the horrible truth rang through Natalie's head as she forced herself to walk normally down the hospital hallway. She wanted to run, to go lick her wounds in private, assimilate what she'd just learned.

She ducked into an empty room and put her face in her hands, biting back tears.

Caleb was Dot's brother-in-law.

All the blood in Natalie's body drained to her feet, making them heavy, making her head spin.

The precious little girl Dot loved so much was Caleb's daughter.

The darling imp Dot had taken to Disneyland was Caleb's child.

All his raving about the hardships of being a single parent, of how it wasn't easy—and yet he hadn't told her *he* was a single parent.

He'd lied to her about who he was. He'd lied to her about where he lived. He sure hadn't told her he had a wife and child.

All because she'd meant nothing to him. Nothing more than a weekend fling. And men didn't tell weekend flings vital details of their life.

Despite all the warm fuzzies he'd given her, Caleb wasn't anything more than a player. A man who'd been looking for an easy fling that weekend.

His eyes had probably lit up like a Christmas tree when he'd spotted Needy Natalie.

She'd simply been another woman in what was probably a long line of weekend flings.

A fling never meant to last more than a weekend despite the things the jerk had said otherwise.

Caleb had been married, had a daughter. Natalie placed her hand protectively over her flat abdomen.

Her baby had a big sister.

CHAPTER EIGHT

CLASPING the chart she held tightly to her chest, Natalie stared at the individually wrapped oatmeal chocolate chip cookie propped on the nurse's station counter and wanted to scream. Without opening the accompanying card she knew who'd left the goody. The same person who'd been leaving her cookies for several weeks now.

What was Caleb trying to prove?

Better yet, why? *Why* was he going to so much effort to "woo" her when he'd gone to such lengths to keep who he really was hidden from her?

For lack of knowing how she wanted to handle the situation with him, Natalie had attempted to avoid him. She wavered between memories of the man she'd spent time with at the walk and the man she now knew him to be.

When he'd said no realities were allowed that weekend, she hadn't realized he was feeding her a bunch of lies.

Unfortunately he came by the hospital each evening—with Dot or alone. Occasionally he'd show up during the daytime if a patient was admitted. Frequently she'd get a glimpse of him before she took off to a patient's room.

Avoiding him was avoiding going to jail for attacking the hospital's newest doctor.

How could he have lied to her that way? She'd opened up her heart to him, even gone so far as to ask him to give her a baby. No wonder he'd freaked out. He'd known what hospital she worked at, known he'd see her again, and yet he'd deceived her. Which meant he'd either not cared for her at all or he was a perpetual liar. Either way, she was best rid of him.

But Caleb seemed determined to step back into her life.

Time and again he attempted to get her alone, tried to strike up conversations with her—had even asked her out to dinner.

As if.

She'd said no, of course. She would not open her heart to more of his lies and the pain he was capable of inflicting.

That was when the cookies had started showing up.

Homemade oatmeal chocolate chip cookies. Each came plastic-wrapped and bearing a humorous card meant to make her smile. Unfortunately the handwritten messages beneath each funny always prevented her laughter.

"Forgive me."

"I'm sorry."

"I miss you."

"Give us a chance."

"Let me make it up to you."

Natalie picked up the cookie, stuck it in her pocket. She should just start throwing away the cards without even opening them—or, better yet, just leave them on the table unopened. But she tore the envelope open, rolled her eyes at the corny joke, then snorted at the scrawled message in the handwriting that was now so familiar to her.

As much as she'd like to throw the cookies in his face, they were her favorite, and she couldn't tolerate Mrs. Baker's wonderful cookies going to waste.

She didn't have to ask how Caleb had gotten to Mary. The woman adored him, and chattered non-stop about her hero and his darling daughter every time Natalie visited Lydia.

Unfortunately her limited ability to avoid him was coming to a swift end. The new call schedule had gone up earlier this morning. Her reprieve from having to work directly with Caleb was over. If any deliveries came in on the nights he was on call she'd most likely be working with him.

Which meant she was going to have to deal with the flip-flopping emotions warring within her. She wavered between anger, hurt, betrayal, joy at seeing him, and surprise that he had a daughter and hadn't told her. Not even when she'd blurted out that she wanted his baby.

If he'd been waiting for an opportune moment to tell her about Emily, that had been it.

Gritting her teeth, she tore the card in two, and then again, tearing it until the pieces were too small to tear again. She tossed the remains into the trash bin.

Caleb strolled into the hospital thinking that, regardless of the fact he'd not convinced Natalie to forgive him, moving to Atlanta had been the best decision he'd made in years.

Emily loved her new school, and already chatted excitedly about several new friends. Most of all she loved being near her Aunt Dot and her grandparents. Not to mention the instant bond she'd formed with the Bakers and Lydia. The endless supply of homemade cookies hadn't hurt, either.

He'd enjoyed his practice in Nashville, but he found working in Atlanta invigorating—a new challenge. He'd always feared being near Jamie's parents and sister, thinking it would be a constant reminder of what he'd lost. Instead, being near them had left him feeling whole, mentally and emotionally. Seeing his daughter's happiness played a huge role in that. Overall, his move south had gone much more smoothly than anticipated. The only blight in his world was the fact Natalie still pretended he didn't exist.

No, not true. She acknowledged he existed all right— by running away any time she spotted him.

Tonight she wouldn't be able to run.

Not that he blamed her. He should have told her about Emily.

He'd been so floored by Natalie's request to have a baby he hadn't been thinking straight—hadn't told her when he should have. Hell, he should have told her from the very start. Because the more time that had passed the harder it had gotten. He'd been going to tell her that last morning, but little had he known Natalie would leave without a backward glance.

Surely if he explained how he'd felt she would forgive him for everything he'd done wrong that weekend? He'd deceived her about who he really was—a father, a man with as complicated a life as she'd professed to have.

Natalie got off work in another hour, but she wouldn't

leave her patient until the woman delivered. Natalie was that kind of nurse, the kind pregnant women prayed for when their time came. After the woman delivered he'd corner Natalie, convince her to let him explain. Somehow. He'd been patient enough, waited long enough for Natalie to give him another chance.

Trish propped herself against the nurses' station, chomping on a piece of gum and entering data on a flow sheet.

"Hi, Dr. Burton," she said, fluffing her hair when she saw him. "Did you come bearing gifts for a certain nurse?"

"Hey, Trish." He smiled at the pretty blonde and ignored her comment. Although he'd attempted to be discreet with the cookies, he was pretty sure all the maternity ward staff knew he had feelings for Natalie. "I hear Betsy Arnold's water broke during her drive home from work?"

"Yep, she's in room 206. Poor woman is terrified, and was screaming she's changed her mind about having a baby. Her husband's military, and apparently she doesn't have family near. Natalie's in with her right now." She glanced at her watch. "I'm the neonatal nurse. You mind if I sneak out for a quick smoke break?"

"You really need to quit, you know."

Trish nodded, winked, then headed toward the elevators.

"Take your time," he offered. Not only would he get to see Natalie tonight, but they'd work side by side together to bring a new life into existence. The corners of his mouth lifted. Maybe, just maybe, he'd make some headway with the stubborn woman.

Because he was beginning to think his feelings ran

much deeper than he'd realized. Why else would he go to so much trouble?

Eventually she would forgive him. After they got past the awkwardness between them he'd do something he'd never done with a woman he was interested in.

He'd introduce Natalie to his daughter.

"Please, just knock me out and wake me up when it's over." Betsy Arnold, a pretty twenty-year-old with soulful brown eyes and a short-cropped bob, pleaded mournfully, grasping Natalie's wrist in a death-hold worthy of a professional wrestler.

Natalie gave the woman a sympathetic smile.

"Now, now—surely it can't be that bad, or women would have quit having babies ages ago." She gently removed her wrist so she could spoon more ice chips. "Besides, you know it's bad form to say such things to a pregnant woman."

Momentarily distracted from her own misery, as Natalie had been hoping, Betsy's gaze lowered to Natalie's belly. "You don't look it."

Natalie grinned. She fed another spoonful of ice chips to Betsy, put the spoon in the cup, and pulled her top closer to her body, outlining her slightly rounded belly. "But I am. Isn't it wonderful?"

Until the past week she'd barely shown even while naked. But she'd practically gone to bed flat-stomached one night and awakened with a belly the next morning. At her check-up yesterday, Dr. Hogroebe had professed surprise at how much her weight had increased. So much so that she'd ordered another ultrasound.

Betsy gave a cross-eyed grimace as another contraction hit.

"Wonderful," she said on a painful moan. A droplet of sweat ran down her cheek. "When's the doctor going to get here?"

"He's here."

Both women turned at Caleb's voice, but only Natalie's eyes were transformed into saucers. Only Natalie's lower jaw fell to the floor. Only Natalie fought the blackness threatening to overcome her senses.

But she kept her head high, daring him to say anything.

"About time," Betsy complained, but only half-heartedly. Stress and pain at her contractions shone on her face. "I was beginning to think I was going to have to deliver this baby alone."

Caleb seemed frozen to the spot where he stood across the room. His disbelieving gaze flickered to her belly, held there, studying, analyzing what he thought he'd seen. Finally he snapped out of what had held him in place and his gaze shifted to his patient—who fortunately hadn't noticed his odd behavior.

"Alone?" His brow rose. "Natalie is an excellent nurse. She has delivered more than a few babies on her own. Right, Natalie?" His words bit into her delicate composure. "You're in good hands."

Betsy's contraction eased and she sighed in relief. She turned a grateful face toward Natalie. "Yes, Natalie's wonderful. Except she's so bloody cheery. Can't you make her wear a normal person expression?"

Caleb didn't crack a smile at Betsy's comment.

"Cheery? You're in luck." He washed his hands, gloved up, and checked Betsy's cervix. "Stealing your nurse's cheeriness seems to be my area of expertise."

"She's completely effaced," Natalie said, hoping to

change the subject away from *her*. In a delivery room wasn't the time for her and Caleb to discuss the future.

Not that they *had* a future. He'd lied to her. Had never really expected to see her again.

Besides, Betsy was nearing delivery. Had he taken another ten minutes he might have missed the delivery altogether, if things progressed as expected.

"Yes," Caleb agreed. "Dilated to ten. Her cervix is completely effaced. And Junior's head is crowning."

Kicking into professional mode, Caleb and Natalie broke the birthing bed apart and placed Betsy in the stirrups in preparation for what was only short moments away.

She reminded Betsy to breathe, and to focus on what Dr. Burton was telling her. The woman's reprieve was short-lived. Panic filled her eyes.

"Don't push yet," Caleb advised. "Wait until I tell you, when your next contraction hits, then push with all your might."

"I wish Isaiah was here," Betsy cried, sweat beading on her forehead. "I want my husband."

Natalie placed the bed straps within Betsy's reach. "Here. You can squeeze these," she soothed. She scanned the bed. Was there something more she could do? She had to distract her patient from the pain and keep her focused on the task at hand. Worrying about Caleb and how he felt about what he'd seen was *not* her top priority.

Despite the way her knees wobbled at Caleb's nearness, she forced a smile and gently patted Betsy's arm. "Good news is that you won't have to listen to him complain about his bruised fingers for the next few weeks."

Betsy shot her a foul look. "There you go with the cheeriness again."

She smiled for real at her patient's remark.

Betsy's expression tightened. "I feel another contraction coming on," she warned. "Right now."

Natalie glanced at the monitor. "Yes, another's starting. Wait until Dr. Burton gives you the go ahead, then push."

"I feel like I need to push now," she cried, her expression pinched with pain. "There's a horrible pressure down there."

"Not yet," Caleb said. After a few seconds, when the moment was right, he gave the go-ahead. "Push."

Betsy bore down, pushing with all she had. Her belly tight, her face crunched in concentrated agony, her fingers twisted into the sheet.

"Breathe, Betsy," Natalie reminded her from beside the woman. "Breathe."

Caleb had everything he needed close at hand, so she stayed at Betsy's side, encouraging the woman, coaching her in place of her soldier husband.

"I can't breathe," Betsy panted, her belly a taut, contracted ball. "I'm too tired. I need to stop. I can't do this. I'm being torn apart."

"You *can* do this. You will." She checked the monitors, glanced toward Caleb to make sure she hadn't missed anything he might need. As the assigned nurse, Trish should have already come into the room, but she was nowhere to be seen. Natalie double-checked the incubator, ensuring suction gear and any emergency equipment that might be needed for the newborn was within easy reach. Just in case.

Betsy gave a hefty cry, grabbing hold of Natalie's hand and crushing her fingers. "I can't…do this."

But she did.

"Stop pushing, Betsy. The baby's head is out."

Natalie's gaze darted back and forth between her patient and Caleb, who was preparing the baby to finish entering the world.

"I want you to rest until your next contraction hits," Caleb said, without glancing up from between the woman's legs. "When your next contraction starts, push. One more big push, you'll be done. Your baby will be here."

A few minutes later a heartfelt cry filled the room. The sweet, musical cry of a baby announcing his arrival into the world.

The most joyous sound, and one that always touched Natalie's heart. No matter that she'd heard the sound hundreds if not thousands of times. A newborn's first cry was magical.

Soon she'd hear that cry from *her* baby.

"You have a beautiful baby boy," Caleb told Betsy, placing the baby on her belly. "Just a sec and you can hold your son."

Adrenaline pumped through the new mother, leaving the dampness of her hair and skin the only signs of her fatigue from moments before. She strained to get a better look at the red-faced baby wailing on her belly.

When Caleb got the cord clamped and cut, Natalie did a quick assessment on the little boy. "Apgar is ten."

"Perfect," Caleb said, flashing a quick look toward Natalie before returning his attention to Betsy.

Natalie wrapped the squinting, red-faced, whimpering baby in a warm blanket and handed him to his mother for a peek before being taken to the nursery for the works.

"He's beautiful," Betsy said, apparently oblivious to what

Caleb was doing between her legs now that she held the prize of her exhausting efforts. "He looks just like his father."

Natalie's eyes misted, and she gave a soft sniffle.

Would she look into her baby's face for the first time and see the man she'd spent the most wonderful weekend of her life with? The man she'd just worked with to ensure the safe entrance of this gorgeous little guy into the world?

She bit the inside of her lower lip. Would she be just as alone in the delivery room as Betsy?

The new mother wrapped her arms lovingly around the baby. She lifted teary eyes to Natalie. "My camera's there. Will you take a picture so I can send it to Isaiah. Please?"

Natalie glanced at Caleb to make sure he didn't need her assistance. He nodded. She turned on the camera, was glad to see it operated in a similar way to her own, and snapped several photos of the new mother and son.

Betsy's eyes glimmered with pride as she stroked her fingers over the infant's cheek. He reflexively rooted toward his mother's hand, and Betsy cooed sweet words of affection.

Natalie's heart fluttered at the sight of mother and child bonding. A new family.

"Photos aren't as good as the real thing," Betsy said in a soft voice, still staring starry-eyed at her baby, "but at least he'll be able to see what he looks like. I can't wait for him to meet our son."

Natalie blinked back tears, shaking off thoughts of her own pregnancy and refocusing on her patient. She took the baby and suppressed the maternal urges soaring through her at the sweetness of the babe. She handed the tiny bundle to Trish, who'd finally entered the room. Where *had* she been?

Natalie gave her a questioning look, but Trish only shrugged, as if her lateness was no big deal.

"What a cutie," Trish cooed as she took the baby to the nursery for a myriad of tests.

Caleb was telling Betsy to push again, so she could deliver the placenta. Natalie made sure her patient was as comfortable as possible, monitored her blood pressure, vitals and her fluid status.

She'd meant to escape the room before Caleb finished with their patient. But instead Caleb finished first, and appeared to be waiting on her.

Oh, he hid it well—talking with Betsy, praising her efforts and her beautiful son, asking if there was anything he could do to make her hospital stay more comfortable.

No longer in pain, Betsy eyed him with the same adoration most women did.

Pretending to ignore him, Natalie made adjustments to her patient's IV line.

"Anything else I can do for you?" she asked, sensing Caleb's scrutinizing gaze on her. On her belly.

When Betsy shook her head, Natalie headed into the hallway without acknowledging him. She needed out of the room before she suffocated. There would be no more questioning of whether or not Caleb knew about their baby.

"Wait."

His voice chilled her insides. She sped up, but not enough. He caught her before she'd taken two steps outside the birthing room. Grabbing her arm, he grasped her so tightly she winced. She turned enough to let her gaze fall to where he held her.

"Yes, Dr. Burton?" she asked pointedly, glaring at the way he held her. His fingers relaxed, but he didn't let go.

Her heart thundered in her chest.

This was it. He was going to ask about their baby.

What was she going to say? Should she tell him *Caleb, we're having a baby?* How would he react? Would he love their baby? And, if he did, could she forgive him for the lies he'd told her?

"I need to talk to you," he said.

"In regards to your patient?" Mostly she was attempting to buy time, to figure out how she'd respond. Not that she'd figured out a response any of the other million times she'd tried, since she'd looked up and seen him for the first time since she'd left his hotel room.

His gaze dropped to her waistline. To the distinct bump beneath her shirt visible to anyone who cared to look closely.

Caleb looked closely.

He also looked horrified.

"You're pregnant."

CHAPTER NINE

CALEB'S stomach plummeted—much in the way he imagined freefalling from a cliff might feel.

He'd thought he'd misheard Natalie when he walked into Betsy's room. Thought he'd misread what he'd seen.

Hoped he had.

He'd searched her waistline at every opportunity he'd gotten during Betsy's delivery. Had prayed that the soft swell of Natalie's stomach wasn't a baby.

Natalie couldn't be pregnant.

Not his Natalie.

"Of course I'm pregnant," she huffed indignantly, unsuccessfully jerking on her arm. "What did you think? That I'd gained weight?"

Any man worth his salt knew there was no good answer to that particular question.

"I—" Truth was, he *had* noticed she'd gained weight, but she'd been so thin before—too thin. She looked wonderful with the extra pounds. He'd thought her the image of vibrant health.

"You did, didn't you?" she correctly accused him. "You thought I was just getting fat."

"I didn't think that."

She gave him a disgusted look. "If I was, I'd blame you and all those cookies." Hurt flickered, but she quickly masked it, inhaled sharply, and rolled her eyes. "Pardon me. I have patients to attend to."

She attempted to pull free of his hold.

"No." The word was choked from deep in his throat, his voice barely recognizable even to himself.

Natalie's brow lifted. Despite the confident image she showed, her eyes shone bright, a glimmer of tears in the corners. Her lower lip trembled, albeit almost imperceptibly. He'd hurt her yet again. From the moment she'd said she wanted him to give her a baby he'd kept on hurting her.

She'd wanted a baby.

Asked him to give her a baby.

Now she was pregnant.

Remembering the used condom packages he'd gone to toss away, only to have his gaze land on the expiration date—the long past expiration date—Caleb felt his blood drain. His whole body tingled, felt numb.

"Is it mine?"

Her face paled. Her mouth dropped. Her gaze narrowed and speared him with emotions akin to hatred. "I was scheduled for IVF long before we even met. Had already gone and failed two rounds of artificial insemination."

This time his mouth dropped. "Artificial insemination? IVF? What for?"

"I'd think that was obvious." While his shock rendered him stupid, she jerked free and flew down the hallway, ducking into the women's bathroom.

Not in his wildest imaginings had Natalie been pregnant.

No, he'd been imagining her forgiving him, them going to dinner, laughing over drinks. Perhaps he'd convince her to go back to his place, where they could talk in private. Do other things in private.

Natalie was pregnant. On purpose. By in vitro fertilization.

The idea blew him away.

Beautiful, fun, sexy Natalie, who he wanted to have a relationship with, to introduce to Emily, was pregnant.

That changed everything.

Natalie pushed into the bathroom, locked the door, and burst into tears. She'd been holding them in, fighting the overwhelming need to crumble. Fighting the horrific panic settling in.

"Just hormones," she blubbered out loud to herself, refusing to admit Caleb's reaction bothered her.

Is it mine? he'd asked. Urgh!

"What did I expect?" she mumbled under her breath. "A shout for joy? An instant moment of recognition that I'm going to have his baby? No, he believed the IVF thing. How convenient. How typical."

A moment of recognition had crossed his face. One of complete horror—right before he'd asked if her baby was his.

Clearly he didn't want her baby to be his. No surprise there. Not after the way he'd acted when she'd asked him to make her pregnant.

"The jerk."

She pulled off a long roll of the thin white tissue paper, dabbed at her eyes and blew her nose.

"The complete and total jerk."

She squeezed her fists together, hating the moisture streaming down her cheeks. Anger at Caleb fueled the tears as much as hurt. Anger at herself blazed just as strong.

Why was she so upset? Had she wanted to believe he really cared? That he was truly sorry for the lies he'd told her? That there was a chance they could be a family? Caleb, his daughter, Natalie and their new baby? His horrified look had killed the hope she'd foolishly had.

She shouldn't be so upset. She'd gotten what she ultimately wanted. She was pregnant. That was all that mattered.

She was pregnant, and had she hand-selected the finest donor from the fertility clinic she still couldn't have given her baby better genes than Caleb's.

She should be ecstatic. He knew about the baby and had bought her noncommittal response about IVF. She wouldn't be like him—wouldn't lie if he ever pressed. But if she could answer honestly without answering at all— well, that wasn't exactly lying. Not really.

Besides, he didn't *want* to know the truth.

She'd seen the relief in his eyes when she'd mentioned IVF. Relief because he was off the hook.

She'd wanted to hook him.

Right through the gizzard.

Despite the cookies and sweet messages, he didn't care about her. She'd been right. She was a bruise to his big, fat, inflated ego because *she'd* been the one to walk away.

"I've been such a fool."

She'd confused him with the wonderful man she'd spent time with at the walk—the wonderfully attentive, sexy man who'd looked at her with…what, exactly? Lust?

No, something in his gaze had said his feelings for her were more than mere lust. But perhaps that was part of Caleb's allure? When he looked at you, he really looked at you, and that made you feel as if you were special, unique, someone he cared about.

She blew her nose again.

Reality was, she'd been an easy fling.

"You can't stay in there forever."

Dear heavens! He was standing outside the door! Could he hear her sobs? Her ramblings to herself?

She searched her brain, trying to separate what she'd rambled on about in her mind versus actual words with her mouth.

"Says who?" The childish response was so unlike her it took a moment to realize she'd been the one to say the words.

"Me."

To Natalie's surprise the bathroom door was pushed open, despite the fact she'd locked it. She *had* locked it. She knew she had.

"How do you keep getting inside locked doors?"

He shrugged as he closed the bathroom door behind him.

She frowned. "You have no right to come in here." Weak, but the best she could muster at the moment.

"You were crying."

He'd heard.

She raised her chin so high her neck arched. "I always cry after a delivery."

"Uh-huh?" He shook his head, turning the lock back into place.

"Why bother? You've already proved just how easy it is to barge right on in, whether you're welcome or not."

She glared at him, wishing the bathroom didn't suddenly feel so tiny. Wishing she didn't feel so overwhelmed by the man towering next to her.

He reached out to cup her face. Gently, he stroked his thumb along her jaw. "We need to talk."

Why was he touching her? Didn't he know that his merest touch sent shockwaves through her? Probably just aftershocks of the phenomenal sex they'd had, but shockwaves all the same.

"I don't want you to touch me."

His hand fell. "You're pregnant."

He said the words so coldly that another wave of hurt swept through her.

"Yes." She gritted her teeth, steeling herself against the pain. "We established that out in the hallway. Go. Away."

"You were serious when you asked me to make you pregnant."

She arched a brow. "Did you think I wasn't?"

"You caught me so off-guard with your request that perhaps I never truly gave it full credence." His gaze met hers. "We'd only known each other for four days."

She refused to let him corner her. "Yet, as I reminded you that morning, we were in bed together. I felt like I knew you quite well for that to happen—like you knew me quite well. Sorry if my perceptions were mistaken."

"We had a wonderful weekend. The best I've had in a long time. A weekend that I thought was the beginning of a relationship." His pupils constricted to fine pinpoints. "But we hadn't reached the point where a woman asks a man to make her pregnant."

She could remind him that not mentioning he had a

wife and daughter wasn't a great way to start a relationship either, but why bother? At this point she just wanted to be as far away from him as possible.

"Obviously our perceptions of when a woman can ask a man to make her pregnant are vastly different. I think after a couple have already risked pregnancy is as good a time as any."

His skin grew pasty, as if he didn't know quite how to take her comments.

"You weren't a virgin," he ground out. "Surely you haven't asked your other lovers to make you pregnant?"

"No." Now wasn't the time to point out her lack of experience—that she'd only had one other lover. "I didn't ask anyone except you." She gave an overly bright smile. "Thank goodness women don't need a man to get pregnant."

Caleb frowned, crossing his arms. "A woman can't get pregnant without male involvement somewhere along the way."

"And thank goodness not all men feel about pregnancy the way you do, then." She put her hands on her hips, giving him a scathing look. "I asked. You said no. Go away and leave me alone, Caleb. I don't need you anymore."

He grimaced. "You don't mean that. You're just upset."

"Upset?" She furrowed her brows. "You followed me into the ladies' room. Why would I be upset?"

"Being upset isn't good for the baby."

His words stabbed into her heart. "Like you care what's good for my baby. You had your fun, Caleb. Move on to the next score. Maybe Trish would like a weekend romp? Only you'll have to come up with a different line, since she already knows who you really are."

His jaw clenched. "You're pushing it."

"Pushing what? *You?*" She snorted. "I didn't ask you to follow me in here. I haven't asked for one bloody thing except for you to give me a baby, and you said no!"

Her words rushed out, rising in accusation and anger with each syllable.

"Why didn't you tell me you were going for IVF? You should have told me, Natalie."

Of all the nerve.

She snorted. "Why didn't you tell me you had a daughter? That you'd been married? That you are a widower? That you're Dot's brother-in-law?" Each question shot out rapid-fire.

"I deserve that." He nodded, as if he'd been waiting for those questions. "Emily isn't something I talk about with women."

"Women? As in plural?" She shook her head in denial. *She'd known.* So why did his admission twist her stomach into knots? "You have a lot of experience with weekends like the one we shared?"

"No," he admitted, shaking his head in exasperation. "No experience of what we shared. But it's been five years, Natalie. You don't expect me to have been a monk?"

She gritted her teeth to keep from hissing at him. "I don't expect anything where you're concerned. Not one thing."

"Apparently you do, or you wouldn't have been crying."

"That?" She gave a fake laugh, knowing she had to wipe the smug look off his face. She wanted this conversation over. She needed not to be closed in with him, before she shattered into a million bits and he saw the truth. "I told you—I cry after all deliveries."

His narrowed gaze dropped to the bump at her waistline. "I'll be sure to bring my wading boots and a box of tissues when it's time for your own delivery."

Thrusting her chin forward, she glared. "You will not be anywhere near when *my* baby is born."

His forehead wrinkled, and although she'd been expecting a snide remark he surprised her yet again.

"Who *will* be there, Natalie? Not this anonymous IVF donor." The furrows across his forehead deepened with thought. "I'm assuming the guy *was* an anonymous donor?"

She made a non-committal sound.

"Who's going to be with you when you bring your baby into the world?"

Good question. But not one she'd dissect with him watching her so intently.

"Perhaps you have me mistaken for some needy, clingy hothouse flower? Think again. I don't need anyone with me," she said huffily. "I don't need anyone, period. Not at my delivery, not ever, and certainly not you."

"Sure you do, Natalie." The insufferable man did the unthinkable. He brushed his fingertip over her lower lip in a sweep that was so soft, so gentle, it could only be called tender. "We all need someone from time to time."

"Not me," she denied, jerking her chin away from his fingers.

He laughed softly. "You don't really believe that."

"You know nothing about me."

"I know enough," he pronounced smugly.

"You know nothing."

"Go to dinner with me tonight, so you can enlighten me about all the things I don't know," he countered smoothly.

Natalie backed up against the sink counter and stared at him. How did he keep doing that? Surprising her?

"But I…I'm pregnant," she stammered, wondering why he asked, why he'd want to go to dinner with her now.

He shrugged. "And I'm a widower and have a five-year-old daughter. It's only dinner. Say yes."

"Why would you want to take me to dinner?" she asked suspiciously.

He paused for a long time. "Maybe we can be friends?"

The bathroom began closing in on her again. She placed her hand on the sink to balance herself. "We can't be friends."

"Why not?"

Because I'm pregnant with your baby! "Because we can't. That's not who I am or how I operate."

"You can't be my friend because we had sex?"

He made it sound ridiculous.

"Something like that."

"You're no longer friends with your past lovers?"

"Lover," she blurted out. "Bob and I are cordial, but not what you'd call friends. Not really."

Oh, Lord.

Caleb's eyes narrowed, honing in on the fact she'd come to some profound conclusion—something that shocked her.

"You've only had one lover?" he asked softly, sounding a little shocked himself.

Why had she opened her big mouth?

"Besides you." She glanced down at the floor tile, at the scrubbed-clean grout.

"Why didn't you tell me?"

"I think we've already established that neither of us

revealed pertinent details of our lives. Besides, it isn't any of your business how many lovers I've had. Nor is it any of *my* business how many lovers *you've* had."

He named a number much lower than she would have guessed.

"Didn't you hear me? I said that information isn't any of my business."

"I disagree."

Wearying of their going back and forth, she closed her eyes, took a deep breath. "What is it you want from me?"

He placed his thumb beneath her chin. "I'm not sure. Why did you have to get pregnant *now?*"

He sounded like a whiny child who'd just been denied his favorite toy.

"Why not now?"

"Because I want you—"

"But now I'm pregnant you don't?"

His pupils narrowed in surprise at her question, his expression growing tortured. "That's the hell of it. Even knowing you're pregnant, I do. I've missed you, Natalie. Friend, lover—however you'll have me, I want you."

This time it was Natalie's turn to be surprised.

CHAPTER TEN

AT THE end of her shift, Natalie grabbed her jacket and the oversized purse she had filled with everything she might need. A small first aid case. A sewing kit. Her wallet. Her cellphone. A small flashlight. A package of peanut butter crackers. Even bottled water. What she quickly discovered she *didn't* have was an excuse to tell Caleb no when she saw him propped against her car.

He'd said he still wanted her—or at least he thought he did—even though she was pregnant.

After she'd met him, her reasons for walking away from Caleb, for not wanting to see where their attraction would take them, had been based upon her desire for a baby. But now, thanks to him, she was pregnant.

What reason did she have not to go to dinner with him? Not to spend time with him?

He'd lied to her. But what if he truly regretted having done so? And weren't his lies similar to her own?

Lies of omission?

He hadn't *said* he was from St. Louis. She'd assumed it and he hadn't corrected her. He hadn't *said* he'd never been married, that he didn't have a daughter. She'd assumed it.

Perhaps she should give him another chance. After all, he had gone to a lot of effort to convince her to forgive him. Even if his efforts *had* been fueled by the need to soothe his ego.

Perhaps he did deserve a second chance. Besides, wouldn't having memories of her baby's father be important later on? Wouldn't her child want to know what its father had been like? Wouldn't he or she want to know as many details as Natalie could share?

Which meant Natalie couldn't say no.

Yet, when her gaze met his, she found herself wanting to run.

Which was ridiculous. She wasn't a timid person. Wasn't a runner. She was a fighter. Just ask anybody.

So why had she spent the last few weeks running from Caleb?

As much as she wanted to buy that it all had to do with the baby, she couldn't convince herself.

"You ready?" he asked, when she stood a few feet away. He'd changed out of his scrubs into loose jeans and a T-shirt advertising "PEACE." He looked more like a hunky college kid than a revered physician.

He took her breath away.

"Are you sure our going to dinner is a good idea?"

"I have to eat. You have to eat. Once upon a time we enjoyed each other's company." He grinned a lopsided smile that added to his appeal. "Only makes sense that we dine together."

"After the walk, you never meant to see me again." She wasn't sure why she was being so confrontational when she'd just decided she should spend time with him. For the baby.

She'd gone from running to attacking.

Perhaps because she wanted to throw herself into his arms, smother him with kisses, place his palms on her belly and let him feel their baby.

"I very specifically recall telling you that I *wanted* to see you again." He straightened from where he leaned against the car. "I told you several times."

She snorted. "We both know you were just saying that because you wanted to get into my pants."

He frowned. "Is that what you believe?"

Did she? He'd said he wanted to see her again even *after* he'd gotten into her pants. Truthfully, she had to admit that maybe she did believe him and that she was wrong. Perhaps he *had* wanted to see her again?

He didn't wait for her answer, just took her hand in his before she could lodge a protest.

Caleb followed Natalie's gaze as it dropped to her belly. She was pregnant. Part of him had difficulty computing that. He was pretty sure part of him was in denial, too.

He dealt with pregnant women every day. It was what obstetricians did. But there was a part of him he kept locked deep inside. The part that blamed himself for getting Jamie pregnant. The part of him that whispered she'd still be alive if not for him.

Of course there was Emily to consider. He couldn't imagine life without his daughter. She *was* his life. His whole world.

What women were willing to risk to hang on to their pregnancies scared him. Yet wouldn't he give his own life for Emily without a second thought?

* * *

Dinner with Caleb started awkwardly, self-consciously, but with his easy smile and good conversation he quickly had Natalie relaxing.

By the time he'd convinced her to order dessert she was almost as at ease with him as she'd been during the walk.

Which scared her. She needed to keep on her guard around him, to watch what she said, to protect her baby.

"Is the baby kicking?"

Natalie's mouth opened to deny him, wondering why he'd ask about the baby when throughout the evening they'd avoided mentioning her pregnancy. Then she realized her gaze had lowered, her hand had dropped to the swell of her belly.

She smiled softly, but didn't comment. He didn't know the exact timing of her pregnancy—didn't realize it was too soon for her to feel the baby's movements.

"What made you decide you wanted a baby, Natalie?"

"I've always wanted a baby," she immediately countered.

"But why now? Why not wait? Go about it the old-fashioned way?"

A million responses ran through her mind, ranging from telling him it was none of his business to telling him the truth. Already too many secrets lay between them. She wouldn't add another.

"My life priorities changed after the car wreck last fall."

"That doesn't explain why you'd go through IVF to get pregnant."

"The wreck damaged my pelvis, and scar tissue formed on my uterus. Dr. Hogroebe told me at my last check-up that I'd probably end up infertile."

Caleb's face softened compassionately, and he reached across the table to touch her cheek. "I'm sorry."

"Don't be. It could have been much worse. I could have already been infertile." She spread her fingers over her belly. "Right now I feel like the luckiest girl alive."

"Because you're with me?" he teased, hinting that he'd regained a semblance of the comfort they'd previously shared as well.

"Because I'm pregnant." *With your baby,* she silently added.

"Was the reason you didn't want to see me again because of your plans to get pregnant?"

She nodded. "The timing wasn't great for starting a relationship."

A serious look came over his face. "Why didn't you tell me why you wanted to get pregnant that morning?"

Her heart quickened. "Would knowing have changed your answer?"

"No," he answered, so quickly she knew it was the truth. "I really don't want more children."

Natalie was saved from having to answer by the waiter showing up with their desserts in hand. He placed an apple streusel with a generous dollop of vanilla ice cream in front of her.

"I shouldn't eat this. Dr. Hogroebe says I'm gaining too much weight."

"You look beautiful, Natalie."

Heat flushed her face at his compliment. Being with Caleb *did* make her feel beautiful. It was how he looked at her. Like she truly was beautiful in his eyes.

Needing to put some distance between them, she changed the subject the moment the waiter walked away.

"Tell me about your daughter."

"Emily?"

"Unless you have another daughter you forgot to mention?" Her words came out harsher than she'd meant them to, and he winced. "I'm sorry—" she began, not wanting the tension to return.

"No." He shook her apology away. "I deserved that. Emily's five, in kindergarten, and she's my whole world. She looks just like her mother."

Glancing down at her plate, Natalie spooned a bite of streusel and ice cream. The rich dessert melted in her mouth, but she barely tasted it. She wondered at the woman who'd once held Caleb's heart, at the little girl who still did. She'd seen the photos Dot had taken at Disneyland. Emily was a dark-haired imp with even darker eyes. Her mother's eyes?

"She's full of spunk." Caleb's voice held pride as he talked of Emily's school, her friends, her natural knack for music, about her excitement at living in Atlanta and being close to her aunt and grandparents.

He practically glowed with love for his daughter.

How could he love Emily so much and not want anymore children?

Natalie loved how his eyes lit, how his face showed such animation as his love for Emily shone through. Any child would be lucky to have such a father. She wanted *her* child to have his love.

"Are you sure you don't want more children?"

The light faded from his eyes. "Positive."

She tried to hide her disappointment, but likely failed. "Is being a father so horrible?"

"Being a father is amazing—the greatest thing I've ever done—but I don't plan on doing it again."

Because he'd loved Jamie and didn't want a child with anyone other than the woman he'd given his heart to? The thought stung, but Natalie couldn't fault him for having loved his wife so much.

Yet he *was* going to have another child.

Would Caleb see their baby as an insult to his wife's memory? An insult to his daughter?

Could she forgive him if he did?

Caleb knocked on Natalie's apartment door, pacing across the stairwell while he waited for her to answer.

He'd dropped her at her car, offered to follow her home, but she'd refused. Perhaps she'd thought he'd push to come inside?

She might be right. Why else would he have sat in his car debating whether or not to go up?

Why else had he come up? Knocked on her door?

Really he should put Natalie out of his mind and heart. She was pregnant.

He still couldn't believe it. He'd met a woman who made him feel whole and she'd gotten pregnant. On purpose.

The mere idea of it gave him hives.

Judging from the size of her belly, she must have gone for IVF immediately after they'd met. Or already been pregnant.

Which would explain the "complicated" life she'd mentioned at the walk.

He'd not planned to become emotionally involved with another woman. Not after Jamie. Particularly not a pregnant woman.

Part of him had wanted to get the hell out of Dodge when he'd seen her belly.

Another part had wanted to shake her and ask her how she could do that to him.

Another part had welled with worry that *he'd* made her pregnant.

He couldn't quite let go of that part.

His condoms had been out of date.

He pulled on the collar of his T-shirt. How could the cotton material suddenly be cutting off his air supply? Making his palms sweat?

Stepping back in front of her door, he knocked again. Harder.

He needed to accept Natalie's explanation and be done with it. Be done with *her.*

She was right.

They couldn't be friends.

Deciding she wasn't going to answer the door, he turned to leave.

"Caleb?" Natalie said through her cracked open door. "What are you doing here?"

Seeing her did funny things to his insides.

"Hi." Did he sound like the world's biggest dork? "I came up to make sure you got home okay."

A short pause.

"Yes, I'm fine." Her brows drew together. "Are you okay?"

Not really. He felt raw, torn apart inside. *Leave. Leave now and be done with it. You can't deal with having feelings for a pregnant woman. Not after what you went through with Jamie,* the voice inside his head warned.

But what if Natalie's baby is yours?

What if you made her pregnant?

Even if you didn't, can you really walk away when she's alone? When she obviously needs you?

Although she looked tentative, she removed the chain and opened the door. "Come inside."

He stepped into Natalie's living room, his hands crammed into the front pockets of his jeans.

With her arms crossed over her breasts, she stayed on the opposite side of the comfy living room, with its over-stuffed furniture, homey throw pillows and various knick-knacks on shelves.

He curled his fingers into his palms, painfully digging his fingernails into his flesh. "Tell me about your IVF."

Her eyes grew huge. "Excuse me?"

"Tell me when you decided to go for IVF. When you picked out your donor. How you chose him. When you had your eggs harvested. When you had the embryos placed. I want to know everything."

She looked at him as if he'd gone mad. "Why?"

Good question. One he wasn't sure he had a good answer for.

Frustrated, he glanced around the living room. His gaze landed on the coffee table.

A coffee table laden with baby items. A fuzzy blue teddy bear. A rattle. A pair of white booties. A multi-colored pastel crochet baby blanket.

She followed his gaze. "Lydia and Mary gave them to me. Every time I visit they send me home with more gifts. I've asked them to stop, but they just keep finding things the baby 'has to have.'"

His baby? He picked up the bear, closed his eyes.

Emotion squeezed his insides, nearly blinding him. Sweat covered his skin and he gripped the bear in tightly closed fists.

Had Natalie really had IVF?

He tossed the bear back onto the table and without a glance toward her headed toward the door. "I've got to go."

Natalie lay on the exam table, shivering as the sonographer squirted a cold conducive gel on her belly.

"You said you wanted to know the sex of the baby?" The sonographer put the wand on her belly and rolled until he found the position he wanted.

"Oh, yes." Excitement surged through her.

Soon, very soon, she'd know if her baby was going to be a boy or a girl.

The sonographer gasped.

Something was wrong. Natalie searched the monitor, trying to figure out what he saw.

Dear Lord.

Without the sonographer saying a word, Natalie knew exactly what had caused his gasp.

"How's this possible?" she asked, her eyes wide, her hand on her temple as the gravity of what she was seeing hit her.

His gaze on the screen, the sonographer continued to run the instrument over Natalie's abdomen. "You know I'm not supposed to discuss this with you. Dr. Hogroebe is supposed to be the one to tell you my findings."

"Hello?" Natalie snapped her fingers, causing the technician to glance at her. "There are two babies on that screen. Tell me how that's possible."

The man shrugged. "It's not uncommon for more than one embryo to take during IVF. You know that. Surely they prepared you for the possibility during the early stages of your fertility treatment?"

Except she'd never made it to the egg-harvesting stage, much less to the implanting of live embryos.

But she *had* been on the medication to cause her to release multiple eggs for harvesting. Why hadn't she ever considered the possibility that more than one egg might have been fertilized?

That Caleb might have given her more than one baby?

She was having twins.

"But why hasn't Dr. Hogroebe heard two heartbeats when she's listened with the Doppler?"

Pausing the instrument to take measurements of what was now labeled Baby One, the sonographer shrugged again. "There are lots of possibilities. You aren't far along, so one could have been hiding behind scar tissue—or perhaps even the other baby."

"At least this explains why I'm gaining more weight than normal," Natalie mused. She'd been so ecstatic over being pregnant that she'd never considered the possibility she might have conceived multiple babies.

"Perhaps Dr. Hogroebe suspected as much, and was verifying her suspicions by ordering this ultrasound. I'm going to finish, make you a copy of the ultrasound, then call her to come have a look."

Dumbfounded, Natalie nodded. She'd prayed for a baby, prayed for a family. She'd been blessed with not just one baby, but two.

Caleb might not want more children, but his family tree had just added a couple of new branches.

Her heart squeezed at the thought of him.

Since the night he'd come to her apartment their roles had completely reversed. He no longer sought her out. No longer left cookies with messages.

Instead, he'd taken to avoiding her when possible.

She'd worked with him on two deliveries since Betsy's,

but he'd remained coolly aloof, professional. He'd shown no signs of anything personal having happened between them. When she'd attempted to talk to him he'd brushed her off, saying he had to go pick up Emily.

"By the way—" the sonographer cut into her thoughts "—looks like both babies are boys."

Boys. She and Caleb were having sons.

Correction, *she* was.

Caleb didn't want their children. She'd never force them upon him—never expose her boys to a father who didn't want them.

Still, she'd count her blessings.

Not only was she having Caleb's son, she was having two.

Two healthy babies. Natalie could hardly wait to tell her friends, to tell Dot.

Caleb would no doubt hear of her news. What would he say when he heard she was having twins?

He'd probably be doubly glad he'd ended things, if that was what his visit to her apartment had been about.

Caleb and Dot's practice was located on an adjacent lot to the hospital, and Natalie walked over to the clinic. She supposed she could call, so she wouldn't bump into Caleb, but she didn't.

Just because he didn't want to be a part of her life, her babies' lives, it didn't mean she'd cower away or avoid Dot. She wanted to tell her friend her good news.

The lobby was filled with a mixture of pregnant women. A few had small children playing in a corner that was equipped with puzzles and playthings. A partitioned area was set up as a breastfeeding area.

"Hi, Elaine," Natalie greeted the receptionist who'd accompanied she and Dot to lunch on several occasions.

Elaine smiled. "You here to see Dot? Go on back to her office. I'll let her know you're here."

"Natalie?" Dot said, spotting her the moment she stepped out of an exam room. Her friend looked her up and down, concern in her eyes. "Are you okay?"

Natalie nodded. "Better than okay."

Dot's eyebrow rose. "Oh?"

"I'm having twins!" Saying the words out loud caused thrilled goosebumps to coat her skin. "Can you believe it?"

"Twins?" Dot's eyes widened. "Natalie, that's wonderful."

Dot wrapped her in an excited hug and they danced giddily around. "You went for your ultrasound today? That's when you found out? Twins! Oh, tell me everything."

Natalie pulled the CD from her purse. "Better yet, I'll show you."

"Caleb," Dot said, as another exam room door opened and a tall man in blue scrubs stepped into the hallway. His gaze immediately met Natalie's and he froze.

"Come congratulate Natalie," Dot ordered him. "She's having twins. Isn't that fabulous?"

Fabulous? Natalie being pregnant, period, fell way short of fabulous—but *twins?*

Twins tremendously increased the risks that went along with pregnancy.

Natalie's bright smile faded. Guilt hit him. He should be happy for her, because truth was, despite how miserable he felt, he wanted her to be happy. Being pregnant made Natalie happy.

Selfishly, he cringed, though.

Twins. Natalie was pregnant with twins. Multiple births were consistent with IVF. Which meant there was less possibility of him being the father. *But she'd been on fertility drugs.*

He grimaced. No, Natalie had said she'd gotten IVF.

"Caleb?" Dot scowled at him, looking back and forth between him and Natalie.

He shoved aside his own misgivings and forced a smile to his face. "Congrats."

Long lashes swept across her cheeks as she glanced down, refusing to meet his gaze any longer. "Thank you."

"Natalie was just about to show me her ultrasound. You want to watch?"

Caleb had seen numerous ultrasound videos during his career—a multitude. Had even done what probably numbered in the thousands in his own office. An ultrasound was no big deal. But he'd rather have his toenails yanked off than view *this* particular ultrasound.

"Uh—no, thanks. I need to finish with my morning patients so I can run by the hospital at lunch."

Dot's brows moved together in a telltale motion that said she saw right through him.

Natalie didn't look up. The excitement that had glowed on her face when he'd stepped into the hallway was gone. In its place was... He couldn't quite label the emotion weighing her down. Sorrow, perhaps?

"Fine. Your loss," Dot said, lacing her arm with Natalie's. "Come on, sweetie. I can't wait to see your babies. Did you find out what you were having? Boys or girls? Or both?"

With one brief glance his way, Natalie nodded. "Boys. Both babies are boys."

They disappeared into Dot's office.

Natalie was pregnant with twin boys.

Natalie sat in the train-themed nursery she'd so lovingly prepared in her spare bedroom and rocked back and forth to Beethoven. Every night she rocked while listening to different musical compositions that reportedly increased babies' intelligence by enhancing synapse production in the brain. Her babies would have every advantage she could give them.

She couldn't believe she was already thirty-three weeks pregnant. Well, looking at her huge belly she'd believe she was a *hundred* weeks pregnant.

She'd seen Dr. Hogroebe just that morning, and everything was going wonderfully with her babies. Unfortunately the obstetrician wanted her to go on medical leave from her job, due to the high risk of early labor.

Medical leave. Thanks to not having to do the IVF she still had some savings, but her funds wouldn't last long. Unfortunately she had very little paid time off built up. Not after the weeks she'd been out following her car wreck.

Somehow she'd manage, though. Where there was a will there was a way. Already Lydia and the Bakers had requested babysitting privileges when Natalie returned to work.

She hated the thought of how soon she'd have to go back, but providing for her children meant more than just physically being there. There would be diapers to buy— lots of diapers—and formula to supplement her breast-feeding. She desperately wanted to breastfeed her boys for at least the first six weeks, if not longer. Statistically, babies who were breastfed the first six weeks of life had higher intelligence, less illness, and even less risk of cancer later in life.

Earlier, Lydia had asked her about names. Natalie couldn't decide. Deep in her heart she wanted to use Caleb's name, but that would never do.

Rarely did a work day go by that she didn't see him. But chasms separated them, even when they were in the same room. Guilt ate at her for not telling him, but she honestly believed he wouldn't hear her even if she did.

He didn't want to know the truth.

From the living room, her phone rang. The time was only a little after nine, but she didn't generally get calls this late.

"I woke you?"

"Caleb?" She didn't bother to hide her surprise. "I wasn't asleep," she assured him. Her heart automatically expanded with renewed hope.

"Dot told me you had a doctor's appointment today."

"Yes." Why had he called? For weeks now he'd pretended she didn't exist. "She said Dr. Hogroebe wants you to go on leave from the hospital."

"Apparently my cervix is starting to efface—but fortunately no dilation."

"You should be on bed rest."

"Bed-rest? With twins? I know it's coming, but I'm not ready for that yet. I'll do as Dr. Hogroebe says and go on leave starting next week."

"Next week? Why not now?" he demanded.

"She gave me permission to finish out the week, so the nursing director can make arrangements for someone to cover me."

"You can't go to work when you should be on bed-rest."

She pushed her hair behind her ear, changed the phone to the opposite ear. "I'm pregnant, Caleb, not an invalid."

"Twins are a high-risk pregnancy. Being on your feet for long periods is not good for you or the babies."

"Everyone has been wonderful in the maternity department," she said defensively. "When I've needed a break, I've taken one."

He acted as if she were purposely trying to make something go wrong, when the truth was the exact opposite. She was doing everything she could to ensure healthy babies. She'd asked Dr. Hogroebe point-blank if it was okay for her to finish out the week. She'd said it was fine.

"Besides, what do you care? My babies have nothing to do with you."

She'd swear static crackled over the phone line.

She'd have thought he'd hung up, except there was no resounding click, no recorded message telling her to hang up and dial again.

"You're right." Anger laced his words. "I shouldn't have called. Goodnight, Natalie."

CHAPTER ELEVEN

THE next evening Natalie caught a glimpse of Caleb, but he was on his way to a delivery and she wasn't assigned to that patient. She waited around for a while after her shift had ended, then decided she was being silly. His call hadn't meant anything.

She went home and binged on Mary's oatmeal chocolate chip cookies. Her friend fixed weekly care packages. Reportedly for the boys.

The following afternoon, Natalie went to lunch with Dot.

Once they were seated at a semi-private table in the hospital cafeteria, Dot poked a straw into her glass of milk.

"So, I've been more than patient, but I'm tired of playing guessing games. What's going on between you and my brother-in-law?"

Natalie forced her gaze to remain on the vegetable soup and sodium-free crackers she'd chosen in the cafeteria line. "Nothing is going on. What makes you ask?"

"Oh, just the fact that he asks me about you, asks about the babies."

"That's just his being concerned about a co-worker."
Caleb asked about her and the babies?

"Yeah, right. Why doesn't he just ask *you?*"

Natalie's stomach fluttered in ways that had nothing to
do with the aroma rising from her soup. "How am I
supposed to know?"

"Oh, you know, all right."

She didn't want to talk about Caleb. Not with Dot. Not
with anyone. What was she supposed to say? That she'd
met him, fallen head-over-heels, gotten pregnant, and been
blown away when he had re-entered her life? That he'd
wanted a relationship with her until he'd found out she was
pregnant? That he'd blindly accepted she'd had IVF?

"You're not going to tell me?" Dot leaned forward and
stared a hole into the top of Natalie's head. "If you're
worried I'm going to be upset, you're wrong."

Natalie looked up and met her friend's expectant stare.
"What do you mean?"

"Oh, don't give me that. There's something going on
between the two of you. I figured that out the moment I
discovered you'd met each other at the walk. Cal asked
about you. Repeatedly. It may have taken him a few
months to get relocated here, but he wasn't taking any
chances on you finding someone else in the meantime."

"I didn't know he was your brother-in-law when we
met."

"Would it have made a difference if you'd known he'd
been married to my sister?"

"Yes." But not the way Dot probably meant. If Caleb had
told her the truth about who he was she might have taken him
seriously—might not have felt used, might have contacted
him to tell him about her pregnancy, to say she missed him.

She *did* miss him.

"He's a good man, Natalie. From the moment he met my sister he didn't have eyes for anyone else." Dot shrugged one elegant shoulder. "You know, I thought if Cal moved to Atlanta I could somehow be closer to Jamie— make her more alive to me, to Emily, maybe even to Cal."

"Oh, Dot." Natalie wasn't sure what else to say.

"What am I doing?" Dot frowned. "I shouldn't be laying this on you. All I wanted was to tell you to give Cal a chance. He deserves to be happy."

Give Caleb a chance? As if he'd let her. "What makes you think I can make him happy?"

"Because he looks at you the way he looked at Jamie. He doesn't see anyone else when you're in the room, Natalie. Doesn't even know any other woman exists. He's fallen for you."

"You're mistaken," Natalie denied, unable to hold in her laugh. "I won't deny he was attracted to me, but that was before he found out I was pregnant. My pregnancy killed any feelings he had for me."

"Which is why I'm being interrogated by him following your doctor's appointments?" Dot stared at her with serious eyes.

"He's an obstetrician. I'm pregnant with twins. It's a professional thing."

Dot rolled her eyes. "Okay, if you're not ready to talk about it yet, fine. I'm here when you are."

Later that evening, Natalie found herself standing speechless in front of Caleb's daughter. Dot had brought the dark-haired darling to the hospital.

The child had stick-straight shiny black hair that was

pulled away from her face with two lilac barrettes that matched her jumper. Her eyes were so inky dark they appeared to be black. Her smile was pure Caleb.

"Emily," Dot said to her niece, "this is my good friend Natalie. I've told her lots of wonderful things about you, and she's wanted to meet you for a long time."

Natalie's throat tightened. What was Dot doing?

Emily's eyes never swayed from Natalie's belly. Natalie's very round belly. "Are you having a baby?"

Giving Dot a questioning look, Natalie pulled herself together and smiled at the child. Caleb might think Emily looked like Jamie, but Natalie saw strong traces of him in Emily's features. Especially in her expressions.

Would their sons have similar expressions?

"Yes," she answered, hoping her voice didn't warble. "I'm having a baby in just a couple of months. Actually, I'm having two."

Your brothers.

"Two?" Emily's black eyes widened. "My friend Macy's mom had a baby, but she only had one."

"Oh? Does Macy have a baby brother or a sister?"

"A sister. She got to wear a special shirt that says she's a big sister."

"A T-shirt, huh? That is pretty special." Natalie smiled at the precious little girl. At that moment one of the babies gave a hearty kick into her ribs, and she placed her hand over the area. Her belly shifted beneath her palm.

Emily's eyes grew even wider. "Are your babies trying to get out?"

Natalie and Dot both laughed.

"No," Natalie assured her. "I think he just heard your voice and wanted to say hello."

"Really?" The idea fascinated Emily. She eyed Natalie's belly with renewed interest. "Hello, in there." She giggled, leaning close. "I'm Emily."

Natalie glanced up, caught Dot's eye, and for a moment thought her friend knew everything. Was that why Dot had taken such an interest in her after the breast cancer walk? Quickly Natalie glanced away, focusing on the giggling little girl addressing her belly.

"Would you like to feel him kick?"

Emily's eyes lit up like a Christmas tree. "Can I really? I promise to be very careful."

Taking Emily's hand, Natalie placed the tiny palm over the spot where Junior was practicing for the NFL.

"Oh!" Emily burst into excited laughter. When she looked up at her aunt her eyes were wide with wonder. "He kicked my hand."

"What are you doing?"

Natalie, Dot and Emily all turned startled eyes toward Caleb's thunderous boom.

"I finished up at the office and needed to make rounds so I brought Emily with me," Dot explained, her defensive stance daring him to make a big deal of it.

But he didn't look at Dot. He stared straight at Natalie, as if *she'd* orchestrated the meet. All along he'd kept Emily from her—didn't trust her with knowledge of his daughter, much less to actually meet her. His anger rammed that fact home. He didn't want her anywhere near his child.

"Daddy, Natlee's baby kicked me!"

Caleb's angry gaze left Natalie's face and dropped to his daughter. His expression momentarily softened. "Why don't you go with Aunt Dot?"

"But, Daddy—"

"Emily, remember the rules for when you're in a hospital. You have to listen the first time I tell you something. Now, go with Aunt Dot and wait with her until I come to get you."

Emily frowned at her father, gave one last lingering look at Natalie's belly, then went with her aunt, pausing briefly to wave at Natalie.

"Bye, Natlee. Bye, babies."

Dot gave an apologetic look to Natalie, and looked like she might say something to Caleb. But she changed her mind, took Emily's hand and led her away.

The moment little ears were out of reach, Natalie scowled at him. "What is *wrong* with you? All she did was feel one of the babies kick."

His expression remained stony. "Dot shouldn't have brought her here."

"Why not? Because you didn't want her to meet me?"

He didn't respond.

"For someone who said so much a few minutes ago, you sure don't have much to say at the moment." She spun on her heels and headed to a patient's room.

Caleb knew he'd messed up the moment the words flew out of his mouth when he spotted Emily's hands on Natalie's belly.

His first thought had been that Natalie had told his daughter about them. Hadn't Emily been asking for a baby brother or sister since her schoolfriend began bragging about how grand it was to be a big sister? He wished this new phase would hurry up and wear off, and the big sister blues would kick in. Maybe add in a little sibling jealousy, so Macy would change her tune. Perhaps then so would Emily.

"Open mouth, insert foot," Dot whispered, as he entered the break room where she'd taken his daughter. Emily sat at a table, drawing a picture with crayons and paper from her schoolbag.

"You shouldn't have brought Emily here. You had no right."

"Why not?" Dot played innocent. "Bringing her here saved you from having to go back by the clinic."

"I didn't mind having to go back by the clinic."

"Caleb, that's ridiculous. I had to check on a lady before going home anyway."

"I don't want Emily here."

"Why not?"

Caleb watched his daughter, realized she was drawing a pregnant woman. A pregnant woman with short blond hair and big blue eyes. Natalie.

"I don't understand why you didn't want Natalie to meet Emily. But then I don't understand a lot of the things you're doing lately. You ask about her, stare at her when you think no one is looking, and yet you ignore her when it's obvious there's something between you."

Caleb blinked. "It's not that. Keep your voice down."

Both of their gazes went to Emily, who seemed content with her drawing. For the moment, at any rate.

"Then what is it?" Dot whispered. "No, don't tell me—because I know. It's not that you don't want Natalie to meet Emily; it's that you didn't want Emily to meet Natalie."

Caleb winced, wanting to deny Dot's claim but unable to.

"Let me get this straight. You've been involved with Natalie for months—and don't you *dare* try denying that you have feelings for her—but you're too ashamed of her to introduce her to your daughter?"

"I'm not ashamed of Natalie."

"Then what?"

He didn't want to tell her, but Dot wouldn't quit. "I don't want Emily hurt."

"Natalie would never hurt Emily."

"Not intentionally."

"What are you talking about?"

"Natalie is *pregnant*."

"Yes, so what? Emily likes babies."

"It would be easy for Emily to become attached to Natalie."

"What would be the problem with that? Natalie's a lovely person." Enlightenment dawned in her eyes. "You think something might happen to Natalie, don't you?"

"Nothing's going to happen to her."

But something in the way he said the words caused Dot's gaze to narrow.

"It's not Emily you're worried about getting hurt, is it, Caleb? It's *you*. Keeping some distance between Emily and Natalie is a way of holding Natalie at arm's length. You're using your daughter as a barrier." Dot gave him a disbelieving look. "Shame on you."

"You're insane."

"No, you are. And if you're not careful you're going to lose the best thing that's happened to you since my sister and Emily."

"My blood pressure's *what?*" Natalie asked, sure she'd misheard Trish's reading. She'd suffered with a headache all morning, but figured stress had triggered it. Today was her last day of work until after the babies arrived. But when she'd noticed her socks were digging into her ankles she hadn't been able to ignore the headache any longer, and had asked Trish to check her pressure.

"A hundred and sixty over ninety."

Natalie's heart lurched. "That can't be right. Take it again."

She thrust her arm out toward Trish. Unfortunately anxiety-induced adrenaline pumped through her body over the first reading, shooting her pressure up even higher.

Looking worried, Trish patted her scrubs pocket, obviously remembered she'd quit smoking, and grunted with frustration. "You need to call your doctor."

"I can't. Dr. Hogroebe is out of town."

"Who's covering for her? I'll call for you," Trish offered.

"Dr. Watson and Dr. Burton, but don't call. I probably just ate something I shouldn't have, and that's why my pressure is up."

Or it was due to the fact that she hadn't slept well since the night Caleb had called—that she'd cried hours on end last night because the father of her babies truly didn't want her to have any interaction with his daughter.

"You should get checked. This could be the first sign of toxemia."

"I'm fine," Natalie denied. No way did she have toxemia, also known as pre-eclampsia. Everything was just fine with her pregnancy. "Just too much sodium, I'm sure."

Had she even *eaten* anything with salt? She was watching her diet, making sure she ate healthily, giving her babies every advantage she could.

"Unless you licked the saltshaker dry, I'm not buying that." Trish shook her head. "We're not real busy at the moment. Go put your feet up, and I'll keep a watch on your patient. If anything changes I'll come get you."

She started to deny the need to, but Trish pointed toward the break room.

"If not for you then for your babies. Go sit down."

When it was put that way, Natalie couldn't argue.

Unfortunately the thought that her pressure was up worried her, and made her symptoms worse. Her temples pounded like banging cymbals. She needed to relax and decrease her pressure. A few minutes of rest and she'd be as good as new.

Propping her feet in the chair next to her, she leaned back, closed her eyes, and practiced the relaxation techniques she'd learned during nursing school. Everything was fine. It was just a fluke that her blood pressure was up. She did *not* have toxemia.

She repeated the phrase over and over, using the words as a calming mantra.

"Natalie?"

Caleb's voice cut into her thoughts, causing her to open her eyes. He stood over her, wearing light blue scrubs that made the color of his eyes all the bolder. His hair was ruffled, like he'd just pulled off a cap.

"Are you okay? Trish caught me coming out of the OR," he explained. "She asked me to check you."

Just being near him caused her belly to do funny things—probably sky-rocketed her pressure. *What if her pressure didn't go down? What if the babies were in trouble?* Unable to hold in the flood of emotions, she burst into tears.

"Natalie?" Caleb dropped to his knees and put his hand on her chin, forcing her to look at him. "What's wrong?"

"Nothing," she lied, keeping her eyes averted while she attempted to get her tears under control. "I'm fine."

"You don't look fine. Apparently Trish didn't think so, either, or she wouldn't have asked me to check you."

"She had no right to say anything. Not to you."

"Dot and I are covering for Dr. Hogroebe. Of course Trish should tell me if you're having problems."

"I'm not having problems," she denied adamantly. But the fact she almost screamed the declaration belied her words, and another wave of tears started.

"Natalie, honey—talk to me. Tell me what's wrong. Trish said your blood pressure is up. Are you hurting anywhere?"

She ignored his "honey," afraid to acknowledge the concern in his voice. Probably the same concern he'd show *any* patient. She met his eyes, longed for the connection they'd shared at the walk, longed for him to hold her and tell her everything was going to be okay with their babies.

"My head." Fear propelled her into speech. "And my hands and feet are swollen, Caleb. My pressure is up and my hands and feet are swollen." The last came out in a panicked cry.

"Shh," he soothed, placing his hand over hers. "Don't go assuming things. Let me check you."

Wiping at her tears, she shook her head. "You aren't checking me."

"I'm just going to listen to your heart. Examine your hands and feet. Recheck your blood pressure."

She nodded. "Okay."

Caleb took the stethoscope from around Natalie's neck and placed it around his. He listened to her heart, taking great care at each spot. Then he took her hands in his, his fingers lingering as he examined her swollen fingers.

Even through her haze of fear, the fact that Caleb held her hands registered, sent shockwaves through her. Particularly when he didn't let her hand go, but instead clasped it tighter.

Just having him hold her hand eased some of the tension curling her insides. She needed his arms around her, but for now this was enough. His hand clasped hers as if he couldn't bring himself to let it go.

But the hand that had felt so strong only moments before now shook. "Natalie, I'm sending you home."

"I can't go home. It's my last day. I'm scheduled to work until seven."

"You can't stay here. Not like this. You need to get off your feet—relax. You need bed-rest." His grip tightened. "You should already *be* on bed-rest."

"I can't go home, Caleb." She gulped, met his eyes. "I don't want to. I'm afraid to be alone."

"You don't have to be alone, Natalie. Not ever. I promise. I'm taking you home, and I'll stay with you until your pressure is down. First, I'm going to call a blood pressure med to the hospital pharmacy. Trish will give you one now."

She closed her eyes, trying to waylay the fear coursing through her. "Why are you being so nice? I thought you were mad at me for meeting Emily."

"Just at myself for being a fool," he admitted, giving her hand a reassuring squeeze. He stared at their hands a long time, his expression tight. Then glancing at his watch, he let go of her hand, straightened, and wiped his palm over his scrubs. "Look, I've got to check on the patient I just operated on. Once I'm done, I'll pick up your prescription, pick up Emily from her grandparents, then come by your place. Is that okay?"

"You're bringing Emily to my apartment?"

"Yes. If you're okay with that?"

Dumbfounded, Natalie nodded.

"Are you going to be okay to drive home?"

She wasn't sure. Her insides shook. From her pressure and from Caleb.

"What am I saying? Of course you're not okay. Your blood pressure is through the roof and you're terrified." He draped the stethoscope back around her neck, let his fingers linger at her nape. "Wait here. I'll come back for you."

What was he *doing?* The last thing Caleb wanted was to take care of Natalie. No, that wasn't true. He *did* want to take care of her. Sort of. But another part of him said he should stay the hell away and protect his heart.

He'd convinced himself that staying away was the best thing he could do for her and her babies. That if he wasn't in the picture nothing would go wrong.

But it already had.

Natalie's blood pressure was up. Dear Lord, did she have toxemia? He suspected so. So did she. He'd seen the fear in her eyes. If so, she'd be confined to total bed-rest. Who would take care of her then?

He didn't want to take care of a woman fighting to keep healthy during pregnancy. Yes, he did it all the time as a physician, caring for his patients, but that was different. This was Natalie.

He was still arguing with himself twenty minutes later when, leaving Natalie in his car, he ran into his in-laws and got his daughter.

"Natlee!" Emily said in surprise when she spotted the passenger in his car. "Did you have your babies?" His daughter peered around the seat, spotted Natalie's large belly, and shook her head. "Nope. They're still in there."

"Natalie is going to go home with us, Em. She's not feeling well and we're going to take care of her."

She turned big, serious eyes toward Caleb. "Like you take care of me when I'm sick?"

"Yes," he explained. "Just like that."

"Caleb?" Natalie looked at him in question.

A question he wasn't able to answer, so he shifted the car into reverse.

Apparently Emily was a natural-born care-taker, because his daughter waited hand and foot on Natalie. Not that Natalie asked for anything. Emily just kept bringing her things and doing things. Things like reading a story to Natalie and the twins. Things like a glass of milk and a banana that Emily had pre-peeled, smashing quite a bit in the process.

All that in the first five minutes they'd been home.

"Uhm, Natalie might want something more filling than a piece of fruit and a cup of milk. Maybe we should cook something?"

He'd meant to stop by and pick up take-out, but in his preoccupation with Natalie's situation he'd forgotten.

"Do you want Daddy and I to cook dinner, Natlee?" His daughter turned imploring eyes on Natalie. An expression he always found to be Jamie-like. His heart lurched as memories assailed him. Memories of Jamie so weak from chemo she could barely lift her head, so sick that she barely had the energy to hold her newborn daughter. Too little, too late, the oncologists had said of his wife's treatment. If only she'd taken therapy earlier.

"I am a little hungry. But—" Natalie took a bite of the banana "—this is wonderful."

"Daddy, you were right." Emily placed her hands on her hips in another Jamie gesture, twisting his heart, reminding him of all the reasons he'd pushed Natalie away after finding out she was pregnant. "We *do* need to cook for Natlee. Her babies are *starved*."

But he couldn't push her away. Not now. She needed him.

"I just got her tucked in," Caleb said, coming back into the living room where Natalie still lay on his sofa. Every time she'd offered to get up, Emily had pointed her back to the sofa. Natalie had given up, and had enjoyed the little girl's attention.

"She's precious, Caleb," Natalie praised softly, resting her head against one of the burgundy throw pillows. "You've done an excellent job raising her."

"I think she's pretty special. But then I'm partial to dark-eyed imps."

"Was that what Jamie looked like? Does Emily look like her mother?"

Caleb sank into the chair across from the sofa. He closed his eyes and didn't speak for a long time.

"At times when Emily smiles my heart breaks. She looks so much like Jamie." Pain, raw and excruciating, emanated from where he sat. "I miss her."

Her heart squeezed at the loss in his voice. "I'm sorry, Caleb."

His eyes didn't open, and the only telltale sign that he'd heard her was the tic at his jaw. Stretched out in the chair, he looked tired, alone, and if she'd thought he'd welcome her she'd have crossed the room to wrap her arms around him.

"I wish you'd told me about Jamie and Emily when we first met."

His eyes opened. "Why? What would have been different?"

"I'm not sure, but it hurts that I didn't know—that we kept secrets from each other." Like how she was still keeping secrets from him. Secrets like his sons.

Natalie lowered her gaze. She should tell him. She suspected deep down he already knew, but that was no excuse.

"I'm glad that weekend happened." She took a deep breath. "That night with you was the most amazing night of my life, Caleb."

"Really?" His eyebrow arched. "You didn't act like it. You ran away so quickly the next morning I felt like I'd pushed you into something you weren't ready for."

She sighed. "How can a person prepare for a tornado? It can drop down on you without warning, turning everything you thought you knew upside down." She clasped her hands together. "I wasn't ready for *you*. For how you made me feel."

"How *do* you feel, Natalie?" He sat up, leaned forward. "Because, despite all the reasons why I shouldn't think of you, you're in my head all the time. My first thought in the mornings. My last thought before I go to sleep."

Her heart hammered at his admission. "What reasons?"

His gaze fell to where her hands rested on the shelf her belly made.

"My babies?"

His expression tightened painfully. "Pregnant women aren't my thing."

Natalie laughed wryly. "You're an obstetrician."

"It's different. *You're* different. You make me feel different. More alive than I thought I'd ever feel again." He stood, paced across the room, then turned earnest eyes toward her. "I'm in love with you, Natalie. It's the only explanation for why I feel this way—why I want to spend every moment with you despite your pregnancy."

"You're in love with me?" Dared she believe him? Her heart soared. He'd barely spoken to her in months. A declaration of love was the last thing she'd expected.

"I think I have been from the moment you started spouting breast cancer statistics at me. I thought I could stay away, not care. But when I saw you with Emily, something snapped inside me."

"Probably a coronary," she reminded him. "You were so upset."

"Upset with myself. You scare me. These babies scare me." His gaze lowered to her belly and his face winced with pain. "They're mine, aren't they?"

Feeling woozy, she let her gaze follow his to her stomach. "Yes."

Her one word shook the foundation of Caleb's world.

Yes. He'd gotten Natalie pregnant. Her life might be in jeopardy because of him, because he hadn't thought to check the dates on his ancient condoms.

If anything happened to her it would be his fault.

Just like it was his fault Jamie had died.

"When we met," Natalie began, her voice low, steady,

"I was on fertility drugs—was scheduled to have my eggs harvested. But I never had the procedure."

Her gaze searched his, yearning for what he wasn't sure he could ever give.

"I was already pregnant."

"By me."

"I wanted to tell you, Caleb, when I first found out I was pregnant. I desperately wanted to tell you. But I decided to wait. Then I discovered you were Dot's brother-in-law, that you had a daughter—despite having led me to believe you didn't want children. I felt used. Like I was nothing more than a weekend fling."

"If I hadn't figured it out, would you ever have told me I was going to be a father again?"

"I don't know," she admitted. "You were very clear on your feelings at the hotel that morning. I didn't want you to feel trapped, to feel like I'd intentionally gotten pregnant."

"You were on fertility drugs, you asked me to get you pregnant, and you did get pregnant," he scoffed. "What else would I think?"

"You may not believe me, but I didn't intentionally get pregnant that night." She searched for the right words to convey how she'd felt that night. "I know it looks bad, but I didn't. When we made love, all I thought of was you. Not of conception or how much I wanted a baby. I've always thought my pregnancy a miracle." She smiled. "Our babies are miracles."

"Not so miraculous. We used expired condoms."

"Expired?" Her mouth dropped. "You used expired condoms?"

He sucked in a deep breath. "A sad testament to just how long it had been for me, I know."

The secret guilt she'd held that she'd somehow wished herself pregnant dissipated. Yes, she'd wanted a baby. Yes, she'd been on fertility drugs. But Caleb had used faulty protection.

"I didn't know." She fought to keep a smile from her face. Their children had been made through a convoluted chain of events. Through love. Caleb had said he loved her, and she no longer had to feel guilty over her pregnancy.

"Now you do." Caleb crossed the room and dropped onto the sofa next to her feet. "When I moved to Atlanta and saw you, realized you were pregnant—" He grimaced. "Deep inside I knew. But you said you'd had IVF, and even Dot said you'd been trying to get pregnant for months. I told myself it was just a bad coincidence."

"Bad?" Her voice squeaked.

"You're pregnant. With my babies."

"And?"

"That's a nightmare, Natalie."

She stiffened. Perhaps her happiness had been premature. Shared responsibility or not, Caleb still didn't want their children. "If you think I'm going to expect anything from you just because you now know the babies are yours, you're wrong. I've never expected anything from you, Caleb. You gave me what I wanted most in the world. I don't need anything from you beyond that."

He leaned toward her. "What about what I expect from myself?"

"You don't have to do anything you don't want to do. I wanted to get pregnant—was planning to go the road alone from the beginning. You knowing they're yours doesn't change that."

"Go the road alone?" he snorted. "You have no idea. If only it were that simple."

"What's so complicated, Caleb?"

"You're pregnant with twins, Natalie. Not only is that high risk, but now your blood pressure is elevated and there's a very real chance you have toxemia. What am I supposed to do about that? Am I supposed to just sit back and watch you die, too?"

Natalie jerked back from Caleb. She didn't understand the vehemence with which he'd directed his words at her. What did he mean about her dying, too? Was he comparing her to Jamie?

"I'm not Jamie," she said softly. "I'm not going to die, Caleb."

"You don't *know* that!"

"Your screaming at me is not helping," she shouted back. Then realized what she'd done, and bit her lower lip. "I'm sorry." She winced, feeling tears well up in her eyes. "It seems our entire relationship has been one mistake after another."

"Because we haven't been honest with each other."

His soft words seemed so incongruous after his earlier shouts that she scowled at him. "You want honest? I'll give you honest. I love you, Caleb. With all my heart and soul. When I first met you I questioned my decision to use an anonymous donor and began wondering what you'd say if I asked *you* to give me a baby. Over the course of the weekend I forgot, and just enjoyed being with you. Just as I forgot about my dream of a baby on the night we made love."

"How can you speak of love? You used me to get pregnant."

"You're the one who used faulty condoms, Caleb. But you're right. I desperately wished for a baby and you gave me my wish." She wrapped her arms protectively around her belly. "These are our boys, Caleb. The babies we made that night. Thank you for giving me my dream—I owe it all to you."

"No." He shook his head in denial.

She glared at him, hating the pain and anger she saw etched on his face. "I'm sorry you don't approve, but the facts remain the same. I'm having your babies."

Tension flared between Caleb and Natalie for the next two days, but he refused to let her go home. Who would take care of her? Her entire life was on hold while she was on bed-rest. He blamed himself. It was his fault.

Despite his increasing her blood pressure medication to the maximum dose considered safe during pregnancy, Natalie's pressure remained elevated.

And, although she didn't say anything, she couldn't hide her headaches from him. He'd caught her rubbing her temples one time too many. The obstinate woman refused to take even a single acetaminophen tablet to ease her pain, citing that she wouldn't risk the babies being exposed to anything they didn't have to be.

Seemingly oblivious to the strain, Emily adored Natalie—adored taking care of her and feeling the babies move. Each day that passed his daughter grew closer to Natalie, and he felt powerless to stop it from happening.

Having returned from her trip, Dr. Hogroebe saw Natalie in her office four days after he'd brought her home with him.

"Caleb's done all the things I'd have done, but your

blood pressure is getting worse despite medication and bed-rest." The specialist gave Natalie an empathetic look. "We've got to consider getting those babies out."

"No," she denied emphatically.

"Natalie—" Caleb began from beside her.

"It's not up for discussion. I'm not far enough along to deliver yet."

"I understand your desire to carry the babies as long as you can," Dr. Hogroebe said, "but continuing your pregnancy is putting your life at risk. I can schedule you for a Cesarean in the morning."

"I'm not willing to have a C-section. Not if it's just me at risk. What about the babies? Are they okay?"

"As a maternity nurse, you know there are risks for the babies as well as to you."

"But those risks can be monitored, and they'll be lower if they're not born prematurely. If I continue on bed-rest, continue with my medication to keep the pressure from going too high, the risks to the babies are minimal, right?"

Dr. Hogroebe looked resigned to Natalie's decision— as if she'd expected it. "If you choose not to deliver, then certainly you'll require close monitoring."

"What about starting steroid injections to build up the babies' lungs?"

Dr. Hogroebe nodded. "Regardless of what you decide, I'd like to inject you today, and again in twelve hours." She turned to Caleb. "Will you give her the second shot tonight?"

Battling a mixture of anger and astonishment that Natalie was being so stubborn, he nodded. Why he was astonished was beyond him. Hadn't he been through this before? Been in love with a woman who'd given her life to bring a baby into the world?

"Since you're staying with an obstetrician, I don't see any reason for you to be admitted for observation, or for you to come in any more often than weekly. But you have to listen to Caleb. If he says it's time to come in, you come."

"Then I say she stays today. Do the C-section this afternoon. Now."

"No." Natalie gave him a staunch look. One that ordered him to butt out. Then she turned back to the doctor. "Another week or two could make all the difference in my babies' chances for a healthy start. I'll do whatever I can to make that happen." She gave Caleb another pointed look. "I'm not having the babies any sooner than is absolutely necessary."

They made it the entire drive back to his place without saying a word. Several times Natalie considered speaking up, saying that she wanted to go anywhere other than his place. But to do that meant leaving Caleb, leaving Emily. She wasn't ready to give up hope yet.

Because, despite everything, her hopes had begun to lift. Even if he could never fully give his heart to her, Caleb did have strong feelings for her. His hang-up was with her pregnancy, with having more children. But once he saw their boys, held them, surely he'd love them as much as she did? Just look at what a great father he was to Emily. She'd just have to be patient.

She settled onto the sofa and stared blankly ahead, waiting for what was sure to come.

"You have to let Dr. Hogroebe do the Cesarean." He broke their silence. "To risk your health, your life like this, is ridiculous."

"No." She didn't say more—couldn't even wrap her tongue around anything more. In her heart she knew these twins would be her only birth children.

"I understand that you don't want to take a chance on the twins being too premature, but have them before something happens to you. They're far enough along, Natalie. The hospital is equipped to take care of thirty-four-week gestation babies. You know that."

Tears welled inside her. "Don't you understand? I can't deliver yet. Not this early. I love these babies and I have to give them every chance possible. They couldn't breathe on their own if I had them now."

"You can't risk your life this way." He lifted her legs from the sofa, slid beneath them to semi-place her in his lap. "With modern technology, your babies have an excellent chance of survival. Greater than ninety-eight percent, Natalie." He took her hand in his. "Please, do this for me."

"You can quote statistics to me on their survival rate— but at what cost to our children?" she tossed back at him. "Each day that passes means less risk of physical and mental disabilities. How can you ask me to deliver early?"

"Endangering your life isn't worth what a few more days will buy the babies. If you weren't at thirty-four weeks, maybe. But not now, Natalie. Let Dr. Hogroebe do the C-section."

She flinched, but held his gaze. "No. I'm going to carry this pregnancy as long as I'm physically able— even if it kills me."

He turned ghostly white. "Don't say that."

Her words had been a figure of speech, but she realized they were true. She *would* give her life for her babies. Not that she believed it would come to that, but if it did there was no choice to be made.

He stared at her in complete and utter horror. "You can't do this. I won't let you."

"I'll follow my doctor's advice. Everything will be fine." God, she hoped so. "Quit overreacting."

"Continuing your pregnancy isn't safe."

"Continuing this conversation isn't safe. Let it go. You want to help keep my blood pressure down? Stop asking me to have the babies early."

He stared at her for a long time. Natalie prayed that any moment he would relent, say he loved her and that everything really would be okay. He'd be by her side and together they'd bring their babies into the world.

"I can't do this, Natalie. I won't do this. Not again. You have to decide." Taking care not to jar her, he moved her legs, stood to stare down at her. "If I matter to you at all, you'll have the C-section."

And with that he left.

With clarity, Natalie knew he'd walked away from much more than just their conversation.

CHAPTER TWELVE

NATALIE knew crying wasn't good for her blood pressure, but she couldn't seem to help herself. After Caleb left—presumably to pick up Emily from her grandparents—Natalie called Dot to come get her. Although she wasn't supposed to be on her feet, she gathered her toiletries, clothes, and the second steroid injection. She threw them into a bag and impatiently waited for Dot, hoping her friend would arrive before Caleb came back. She couldn't deal with another confrontation.

She considered writing a note—but what was the point? She'd thought he'd change his mind about the babies, that he'd get beyond his aversion to the idea, but he wanted her to deliver early even knowing what that would mean. How could someone who was such an excellent father to Emily be so callous as to want her to deliver when their babies couldn't even breathe yet?

Ten minutes later she was seated in Dot's SUV.

"You're sure about this?" Dot asked from the driver's seat.

Natalie blinked. "Sure about what?"

"Leaving Cal. He's not going to be happy when he finds out you've left."

"Left? I don't live with him, Dot. He brought me to his place because he was on call for Dr. Hogroebe the night my pressure shot up. Somehow that night turned into days. Then he insisted upon going with me to my appointment today. But I do not live with him."

"Newsflash: Cal and I are not in the habit of bringing our patients home with us."

Natalie shot her a look. "You know what I'm trying to say. He brought me to his place because he wanted to keep an eye on me. That's all."

"Because you're pregnant with his babies?"

Natalie tried to hide her surprise at Dot's comment. Had Caleb told her the truth?

"Do you really think I didn't work out that you got pregnant the weekend of the walk? I'm a gynecologist! A good one. I suspected something had happened the moment Cal asked me about you. Then asked again. And again."

"I…"

"It's okay, Natalie. There are some things that are meant to be private. I understand your reasons for not saying anything. I'm happy for you and Cal. For me, too, as in a roundabout way I'm going to be an aunt again."

Her heart swelled with love for her friend. "Thank you, but Caleb and I aren't a couple."

"You love each other. You're pregnant with his babies. How much more together can you get?"

She didn't deny Dot's claim of love. "Everything is so complicated."

"Fine. You can explain why you think you aren't a couple later. For now, can you tell me why you're leaving him?" Dot stopped at a red light and glanced toward her. "If you tell me it's private, I won't push," her friend said gently. "But I hate to see you hurting, and I know Cal is going to be hurt when he realizes you've gone."

Natalie sighed. Dot was the best friend she had, and the truth was her emotions threatened to burst open. She needed to talk.

"I'll tell you everything when we get to your place."

The sofa was empty. Caleb stopped mid-step in the living room and stared at the bare piece of furniture.

Emily tugged on his hand.

"Is Natlee sleeping?" she asked, apparently just as confused that their guest wasn't in her usual spot of honor.

Caleb's heart sank. Without having to be told, he knew Natalie wasn't in bed. She was gone. Didn't she know she wasn't supposed to be on her feet? As a nurse, you'd think she'd understand complete bed-rest meant complete bed-rest.

"No, honey. Natalie has gone home."

"Why?" Emily scowled, her dark eyes going from the empty sofa to his face for an explanation. "Doesn't she need us to take care of her and her babies anymore?"

Together they walked to the sofa, and he pulled Emily into his lap, kissing the top of her head. "Natalie has her own home, Em. She was only here for a little while. She really appreciates all the care you gave her, but she needed to go home."

How was Natalie going to take care of herself when she wasn't supposed to be on her feet? She needed twenty-four-hour care. Yes, he'd told her he couldn't do this. But he hadn't meant for her to leave. Was he cursed to always mess up when it came to the women in his life?

"But she promised to let me read my reading book to

the babies tonight," Emily said with a pout to her lower lip. "Natlee wouldn't break a promise to me. She wouldn't."

He hugged his daughter. "I'll read your book with you, Em."

"But I want to read to the babies. They like me to read to them. Natlee said so. She said they listen to me."

"I'm sure they do."

"Daddy, Natlee *needs* us."

Caleb's chest hurt. Hurt so severely he almost thought he was having a heart attack. But his heart wasn't suffering an infarction, just writhing in agony. Natalie had left him.

He'd practically pushed her out the door. How could he have been so stupid? So selfish?

Emily pulled back to look at him. "I've got an idea, Daddy. Let's go get Natlee and bring her back."

The earnest gleam in Emily's eyes spoke of a little girl who needed Natalie, too. Damn it, he was trying. Trying to be a good father and to give Emily all the love she'd have had if Jamie had lived.

Damn you, Jamie, for leaving me.

A wet trickle hit his cheek. Another. Emily's astute gaze honed in on the droplets and she wrapped her little arms around his neck. "It's okay, Daddy. Natlee will come home," she assured him with unwavering confidence. "When I asked if I could be her babies' big sister, she said yes. She has to come back so I can get my T-shirt."

Emily planted a kiss on his cheek and Caleb's heart cracked, letting out all the pain he'd held in since Jamie's death. Letting out all the guilt over her death, all his helplessness. Grief unlike any he'd known consumed him, and he held onto Emily, rocking her like she was still a tiny babe.

Whether from an innate understanding that belied her young age, or just from shock at his uncharacteristic behavior, Emily continued to attempt to soothe him with sweet words of love, pats of her little hands and kisses.

"Shh, it'll be okay. I'm here for you. I won't let anything bad happen to you."

Words he'd often whispered to her after various tumbles or bad dreams. Words that held love.

The gift of love Jamie had given him through this beautiful little girl they'd made. A gift Natalie had offered him and that he'd rejected at every turn. Now she was gone.

His daughter was wise beyond her tender years. Natalie needed them. But they also needed her—needed to bring her home.

Home. Because she and the twins belonged with them, as part of their family, forever.

CHAPTER THIRTEEN

THE sharp pain in Natalie's right side wouldn't stop, no matter how she repositioned herself. She curled into the cartoon-covered pillow and fought tears as she caught a whiff of Emily's shampoo fragrance.

Dot's condo was a lovely three-bedroom, two bath. Dot had one of the spare bedrooms done up as a home office, and the other as Emily's room. The entire room had been decorated as per Emily's direction, and a Disney Princesses motif abounded.

After a long pouring out of her heart, Dot had helped Natalie to Emily's room. Whether her eyes were open or closed she felt the little girl's presence, and her heart ached. She missed Caleb's daughter. Missed the sweet way Emily touched her belly, giggling when one of the boys gave a hearty push against her palm. Missed how Emily would curl on the sofa next to her and entertain her for hours on end with tales of kindergarten, piano practice, trips with Aunt Dot. Missed the sweet, short-sentenced books Emily read to the twins. Missed the way the little girl had started kissing her goodnight and telling her she loved her before going off to be tucked in by Caleb.

Just the night before, Emily had asked if she could be the twins' big sister.

Natalie's heart had swollen and she'd choked up prior to telling Emily she'd be honored for her to be the twins' big sister. Emily had then pronounced that she needed a T-shirt just like her friend Macy's. Only perhaps, since she'd be a big sister to *two* babies, she'd need two T-shirts.

The pain in her side stabbed deeper, and Natalie couldn't squelch her gasp. That was when she realized the almost constant roiling of her belly wasn't roiling anymore. Was it possible that both of the boys had decided to sleep at the same time? They'd never managed that in the past.

She didn't want to wake Dot, but her fear escalated. And fear would cause her blood pressure to soar higher. She needed to get to the hospital and get an ultrasound to check on the babies' movements.

Making her way across the hallway, she knocked on Dot's bedroom door. "Dot? I'm sorry to wake you, but I think something's wrong."

The next couple of hours passed in a painful blur. Dr. Hogroebe met them at the hospital. Both of the babies were alive, but in distress. Dr. Hogroebe admitted Natalie and started IV meds. She wanted to do a Cesarean—immediately.

"But the steroids haven't had time to kick in. If I deliver now both babies will be in the NICU for Lord only knows how long." And that was if things went well. She wouldn't consider the alternative.

"Natalie, your blood pressure is through the roof. I'm insisting we proceed with a Cesarean."

Although she'd disappeared for a short while, Dot now sat with Natalie, holding her hand in a death grip. "You have to listen to Dr. Hogroebe, Nat. The hospital has an excellent NICU. The twins will get the best of care and will do fine."

Her eyes watery, Natalie nodded. She wasn't thinking clearly—couldn't think clearly. No doubt she'd been given something to calm her down. She'd been on the verge of hysteria when she'd arrived at the hospital. Her boys hadn't been moving.

Even now they were scarily still. But the reassuring beat of the heart monitors prevented her from getting more wound up. That and the drugs they were feeding into her IV.

She closed her eyes and slept. For how long she wasn't sure. A nurse coming in to record her vitals awakened her. Caleb sat in the chair next to the hospital bed.

"Hey, Sleeping Beauty."

Even now she felt groggy, not completely in control of her wits. "Was I out for long?"

"Not long."

Natalie's gaze went to the monitoring strips running next to the bed. Both babies were still okay. Thank God.

"How's my pressure?" she asked, trying not to wince when she looked at the electronic read-out from the cuff intermittently checking her pressure.

"Down from when you came in, but still knocking two-hundred systolic."

"How did you know?"

"Dot called after you got to the hospital."

So that was where her friend had disappeared off to.

"I don't want you here." She'd thought he could love

her, could learn to let her into his family. But the truth was, Caleb didn't want his family expanded. Didn't want their boys. He had Emily, and that was all he needed.

She would move on—would eventually get past the pain of losing Caleb and Emily. Soon she'd have her hands full with two baby boys who were going to need a lot of medical care for the first few weeks of their lives. Possibly longer.

Her children needed her focus on *them,* not distracted by a man who couldn't accept her love.

"That's what Dot told me."

Natalie stared into Caleb's tightly drawn face. "Then why are you here?"

"They're coming to take you to the OR in just a few minutes. I need to be there."

He wanted to go in the OR with her? "Why?"

"Those are my babies, Natalie. I want be there when they're born."

Hello? That was a different tune from the one she'd been hearing. She stared at him suspiciously. "You told me you didn't want any more children. Just last night you were trying to force me into agreeing to this. Well, congratulations, Caleb. Looks like you're getting what you want. I'm having a Cesarean. Our boys will have to fight for each and every breath, will likely be on ventilators, and will have to deal with all sorts of complications caused by being premature."

"Natalie, you haven't paid attention to anything I've said. I don't want anything to happen to our babies." He glanced away, flexed his jaw, then re-met her gaze with glistening eyes. "I thought by staying away you and the boys would somehow be safer, but things have gone wrong anyway. I don't want to lose you, Natalie. I love you."

"I don't understand."

"Natalie, Jamie was six weeks pregnant with Emily when they found her cancer." He closed his eyes, took a deep breath. "She refused to take any treatments that might harm her unborn baby—Emily. From the beginning she thought she was going to die regardless, and she wanted to live on through her baby. She might have died anyway, but with waiting her cancer spread fast."

Natalie had known Jamie had died of breast cancer, but hadn't realized she'd been pregnant at diagnosis. "The situation is not the same. I'm not going to die."

"You don't know that. I've been blinded by fear that I'd lose you the way I lost Jamie. I thought I'd spend my life alone after I lost her, because I was sure I'd lost my ability to love anyone other than Emily. Truth is, I love you more than life itself, Natalie. Do you hear me? It isn't that I don't want our children. Hell, I'd love making dozens of babies with you. But not at the risk of losing you. Never that."

"You *want* our babies?"

He placed his hands over her very round belly. "How could I not? They're the best parts of you and me."

"But all those things you said…"

"Words of a man blinded by pain and desperation. I want to be there with you today. To be with you every day for the rest of our lives."

What kind of drugs did they have her on? She had to be hallucinating. Her eyes stretched open, she stared at him. "What are you saying?"

"*Love* me, Natalie. Despite all my flaws, love me and let me love you and our babies."

"I do love you, Caleb."

THE NURSE'S BABY MIRACLE

"Then you'll marry me? Be my wife and Emily's mother?"

"You want to marry me? You're sure?"

"If you'll have me."

Tears streamed down Natalie's face. "Why now? Why are you asking this now?"

"Because I want you to know that I'm really with you in that OR. Not just physically, but pulling for you and our boys emotionally, mentally, spiritually. I want you to know that you have a lot to live for, Natalie. And that we need you. Me, Emily, our boys."

"I'm not sure what to say."

"Say yes."

She wanted to. Desperately she wanted to. But reason said she shouldn't make an emotional decision. Nor should she make such a decision while under the influence of whatever medication they'd given her.

"I need to think about it."

"I understand." But he didn't look as if he did.

The OR tech stepped into the room. "I'm here to take you to the OR. You ready?"

Her gaze not leaving Caleb's, she nodded. "You promised I wouldn't be alone," she reminded him, lacing her fingers with his. "I'm holding you to that promise."

He lifted her hand to his lips. "There's no place I'd rather be."

EPILOGUE

"NATLEE!" Emily called, bouncing into the family room of the NICU unit, where Natalie rocked Thomas in one arm and Jeremy in the other. "Daddy says we get to bring the babies home today!"

Two stressful weeks had passed since Natalie's C-section. Following their birth, both boys had been rushed to the NICU and placed on ventilators, to help their under-developed lungs. Thomas, the smallest twin, had tempo-rarily had to have a colostomy, due to a paralytic bowel, but the surgical opening had now been closed with no complications.

Natalie had stayed at the hospital almost around the clock, holding the babies and feeding them nutrient-rich breast milk through a preemie bottle. Just this week Jeremy had successfully breastfed for the first time, and continued to do so. Both babies were thriving.

"Today?" Natalie asked, her gaze meeting Caleb's. The neonatologist had talked about letting them take the boys home soon—but today? "Can we really?"

"Yep," Emily answered for her father. "And look what I got." Emily puffed her chest out, showcasing a pink T-shirt with bright blue letters announcing to the world that she was a big sister. "Daddy got me a blue one with pink letters, too."

"Very nice," Natalie praised, unable to keep the smile from her face.

"Look, Natlee." Emily drew her attention again, spinning around so Natalie could read the boys' names on the back of the shirt. "Macy's shirt didn't have *her* baby's name," Emily smugly declared, with the one-upmanship only a small child could pull off and still be cute. "Daddy says mine does because our family is extra special. I'm getting a new mommy along with my baby brothers."

"Maybe we should have put Natalie's name on your T-shirt, too?" Caleb suggested, smothering a grin at his daughter's excitement.

"Could we really?" Emily latched onto his suggestion.

Caleb walked over to Natalie and took Jeremy from her, kissing the baby's soft peach-fuzz-covered head. "I tell you what, Em, Natalie and I will get you a T-shirt proclaiming you to be our flower girl. How about it, Natalie? You ready to make an honest man of me?"

"Gee," she teased, her insides fluttering with excitement at the way he looked at her, then down at their son, with eyes full of love and pride, "do I get a T-shirt, too, if I say yes?"

As if he'd known she'd ask, he reached behind him and pulled out a T-shirt he'd apparently had tucked into the back of his jeans. "Of course." He grinned. "Got to have a T-shirt."

Natalie eyed him suspiciously, her heart thudding in her chest at what the shirt might have on it. He'd already resumed his daily cookies, but this time each accompanying card held the same message: *Marry me.*

Shifting Thomas so she had two free hands, she smoothed out the T-shirt.

"I knew 'bout that." Emily grinned from ear to ear, bouncing next to Natalie's rocker. "Lydia, Mrs. Baker and me made it. Daddy helped a little."

Staring at the shirt, Natalie felt tears well in her eyes. Tears of joy.

On the T-shirt were five simple stick-figure drawings made with fabric paint. Above each easily discernible person was a word: Daddy. Mommy. Emily. Thomas. Jeremy.

Below the drawings were two of the most precious words Natalie had ever seen.

My Family.